# THREADING THE NEEDLE

# JOSHUA PALMATIER

**DAW BOOKS, INC.**
DONALD A. WOLLHEIM, FOUNDER
375 Hudson Street, New York, NY 10014

**ELIZABETH R. WOLLHEIM**
**SHEILA E. GILBERT**
**PUBLISHERS**
www.dawbooks.com

*This book is dedicated to fellow author, co-editor, and loyal friend, Patricia Bray. She's withstood all of my wild dreams, from the flights of fantasy that become the books you're reading, to the small press Zombies Need Brains.*

# *Acknowledgments*

This book was made possible by many people—readers, friends, family—all of whom supported me in some way during the writing process. readers for rooting me on when the writing felt tough; friends for keeping me sane and providing me with drinks when required; and family for encouraging me to do what others might only dream. Thank you all.

A few deserve particular mention, though:

My agent, Joshua Bilmes, who took me on mid-series and who shares my dreams of what my writing career could be. He forced me—at the eleventh hour—to cut over 25,000 words from this book, which only made it better.

My editor, Sheila Gilbert, who continues to push me—sometimes kicking and screaming—along the writing path.

David J. Fortier, who suffered through the first draft of this book and sent me feedback. And that first draft was . . . *shudder*

Missy Gunnels Katano, loyal minion (we'll just ignore that previous claim on minion-ship by Gini Koch), who never fails to support me at cons with chocolate and enthusiasm.

My mom, who's also helped tremendously at cons by helping out at my dealer's room table. Plus, you know, that whole "raising me since I was born" thing.

And lastly, my partner, George, who's dealt with all of my writing highs and lows from first publication onward.

All of these people helped bring this book about. It may have been published without them, but it wouldn't have been nearly as good, nor as fun to write.

# PART I:

## Erenthrall

# One

KARA TREMAIN KNELT ON THE STONES at the edge of the creek, reached into the chill water with the shirt she held, and scrubbed it vigorously. Banks of stone and sand rose up on either side of the creek, and a large pool spread out before her where the water ran slower and deeper. A few of the youngest children of the Hollow were splashing in the pool, their mothers or fathers watching from the shore while working on their own laundry.

Kara pulled the shirt out of the current, wrung it, then tossed it into the basket on her left while reaching for another. This one was Cory's, smelling of his sweat. She breathed in his scent before soaking it, pausing to sprinkle some of the dried soap into its center before scrubbing it again.

The first time she'd done this, her shoulders had ached for a week. Now her arms were tanned and muscled. Someone else had always handled her laundry in Erenthrall, before the Shattering: her mother when she was younger, but after her parents had died at the hands of the Kormanley, one of the servants of the Wielder's college had seen to it. Same for all of the nodes she'd worked at after that. She hadn't even noticed when they came to empty the hampers or return the cleaned clothes; the servants had been nearly invisible.

Of course, her mother and the other servants would have had the help of the ley in Erenthrall.

Instinctively, she reached for it. But unlike in Erenthrall, here in the Hollow the ley wasn't waiting, ready to be used at a mere thought. There was no Nexus, nor any nodes to augment the ley's power, but the ley was there. She'd managed—with the other Wielders in their group—to stabilize it into its own network, against the wishes of some of those in the Hollow. It had run strong enough to provide the refugees from the Shattering enough heating stones for their tents during the harshest winter months. Kara doubted many of them would have survived, especially during the unnaturally bitter cold snap they'd endured for nearly two weeks at the end of the year. Even then, they'd lost two, and another dozen had suffered frostbite.

Shaking herself, she pulled herself up out of the ley. One of the children splashed her and she snapped the shirt at the girl in mock anger. The girl shrieked and surged away through the water. Smiling, Kara dropped the shirt into the wet basket and reached for another, only to discover she was finished.

The other members of the Hollow called out to her as she tucked the basket onto her hip and hiked up the steep incline that led to the main group of buildings, wiping the sweat from her brow as she ducked beneath the limbs of the surrounding trees. Emerging at the top into the sunlight, she cut to the left, between two cottages with women and children working in the small herb gardens. A couple of dogs barked at her, trotting alongside before breaking away. But the small village was mostly empty, the regular tenants— along with those who'd sought refuge here after the Shattering—already out in the fields, sowing the rest of the spring crops.

Kara didn't know why they were bothering. She intended to repair the distortion that currently engulfed Erenthrall and then return, to reestablish some semblance of the city where she'd grown up. The only reason she'd left was because the city had become too dangerous. Violent groups of survivors had begun killing indiscriminately, while packs of feral Wolves roamed the streets. The quakes, the unpredictable eruptions of ley, and the random auroral light storms only added to the danger.

It had been safer to retreat to the Hollow.

When their wagons had halted on the narrow dirt path that was the Hollow's only road, they'd found the two elders—Paul and Sophia—waiting for them. Sophia, over half a century old, with the wispy white hair, wrinkles, and age spots to prove it, had stepped up to Allan immediately and welcomed him with a hug and kiss on the cheek, reaching to pull his daughter Morrell into the embrace. Morrell had burst into tears and clung to her. Sophia had stroked her hair, then turned her sharp, intelligent eyes on the rest.

"And who do we have here, Allan? Guests?"

"I'm afraid not. They're all refugees from Erenthrall."

Sophia shot him a hard look. "Erenthrall?"

Allan's shoulders slumped. "It's gone. Destroyed."

"Serves them all right," Paul snapped. "The use of the ley brought them to this. We shouldn't let them into the Hollow. They should deal with the consequences on their own."

"Hush, Paul." Sophia's voice was soft, but it had an iron core, and Kara realized they already knew about Erenthrall. They would have felt the Shattering, or heard it, even here in the hills a few weeks of hard travel to the northwest.

Paul quieted, but kept his arms crossed over his chest.

"We don't intend to stay," Kara had said.

The elderly woman took in Kara's tattered and road-stained purple Wielder's jacket, then met her gaze. "I suppose we can make room for a few more."

The surge of relief from the wagon train behind had been palpable. Kara had dropped her head, tears burning in her eyes. But then Cory had wrapped his arm around her waist and she'd leaned into him, into his strength. She'd heard sobbing as Sophia, Paul, and a slew of other villagers who'd been watching from a distance came forward and led them toward a wide meadow to the west, within walking distance of the village.

Kara now passed between cottages whose residents she'd come to know by name and entered the greenbelt that separated the Hollow from that meadow. A moment later she stepped out of the trees.

Tents were pitched across the entire length of the sward. Toward the back, a group of Kara's fellow refugees were building a set of cottages, smaller than those in the Hollow proper, but far more permanent than the tents. Two had already been completed, with a third close, and two others mere skeletons of braces and supports. Nothing like any of the buildings they were used to in Erenthrall, but still more *solid* than Kara liked.

She shrugged her unease aside and headed toward the tent she and Cory had claimed, pushing the basket with the wet clothes through the flap, then crawling in afterward. Setting the basket to one side, she touched the wide, rounded heating stone and reached for the ley. The stone began to warm beneath her fingers. Humming to herself, she began pinning some of the clothes up on lines running across the tent over the stone.

She had just hung the last of the shirts when she caught movement out of the corner of her eye. Shading her gaze with one hand, she squinted.

Her heart skipped when she recognized Cory. "Why are you not helping in the fields, Cory?" He was moving fast, not quite running. Max, the little mutt who had attached himself to Kara after she'd saved him from a distortion, raced along at Cory's heels.

They were headed straight toward her.

She reached for the ley, but it told her nothing, and Cory wouldn't be looking for her if there'd been an accident, he'd be looking for Logan or Morrell.

Which left only one other option.

She tossed the unused clothespins into the basket and tucked it inside the tent. Then she grabbed her purple Wielder's jacket and shrugged into it, snatching up a water skin.

Cory saw her waiting and waved. Max barked and tore away from him. She knelt as the little dog leaped up into her arms and attempted to lick her face. She fended him off with one hand, his tail a blur.

"It's the group sent to Erenthrall, isn't it?" she asked when Cory was near enough to hear. "Allan, Bryce, and the others are back."

"The sentries report they'll be here shortly. Sophia

thought you should be there to meet them when they reach the Hollow."

Kara passed him the skin. "Did you run from the fields?"

Cory drank deeply, then wiped his mouth with the back of his hand. "Of course."

Shaking her head, Kara snagged his arm. "You'd better come with me. I'm certain they sent for Paul, Hernande, and Sovaan already."

They wove back through the tents toward the Hollow, emerging onto the dirt road just outside of the village. Sophia was waiting, Sovaan and Hernande to one side. The elderly woman reached up to tuck a few strands of her hair back behind one ear as Kara and Cory approached.

"Good to see you," she said. "I thought you'd be in the fields, but I'm glad Cory found you."

"Laundry day today."

"The washing never ends."

They halted beside Hernande, Cory's mentor, who nodded in greeting. Sovaan, another mentor from the University, merely frowned. Kara had never found out why Sovaan disliked Hernande. They'd been at odds long before the Shattering, and Hernande had merely waved Kara's question aside when she'd asked, saying it was an old grudge, petty and stupid.

"How goes the work on the new cabins?" Sophia asked.

"Two finished, another close behind. Two more going up now. It will take most of the rest of spring and summer to get them all done."

"As long as they're up before winter," Sovaan interjected. "I nearly froze to death in those tents."

Kara thought about the two people they *had* found frozen, but she kept quiet.

Max suddenly began barking, startling her, before he streaked away from the group, down the rutted road, and into the trees. "Max!" Kara swore when the dog ignored her. He vanished, although Kara could still hear him barking. The angry protectiveness in the sound, undercut with a growl, suddenly changed to excitement, and everyone in the group relaxed.

A moment later, they could all hear the creak of a wagon and the shouts and curses of those who'd left for Erenthrall to scavenge for supplies. A figure emerged from the trees, running toward them, his face lined with urgency.

"That's Jasom," Sovaan said.

As soon as Jasom saw them, he shouted, "Find Logan! We have wounded!"

Sophia snapped around, but Cory was already rushing to the east. "He's in the fields!" the elderly woman called out after him.

The rest of them ran down the road toward Jasom as the wagon appeared, the Dog Bryce holding the reins, grim-faced and hard, two others in the back of the wagon, holding on tight. As soon as Bryce saw them, he pulled back on the reins, shouting for the horses to halt, then leaped from the wagon before it had completely stopped.

"Who is it?" There had been at least fifteen members in the group; Kara could see only three others besides Jasom. "Who's been hurt?"

"Claye. A few others were injured, but not seriously. Terrim is dead."

Bryce led them around the back of the open wagon. Two men were hovering over Claye's body, their hands and clothes covered in blood as they pressed down against a wound on Claye's side to stanch the blood flow. An arrow jutted from his gut, just beneath his rib cage.

Sophia swore as the thick scent of blood struck them all, then heaved herself up into the wagon. "Hold him. Don't let up the pressure."

"What happened?" Sovaan asked.

Bryce wiped a hand down his scarred face. "We were attacked on the outskirts of the plains, just before reaching the hills."

"By who?"

Bryce shrugged. "They rode out of the northeast on horses, hit us hard, tried to take the wagon. Terrim was dead before we knew what was happening. He was driving the wagon. The next thing I knew, I was fighting off two of them while a third was whipping the horses, trying to draw the wagon away. Claye and Allan charged from the side and managed to climb into the back, while the rest of us fended off the others. As soon as they saw their man killed by Claye and Allan bringing the wagon to a halt, they broke off the attack and fled, firing arrows as they left. That's when Claye was hit. He was an easy target, standing on top of the wagon."

They all watched as Sophia gently probed the flesh around the arrow. Claye moaned and twisted beneath the touch, and Sophia's jaw muscles clenched. She sat back.

"There's nothing I can do. We need Logan."

"Where is he?" Bryce demanded.

"Cory ran to fetch him from the fields. But we can move Claye to Logan's place, get him set up on the table." Sophia clambered down from the wagon. "Hernande, get fresh water from the creek. Sovaan, get the fire started. And Kara—"

"Fresh linens."

Sophia nodded. "Go. The rest of you, bring the wagon as close to Logan's as possible and then help me carry him inside."

Sophia continued giving orders, but Kara ran toward Logan's cottage behind Sovaan. They burst through the outer door into the inner room, the scent of crushed herbs and medicine overpowering. Sovaan moved around the table in the center of the room to the hearth, muttering under his breath. Kara cut left and swung open the main doors of the massive cabinet against one wall. Linen was stacked to one side, and she pulled out the first few sets of folded cloth, snapping them open and beginning to tear them into strips. She felt a tug on the Tapestry from Sovaan, and firelight spilled from the hearth.

She had a respectable pile of bandages when the door cracked open and Sophia rushed into the room, holding the door while Bryce and the other two men carried Claye's limp figure inside and set him on the table. The Dog groaned, but Kara could tell he was nearly unconscious. Sophia shooed Bryce aside and ordered the others to continue putting pressure on the wound. Kara immediately handed over the torn cloth, then continued to rip the material into additional bandages. With the amount of blood she could see, Logan was going to need them. Both Sovaan and Bryce had retreated, backs up against one wall, uncertain what they could do to help.

"Where are the others?" Kara asked.

Bryce's eyes were focused on Claye. "What others?"

"Allan, Glenn, the rest of those that went with you?"

Bryce stared at her a moment, as if he still hadn't heard, then blinked and shook himself. "We handed over some of the supplies for them to carry, to make room in the wagon for Claye, then we sprinted out ahead of them. They should be coming into the Hollow shortly."

"Did the attackers follow you?"

"I left that to Allan and the other Dogs. Ask him."

He turned toward the door.

"Where are you going?" Kara asked. The Dog stopped at the entrance, half turned. "Someone needs to tell Terrim's wife that he's dead."

Then he was gone, replaced by the bright sunlight of midday.

Kara stood stock still, a hot ache in the center of her chest. She'd forgotten about Terrim in the rush to help Claye.

Hernande appeared in the door. He heaved two buckets of water up onto a smaller table set off to the side of the door, some of it sloshing onto the floor. He panted, his dark complexion tinged a deeper shade of red.

"I'll be fine," he said. "I should have brought the buckets one at a time."

Kara didn't have a chance to answer as Logan entered. He took in everything with a quick glance.

"Everyone out," he ordered, his voice deep and booming. He shifted to the table, two others coming in behind him. One of them was Morrell, Allan's daughter. "Even you, Sophia. I'll handle it from here. You'd only hover and be in the way."

Sophia gave Logan a hard stare, which he ignored, already intent on his patient. Sniffing, she pulled back and let Logan and Morrell take her place. "We'll be waiting in the meeting hall." She ushered the others out before her, snagging one of Kara's unused cloths to wipe her hands clean. Morrell took Kara's place with a worried frown.

Kara gripped her hand and squeezed. "Bryce said your father was fine."

Morrell gave her a relieved smile, then began tearing more bandages.

Kara stepped outside, exhaling harshly as tension sloughed

from her shoulders. Sovaan, Hernande, and Sophia were standing with Cory, waiting for her. A few other members of the Hollow had gathered to see what the commotion was about.

"Will he be all right?" Hernande asked quietly, one hand stroking his scraggly beard as he contemplated the small cottage. A ragged bellow came from the open doorway, and Kara flinched.

"It's hard to say. The arrow hadn't penetrated that deeply. Thankfully, it was close to his side. I know there was a lot of blood, but he hadn't yet passed out, which is a good sign. It will depend on whether Logan can get the arrow removed and the bleeding stopped."

"Where did Bryce go?"

"To tell Sara that her husband is dead."

"And the others?"

"Left behind to travel on foot."

Hernande nodded. "Then there's nothing we can do but wait."

"Agreed." Sophia paused long enough to eye the Hollowers watching, then announced, "The expedition to Erenthrall was attacked on their way back, and Claye was wounded. Logan's seeing to him now. If you'd like to make yourselves useful, I'm certain Jasom could use some help unloading the new supplies from the wagon." She lifted one eyebrow meaningfully. Those who'd gathered started, with some guilt, then began to disband.

Sophia shook her head, mumbling, "Gawkers and gossips, all of them," under her breath, before heading to the long stone building that served as the village's meeting hall. Kara and the others followed. "I don't like the news that there's a group operating so near the foothills, especially one proficient with the bow and arrow."

"It does mark a change in tactics," Hernande agreed.

"And a shift away from the city."

"What do you mean?" Sovaan asked as they entered the meeting hall. Sunlight poured in through the windows in shafts, revealing rows of seats scattered in the center of the room, tables shoved up against the walls, and a raised platform at the far end. A few of the decorations left over from the harvest festival months before remained—sheaves of grain tied with ribbons, gourds, cornstalks, a few dried flowers. The wooden floorboards creaked underfoot as they moved down the center of the room toward the platform.

Sophia began pulling wooden chairs into a rough circle. "After the Shattering, most of the people who'd lived within Erenthrall returned to the city, even with all of its dangers. Or they fled to some of the outlying towns, those connected to the ley lines near the city.

"Nearly all of you came from the University or were Wielders before. You were taken from your homes, from your families and familiar surroundings, and thrust into studies at the college or the University, exposed to new things, new ideas. Most of those in Erenthrall would have grown up and lived within only a few districts. Being forced to abandon everything would be terrifying."

"Yes, yes." Sovaan waved a hand impatiently. "So they returned to Erenthrall. Or as close as they could get. What's your point?"

Sophia's mouth pinched in annoyance. "My point is, now they're leaving again. Why?"

"There isn't enough food."

All of them turned toward the still-opened doors, where Bryce stood in silhouette before moving deeper into the room. His entire stance radiated tension, danger. He reminded her of the Dogs combing the streets before the Shattering, following the Wielders, following her.

"The entire city has changed. It's dividing up into sectors, each controlled by different groups—the Temerite enclave to the northeast, the Gorrani to the southwest, others. The Wolves have expanded into new territory. We heard them toward the end of our excursion. Allan was hunted and only escaped by going into the distortion and hiding out."

"Is he all right?" Kara asked.

"A few cuts and bruises, nothing serious."

"And how did the expedition go?" Sophia asked.

"It's getting harder and harder to find anything of worth, especially food. There isn't much that hasn't spoiled in the parts of the city left unclaimed."

"Which is why people are leaving," Hernande said. "If they aren't part of one of the main groups, then they're running short on supplies. They're being forced out, like we were."

"And the attack on our wagon near the foothills means it isn't only the city that's dangerous. It's spread to the plains." Bryce sank into a chair and leaned forward. "They're beginning to form larger, more organized groups in the towns surrounding the city. Our safe little haven here in the Hollow isn't so safe anymore. We need to come up with some defenses. We need to protect ourselves."

"We have sentries—" Sophia began.

"Four!" Bryce interrupted in frustration. "Watching the most obvious paths into the valley! That isn't going to cut it. We need to come up with something better—scouts, patrols, expand the ranks of those who can fight beyond the few Dogs in my group. We need to protect ourselves before one of these bands finds us and attacks us here on our own turf!"

No one moved, facing each other across the rough circle of chairs.

Then Sophia shifted uneasily. "The Hollowers aren't going to like that. We settled here to escape violence and the misuse of power."

"Would you rather let the thieves and brigands overrun us all?"

"We're deep enough in the foothills that I don't think we'll have to worry about it immediately," Hernande said as Sophia stiffened. "But it is something we'll have to consider as people become more desperate. Bryce is right: this valley is not easily defended."

Sophia's body didn't loosen, but she said nothing. It was clear to Kara there would be resistance from the original Hollowers.

"What about the distortion?" Kara asked.

"What about it?"

Kara shot Bryce a black look. "Has Erenthrall's distortion changed at all? Does it show any signs of weakening? We won't be able to return and rebuild Erenthrall if the distortion collapses and destroys everything inside before we find a way to heal it."

"How in hells should I know? I'm not a damned Wielder."

Shouts rang out from outside the meeting hall.

"Sounds like the rest of the expedition has returned," Bryce muttered.

Kara almost pursued her questions about the distortion, but dropped the topic with a shake of her head. She rose and moved to the door, along with Hernande and Cory. Outside, the rest of those in the Erenthrall expedition were straggling in, some of them carrying the supplies Bryce had thrown from the wagon to make room for Claye, others helping a few wounded. Those in the Hollow rushed forward, taking the supplies and setting them aside or offering up water skins. A few of the expedition collapsed to the rutted road, their exhaustion evident in the lines of their faces.

The last stumbled in, with Allan and two other Dogs at their back. Kara sagged in relief. "I'll go get Allan."

Hernande caught her arm. "No need. He's headed this way."

The ex-Dog had seen them standing in the doorway and, after saying something to the other two Dogs, moved toward the meeting hall, accepting a skin from one of the boys.

"Claye?" Allan asked as soon as he was within range.

Hernande nodded toward the healer's cottage. "Logan is working on him now. Bryce already informed Sara about Terrim."

Allan's shoulders sagged. He looked weary, dark smudges under his eyes. Kara noticed a few new cuts on his face, mostly healed, and the yellowed remnants of fading bruises.

"Did anyone follow you?"

"Not as far as I could tell. They retreated onto the plains, to the east." His glance shot over Kara's head, to the others waiting inside. He thrust his chin forward. "We should join them."

They shifted back into the room.

"Did they attack again?" Sophia asked immediately.

"No, and no one followed us into the foothills." He looked toward Bryce. "Have you told them about the city?"

"About the Wolves, yes. I tried to convince them to increase our defenses, but they're being stubborn."

Sophia bristled.

Allan grabbed a chair and settled in with the rest, slinging the bag he carried over one shoulder to the floor. "What about the quakes?"

Hernande and Cory glanced toward each other.

"Quakes?"

"They haven't ended. You may not have felt anything here, but they're continuing in and around Erenthrall. We felt one on our way out, strong enough to collapse a few buildings."

"We thought the earth was settling. Stabilizing."

"I don't think so."

Hernande leaned forward. "We'll have to take a look at the sands again, see if the ley has been disturbed."

"Does it matter?" Sovaan demanded. "If the city has run out of supplies, then why would we want to go back?"

And there it was, what Kara had feared since the discussion began.

"We have to go back."

"Why?"

"Because we have to heal the distortion. We have to repair the damage that we caused."

Sovaan straightened in affront. "*We* didn't cause this damage. The Nexus exploded because of the Baron and his Prime Wielders and the damned Kormanley. We are simply suffering the consequences. I say we leave the city to the Wolves and the scavengers, let them tear each other apart. We can start fresh here. The Hollow has everything we need."

Sophia cut off Kara's response. "The Hollow barely had enough food to feed those of us originally from here this past winter. We certainly didn't have enough to feed those of you we took in. We survived on what was gathered from Erenthrall."

"I thought that's what the new fields were for," Sovaan countered, "to grow enough food for all of us."

Sophia's eyes narrowed. "Crops and harvests are anything but certain. Weather, disease, drought—any of it could destroy everything. We need those supplies from the city. Besides, I don't recall us agreeing to let you stay here longterm in the first place."

Allan reached for his bag. "The city provides more than just food. I found these in an apothecary." He pulled out a few small bottles and handed them around.

Sophia gasped as they reached her. "Logan would kill

for this bottle of seranin alone. And I ran out of devil's claw before the Shattering." She clutched the small vial close to her chest. "It helps with the arthritis in my hands."

"I don't understand," Kara said. "I thought you'd already raided all of the apothecaries in the uncontrolled areas of the city. Where did you get these?"

"Inside one of the shards."

It took a moment for it to sink in, but when it did Kara's eyes widened. "You pulled these out of the distortion?"

"The Wolves trapped me close to the distortion. The only way to escape was to go inside. But the pack's leader—a man half-transformed, like Hagger—set the Wolves on watch around the shard, waiting for me to come back out. I was forced to move deeper into the distortion to bypass them, and along the way I found the apothecary." He pulled out a glass jar of peaches. "Along with this. There was enough food in that shard to last us a few days, perhaps a week. None of the others in Erenthrall can reach it."

Hernande was chewing on the end of his beard now, head bowed in thought. "Is there another way to gain access to these supplies?"

"I can take someone into the distortion with me, but getting them in and back out would be unpleasant."

"That's not what I meant. We've been discussing how to heal the distortion. While we all agree we don't have enough Wielders or mentors to take it down all at once, what about healing a single shard at a time?"

Kara drew breath to protest, but paused.

They'd never considered healing it piece by piece.

She glanced up at the others, all waiting expectantly. "It might work. But we'd never be able to heal the entire distortion this way. There are hundreds of shards, if not thousands. It would take too long."

"What could go wrong?"

"Distortions are delicate. Any change in its configuration, like the removal of a shard, could cause it to unbalance. We may unwittingly set off its closure. And then everything and everyone currently trapped inside would be killed or destroyed. We'd never be able to recover the central part of Erenthrall."

The group grew somber.

"It doesn't matter," Bryce said abruptly. "We can't pin all of our hopes on the crops. And we can't count on remaining hidden here in the foothills, not with these groups arming themselves and venturing out onto the plains. We need those supplies trapped in the distortion, and we need to start work on defending ourselves here, at the Hollow."

"What do you propose?" Sophia asked.

Bryce stood, reaching for the bag Allan still held. The ex-Dog handed it over.

"We need to send some of the Wielders, with protection, to Erenthrall, to see if they can get at the supplies in the shards. As for the Hollow, I don't have enough Dogs here to protect it fully. We need to start training some of the others to fight. With swords, bows, anything else we can find. Crops will be worthless if we get raided."

He slung the bag of medicine and food up over his shoulder and headed for the door. "I'm going to hand this over to Logan and then go to my tent. It's been a long, bitter few days."

They watched as he stepped outside and turned left, out of sight.

"He's right," Allan said grudgingly. "The attack on the wagon only emphasizes what we saw in the city. We need better defenses."

"Paul won't like it," Sophia said. "Nor some of the others. They'll claim that the only reason we're at risk is that we took you in, and we should kick you out now."

"These groups would be coming whether we'd come here or not. Would Paul and the rest rather wait to have their throats slit one night, when one of the groups finds the Hollow? Because that's what will happen eventually."

Sophia's lips pursed at the gruesome image. "No, I suppose not."

"Then I suggest you start training people to wield swords and handle bows."

The elderly woman still appeared resistant. "I'll have our trackers start drilling those interested in archery. At worst, we could always use additional help with the hunting. And I'll tell the rest they can go to the Dogs for training with swords if they want."

"Good." Allan turned to Kara. "You need to speak to

the Wielders and figure out how to heal one of the shards. I don't want to wait too long before returning to the city."

Kara contained a surge of excitement. They'd become too complacent here in the Hollow. They needed to begin work on retrieving Erenthrall before that complacency spread. "I'll meet with them right away. Working to heal a few shards may give us an idea of how to heal the entire distortion, something we haven't thought of yet. We won't lack in volunteers, even if Erenthrall is still dangerous."

"It's still dangerous. Perhaps more so than before the Shattering."

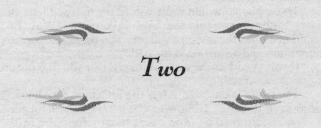

# Two

KARA LAY IN THE DARKNESS of her and Cory's tent, listening to Cory's deep breathing and the utter quiet of the night. It was close to dawn; she could taste the dew on the chill air. Earlier she'd heard others rousing to relieve the patrols Bryce had set up. He'd paired one of his Dogs with one of the Hollower trackers and a third untrained man or woman, each team walking the edge of the valley at set intervals. There were at least three such teams on patrol at any one time, in addition to the two set to watch the passes where the creek entered and left the valley. In another hour, she knew she'd hear the muted clang of those practicing with swords at the far end of the meadow. Kara and Cory's tent was too distant to hear the thunk of the arrows hitting the practice targets.

"Can't sleep?" Cory's breath felt warm against her neck.

"No. I've been awake for hours."

He kissed the nape of her neck, then rolled away with a sigh. She twisted to face him.

"Worried about going to Erenthrall?"

"Yes. I'm worried about the distortion, about our attempts to heal it. What if we trigger the distortion's collapse? I know we can't restore Erenthrall completely, not after what's happened, but we could at least make it a refuge, a place of safety for the survivors. Think about all of the people who are trapped inside it. We saved a few, but if the distortion collapses . . ."

"Those people would want you to try to free them. Besides, I thought you said that even if you can't release one shard at a time, the attempt will give you more information about how the distortion is formed."

"It will. And I know we have to try. But still, the distortions are so unstable."

"The *world* is unstable. After the attack on the wagon, I don't even think the Hollow will be a haven much longer."

Kara heard rustling from a tent nearby, followed by the slap of a tent flap being thrust aside, then silence. Cory stilled, both of them listening. Someone yawned and shook themselves, then there was a clank of metal against metal before the sounds moved off.

"Sword practice," Cory murmured softly.

Outside, they heard more rustling as others rose and headed toward the practice yard.

"I haven't been back to Erenthrall since the Shattering," Kara said. "From what Allan and the others describe, it isn't remotely like it was before. Confluence, Eld, Stone, even Grass and Copper. I'm not certain I want to see it now. I don't want to see the damage that the Wielders have done."

Cory sat up. "The Wielders didn't cause the Shattering. The Baron did, and the Kormanley."

"Did they? I know that Marcus did something to cause the blackout just before the Shattering. What if he unbalanced something in the Nexus? What if that's what caused the explosion?"

"You don't know it was Marcus who caused the blackout. You only know it was someone in Eld, based on what you saw in the sands before the Dogs took you."

"It was Marcus. I know it."

Cory gave a weary groan; they'd had this argument before, many times. "It doesn't matter now, does it?" She could hear him shifting around the tent, pulling on clothes. "The Nexus is destroyed. We'll likely never know exactly what caused it, or who brought it down—Marcus, the Kormanley, the Baron. We have to deal with what's happening now."

Kara tensed, ready to keep the argument going, but then relented. Marcus, the Baron—all of them were dead.

"Where are you going?"

"To the practice yard."

Kara suddenly sat up. "The yard?"

"I need to learn how to use a sword. At least the basics."

"Of course." She wasn't even certain what was bothering her. Except, like the cottages, it was one more sign that they were moving further and further away from Erenthrall.

She reached out and caught Cory's arm in the darkness. "Don't go today."

"Why not?"

"Because . . ." She fumbled for a reason. "Because I need you to show me the ley system in Erenthrall in the sands again."

"It won't do any good. The ley is changing too fast. It won't be remotely the same by the time you reach the city."

"I know."

Cory was silent, then sighed. "Get dressed then."

Kara threw the blanket aside and scrambled into clothes, touching the heating stone to turn it off.

When they stepped out into the predawn darkness, the chill air sucked Kara's breath away. She rubbed at her arms as Cory pulled the tent flap back into place and secured it, then they headed toward the village, many of its residents already up and doing chores.

They reached the barns, lamplight glowing from inside the last of the stone-lined stalls. When she and Cory rounded the corner, they found Hernande and Artras leaning over the sand pit, scrutinizing the shifting sands beneath them. Both of them looked up.

"Kara!" Artras said, rising stiffly from her crouch. The elder Wielder pulled Kara into a tight hug, then held her at arm's length. "Are you ready to return to Erenthrall?"

"No. But I am eager to see if we can finally do something about the distortion."

"So am I. Not all of us want to remain here in the Hollow like Sovaan." She motioned toward the sand pit. "I asked Hernande to show me the state of the ley before we depart. I assume you had the same idea?"

"That's why we're here."

"Then take a look." Artras hunkered down at the edge of the pit, Cory joining her. Kara moved around to the far side with Hernande.

"The chaos of the ley lines is rather interesting." Hernande's tone was that of a University mentor. "I am convinced there is a pattern here. Nature is not generally prone to complete disarray. The ley lines must be attempting to establish a new network."

Kara knelt down, knees pressed into the stone they'd used to line the floor and pit. The sands that filled it had already been set to Erenthrall and were moving in eddies and swirls, some of them slow, others accelerated, the lines merging and flowing. Occasionally, a spurt of sand erupted upward, like a geyser. The shifting sand created a soft hissing sound that Kara found soothing most of the time, but today the noise irritated her.

The center of the pit was nearly static, the active ley lines cut off by the distortion in a perfect circle. Inside that circle, where reality was shattered, there were only a few localized areas where the sand shifted, indicating a shard where time was still moving forward and the ley trapped there was attempting to realign itself. Kara, Hernande, and the others all agreed that the ley in these shards was attempting to form its own network, but in most, there wasn't enough ley for it to organize. A few of the shards were completely full, edges well defined, as if something had ruptured and flooded the region.

Hernande pointed toward the distortion. "I believe, from what Allan has been able to tell us, that this is the section where he was forced inside the distortion by the Wolves."

"It doesn't appear those shards are holding much ley."

"No," Artras said, "which is a good thing. My guess would be that fixing a shard that contains active ley would be more difficult than one without. We wouldn't want to break down the walls of a shard flooded with ley, for example, only to have it rush unrestricted into a section of the city that may be occupied."

Kara shivered at the image. Ley was harmless in its natural state, but if it were concentrated, it could be deadly. She recalled the stories about the sowing of the towers in Grass before the Shattering, where some of the lords and ladies of the city and surrounding areas had risked exposure to the ley by watching from unprotected balconies. They'd been killed, their bodies consumed by the ley when it touched them.

And then there was the Shattering itself. When the Nexus had exploded, the ley had devoured everything organic within a certain radius of the center that wasn't protected in some way. Kara and most of her fellow Wielders in the Hollow had only survived because they were locked away in cells beneath the Amber Tower. The same was true for Allan, Morrell, and the Dogs in their group. If Kara had been out in the streets, doing her rounds as a Wielder, she would have been killed. Most of the other survivors who had found their way to the University and then the Hollow had also been protected in some way.

She pushed aside the grim thought of what would have happened had she not been captured by the Dogs and shifted her attention to the rest of the ley. "It looks like the two rivers have settled into new courses."

"They're flowing through what were once streets, their banks now defined by buildings and the debris collected at their edges. But note these areas here and here." Hernande pointed to two locations outside the distortion. "They appear to be stable points in the general chaos of the ley."

"How can you tell?" They didn't appear any different than the rest of the ley.

Cory answered. "We've been watching them for the past few months. Everything else is shifting, reorganizing, but these two locations haven't moved."

"So the ley is attempting to establish a new system around the distortion, as we thought," Artras said brusquely.

"Why hasn't it stabilized, then?"

Artras shrugged. "Who knows how long it will take? We have no point of reference. The ley system we were using was always there. Only recently did we humans have the arrogance to try to manipulate and change it. And look where it got us."

Kara glanced up at the older woman's stern expression. For a moment, she'd sounded like Ischua, the Tender who had discovered Kara's talent and guided her after her parents' deaths.

Kara motioned toward the map. "I don't see anything around the area Allan found that will cause us any problems. The ley there appears relatively stable."

"Yes," Hernande agreed, "but remember that it is always changing. By the time your group arrives, it may be more volatile. Especially if the earthquakes have continued. We'll keep watch here, of course, but we won't be able to send word if something changes."

"I know." Kara rose. "Allan and the others are probably ready now. We'd better gather our things."

Now that she'd seen the ley system, the fears and anxiety she'd felt before dawn had receded, replaced by resolve. The same resolve she'd felt standing on top of the building after being pulled from the distortion by Allan and seeing the blazing white lights of the unquickened distortions over Tumbor, Farrade, and the other cities in the distance. She'd set it aside over the past few months to focus on survival, but it gripped her again now.

Kara bit her lip at the stricken look on Cory's face, but turned and left with Artras, the older Wielder taking her arm as soon as they were out of sight. "He'll be fine. You simply haven't been farther away from each other than a few minutes' walk in a few months. He'll adjust."

Kara didn't trust her voice enough to say anything.

Artras and Kara hustled to the refugee's meadow. Artras broke away from Kara and headed toward her own tent, shared with Dylan. Kara thrust her own tent flap back and reached inside, her pack waiting. She pulled it toward her, ready to step back outside into the dew-laden air, but she paused. The inside of the tent, still warm from the heating stone, smelled like Cory, his musk like earthen loam mixed with a faint spice that tickled her nose. She drew it in, committed it to memory, then released it and closed the tent again. Swiveling on the balls of her feet, she pulled her arms through the straps on her pack and settled it as she wove through the tents back toward the village.

As soon as she rounded Logan's cottage, she saw Cory, Hernande, Artras, Allan, and the rest of the group surrounding the single wagon they were taking into the city. It was already loaded with the few supplies they weren't carrying in their own packs. Two horses were hitched and stamping their feet, impatient to get moving. Kara noted four Dogs, all grouped around Allan. Aside from Artras, two other Wielders were going with them: Dylan and a younger Wielder named Carter. Two men from the refugees and two others originally from the Hollow—none of whom Kara knew well—would help gather the supplies once they were freed.

She noted Morrell standing close to her father. As she watched, the young girl—young woman, she realized with a start—suddenly reached out and hugged her father close before pulling back. Allan stroked her long golden hair, but caught her shoulders when she pulled away, saying something to her that Kara couldn't hear, a serious expression on his face. Morrell nodded and Allan nearly patted her head before catching himself.

Both Sophia and Paul were standing to one side, Paul scowling as usual.

Allan glanced around. "We're all here. Let's head out so we reach the plains before nightfall."

"Don't take any risks." Sophia gripped Kara's hands in her own. "We need you here more than you need to heal the distortions."

Behind her, Paul grunted in disdain.

Hernande shifted a discreet distance away as Kara turned to Cory.

"I'll be careful." She wrapped her arms around his waist and drew him in close. "And I'll be fine." She kissed him, then pulled away before her confident facade could crack.

One Dog and one Hollower had already taken the driver's seat and hied the horses to the edge of the forest, the rest trailing behind or already out in front. Artras was waiting for Kara to catch up. She said nothing as Kara rubbed at her face with her sleeves.

Then the group passed into the shadow of the trees, and the Hollow fell behind.

"Should we camp within the tree line, since there's only an hour or so before dusk?"

Allan stared out at the rolling edge of the plains. "We'll be traveling the grass for days. If there's someone out there, watching for us, they'll see us whether we move now or later." He met the Dog's gaze. "Be on your guard."

Glenn nodded, the gesture the sharp acknowledgment of a Dog to his superior, before retreating back into the woods to fetch the wagon and the others. Allan had been concerned the Dogs would assume Bryce's disdain for him and be insubordinate, but without Bryce here to goad them, they'd settled into the familiar framework that had existed in their packs before the Shattering. It was like the den before, with Hagger. Allan's old partner had been the instigator, gathering around him those that would follow his lead. But Bryce wasn't half as bad as Hagger had been.

He continued to scan the horizon as he heard the wagon trundling up from behind. Glenn and Adder appeared in his peripheral vision, and he motioned them out onto the plains, one to either side. They trotted up to the nearest rise, hands raised to shield their eyes from the sun, then signaled all clear.

Allan sought out Gaven, who was driving the wagon. "Everyone stay close to the wagon. We don't see anyone, but that doesn't mean they aren't there. Tim and Kent, form up behind. Glenn, Adder, and I will take the lead."

Gaven snapped the reins, and the horses pulled the wagon out from the protection of the trees. Allan waited until Tim and Kent were settled a short distance behind the main group, then trotted forward to where Glenn and Adder were already ranging out into the distance.

An hour later, with the sun sinking into the horizon, he called a halt in a shallow depression that would provide them some cover. The group broke into action with a palpable sense of relief. The Hollowers and Dogs immediately began setting up the camp, unloading the few supplies they had and establishing a perimeter and guard positions. Gaven unhitched the horses, leading them off to be fed. The Wielders looked bewildered.

As Allan returned to the wagon, Kara stepped forward, the Wielders behind her.

"What can we do?"

He paused to consider, noting the Hollowers already clearing a space for the fire to one side. "Can you create a heating stone out here? I have us camped out of the line of sight of anyone on the plains, but a fire would still be risky."

"We can try."

"Do it. Otherwise, you can help with the cooking. We won't be using the tents tonight, only pallets." He motioned toward the clear sky.

Kara turned to the others, already issuing orders. They broke up into groups, two heading toward where the Hollowers were trampling down grass in a rough circle, Kara and Artras toward where the grass had been cleared and a pit dug for the fire. They both hunkered down and closed their eyes, after ordering one of the younger Hollowers to search for a large stone.

When nothing happened for a long moment, except subtle shifts in their expressions, Allan shook his head and made the rounds of the camp, checking in on the Dogs.

By the time the sun had set in a blaze of blood red, the stars brittle overhead, half-moon to one side, Kara and Artras were holding their hands out to the glowing heating stone with smug grins on their faces and the Wielders and Hollowers were already setting up a tripod with a hook over it. A husk of corn was soaked and laid over the stone, cuts of venison spread out, filling the small depression with the scent of cooking meat.

Allan steered clear of the heating stone, knowing he'd disrupt it, and drifted out to the edge of their camp, passing Glenn in the darkness. He settled down into the ankle-high grass on a knoll and stared into the distance, toward the bright dome of the distortion in Erenthrall. The varied lights from its shards appeared to pulse, as bright as the moon, although it was a pinkish orange color, striated with streaks of brighter greens and purples. Off to the right, low on the horizon, he could make out a faint star: the distortion hovering over Farrade. Farther to the west, he could see the much brighter white light of the distortion over Tumbor. It was only marginally closer than Farrade. The fact that it shown so much brighter meant that it was significantly more powerful than the one in its sister city. When it quickened . . .

Allan reached forward to pluck at the grass before him.

He pulled a stalk and stuck it in his mouth, chewing on the tender end. A short time later, he heard someone approaching from behind, feet swishing through the grass. Kara settled down, cross-legged, beside him. There was just enough light from the moon and distortion to see her shadowed features.

"Beautiful, isn't it?" Kara said.

"And deadly."

"I know that, more than most. But it's still beautiful. I remember when I first saw one, there in Erenthrall, when I was younger. It bloomed in the air before me and Cory and—" Her voice caught. Then she continued: "It just appeared, in the middle of the street, no bigger than my fist. I wanted to reach out to touch it, to heal it, more instinct than anything else. I wasn't a Wielder yet. But the adults nearby stopped me." A wry smile turned her lips. "We were running from the Dogs at the time."

Allan looked toward her, eyebrows raised, and she burst into a laugh, shaking her head.

"It's not what you think. We were playing Thistles in the square when the Dogs came to raid a nearby flat. We ran, even though they weren't after us. We were kids."

Allan wanted to ask her about the name she'd swallowed, but didn't. "If the Wielders knew about the distortions that early, why didn't they stop them?"

"I don't think they knew how. All we could do was heal them. Now the Primes . . . I don't know what they knew. Even if Prime Wielder Augustus knew what was causing them—and I'd guess that it had something to do with the Nexus and the overuse of the ley system—do you really think Baron Arent would have allowed him to fix it if it threatened his hold on the ley and the other Barons?"

Allan thought about his few meetings with the Baron and the Prime Wielder. "No, he wouldn't. But Augustus was obsessed with the Nexus. If it were unstable, he would have attempted to repair it."

"If he could have repaired it, he would have."

"Maybe it wasn't the Wielders or the Primes. Maybe the Nexus didn't need to be fixed."

Kara looked toward him, half of her face in shadow, her body tense. "You mean the Kormanley?"

"They certainly caused enough havoc before I left for the Hollow."

Kara's hand tore viciously at the grass before her. He expected her to launch into a tirade about how destructive they'd been, but she surprised him.

She stopped shredding the grass and looked toward Erenthrall. "Do you think we deserved it?"

"What do you mean?"

"Some of those in the Hollow believe that the Shattering was a punishment, the vengeance of the gods, brought down upon us for our abuse of the ley."

"It wasn't the act of a god. It was Prime Wielder Augustus' arrogance and Baron Arent's greed. I was in the Amber Tower. I saw it."

"And some of them—not just the Hollowers, but a few of the refugees who came with us—believe that it's the Wielders' fault."

"They're fools."

"But we *were* misusing the ley. The distortions, the blackouts—they were all signs that we'd pushed the network too far. Yet we didn't stop. Nature tried to warn us and we didn't listen. Look what happened."

She gestured out toward the plains, toward the distant glaring dome of the distortion. They sat in silence, the stillness of the plains interrupted from behind by those in the camp.

Then Allan said, "It's changed completely. And I don't mean just Erenthrall. On my excursions to the city before the Shattering, to gather supplies for the Hollow, I'd sit on the hilltops and look down at it from afar. Ley lines spread out from it in all directions, like a web stretching to the towns and villages that dotted the plains. The web is gone now. The plains are dark."

Kara shifted her attention to the rest of the plains. There were a few spots of light scattered here and there outside the dome, close to the city; places where the ley system was intact, but obviously wild. White light flickered to the east, where Allan knew a plume of ley shot into the sky a hundred feet high. Almost directly on the path between the Hollow and the distortion, a large lake of ley had pooled in a low-lying area, what had once been a village. The spire of the town's stone meeting hall jutted out of the center of the lake, a few of the larger buildings' roofs visible as well. Besides pinpricks of white ley light in various other locations, they could make out a few outcroppings of firelight—again, all close to the city.

Kara pointed toward the brightest of the firelit sections. "What's that?"

"The Temerite's enclave. They were the most organized right after the Shattering. They seized hold of a few districts that hadn't been as severely damaged as the others and walled them in using the stone from collapsed buildings. The fire you see is actually dozens of bonfires set on the walls. They keep them lit so they can patrol and keep scavengers out. The smaller fire, farther to the south, is the Gorrani camp. There are rumors of an Archipelago compound on the far side of the distortion. And of course there are other encampments scattered between them all. But before the Shattering, there were ley lights three or four times that distance out into the plains, especially along the Tiana and Urate, and southward toward Farrade and Tumbor. All of those towns and villages are dark now."

"The ley is still there, running through those towns. It's just not being augmented by the Nexus like it was before."

"Is that what you intend to do if you can heal the distortion? Create a new network?"

"Not like what the Baron and Prime Wielder Augustus had," Kara said harshly. "They abused the ley to retain their power. But the world needs somewhere safe to travel, somewhere the ley is stable and that can be easily protected. If we can heal the distortion, we can make Erenthrall a home again, without the Baron and the Dogs and the Primes controlling everything."

"And you think we can do that, those of us in the Hollow."

"Why not? We have you and the Dogs. We'll have resources, once the distortion is gone. And we have Wielders."

Allan was going to point out that Erenthrall may have changed too much to be recovered when one of the guards shouted a warning.

He was moving, sword drawn, before Kara had even turned. He charged through the startled camp. Without thought, he noted who was frozen in shock and who was grabbing for weapons. Then he caught sight of Tim's shadowed form and slowed. "Report."

"Something on the plains to the northeast." Tim pointed toward the direction of Dunmara and the Reaches. "Looks like a fire of some kind."

Allan picked the faint, flickering light out of the darkness, surprised Tim had noticed it at all. Muscles in his back and shoulders relaxed as he realized how distant the fire was, too far for whoever it was to have seen or heard them.

Gaven, Carter, and Artras appeared behind them, knives or swords readied.

"Is it the raiders?" Gaven demanded.

"No. At least, not near enough to threaten us."

Gaven looked disappointed.

"What should we do?" Artras asked.

Allan sheathed his sword and the others lowered their weapons in response. He motioned to Kent and Adder. "We'll go check it out."

"I'll come as well," Gaven said, stepping forward.

Allan halted him with a hard grip on his shoulder. "I need you here, Gaven." He looked the older wagon driver in the eye. "I know you want to hurt them for killing Terrim, but with three Dogs gone, and Jack and Cutter out hunting, you'll need to help guard the others."

Gaven glared out at the faint fire, but nodded.

Allan, Kent, and Adder struck out across the grassland, moving at a steady, ground-eating pace. The camp fell behind, lost within a few hundred yards, the depression obscuring the glow of the heating stone. Allan focused on the dim firelight ahead, flickering low enough that occasionally it vanished. As they drew closer, it strengthened into a steady fire, larger than a campfire. Smoke billowed up toward the stars in a thick column, lit from beneath by angry red-orange flames. A gust of breeze brought the acrid reek of smoke and the stench of burning bodies. Allan swallowed against the smell, then gestured toward the two Dogs.

Kent and Adder angled toward Allan as he slowed. They edged forward cautiously, the wind shifting again, blowing the smoke away from them. All three dropped to the ground as they came up on the edge of a knoll, inching forward on hands and knees, then stomachs, using the grass as a screen.

Ten wagons lined the wide wash of the creek bed below, a thin trickle running through its center now, but a much wider flood path carved out of the plains on either side. Four of the wagons were burning, the fire crackling and snapping as it ate at the wooden walls and roofs, billowing out from beneath miniature eaves. At least twenty men were tossing trunks and barrels into four of the remaining wagons through the small open doors at their backs, a few others dragging more supplies from the remaining two. Five others held twelve men, women, and children captive near the center of the camp, a few of the women sobbing, one screaming, held back by two others as she struggled toward a body lying not far distant. More bodies riddled the wash, most obviously belonging to men from the wagons, killed before they could mount a defense.

The group's leader suddenly spun. "Shut that bitch up." When no one moved, he took two long strides toward the woman and slapped her hard across the face, flinging her back into the men holding her. They both lurched to their feet, fists clenched, but the five men guarding them leaped forward, swords bared, and they backed down.

The leader—a tall man with broad shoulders and a regal bearing, hints of Temerite in his face—turned away. His gaze swept the area, passing over Allan's position without pause, fastening on the men holding the skittish horses being hitched to the four wagons. "Where are Ghent and Harrison? Haven't they returned with the horses that bolted yet?"

Someone answered, but Kent tugged on Allan's shirt. The Dog pointed to a few of the bodies, then jerked his head toward the edges of the wash.

It took a moment for Allan to realize that the men had been killed by archers. None of the men below dealing with the supplies and horses had bows.

Which meant the archers were likely still watching from the darkness above the wash.

He passed the word on to Adder. They'd been lucky not to run into them on their approach. The smoke must have obscured them in the darkness, along with the grasses as they edged up to the knoll.

Adder gave him a questioning look, tilting his head toward the darkness behind them, but Allan shook his head.

He didn't want to risk exposing their position by retreating now that he knew there were others behind them.

Below, one of the men shouted, "It's empty," and climbed down from a wagon.

"Torch it."

Three men stepped forward with firebrands, one of them tossing a glass object inside with enough force Allan heard it shatter on impact. The others threw in their brands, and flame gushed out of the door with a feral whoosh, the men ducking as they backed away.

Allan focused on the leader, watching his movements. The Temerite lord stayed back from the main activity, but shifted from position to position, completely in control. The men were efficient, methodical, speaking to one another in curt sentences. No one laughed or joked. The leader rarely spoke. Everyone already knew what they were supposed to do.

The sixth wagon was finally emptied, the man inside hopping out mere moments before it was torched like the other. The leader began shouting orders, the others picking up the pace as the last of the supplies were loaded into the remaining wagons. Allan felt Kent tense as the men below regrouped. Two of the wagons began to trundle out of the wash, heading northeast. The men who'd been loading it drifted to surround the captives, glances passing among those with swords already drawn.

Allan placed a hand on Kent's shoulder and the man's eyes narrowed. Allan shook his head. Kent tried to pull away, but Allan clamped down hard, shoving him flat against the grass, leaning in close when he began to struggle.

"There's too many of them. We'd only get ourselves killed."

"Like hells," Kent spat. Allan shot a glance at the wash to see if anyone had heard, then tightened his grip until pain lanced across Kent's face.

"Do you want them to find our own camp?" Adder snapped from Allan's other side. "Or the Hollow?"

Kent fought a moment more, then relented. "They don't have a chance."

Allan loosened his grip, fingers aching. "They were all dead as soon as this group found them."

Below, someone barked a command and slapped their hand to the back of the last wagon. It began pulling away, after a shove from three of the men when one wheel stuck in the sandy bottom.

As soon as it began to move, the leader raised a hand and gave a curt signal.

Arrows shot out of the darkness from six different locations, each finding a mark among the captives. Four fell without a sound, including both children, arrows protruding from chests, a neck, an eye. Two others screamed, clutching at an arm, a stomach, but before the rest of the captives could react, more arrows found marks. The few survivors leaped up, men roaring, women screaming, and the men that circled them closed in. It was a slaughter, over in seconds.

The leader watched in silence. As soon as the last body slumped to the ground, the woman clawing at her attacker's arm even as she fell, he ordered, "Back to Haven."

The men stepped away from the slew of bodies, heading toward the edge of the wash. Conversations broke out, a few bursting out in laughter as they scrambled up the cut's far slope. Allan tasted bile in the back of his throat.

"What about Ghent and Harrison?" someone asked.

The leader scanned the darkness. "They'll find us on our way."

Allan, Adder, and Kent hunkered down even further as the six archers leaped down to join their fellows. Within moments, the wash was clear, only the dead and the six burning wagons left behind. The crackle of the flames eating away at the wood was loud in Allan's ears. To one side, he heard Adder dry retching.

"Should we leave now?" Kent jerked out from beneath Allan's hand. "I think the slaughter is over."

"Not yet. We don't know whether they've all left."

"They're gone."

All three of them lurched to a seated position, Allan managing to draw his blade and point it toward the figure standing over them, but an arrow was trained at his head.

"It's Cutter."

Kent swore as Cutter lowered his bow to the ground. The tracker scanned the darkness, eyes settling on the dead. "They've all headed northeast."

"Even the two after the horses?"

Cutter nodded, and Allan rose into a crouch. "Then let's get back to camp. Cutter, follow them discreetly, find out where they're headed."

Cutter pulled a string of dangling hares attached to his belt and handed them over to Allan. "I'll be back before you break camp." Then he vanished into the darkness.

"What about the dead?" Adder asked, staring down into the wash.

"We don't have time to bury them."

"We can at least pray for them."

"Pray as we walk."

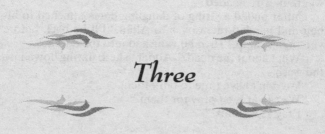

# Three

MORRELL FINISHED LABELING the last of the medicine bottles and placed them back in the wooden cabinet inside the healer's cottage. The wooden door creaked as she closed it and slid the string over the knob to keep it secured. She turned to brush the small cutting board free of the dusty remnants of crumbled wormroot, but a moan interrupted her.

She sucked in a harsh breath of fear, then remembered that she wasn't alone in the cottage. Claye was still here.

She rounded the central table where Logan had cut the arrow free of Claye's side and entered the small side room where the Dog rested on a plain cot, a blanket thrown over him. He'd been unconscious and feverish since the day he'd been rushed into the cabin. She knelt down next to the cot and placed a hand against Claye's flushed forehead. He tried to flinch away, one hand flapping weakly against the blanket.

"Stop it."

"What—?" His bloodshot and grit-crusted eyes caught hers briefly, registering confusion but no recognition, then flicked away, taking in the room. His breath was a phlegmy rasp, rattling deep in his chest. His skin was hot to the touch.

Morrell pulled her hand away and frowned. "You're in Logan's cottage. You were attacked, shot with an arrow. Remember?"

Edges of panic lined his face. "Logan? Attacked?"

"You were returning from Erenthrall with the wagon. Bandits tried to take it."

He sucked in a breath and held it, but then something clicked and he sank back into the cot. "Yes. Yes, I remember. They killed Terrim." He broke into a fit of coughing.

Morrell reached for the damp cloth in a small basin of water to one side, used it to remove the gunk from around his eyes. "You were hit, in the side."

He scrabbled at her arm. "Bryce? The others?"

"Everyone else is fine."

His eyes fluttered closed in relief.

She continued to wash his face, then set the cloth aside. Raising one of his arms —it felt strangely weightless, as if it were hollow—she pulled back the blanket to check the bandages wrapped around his chest. Fresh blood stained them in three places; his activity had reopened the wounds. But it was the putrid smell that bothered her.

"How bad is it?" Claye asked, startling her. She'd thought he'd slipped back into unconsciousness.

"It's festering. Logan's done all he can."

His head sank back to the cot. A moment later, he chuckled. "Killed by infection. How stupid."

Morrell pulled the blanket back further, then rose.

Claye had enough strength to catch her wrist. "Where are you going?"

She pulled his hand free. "I'm going to send for Logan. And I'm going to change your bandages. I'll be back."

She slipped into the outer room, then out the front door into bright sunlight. She squinted, catching sight of Jasom running across the rutted street in the direction of the barns.

"Jasom, come here!"

Normally, Jasom wouldn't pay her any attention, but the harshness in her voice halted him in his tracks.

"What is it? I'm busy."

"I'll bet. Claye's conscious. Fetch healer Logan. He'll want to take a look at him."

Jasom's eyes widened. "I think he's in the fields. I'll bring him right back!"

Morrell ducked back inside the cottage, moving swiftly. She set a pot of water over the coals banked in the small fireplace, then gathered up fresh bandages. She pulled the water from the coals, tested it, then moved into Claye's room, dragging a stool closer to his cot with one foot. Claye watched her warily.

"Should you be doing this without Logan here? I know you've been working with him, but—"

"I'm almost thirteen, and I've been changing your bandages for the past few days."

"Oh."

She squashed the pang of guilt about not mentioning that she'd never been *alone* while doing it and settled herself onto the stool. Claye swallowed once and stared at the ceiling.

When she pulled back the wrap, the smell of putrescence nearly made her gag. Claye moaned as the cloth stuck, then gave. The wound beneath oozed sickly yellow-green pus, the skin at the edges inflamed. Morrell leaned in closer, a curious detachment falling over her. She reached forward and pressed her fingers gently to either side of the wound just beneath his rib cage. Pus erupted from the hole, draining down the Dog's side and staining the bandage beneath. Claye's hands gripped the edges of the cot as he tried not to thrash about, but Morrell only increased the pressure, her fingers moving around the inflamed area, kneading the flesh, working as much of the pus out as she could. Claye writhed, his body instinctively pulling away. Another moan escaped him.

"Hush. I need to clean it out as much as possible."

The pus began to streak with blood, but she didn't stop. As her fingers moved around the wound, she found she could *feel* the infection, like flecks of darkness inside the flesh. Her fingertips prickled as she worked, as if they were being pricked by a thousand pins, the sensation not unpleasant. The infection had striated into the surrounding skin, lines of red obvious on the surface, but she could feel it seeping deeper inside Claye's body as well. A pocket of virulence here. A thread of invasion there. It was working its way into his bloodstream, through the tissues around his stomach. It was killing him.

It was too deep. Logan would never be able to cut it out. But she could feel it. It was *right there*. If only she could reach in and pull it out herself, drag it from his body, now, before it reached something vital.

Her fingertips flared, the prickling sensation suddenly intense, burning like fire. She gasped and jerked backward. A shiver of vivid colors enveloped Claye's wound.

"What is it? What happened?"

Morrell's mouth was dry, her tongue stuck to its roof. She stared at her hands. "Nothing. Nothing happened."

"I felt something. Like a tug."

"I didn't do anything."

Claye met her gaze, his skin beaded with sweat. Then his eyes dropped to his side. "Well, whatever you did, it doesn't hurt as much now." He collapsed back onto the cot. "Don't get me wrong, it still hurts like a son of a bitch, but it isn't throbbing like it was before."

Morrell didn't answer, leaning forward over the wound again. She placed her fingers next to the gaping hole. More pus had drained out into the used bandage beneath, but the yellow-green was now a brownish sludge. No new pus appeared as she prodded the edges of the wound, but it did bleed. The flow was sluggish. Claye didn't flinch away as much as before, and even Morrell could tell that the skin around the wound wasn't as inflamed.

She prodded the wound more, the prickling sensation returning to her fingertips, but she couldn't feel the infection anymore.

"Morrell?"

She jerked, the stool rocking beneath her. "In here!" She fumbled for a cloth, dipped it in the warm water, and began wringing the cloth out over the wound, washing as much of the blood away as she could. The familiar motions of washing the wound in preparation for a new bandage did little to calm her.

When Logan's shadow fell over her, she tried to lurch to her feet, but he put a hand on her shoulder. "Keep working. You're doing fine." He reached to touch Claye's forehead. "Fever's down. Good to see you're awake, Claye. I was beginning to think you'd never return to us. How are you feeling?"

"Like hell. But better now than when I first woke up."

Logan twisted so he could see the exposed wound, Morrell pulling the wet cloth back.

The healer's grim expression collapsed into confusion and Morrell's heart sank. "What did you do?" He shoved Morrell aside.

"N—nothing. I removed the bandage. Then worked as much of the pus out as possible. More came out than I expected, and it wasn't all yellow-green. It was brown at the end. And then it started bleeding."

Logan was pressing against the edges of the wound, persistent, making small noises beneath his breath.

Finally he sat back, hands dropping to his thighs, his gaze lingering on the wound before flicking toward Claye's face, then Morrell's.

"I don't know how it happened, but the infection is gone."

"That's good, isn't it?" Claye asked.

Logan was staring at Morrell. "Yes. Yes, it is good. I didn't think the poultices and salves I was using were working, but apparently I was wrong."

The statement hung in the air. Morrell returned his penetrating look with what she hoped was a wide-eyed, innocent expression.

More blood trickled down Claye's side, pooling on the already pus- and blood-stained bandage beneath. Logan reached for one of the new bandages Morrell had brought, using it to clean up, suddenly all business.

"I think I can safely close the wound now. Morrell, fetch me my needle and some thread. Sterilize the needle. I don't want the infection to return."

Morrell leaped up from her stool, Logan taking her place. She rushed into the outer room, grabbed a needle and thread, then held the needle in a candle flame. When she ducked back into the room, Logan had already prepped Claye's side. The healer took the needle and thread and began working, Claye hissing each time Logan passed the needle through flesh.

"Find Sophia, Morrell. She'll want an update."

Morrell backed out of the room. She hesitated in the doorway until Claye yelped and cursed, Logan apologizing without pausing. Then she turned and fled.

The sunlight blinded her again as she raced across the street, between the buildings of the Hollow, and down to the creek. She fell to her knees in the mud along the bank and dunked her hands into the frigid water, scrubbing away what little pus and blood remained. Then she continued scrubbing, until her hands were raw. Her breath quickened as she thought about the prickling sensation in her fingers, about the shimmer of light she'd seen after she'd withdrawn her hands from the wound. She'd seen the vivid colors before. They reminded her of the terrifying auroral lights that had plagued Erenthrall and the surrounding plains since the Shattering.

She clutched her hands to her chest, hunched forward over them. When a hand fell onto her shoulder she screamed and slipped on the slick stones of the creek's bank, half tumbling into the frigid water.

"Morrell, it's me! Cory!"

Morrell scrambled backward on the bank a few more steps before the words registered, then blinked up into the sunlight until she picked out Cory. He had his hands spread out toward her, as if trying to placate a spooked animal.

"Are you all right?"

"I'm fine."

He straightened slightly, hands lowering. "You should probably get out of the water then. You'll catch a chill."

She realized she was leaning on her elbow, left arm submerged, side soaked. Her arm was already numb.

She rolled out of the water, Cory helping her up onto the bank again.

"A few scrapes, but nothing serious," Cory muttered, checking out her arm. He paused when he realized her hands had been scrubbed raw.

"I'm fine."

"It doesn't look like it."

"I'm fine. It's just . . ." She waved her hand, tears threatening.

Cory glanced away. "I've been struggling, too. I'm worried. For all of them." He turned back. "But I know Kara's with your father, and he'll keep her safe. That's the only thing keeping me together. He'll bring her back. And he *will* come back, Morrell. He always has before."

She stared at him, realizing he thought she was upset over her father heading to Erenthrall. She seized on his assumption. "I know he'll be back. It just gets overwhelming sometimes. I was helping with Claye and—" Her eyes shot open in shock. "Claye! I was supposed to be fetching Sophia!"

She turned and charged up the bank, through the trees and into the Hollow. Cory called after her, but she ignored him. She didn't even know how long it had been since she'd left.

She was hustling past Logan's cottage when she heard Sophia's voice coming from inside. But then Logan spoke and she froze just outside the open door.

"I think it was Morrell."

"What do you mean? How could it have been Morrell?"

"I don't know. She claimed she was only cleaning the wound, draining the pus. But I checked the wound this morning and it was deeply infected. I don't see how it could have reversed course so quickly. Morrell *must* have done something."

"What are you suggesting?"

Morrell shifted closer to the doorway.

"I think Morrell healed him somehow."

Morrell's chest suddenly felt hollow and empty. What would the Hollowers think of her now? They abhorred the ley and anything associated with it. And it had to be something to do with the ley. She'd seen the shimmering auroral lights.

She slid along the cottage wall to the corner, then broke for the trees behind, passing through Logan's precious herb garden. She brushed up against one of the plants, the pungent scent of spearmint following her.

Then she was in the trees, crashing through the underbrush. She didn't know where she was going, but she knew she had to get away, to escape, to *think*.

Janis emerged from the edge of the trees onto the stone outcropping that overlooked the hills south of the Hollow, the sun just above the jagged peaks of the mountains to the west. The harsh colors of the distortion over Erenthrall glittered on the horizon. Sophia had found her in the cottage she shared with Allan and Morrell, had told her what had happened with Claye. She'd been concerned Morrell had overheard them and run away, but Janis had brushed her fears aside. Now dread clutched her chest at the thought that Sophia might have been right. She'd already checked all of the other places Morrell would run to when upset.

Then she heard a muffled scratch of cloth against stone. She stepped farther out onto the rocky outcropping and found Morrell seated, leaning against an upthrust ridge of granite, staring out into the distance.

Toward Erenthrall.

Morrell didn't move as Janis settled into position beside her. Tears sheened the young girl's cheeks. Her hands lay in her lap, palms up.

They sat in silence for ten minutes before Morrell said, "They told you, didn't they?"

"Of course they did. They were worried. They thought you'd run away."

Morrell's breath caught. "I didn't have anywhere to run to!"

"Oh, my dear child." She placed her arm around Morrell's shoulders, and to her surprise the recently willful and independent girl she had helped raise tucked herself into her side. Janis brushed her silken hair, and a sudden image of Morrell at half her current age stabbed into her heart with a sharp pain. She made soothing nonsense noises, watching the distance without really seeing it. The sun sank closer to the mountains, the shadows of the trees growing long and thin and diffuse, the lights of Erenthrall brighter.

"Did you think Logan and Sophia and the others would throw you out of the Hollow?"

Morrell snuffled and nodded, the motion against Janis' chest felt more than seen.

"Why would they do that? They've known you since you were a baby."

"Because they don't like the ley or anyone who can wield it. Look at how Paul treats Kara and the other Wielders."

"The Baron and the Prime Wielders forced Paul from his land, hurt his family. He's bitter. It has nothing to do with you. He accepted your father, didn't he?"

"That's different," Morrell said hotly, pulling away from her, sitting up straight. Her face was red and splotched from crying. "My father kills the ley, blocks it somehow. Of course everyone in the Hollow likes him."

Janis' eyes narrowed. "Sometimes you're too smart for your own good." She shifted tactics. "It won't matter. Paul won't find out what you've done. Logan, Sophia, and I have agreed to keep quiet about it."

"They won't tell anyone?"

"Why would they? What would they say? They don't know exactly what you did."

Morrell glanced down at her hands. "All I did was touch him."

"From what Logan says, you healed him. Cured his infection, at least."

"But I don't know how I did it."

"My point exactly. Why would they tell anyone if they aren't even certain you can do it again?"

"I *won't* do it again. I refuse to."

Janis' skin prickled in sudden unease. "Why not? You saved Claye's life, didn't you?"

"Yes. But when it happened, I saw—"

Morrell's jaw snapped shut.

Janis touched her arm, drawing Morrell's attention from the distant plains, now cast mostly in shadow, to her own eyes.

"What did you see?"

In a quiet voice—not childlike, but adult; more adult than anything she'd seen or heard from Morrell the entire time they'd spoken—she said, "Lights. I saw auroral lights. Like those we sometimes see on the plains."

"Is it going to hit us?" Allan asked.

Kara reached for the ley as she shaded her eyes with one hand, staring hard toward the shifting auroral light rolling across the plains between their position and Erenthrall like an eerily beautiful fog bank. A hideous prickling sensation crawled across her skin and down her back at the sight, like a thousand fire ants scuttling beneath her shirt. "I don't think so. But it's too close already. We should be careful."

They were standing on the outskirts of an abandoned town, long since raided for whatever supplies it might have held. As Kara lowered her hand, something tugged at her attention on the ley and she turned to face the west.

Allan caught her sudden tension. "What is it?"

"A ley line, stronger than anything we've encountered since leaving Erenthrall." She hesitated, dancing down its length, then gasped. "And a node." She turned to Allan in astonishment. "An *active* node. I have to see it."

Allan drew breath to protest, glancing toward the auroral storm in the distance, now blotting out half of the distortion over the city, then sagged in defeat. "Make it quick—"

Kara had already spun away from him, stalking toward the wagon and the rest of their group hovering on the edge of the town. "Artras, come with me. There's a ley line and node not too far from here. We need to check it out."

Artras gaped a moment, then hustled down from the wagon to meet her. Dylan and Carter both perked up.

"I can help," Carter called, hopping out of the back of the wagon as well.

"No need." Kara waved the young Wielder off. "Artras and I can handle it."

A look of irritation flashed across Carter's face, but then Dylan placed a hand on his shoulder and said something and he turned away.

"Where is it?" Artras asked as she approached.

"West of the village and the road, away from the main buildings."

"I can feel it. Not that strong."

"But stronger than anything near the Hollow."

Artras didn't answer. They stepped off the stone of the road and between two buildings, storefronts of some kind. Behind were a few storage buildings, scattered cottages with gardens now growing wild. Beyond, the terrain was rougher, but Kara could sense the pull of the ley. They brushed through grass, the knee-high stalks pattering against their legs, only rolling grassland interrupted by a few trees stretching into the distance.

"What's that?"

Kara squinted. "I don't know."

They stumbled onto the lip of a depression surrounded by a low wall of stacked stones. A break in the wall acted as a gate, and in the center of the shallow bowl of carved-out earth sat a rough-hewn triangular boulder resting on three squat round stones.

"It's like the bowl around the Nexus in Erenthrall. Not on the same scale, and that rock doesn't look anything like the Nexus when we found it, but close enough." Kara descended down into the depression. The ley grew stronger as she approached. She laid her hand on the rough surface. "It's the node," she said, then corrected herself. "No, it's not. But the node is directly beneath it."

Artras had laid her hand on the stone as well, brushing her hands across its surface as she moved around its three sides, eyes narrowed, searching. Most of the bowl was shadowed, deep enough it wasn't catching the light from the distortion. "I don't see any markings."

Kara realized what she was looking for and began searching as well. Within two steps, she stumbled on a stone hidden in the darkness. She felt it roll away—

And the energy within the bowl shifted. It was a subtle change, but Kara suddenly remembered Ischua, her father, and the test the Tender had given her in the middle of Halliel's Park when she was twelve. Her eyes widened as the memory poured in.

"It must be an old node." She reached down to pick up the displaced stone and returned it to its proper position. "One that was probably part of the ley network before Prime Augustus and Baron Arent subjugated the ley by forming the Nexus."

"But Hernande and Cory have been checking the network using the sands. They haven't seen many pockets of stability at all." Artras patted the rock between them. "This node feels stable."

"I don't think they've been monitoring it this far out. There's nothing here, after all." Then, in a softer voice, "Or there wasn't."

Kara shifted, reaching for the ley as she sighted along one of the ley lines. It angled straight for Erenthrall, the massive distortion looming on the horizon now, the auroral storm in between. It didn't surprise her that the node was connected to the city. But it couldn't be attached to the Nexus, or even Halliel's Park; both of those nodes were locked inside the distortion. It had to be connected to something else. But what?

And then there was the branching line.

She twisted, stepping away from the node toward the west, sighting along the second line. Unseen, it streaked straight across the plains, toward the mountains.

She'd started to reach out to follow it, perhaps to its destination, when Artras touched her arm.

"Look," the elder Wielder said, motioning toward the stone.

"What? I don't see . . ."

"The stone. It's pointing in the direction of the lines."

The stone had been oriented so that two of its vertices were pointed directly along the paths of the ley lines. The third . . .

"There must have been another ley line in the past." She stepped around Artras, lined herself up with the third point of the triangle, kneeling down so she could touch the earth there, reaching into it, feeling the energies that surrounded them. "Yes. You can feel it. The energies aren't quite in synch."

Artras crouched down at her side and she felt the older woman reaching into the eddies. "Something must have happened to the node at the other end, something to cut off the natural flow." Artras stood, staring off into the northeast. "It's pointing toward the Reaches."

"Dunmara?" Kara asked. But she didn't think so. The angle wasn't quite right.

Artras shrugged.

A shout came from the direction of the abandoned town, faint with distance. Kara patted the stone as she said, "We should head back."

They climbed up out of the node's bowl and entered the town to find Allan and the others already rolling out.

"We saw you coming," Allan said as they emerged between two of the faded storefronts to join him. They began to follow the wagon. "Did you find what you were looking for?"

"We found the node. But it didn't offer us any answers, only more questions."

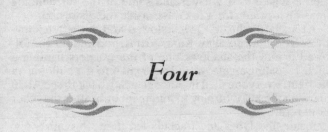

# *Four*

AFTER TWO WEEKS OF TRAVEL, Kara, Allan, and the rest of the group entered the edge of the sprawling streets of Erenthrall. Two of the Dogs loped out in front of the group, vanishing into side streets to scout the way Kara and the Wielders stayed with the wagon.

Kara eyed the buildings as they passed: windows gaped down at them, empty and hollow, their panes shattered; a few doors hung from hinges, some completely missing; shutters creaked in the wind coming from the east. But the streets were mostly clear, the buildings intact. The destruction of the Nexus hadn't been felt as badly this far from the center. Kara swallowed back a bitter taste nonetheless. She knew this was far from the worst, but she could sense how much the city had changed since she'd last been here. It felt wrong. The streets should be alive with people, with activity, with *life*.

One of the scouts returned and gestured to Allan. The ex-Dog motioned Gaven toward a secondary street, branching away from the main thoroughfare heading toward the city center. Gaven picked up the wagon's pace, forcing Kara and the others into a trot to keep up. They reached their destination within five blocks, making two more turns at odd intersections. Kara didn't even know what district they were in, much less what street they were on. But then, she didn't know all of Erenthrall, only the few districts she'd been assigned as a Wielder and some of the surrounding areas, all located closer to Grass, inside the distortion.

At a sharp whistle, Gaven slowed and cut left, leading the wagon into an alley. Kara, Artras, and the others followed it into the shadows, one of the trackers lighting a torch, revealing an alcove and door cut into the building on the right. Everyone filed in, Kara glancing back to see Allan guarding the alley, turning to join them only after the other scout returned.

Inside, the Dogs and trackers led them through a few hallways, then up stairs to the higher levels. They halted in a vacant interior room, doors opening off to either side into other rooms.

Kara turned to Allan. "What are we doing here? There are still a few hours of dark left. Shouldn't we head deeper into the city?"

"Not until we find out what the situation is at the moment."

"What do you mean?"

Allan glanced toward Glenn and Adder, who ducked into two of the side rooms. Kent and Jack headed toward the stairs leading higher up. "Tim, Cutter, keep watch outside." Both headed back downstairs as Gaven and Aaron returned from taking care of the horses.

Only then did Allan turn back to her. "The boundaries of the groups still here in Erenthrall change constantly. The section we're in right now is controlled by the Wolves. That's why there's no one around. We don't know where the Wolves have holed up, but they roam the streets in this area and take out whoever they find. But the Temerites have been pressing into this area from the east, and there are smaller groups scattered here and there who hound them as well. The last time we were here, this building and area were safe, but that may have changed since then. We need to make certain before we try to move in closer to the distortion."

"You've used this building before?"

"It's one of many we've set up throughout the city." He

moved to the side of the room, where the wall was covered in cupboards. He opened a few, removing some blankets, passing them around. Gaven opened others, revealing stored food, a few candles, other supplies.

Kara caught a glint of torchlight on glass and her hand shot forward, her fingers slipping over the object almost reverently. "A ley globe. I haven't seen one of these in months."

All of the Wielders paused, Dylan and Carter rising and drifting forward.

"Should we see if we can light it?" Dylan asked.

They all looked to Allan. He shrugged. "It would save us using the candles or lanterns."

Carter reached for the globe, but Dylan grabbed his hand. "You should do it, Kara."

He didn't notice Carter's look of resentment.

Kara's brow furrowed. "Why me?" She placed the globe in Carter's hands. "You and Dylan see if you can get it to work. See if you can get a heating stone going as well. Just be careful with the ley. We know it's unstable and erratic here."

Carter accepted the globe and they shifted into a corner, already arguing over how to get the globe activated when they didn't know the layout of the ley and how to keep it lit without constant monitoring if the ley was unstable.

"Will they be able to do it?"

Kara reached for the ley in the area, felt it throbbing against her skin. This close to Erenthrall, it surrounded her on all sides, but there was no order to it. The stable ley line they'd found in the abandoned town days before still lay off to their northwest. There were a few other points of stability nearby, possibly nodes, but there was no network, not even a significant locus of power. Somewhere close, ley was pooling beneath the streets, probably in one of the ley barge stations or one of the system's tunnels. Farther out, ley exploded from the earth in a geyser, the fountain already abating.

"They should be able to get this room stabilized, maybe the building, but it's too chaotic beyond that. And it won't last. As soon as we leave, it will collapse."

"It's better than nothing. Just make certain they keep the

globe in here. This room is central enough that the light can't be seen from outside." Allan headed toward one of the side doors, weaving through the others, who had already claimed sleeping space around the room. "They won't be able to do anything if I'm here."

Kara hesitated, then followed him out into the corridors and rooms beyond. As they passed through the apartments and flats, she noted that tables and chairs and other furniture had been rearranged, blocking doorways and halls, creating a maze with dead ends and false turns. Most of the rooms had been cleared, floors and walls bare, only the tracks in the dust from the guards indicating any signs of life.

Allan passed through a door into a room where Glenn stood guard to one side of a shattered window, a faded curtain fluttering back from the broken glass. Allan joined him, Kara hanging back. She could see the variegated lights of the distortion through the opening, blocks of streets and buildings in between. The city rose and fell, following the hills and the natural landscape, but from this vantage, Kara could see all the way to the distortion, the view unobstructed except for a few taller buildings to either side. The land dipped down in a shallow valley, interrupted only by the cut of the Tiana River. The distortion illuminated it all in blocky rooftops and black shadow.

"Anything?" Allan asked Glenn.

"No activity nearby." He pointed. "That ley geyser is new, so we should avoid the Backway District and probably Harker Street. There are torches along the Temerite walls to the east, and a few fires between here and there, smaller groups holding out in a few buildings. The River Rats appear to still hold their small island in the middle of the Tiana to the southwest."

Kara shifted forward as he spoke, until she could see into the distance to the left of the distortion. The view wasn't as clear here, rises in the land cutting off the sightline, but there were numerous groupings of firelight, all on the far side of the Tiana and all too distant to make out any clear details. The ley geyser she'd felt earlier spouted up between a set of buildings much closer to their own, the white light harsh, near blinding.

Sliding to the left, closer to Allan and Glenn, she picked

out the island. Not a true island, merely a long section of buildings where the river had split as it gouged a path through the city. She couldn't tell if there were other groups besides the River Rats in that direction.

"This entire area is controlled by the Wolves?"

"Yes."

Kara straightened in mild shock. "But their territory covers at least four districts, if not more!"

"Which is the only reason we've been able to infiltrate the city and return to the Hollow with supplies all this time. The territory is too large for them to patrol easily. We've been able to slip in and out without notice."

"Most of the time," Glenn added, casting Allan a significant glance.

"Yes, most of the time. But their hold on the others is based on fear. It won't last." It looked as if he were about to say more, but then his shoulders slumped. "You should rest. Tomorrow, I want to take you and the others to the distortion. We need to see whether or not you can release individual shards as soon as possible. If this has been a fool's errand, I don't want to linger in the city."

Kara edged toward the window and looked across the Wolves' territory at the distortion, at the jagged edges of lightning that shot through it and the faces of the shards of fractured reality. Exhaustion brought on by the weeks of travel settled into her bones, but now that she was this close she wanted to be there, at the base of the distortion, acting to bring it down.

But it would do no good working on the distortion when she was already tired. It would only drain her further.

She returned to the inner room, where Dylan and Carter had managed to light the ley globe, its soft white radiance—so different from firelight—suffusing the room. After so long, the light felt strange and unfamiliar. They'd set up the heating stone in the center of the room.

Everyone had slumped down onto their makeshift pallets, a few even snoring. Only Artras stirred as Kara knelt to warm herself.

"This is for you." Artras patted a set of blankets already arranged to one side before rolling over and pulling her own tighter over her shoulders.

Kara sank to the pallet gratefully. She thought the light of the ley globe would keep her awake, but she instantly fell asleep.

Drayden loped along the street in the darkness, his paws making no sound as he padded down the length of a building, winding through debris. The stars out over the plains to the north glinted like pinpricks of broken glass. To the south, the glare of the distortion washed most of the stars out. Dawn was an hour away.

He reached the end of the block and paused, staring out over the plaza to his right. The statue of a man stood on a pedestal at its center, right hand extended toward the heavens, a globe in his left. His lip curled and a low rumble rolled down through his chest. Something about the plaza, the statue, tugged at his memory. As if he knew this place, this person, the meaning deeper than simply a checkpoint on his patrol or a feature of the pack's hunting ground. A flare of sunlight in his mind brought the sound of a crowded bazaar, a girl's childish laughter, the touch of a woman, the scent of roasted meats and pungent ale.

His mind grasped for the images . . .

But he couldn't dredge them up from the depths, and the illusory sensations slipped away. His growl faded. He sniffed the air, the scents of *now* prickling his nose in layers. Dust and stone, dried wood, a dampness that remained from the rain two days before. The musk of his fellow pack mates who'd passed this way recently. Rat shit and urine, the tang of rabbit and vole, the dry slickness of snake.

Wind gusted, plucked at his fur, and he turned his nose into it, breathed in deep—

And slid instantly into a low crouch, neck fur bristling, ears pricked forward, as the scent of humans slammed into him. Many of them, their reek individual, distinct, and close. He pinpointed the direction and scrambled across the openness of the plaza, slinking around the statue that disturbed him with its dark familiarity and hints of lost memories and into the streets beyond. He prowled through the shadows, the noise of his claws against the stone suddenly too loud.

Two blocks further on, he slowed, the scent of humans—and horse—stronger now, almost overpowering. Reaching an intersection, he paused, searched both directions, but saw nothing. He trotted out into the street, nose to the ground, weaving back and forth, circling, picking out six, seven, no, a dozen distinct scents, maybe more if the group had scouts, plus the horses. Metal as well. A wagon, its wheels scraping the stone cobbles.

And one of those scents tickled another memory, more recent than the statue, more permanent.

He snuffled along the track, trying to place it—

Then images exploded across his vision and he jerked to attention, his lips drawing back from his teeth, an angry growl uncurling from deep inside: a frantic chase through debris-cluttered streets, a leap from one building to the next, and then a burst of pain as he slammed into the side of the distortion, followed by seething rage at the prey's escape.

The alpha had been furious, had punished them all severely.

The alpha had ordered them to warn him if the scent of the man were picked up again.

Drayden's anger banked like a fire and, still snarling, he backed away from the direction the man had taken before twisting around and racing toward the den.

The alpha would want to know immediately that the man who had escaped them so recently had returned.

At dusk, Allan, Kara, Dylan, two of the Dogs, and Cutter headed out. Those left behind were to gather the wagon and move to another of Allan's safe houses closer to the distortion, while the main group investigated the shard Allan had discovered the last time he'd been in Erenthrall. Kara wanted to see if it could be healed. She'd brought Dylan in case she needed help.

In the odd half-light of falling twilight and the backwash from the distortion, they edged to the end of an alley, Allan searching the street beyond before motioning Cutter out before them. The tracker sprinted across the street and vanished in the deepening shadows of the buildings. Allan waited to give him a lead and then followed.

They dashed across the street, Kara feeling more exposed now than she had the day before. But no one leaped out of the vacant windows of the buildings and no howl rose from the Wolves. She relaxed once she ducked into the doorway of the far building, tracking Allan by his footprints in the dust and the scrapes and rustlings of his movements ahead. He led them out the back of the building, through a series of rear gardens already ragged and wild, then into another tenement.

They moved swiftly, stayed inside buildings as much as possible, near windows so they could see by the light thrown by the distortion. At one point they descended into a basement, the way forward blocked by a building that had collapsed. Another time, they ascended to the rooftop, jumping over the firewalls and the narrow alleys between buildings. Allan and the Dogs didn't hesitate, as if they'd done this a hundred times; the first few jumps, Kara's heart was in her throat. She was grateful when they returned to the eerily vacant rooms below again. Before stepping into the small enclosure that covered the stairwell, she glanced toward the distortion and realized they were nearly halfway to its base.

The worst part came when they reached the river. The Tiana was wide, the only way to cross one of the many bridges that spanned it. But the bridges were completely exposed, worse than the streets and plazas. And they were deeper inside Erenthrall now, closer to where the fires of the other groups had been.

When they reached the buildings closest to one of the bridges, Allan halted the group. Cutter was waiting for them. They huddled down behind the windows of what had once been a bakery.

They looked out on a wide park, the street leading to the bridge cutting through the low walls, benches, and patches of greenery and trees. The bridge arched up slightly, a wide section for pedestrians on either side. Stone statues rose at intervals, each figure holding a ley globe, most of them still intact but not currently lit. Farther up the river, she could see another bridge, although a section of that one had collapsed.

"Report."

"I didn't see any Wolves, and there's no activity on this side of the river."

"What about the far side?"

"Hard to tell. I hit the roof and watched until I heard you approaching. I didn't see anything near here. There's something happening about ten blocks northeast—a fire, perhaps a clash between a few of the groups we noted in this area last night."

"Maybe that's what pulled them away from the bridge."

"There aren't enough of them to watch all of the bridges normally anyway."

Dylan shifted closer to both of them, crouching down beside Kara. "Do we have to cross the river here? It's too exposed."

"We could head closer to the distortion along the river's edge and try for another bridge, but then we'll be closer to the River Rats," Allan explained, never taking his eyes off the bridge and the river beyond. "I'd rather risk the smaller, less organized groups here. The Rats can be vicious."

Glenn's eyebrows rose. "And these groups aren't?"

"We'll cross here, all in one group, all at once." Allan motioned toward the window. "Same order as before. Cutter, aim for the southern edge of the bridge. We can use the shadow of the bridge's wall as we cross."

Cutter nodded, already scanning out the window. Kara felt for the knife sheathed at her side, although she barely knew how to use it, then drew her hand across her slick forehead.

At a gesture from Allan, Cutter slid down to the empty doorway and out into the street, Kara following the rest in a line. She stayed hunched over, like Allan and Cutter before her, gaze cutting left and right until she reached the hedges of the park. Leaves brushed her shoulders and branches caught in the cloth of her shirt, but she didn't want to move out of the shadows.

They reached the end of the park, clustering in a corner, the bridge twenty steps away. In the distance, she could now see a column of smoke rolling into the sky, lit from beneath by the pulsing orange of a fire.

As soon as Glenn and Tim had joined them, Allan touched Cutter's shoulder, and the tracker sprinted across the walkway to the lee of the bridge wall. The rest were on his heels. The first statue—an elderly man in Prime

Wielder's robes—slid by overhead, hands on either side of the dead globe. Kara glanced up at him, at his faintly arrogant features, then behind—

And caught a hint of movement in one of the buildings beyond the park.

She cried out, but caught herself, choking it off. It still snagged Allan's attention. She halted, crouched low, weight on her heels. He hesitated, then returned.

"What is it?"

"Movement, in the shadows of the café two buildings to the left of the bakery."

Dylan and the others had caught up to them, but Allan motioned them to keep moving.

"What was it? Did you see?"

"It was too quick. But whatever it was, it kept low to the ground."

It could have been anything. Someone crouched down low, like them, or an animal now living in the abandoned city.

Or one of the Wolves.

They waited, but twenty breaths later there had been no other sign of movement.

"Maybe it was nothing."

Allan gripped her arm, pulled her toward the far end of the bridge. "Come on. Go ahead of me. I'll watch as we move."

They reached the far side, Allan pointing toward a mercantile of quarried white granite. As they crossed the thoroughfare to duck into its huge wooden double doors, Kara heard an echo of people shouting and the roar of a fire, far distant. But the sounds died out as soon as she entered the building.

"What did you see?" Dylan asked.

"Nothing. There wasn't anything there."

Dylan looked skeptical, but Allan said, "Go up Traveler's Row," cutting off anything else he might have asked. "It's nearly a straight shot to the area we want."

They stuck to the shadows in the street after leaving the mercantile through a different set of doors. The fire and noise from the fighting receded as they skirted block after block. The distortion neared, its fractured sides rising into the night sky.

A hiss from Cutter and Allan's arm shoving Kara against the nearest wall brought her attention back to the street. Allan motioned toward the rooftops opposite their position.

Figures were silhouetted against the glow of the distortion. Kara hunched down farther into the darkness as the figures leaped from roof to roof. They moved with a fluid, eerie silence, racing toward the disturbance farther up the street. She couldn't see individual faces, but as they passed directly across from her, shifting from the diffuse light of the distortion into darkness, then vanishing, she realized they were dressed in rags, carried spears, a few with bows, and they were all children, or at least young adults.

Kara waited until Allan gave the signal to move again, then grabbed his arm. "Who were they?"

"River Rats."

"They were Morrell's age!"

"And they're dangerous."

Kara didn't need him to elaborate. She'd felt it as they ran past, even from four stories down and a street away.

She glanced behind them as they continued down Traveler's Row, but saw no sign of the River Rats again. At one point, she thought she saw movement between the columns of another mercantile, but she said nothing.

Then Cutter slowed. They diverged from the Row and the trading houses vanished, replaced by more domestic housing—apartments and smaller shops, inns and taverns. They were in a neighborhood similar to the one Kara had grown up in within Eld. The streets were littered with abandoned or broken carts and the detritus of a thousand lives interrupted or destroyed by the Shattering. Trunks and household items were scattered in the dust, dropped as people fled. Kara stepped over discarded clothes, a child's rag doll, a broken urn, as they crossed a street to another building, where Cutter halted inside.

"You'll have to lead us from here, Allan."

"This is close enough."

Allan motioned them deeper into the apartment building, across the foyer, and into the back halls. They exited through the back.

As they continued, Kara noticed that the buildings were

more damaged than they had been earlier, now that they were closer to the distortion. Walls were cracked, entire sections collapsed, leaving gaping holes into the rooms beyond. Roofs had caved in, along with some of the upper floors. They crawled over heaps of stone before entering another building and emerging onto another street. Allan halted and glanced around, orienting himself, then headed toward the distortion at a trot, Cutter a few paces behind him with bow ready. Glenn and Tim brought up the rear, both with swords drawn, but they saw nothing.

A short time later, the distortion appeared ahead, slicing down from the sky, cutting through half of a building to the right and into the cobbles of the street. Kara knew without reaching out with her Wielder senses that the distortion sliced through the ground beneath, probably through the ley tunnels and underground barge system itself.

Allan stopped a few paces from the shard. Both Kara and Dylan drifted up behind him. Through the strangely flat facet, tinged a pale orange, Kara could see the street continuing on as if uninterrupted. Same for the buildings to either side. Much farther ahead, the street ended at a square.

"This is it." Allan pointed. "The apothecary I found is to the left, just before the square. We should probably hit that first. If you can release the shard without destroying what's inside, that is."

"Let's find out."

Allan stepped back, ordering the Dogs into defensive positions around them. Kara let the sounds wash over her as she stared up the wall of the shard, her blood thrumming in her veins. She couldn't help smiling a little, even with the threat of the Wolves and River Rats and others hanging over them.

"It's a little thrilling, isn't it?" Dylan said.

"And daunting. We haven't practiced with the ley in a while. We should take it slow. Let's both investigate it separately first. Then we'll compare what we've found."

"Agreed."

Dylan stepped away from her, moving along the shard's edge. Kara reached out with her hands, although she couldn't bring herself to touch what appeared to be a hard surface; she'd experienced too much horror as a Wielder in the city when it came to the distortions. Instead, she closed her eyes and felt the distortion through what Hernande and the University mentors called the Tapestry.

It felt like every other distortion she'd ever encountered. She could sense the cracks all around her, radiating outward from the center, slicing the remains of the city into distinct pieces. If this had been a normal-sized distortion, she would have attempted to surround it, trace out the damage, and then begin to repair it, healing each fracture one careful step at a time, all while anticipating the destabilization of the distortion and its sudden closure. But she couldn't do that here. She would never be able to sense all of its edges, never be able to piece together what needed to be repaired first.

She focused on the single shard before her instead. It was three times the size of the largest distortion she'd handled in Erenthrall before the Shattering, and oddly shaped. Four sides were relatively flat, like the sides of a gemstone, but the far side was broken up into a dozen or more facets with no obvious pattern of formation. She couldn't visualize how these fractures related to the surrounding shards, to the distortion as a whole.

She pulled back in frustration, opened her eyes and grounded herself again. Dylan was still working silently to one side, his face creased in concentration.

Allan came up to her side. "Well?"

"I don't know. We can't approach it the same way we did before, that's for certain. If we collapse the inner walls, we'll be healing parts of the adjacent shards as well, releasing them. It might set off a cascade reaction, each shard collapsing into the next, until the entire distortion folds in on itself."

Dylan gasped and staggered back a step, one hand rising to massage his temple. He drifted toward them. "This is going to require a delicate touch."

"What were you thinking?"

"As you said, we can't heal all of the sides. But we can leave all of those touching adjacent shards standing and just release the faces that are free, like this one."

"Then do it."

Both Wielders turned to Allan. He shrugged. "That's what we're here for. And the longer we wait, the more likely someone will find us."

The ex-Dog walked away, leaving Dylan and Kara alone.

"You'd better take the lead, Kara. The ley here isn't stable, and it's not as strong as it was before."

Kara had noticed that as well. "I'm going to try to heal this one face. I'll need you to stabilize the sides."

She reached for the Tapestry again, while at the same time stretching out to the nearest source of ley. There were a few weak lines running beneath them, not strong enough to help her if she needed the ley's power. An immense pool stood off to their left, but south of them, caught in the distortion, so she couldn't access it. Another had formed outside the distortion to the west. She linked herself to it, noting that it acted like one of the pits inside one of Erenthrall's old nodes. In fact, a strong line branched out from it, angled west, away from them.

Then she concentrated on the shard before her. Dylan joined her, connecting his strength to hers. The shard's face had five edges, none of them the same length, and as she prodded the surface she realized it was weaker farther from the edges. She found the weakest point, a spot a foot above the cobblestones of the street to their right.

Glancing toward Dylan, whose jaw clenched to indicate he was ready, she began putting pressure on the weak spot.

It resisted. A ripple ran through the face of the shard. She pushed harder, but the face merely bowed inward.

She pulled back. She didn't understand. She was doing what she'd always done to heal a distortion—reach out and encompass the shattered reality, then smooth out the edges, from the outside in.

But she couldn't surround the face. And she didn't think she could pry one of the edges free, not without also affecting the connecting shards.

She needed to pierce the face somehow, then work with the hole she'd create.

Gathering herself, she formed the Tapestry into a sharp point, like a needle, then jabbed the needle forward—

And felt it punch through.

She jerked back, half expecting the face of the shard to

burst like a bubble, but it held. Reaching forward, she pried mental fingers into the tiny hole she'd created and began healing. One of the Dogs swore when the hole she'd created became visible. Sweat broke out on her forehead as she continued, but Dylan added his own strength to hers. She drew some from the distant ley as well, and the hole widened, large enough now for them to step through.

After a certain point, the healing sped up on its own and Kara pulled back, watching the rest of the face disappear into the edges of the shard on either side, as if she'd reached a critical limit after which the shard could heal itself. Dylan tensed as it reached the edges of the adjacent faces, but the healing halted as soon as it hit the face's boundaries.

Kara stood silent, breath held. A breeze brushed past her, coming from inside the shard. She exhaled, tasted the stale air as it escaped, dry and dusty. It smelled of death and decay.

She glanced down. Where the shard had intersected the street, a thick line cut through the cobbles, the earth churned and broken where the shard's wall had been.

A hand on her shoulder made her jump.

"Is it safe?" Allan asked. The rest of the Dogs were grouped behind her and Dylan, blades drawn, eyes searching the newly revealed street, their mostly empty satchels ready.

"It's stable."

"Then let's move."

The Dogs crossed the old threshold cautiously, but broke into a trot on the far side, following Allan as he led them toward the apothecary. Kara grabbed Dylan's arm and hauled him inside as well. They hugged the buildings on the left until they neared the square. The apothecary stood with its door open and Allan and the others ducked inside without hesitation. They stuffed bottles into their satchels, glass vials clinking together. But the fountain in the square snagged Kara's attention, the angel statue with wings spread and face lifted to the sky making her pause. The stone ledge of the basin beneath circled the statue, and leaning up against the basin—

Her breath caught. She could see at least two bodies at this distance, what might be a third lying on the ground at their feet, stacks of supplies surrounding them.

"They killed themselves," Allan said from behind her, making her start. "They waited for someone to come and then they gave up."

"How long?"

"Long enough to scrounge and gather up all of the useful supplies in the area. But time was moving faster in this shard, so it could have been weeks or months, maybe even a year from their perspective. How long would you wait if you couldn't get out?"

Kara didn't know.

"We need to get as many of the supplies they gathered as we can carry. Stay here if you want."

"No. I'll go. If we keep opening up shards, we're likely to find much worse than this."

Allan said nothing, but stepped around her and moved toward the fountain. Kara followed.

He hadn't warned her about the baby, clutched in its mother's arms. Kara hesitated, thinking that something should be done for them, but she didn't know what. They couldn't bury them here, in the middle of the city. They couldn't burn them without drawing attention to the shard and their activities.

Finally, she whispered a small prayer she'd heard her mother use on occasion and then began filling her empty satchel with jars. Pickled eggs, cauliflower, crushed tomatoes. When she tried to pick up a sack of rice it split down the center, the grains scattering in all directions. She swore and began scooping it up into the sack's two halves, tying the wide ripped mouths together with twine they'd brought with them. She used a cup to scrape what was left directly into her satchel.

By the time she'd finished and filled the rest of her sack with more jars, the others from the apothecary had joined them and were topping off their own bags.

"Did you empty the apothecary?" Allan asked Cutter.

"Everything we could find that wasn't broken or obviously spoiled."

"Good. We won't be able to take everything that's here, but we can come back for the rest tomorrow night."

"Assuming that it's still here," Glenn said. "It might not

take long for the other groups to realize this shard is now open."

"We're in the middle of Wolf territory. No one will likely come here. And the Wolves aren't interested in food like this. They want meat."

"We should have brought the others with us. We could have taken nearly all of this with us."

"I doubt we would have gotten here unnoticed with the entire group," Allan said, "especially if we'd brought the wagon. Besides, this isn't enough to make the trip from the Hollow worth it. We're going to have to open up more shards before we head back. We've got time."

They fell into the same order they'd used to get there, returning down the same side of the street. But once they left the shard, Allan motioned Cutter onto a different route, although they would need to return to the same bridge.

As they left the shard behind, Kara glanced back once, the opening in the side of the distortion like a wound. But they'd done it. They'd healed part of the distortion. It was only one of thousands of shards, but it had been repaired.

Drayden growled low in his throat as the group left the healed shard, but Grant—his alpha, standing on two legs beside him—gripped the scruff of his neck and held him back as he began to stalk forward. He whined in protest and confusion. The humans had invaded their territory! They needed to be slaughtered! Drayden could smell their blood from here, wanted to taste its warm, metallic slickness.

"No." Drayden heard both the human word and the guttural wolf command beneath. "We can't kill them yet. We have brethren captured inside the distortion. This man—and these others—may be able to free them."

Drayden understood the words, the intent, but struggled to contain the feral animal that wanted nothing more than to tear and shred with his teeth, to roll in the humans' thick blood as it gushed from their ripped-out throats. The two other pack mates with him struggled as well. One of them began to howl a protest and lunged forward.

Grant kicked his pack mate into the crumbling wall of

the room where they hid. The Wolf—he had no human name, had been changed too much into a wolf to remember it—yelped and twisted around, teeth lashing at Grant's foot. But Grant—more human than wolf, but still part wolf—was too quick. He cuffed Drayden's pack mate hard enough that his snout snapped back into the wall, then knelt and captured the Wolf's neck with one arm before he could recover. The captured Wolf braced his feet, eyes filled with hate, and prepared to break free, head snapping to the side in an attempt to capture their leader's half-human, half-wolf body. Grant's wolf-ear twitched and Drayden and his other pack mate circled the two, Drayden growling low and deep in his chest in warning. He didn't understand why Grant chose to wear the human clothes, but he'd understood almost immediately that Grant was their alpha.

This pack mate had forgotten.

"We will wait." The human words were almost lost in the rumbling wolf command. "And we will watch. We need to know if they belong to the White Cloaks. If they do, then we will kill them."

Drayden flinched at the naming of the White Cloaks, but he remained focused on the pair, ready to lunge and kill his pack mate if necessary. But after growling and thrashing a moment more in Grant's chokehold, the Wolf suddenly yipped and cowered, lying flat, panting in submission.

Grant retained the chokehold for another twenty heartbeats, until his dominance was clear, then thrust Drayden's pack mate away as he stood. Drayden kept his eyes on his mate as Grant dusted off, but the Wolf remained cowed.

Grant caught Drayden's attention with a flick of his hand. "Follow them, but don't be seen. Report back to me."

Drayden huffed agreement, scanned the now-empty street below, then trotted off into the ruins of the building. He'd have to pick up their scent and track them from there.

# Five

"SO IT WORKED?" Artras asked as soon as the group entered the new safe house. "You managed to release one of the shards?" Her gaze dropped to Kara's satchel before she'd finished speaking. She saw the bulging sack and grinned, her shoulders slumping in relief.

Behind her, Carter glared—still ticked that he hadn't been taken on the first run. The two Hollowers—Gaven and Aaron—both came forward to take the retrieved supplies from the rest of the group as they entered. They began to unpack and sort them over where the rest of their supplies had been stored in the new rooms. Unlike the previous apartment building, this hideout was in the back rooms of a mercantile, all on the first level. Kara had seen Adder guarding horses, cart, and the back entrance as Allan led them through the alleys and loading docks, but knew that Kent and Jack would also be on watch, probably on the building's roof.

Kara handed Artras her satchel. "It was easier than expected, although we'll have to proceed carefully. And I think, for safety, we should always work on a shard in pairs, so that one can hold the edges of a face while the other works to heal it."

"I don't understand."

"It will be easier to show you when we head out next, but we'll try to explain."

From near the supplies, Allan broke in with, "You'll have some time. We'll have to hole up here while I search for another shard that's worth opening."

Artras was already shaking her head. "No, we won't."

"Why not?"

"We didn't come here just to gather supplies. We came to start healing the distortion. While you're out searching for shards with food and medicine, we can be healing whatever shards we run across. Think of it as practice for when you find one we really want to reach."

"And I don't relish sitting here doing nothing until you return," Carter threw in, his tone harsh.

Allan bristled, but Kara raised a hand to halt his response. "We'll go crazy if we're forced to wait, especially now that we know we can start repairing the damage. And we do need the practice. All of us."

Allan's gaze shot between Kara and Carter, but he backed down. "You'll have to take Cutter and some of the Dogs with you for protection. Do whatever they say, no matter what. They know the city better than you do. They've been here before."

"Of course."

Mollified, Allan went back to unpacking supplies. Kara turned back to the Wielders.

"I would have wanted the guards along anyway," Artras said, running her hands up and down her arms. "Getting the cart and horses here was . . ." She shook her head grimly. "I don't recognize Erenthrall anymore. We passed one of the old nodes on our way here. It was dead, Kara. Completely dead. I couldn't sense any of the ley beneath it at all, not in the pit, nor in the lines that used to connect it to the Nexus."

"Maybe we're too close to the distortion. It may have cut the node off from its main source."

"Probably. But it's still wrong."

"We'll check it out tomorrow."

Artras waved her discomfort aside. "Tell us about the shard, and what you did to heal it."

"Dylan?"

The other Wielder hadn't expected her to hand the discussion over to him, but after a stumbling start, he began relating everything that had happened after leaving the old safe house. Kara interjected once or twice, and answered a few direct questions, but mostly just listened. She found herself thinking of the men, woman, and child at the fountain inside the shard as she stared into the fire that burned in the center of the large room. Would they find others like that, people who'd been trapped and given up hope? How many had been caught in the distortion when it quickened? Hundreds? Thousands?

"Hmm," Artras said, drawing Kara back to the conversation. "I'm not certain I understand exactly what you did, Kara, but I think I've got the basics. We'll have to see whether we can duplicate it tomorrow."

Before Kara could respond, Jack came into the room.

"It's starting to get light out. We should douse the fire."

Gaven and Aaron poured two buckets of water that had been set aside onto the flames, then stamped out most of the coals. A few were scraped around a flat stone on one side, Glenn setting a frying pan on its surface. He cracked a few eggs and began scrambling them, while Aaron passed around some dried meat. It was tough and salty, but edible. Kara's stomach growled as the smell of the cooked eggs filled the room. Glenn seasoned them with salt and pepper found at the apothecary.

An hour later, everyone had settled onto their pallets, at least three of them snoring heavily. Kara thought she wouldn't be able to sleep, but the moment she closed her eyes, consciousness fled.

Kara woke before the others. She couldn't tell by the banked embers of the fire what time it was. Cutter was asleep in one corner, so she knew those on watch had changed. She didn't see Allan, Glenn, or Tim.

Rising, she grabbed her water skin and made her way to the next room, tripping over Carter on the way. He grunted, slit open one eye as she hissed an apology, then rolled over and went back to sleep. She hesitated in the darkness of the outer room, uncertain where she intended to go, then decided the roof would be safest. The stairs were pitch black, but she stumbled only twice before noting the sunlight filtering down from above. She slowed and emerged onto the roof in a low crouch.

The distortion reared up overhead, much closer than at their last safe house. On the far side of the slanted roof, she saw Allan crouched down behind the outer facade. His head turned toward her as she emerged, then he motioned her forward.

She scrambled across the distance, coming to rest in the sunlight, back against the low wall that ran around the entire roof. Tim sat hunched down opposite them, facing outward. Kara shaded her eyes and measured where the sun stood, a hand above the horizon to the west.

"An hour until dusk," Allan said, although she hadn't seen him take his eyes off the streets below.

"No use returning to sleep then." Kara twisted so she could look out over the edge.

Allan's position faced south, toward where they'd opened up the shard, although Kara couldn't see the opening from here. The Tiana River cut diagonally across the streets before them, along with a ley channel. She could see a ley barge station a few blocks away, the building larger than any of those around it. Most of the nearest buildings were mercantiles or warehouses. Kara thought this used to be the Tinker District, before the Shattering, named for the small repair shops that had riddled the buildings before the ley system had made it a hub for trade and pushed them out.

The distortion cut through the buildings about ten blocks to the southeast. Kara could only see a few patches of the Tiana between here and there.

"Aren't we close to the River Rats? I thought you wanted to avoid them."

"I do. See that section of buildings there?" Allan pointed. "The ones with darker roofs? Those belong to the River Rats. The Tiana splits and surrounds them on both sides. If you look closely enough, you can see where the Rats have run makeshift gangways from roof to roof. It's one of the ways they leave their little island."

"Only one of the ways?"

"They also use boats."

Kara recalled how the Rats had vaulted from roof to roof silently, headed toward the fighting the night before. "They're only ten blocks away. Are we safe here?"

"We aren't safe anywhere in the city anymore. But the River Rats are actually about fifteen blocks away. The section just north and west of them is run by the Wolves. We're outside of both of their territories right now. This is the safest section to be in if we're going to be experimenting with the distortion."

Kara said nothing, chewing on her lower lip as she searched the distance. She didn't see anything moving. There wasn't even a geyser of Icy spewing up from the earth anywhere. And yet she felt a tension on the air. Anticipatory, like a held breath.

"We want to check out the local node before we head to the distortion tonight. Artras said they passed it on the way here and that it was dead. I'd like to see for myself."

"I'll inform Cutter. He'll be leading your group."

"We'll work together tonight, but once I think Artras and Carter are ready, we should split into two groups. We can cover more ground that way, and I don't see why we'd need all four of us together for any one shard."

"That makes sense. I'll try to find more than one shard worth raiding while I'm out."

"Good. I'll go wake the others and get them ready." Kara shifted away from the wall, still crouched low, even though the sun was starting to settle into the horizon, the clouds to the west beginning to color orange and pink. She cursed as she hit the darkness of the stairs, forced to halt until her eyes adjusted.

When she emerged into the main room, she found Artras leaning over a flat heating stone, Carter and Gaven beside her. Dylan was still curled into a ball to one side, ignoring the rest of them. The Hollowers and Dogs were already up, although at various stages of wakefulness.

"It's no use." Artras leaned back. Sweat beaded her brow. "Like last night, there just isn't enough ley in the immediate area for me to create a network to heat the stone."

Gaven waved a hand. "No problem. We'll just have to stoke up the fire again." He looked up as Kara moved toward them. "Is it dark enough outside yet to hide the smoke?"

"Not yet. I'd wait."

He called to Aaron. "Start unpacking something to eat. Maybe those travel biscuits."

Carter groaned. "They're hard as rocks!"

Gaven patted him on the back. "Don't worry. We'll get some broth started, so you can dip them and soften them up."

Carter rolled his eyes.

By the time Allan descended from the roof, replaced by Kent, everyone had eaten and was ready to depart. Allan grabbed a cup of the seasoned broth, dunked his biscuit in it, and ate it as they left, drinking the last of the broth as they passed by Jack on their way out. He handed the tracker his empty cup.

They headed west, cutting through the back alleys, until they reached a main thoroughfare. After a few words with Cutter, Allan split off, heading south, the rest following Adder as he led them toward the node to the north. Glenn kept the four Wielders in line, while Cutter trailed behind.

They reached the node without running into anyone, the streets seemingly more deserted than they'd been since they'd entered the city. Even though they hadn't seen anyone while traveling to reach the first safe house, it had still felt as if they'd been watched or followed. Kara thought part of it had to do with the residential districts they'd traveled through on their way in. The buildings had felt haunted, as if the ghosts of their residents were still walking the halls, peering from the windows.

This was a trade district, the buildings large and blocky and empty. There were few windows, fewer doors, and the facades were stark, flat stone. Some had chiseled statuary and other architectural features along their columns and up their sides, but they'd become nesting grounds for birds and rodents.

They halted outside the node's entrance, Adder deferring to Kara. "I've never been inside."

"I haven't either. None of us came from Tinker. But all of the nodes were built using the same essential layout. There were only minor differences between them."

"How do you know that?" Carter asked. "Wielders are only assigned to one node. We never shifted around."

"Not all of us." Artras kept her eyes on Kara. "Some of us were meant to be Master Wielders, perhaps even Primes. They were transferred from node to node, to make them more familiar with the system and how it all connected. Remember?"

Carter glanced at Kara. "Were you a Master? A Prime?"

"No, but my mentor at the college told me I would be, some day. I worked at several nodes—Eld, Stone, Tallow, a few others."

Artras' eyebrows shot up. "Quite a few, for one so young."

"The transfers didn't all come from the Primes. I requested a few of them myself. But it doesn't matter now, does it?"

Not wanting to answer any further questions, Kara pushed open the node's wooden door, surprised that it was still intact. But it faced away from the Nexus and the explosion, had been protected in the lee of the stone building. Besides, they were fairly far from the center; the ley that had surged through the city would not have been as strong here as it had been near Grass.

They entered the foyer, then passed into the outer room. The node was circular, two corridors branching off to either side. Both led to the Wielders' individual chambers, small boarding rooms with little more than a cot, a table, and a stool. The main hall was where all of the general activity took place, Wielders checking in as they returned from their runs, reporting what they'd repaired and, near the end, any anomalies they'd run into, like the distortions or the blackouts that had plagued the city in the years leading up to the Shattering.

But the real purpose of the node lay at its center, through the heavier iron doors at the far side of the main hall.

The pit.

That was where Kara headed, the others trailing behind, Cutter and the two Dogs scanning the room and watching their backs. She noted that the doors were barred from the outside, and hesitated. That meant someone had sealed them, either because they'd realized what was happening when the Nexus was collapsing, or as a precaution after it had Shattered. With help from Dylan, she raised the metal bar and leaned it against the wall to one side, then pulled the door open.

She should have felt the power of the ley surging upward from the pit. Instead, there was nothing. Not even a flicker. The interior of the pit was nearly pitch black, only the scant light from the distortion filtering in from the door they'd left open behind them.

"Adder." Kara's voice echoed in the chamber beyond. "Torches."

Glenn trotted back to the front entrance and swung the doors closed, while Adder dug out and lit one of the torches they'd brought.

Kara stepped into the darkness, Adder on her heels with the torch held high. They moved up to the edge of the pit and stared down into its depths, a stairwell spiraling along the chamber's side off to their left. The others clustered behind them.

The pit was twenty feet wide, made from river stone, each placed according to the way it affected the natural ley in the area. At its base, barely discernible in the flickering light, round tunnels shot off in three different directions, connecting the pit to the rest of the system. In all of the previous nodes Kara had worked in, she'd been able to sense the flaws in the stones that formed the pit, places where the wrong stone had been used, or where a stone had been oriented incorrectly. The imperfections were always minor and were probably unnoticed by most.

But here, she could sense nothing. Not because the pit had been made perfectly, but because there was no ley system connected to the node at all. As Artras had said, it was dead.

"Absolutely nothing."

"I told you," Artras said. "It's like the blackouts before the Shattering."

"Not quite. Even during the blackouts, the ley was there. It wasn't strong, but it was there."

"This isn't natural." Carter looked unsettled.

"No, it isn't." Kara began descending the stairs. Most of

the others followed, only Cutter and Glenn remaining up top.

The sense of wrongness increased until Kara reached the floor, stepping out into the center of the pit. Whoever was on pit duty was responsible for immersing themselves in the local ley network, centered here at the node. They would ride the ley, regulating it, searching out disturbances and correcting them if they could. If they couldn't, one of the Wielders on duty would be assigned to check out the anomaly in person. The concentration of ley in the district should have been the strongest where Kara stood, the node the focal point, but again she felt nothing.

The others had begun circling the pit, Artras brushing her hands along the stone sides. She halted near one of the openings to a channel.

"Artras, Carter, Dylan, each of you take one of the channels and see if you can find the ley along its path. I'll do the same."

"What are we looking for?" Dylan asked, stepping up to the channel closest to Artras.

"A reason why the node is dead."

All three of them halted, then stilled, a sign they were reaching through the Tapestry in search of the ley. Kara closed her eyes and chose the northern channel near Artras at random, flying down its length. The unnatural emptiness continued for nearly four thousand paces before she ran up against a barrier blocking the channel. She felt along its edges, but discovered she could pass through it—

She gasped. There was ley on the far side. An entire pool of it. It wanted to flow toward the node in Tinker, but the barrier kept it back, funneled it away instead, toward the southwest.

She took a moment to trace along the northern path, then toward where it had been redirected, before returning to the pit. None of the others had returned. Adder stood beside her, obviously uncomfortable. He fidgeted and glanced up to where Cutter and Glenn stood, each occasionally casting a look downward.

Dylan returned first. As soon as his eyes opened, he shrugged. "Nothing. The line runs into the distortion. After that, it's fractured by the shards. Some of it contains ley, some doesn't."

"You didn't encounter a barrier?"

"Not unless you count the distortion."

"There's some type of barrier on this line," Carter said. "I can't penetrate it, although I can sense that there's ley on the far side."

Artras sucked in a deep breath and released it with a shudder. "There's a barrier here as well. But you already know that, don't you, Kara? I sensed you when you returned. You flew right past me." She turned to Dylan and Carter. "There's a pool of ley on the far side, and the flow's been redirected."

"Where?" Dylan moved toward Kara.

"Southwest somewhere. I'd guess another node. I didn't travel to its end."

"But why? Was the barrier natural?"

"No. Someone put it there specifically to alter the flow of the ley." Artras caught Kara's eye. "We've wondered if any other Wielders survived the Shattering. I'd say this answers that question. Only a Wielder could have set up that barrier."

"Or one of the Primes." None of the other three liked that thought. Tensions between the Primes and the Wielders had escalated before the Shattering. The only reason Kara, Artras, and Dylan had survived the explosion of the Nexus was because they'd been arrested by the Dogs and placed in the cells beneath the Amber Tower. None of them had ever found out why they'd been arrested, but Kara would bet the orders had come from Prime Augustus.

"Should we take the barriers down?"

They all looked at Kara.

"We don't know why they were put up. Or when. Something may have happened immediately after the Shattering that forced the survivors here in Tinker to set them up to protect the area. Remember, the pit was sealed from the outside."

"The ley was extremely unstable after the Shattering," Artras added. "Maybe it was overflowing here, surging out of control."

"If we release the barriers, who knows what would happen. I think we should leave them. For now, at least."

The others nodded. Taking that as a signal, Adder began herding them toward the stairs, anxious to be out of the pit. They closed the metal doors behind them, replaced the bar, then Adder doused the torch before cracking the front doors. Cutter scanned the street, then waved them out.

They skirted the ley station, circling away from the River Rats' location before angling back toward the distortion. Again, they saw and heard nothing except an explosion and brightening of the sky much farther south, where the city had burned after the fire started in West Forks. By the white light that lit the thickening clouds overhead, Kara assumed it had something to do with the ley, but it was too far away to investigate.

They were almost at the base of the distortion when they rounded a corner and were brought up short.

She'd forgotten about the Tiana.

The street they'd turned onto sloped downward here, toward what had once been an intersection. Except now, twenty steps away, it was submerged under water. Kara couldn't tell how deep it was, but the river had flooded at least one level of the buildings below, rushing through doors and windows, lapping against stone siding and steps. At the center, where the five streets came together in an odd shaped star, the hands of a statue rose from the water, holding the base of an urn. On each of the street corners, the tops of ley lamps hooked up and out over the rippling surface, the dead ley globes nestled in ornate ironwork at their ends.

"How do we get across? There aren't any bridges here."

"Do you think we would have brought you this way if there wasn't a way across?"

Adder motioned them down the street and up the wide shallow steps of a trading house. The main doors, twice the height of regular doors, stood open behind thick colonnades and spilled out into a grand main hall, the marble floor stretching toward a series of work tables to either side. The room was littered with discarded papers, the winds blowing them into drifts against the far corners. The room lay open overhead for three floors, walkways surrounding the hall on every side, with numerous doors opening onto what Kara assumed were offices.

Adder headed straight toward the three doors in the wall opposite the main entrance, angling toward the left. Cutter had fallen into the rear position, Glenn in between. Kara's feet scuffed through the papers as she cut between the tables, noticing abandoned ledgers, bottles of ink, and quills. Some of the ledgers were open, as if the traders had been interrupted in the middle of recording transactions. On one table, the ink bottle had tipped, long-dried black ink caking the open pages of the entire ledger in a smear. A black palm print from someone's hand stood out on the light wood of the table to one side.

The rooms beyond the main hall were small, the corridors maze-like. They ascended to the third floor, Kara catching glimpses of the black surface of the river through the windows as they climbed.

At the top, Adder halted, letting everyone catch their breath. Cutter slid past him and vanished into a corridor to the left.

The main part of the building stood to their right. There should have been nothing to the left but a drop to the street below.

Kara stepped forward, around Artras.

A large opening led to an arched walking bridge, enclosed in a glass tunnel made up of diamond-shaped panes. Scattered sections of glass were tinted various colors. Some of the panes were cracked or missing. The walkway was made of sheets of metal, iron rails on either side. A horse and cart could have traversed it, with room to spare. It arched over the street—now the Tiana—to the building on the far side.

"The buildings were owned by the same trading house," Adder said. "They added the walking bridge later. It was the pride of Tinker, for a few months." He stood with hands on hips, surveying the bridge. "I grew up here. Well, not *in* Tinker. In Issard's Row, the next district over. Those in Tinker would have nothing to do with us."

Kara didn't know what to say to the bitterness in his tone. But a harsh whistle sounded from the far side of the walk, and Adder motioned her forward. She trotted across the bridge, glancing toward the river below.

Then they were in the second building, descending back toward street level. They passed through a set of offices and corridors like the first, into another main hall with the same layout of tables and tall doors, but with a circular stained glass window in the ceiling overhead.

Once they reached the street, the Tiana behind them now, it took only minutes to reach the base of the distortion.

Carter stared up at it in awe. Unlike Kara, Artras, and Dylan, he'd never been this close to it; the group who'd fled the University with Hagger and the Wolves on their heels had already been beyond its reach before it quickened.

"It's huge." He raised one hand toward the nearest face as Kara had done the night before.

"You couldn't tell that from a distance?"

Carter shot the elder woman a disdainful look.

"Spread out a little." Kara motioned in both directions. "Let's check out the shards and see if there's one we should work on first."

The other Wielders dispersed, the Dogs and tracker keeping an eye on the surrounding buildings and streets. Kara walked up to the nearest section of the distortion and peered through its slanted face. The fractures here were more numerous, probably because one of the main swirling arms of the distortion seared the air a brilliant green overhead. When a distortion opened, it bloomed like a flower, the edges of its petals curling out from its center in curved arms of various colors. Too high for Kara to reach, she could still feel the weight of this particular arm pressing down on her, even without reaching out to touch the Tapestry.

The shard immediately before her contained a corner of a square, an edge of a park, part of a side street, and the corner of a building that looked like a café. The trunk of a tree in the park had been sliced in half, along with several branches and a bench. The small round tables and numerous chairs at the café had been scattered and overturned, some lying in the street. Two of the chairs had been broken, jagged edges pointed in all directions, as if they had been run over by a cart. A breeze rustled the leaves of the tree, although Kara couldn't hear or feel it herself.

She moved down the edge of the distortion to the next shard, toward the park, but here one of the jagged edges of lightning cut almost horizontally at chest height. She ducked down and noted that the park continued, only a small portion of the square captured on the right side. There were a few shrubs and pathways, and the rest of the bench, all lit by what appeared to be midday sunlight.

She straightened. Above the edge, the shard was dark and the leaves of the trees captured inside were dried and dead.

The contrast between the two shards disturbed Kara at a gut-churning level. She began to move on, but Artras suddenly cried out, "Oh, gods!" and staggered back.

Everyone converged on her position.

Inside the shard—a continuation of the square and street Kara had looked at first—a cart with five people loaded in back, bundled in ragged clothing and covered in soot, raced away from three Wolves, the malformed animals caught in midsnarl. The two men, one woman, and two children had looks of terror on their faces. The driver of the cart half stood in the seat, reins in midsnap. The horses attached to the cart were straining forward, their hides flecked with sweat, their eyes white with fear. All of them were frozen, locked in time.

And slicing through the center of the cart and the two horses, cutting through the woman and the small boy clutched to her chest, through the legs of the driver and the two horses, were multiple planes of the distortion.

"We have to get them out," Artras said.

"We can't. The cart and the people must be in at least three different shards."

Artras turned on Kara, angry. "If the distortion closes—"

"I know what will happen! But we can't save them. Not yet. We barely know how to free a single shard. This—" She waved to the cart and shook her head. "We can't free one shard alone, it would kill anyone already caught in both it and one of the other shards."

"Not to mention you'd free the Wolves at some point," Adder added. "I don't know if we could handle three at once."

"We'll have to free all of the shards at once, and have

everyone ready to handle the Wolves when we do. We aren't ready for that yet. We'll have to come back for them."

Artras subsided, disgruntled.

"I found a few shards we can practice on. They seem harmless."

"There's one that appears to have filled up completely with water."

"We'll work around it. Dylan and I will show you how it works and then we'll have the rest of you try one on your own."

She led them back to the first shard she'd looked into, the one with the café. As soon as Dylan was ready, she reached out and pierced the nearest face, Dylan supporting the edges. A breath of heated summer air washed over them as the face fell away.

Two hours later, they'd cleared all of the shards surrounding the cart and the Wolves, completely isolating the group from the rest of the distortion, with only one terrifying moment when Artras lost hold of an edge and three faces collapsed at once in the space of a breath. For that blinding moment, Kara saw the entire distortion closing in her mind's eye, taking the central part of Erenthrall with it.

But after the three faces fell, the surrounding shards had stabilized, only a minor tremor vibrating through the nearby structures.

After that, she ended the practice and had Cutter and the Dogs lead them back to the safe house.

Allan didn't head straight for the distortion after breaking away from Kara and the others. He trotted east for a few blocks, until he neared where the Tiana cut through the middle of the district, and then headed north.

He wanted to check on the River Rats.

He'd been surprised when he'd seen them scrambling toward the clash near the Temerites the night before. The River Rats had always run from conflict, acting more like scavengers, looting the dead afterward and stealing whatever they could. But last night they'd been sprinting *toward* the conflict. And they'd been prepared to fight.

Something in the group had changed. They could have

simply been running toward the fight in hopes of taking advantage after it ended, but he didn't think so. Not the way they'd carried themselves.

He followed the river, paralleling it through side streets as it cut through markets, down plazas and squares, and through the center of an entire block of tenements once he left Tinker behind. When he neared River Rat territory, he slowed, then chose one of the taller buildings and ascended to the roof.

This section of Erenthrall had been built in a different style to the squat warehouses of Tinker. Instead of flat stone or brick facades, the buildings here were adorned with bay windows and wrought-iron balconies. Windows were capped with stone designs, or had wide ledges for plants, and the brick walls were inlaid with intricate patterns. The roofs were gabled, and a few had mock crenellations at the edges and miniature rounded towers at the corners.

Allan emerged onto a sloped roof through a trapdoor at the top of the stairs, keeping low as he slid down the tiles to the crenellated edge. In the shadows thrown by the light from the distortion, he slunk to the nearest stunted tower and climbed up onto its flat, rounded top.

From there, he could see down into the River Rats' island.

They'd taken over an entire block of apartments built on a small rise where the Tiana split at one end, surging around the compound before merging again on the far side. The water flowed briskly. The buildings at the edge were partially submerged, the water rising halfway up the first level, swirling in and out of doors and windows, but the tenements in the interior weren't flooded.

Firelight glowed in some of the windows in the higher levels of the buildings, with watch fires along the roofs. Makeshift bridges connected each of the buildings, with ladders between those at separate levels. Allan counted a dozen of the young Rats on watch, their silhouettes passing before the flames of the fires as they patrolled. They carried bows, and one or two had spears. Others were roasting what looked like birds on spits around a firepit at the center building, with a few large pots set in the coals to one side.

Nothing seemed out of the ordinary.

Before he turned, though, a drum sounded a warning.

Those on patrol reacted instantly, the closest rushing toward the drummer. Shouts rang out, the words unintelligible at this distance. Allan couldn't see what had caught the Rats' attention at first, but then a group appeared on the closest roofline—more Rats, fifteen at least, herding along a group of five others, trussed up. The prisoners stumbled to a halt at the roof's edge, surrounded, and hand signals were passed from Rat to Rat between the buildings. The street below was flooded by the Tiana, the gap too wide to jump.

A moment later, orders were shouted and Rats came running—half of those on patrol, along with a few from the buildings below. They raced to something lying flat, grabbed handles on either side, and dragged it to the edge of the roof. Angling it upward, they shoved it out over the edge, the Rats at one end dropping back as they reached the roofline to help those behind. They kept it balanced until only ten feet of it remained on the roof, the rest jutting out over the flooded street.

Then they lowered it, its end touching the roof on the far side. The bridge slanted downward slightly, but those waiting didn't hesitate, scrambling up over it to the safety of the island. Others prodded the prisoners onto it with their spears. The prisoners weren't as confident, edging along its length cautiously as the Rats harried them.

As soon as everyone crossed, the Rats piled on the end of the bridge, lifted it up, and dragged it back onto the roof. The prisoners were led toward the central fire, the Rats harassing them the entire way with hoots and mocking shouts, a few smacking them with their spears, dancing around them. Only the leader of the group and the two walking with him remained calm. They grabbed one of the spits and bit off a piece of charred meat, settling in, while the rest yanked the prisoners to a halt and shoved them down to their knees.

The prisoners were close enough to the fire to recognize now. Temerites—the trimmed beards of the men stood out against their lighter-skinned faces. And not simply members of the group that had laid claim to the largest section of the destroyed Erenthrall; the Rats had captured guards.

Allan swore.

The Rat's leader ate as more and more of his fellow Rats gathered, pouring out of the buildings on all sides. They surrounded the group, the noise rising. Allan shifted, anxious to leave, but unable to step away. He needed to see how much more dangerous the Rats had become since he'd last been here, how much control this new leader had over them.

As soon as the leader finished eating, he tossed the bone aside and turned toward the prisoners. The roar from those gathered escalated, and someone handed the leader a spear. He advanced on the nearest of the Temerite guards, halting a pace away.

He planted the butt of the spear onto the roof and the entire group fell silent.

Allan couldn't hear the words when he spoke, but he knew their intent. He'd seen this happen before, when he was part of the Dogs. He'd participated himself. The interrogations done by Hagger in particular had been brutal. He still remembered how Hagger had forced him to beat their captured Kormanley terrorists in an attempt to discover where the group intended to strike next. It had been one of the main reasons he'd left the Dogs behind and fled.

Below, the leader motioned to one of his betas, who stepped behind the man they were interrogating and wrapped his arm around the man's neck. One of the other prisoners protested, half rising, but without even an order from the leader one of the Rats slammed the butt of their spear into the protestor's shoulder. Allan heard the scream as the guard crumpled to the roof. The first man struggled against the arm choking him, although Allan could tell they weren't trying to strangle him. Not yet. The Rat's arm wasn't tight enough. The Temerite guard realized it as well and settled, although his face was now flushed.

A Rat stepped forward and pinned down the guard writhing on the roof. The screams died down. The leader began asking questions again, pacing back and forth. The man in the chokehold answered, but it must not have been what the leader was looking for. He spun, casually, and sank the end of his spear into a third guard's gut.

No scream this time. The man hunched forward, hands flying to the handle jutting from his stomach. He looked up toward the leader, opened his mouth as if to speak, but only blood poured out.

The leader jerked his spear free and the man fell forward and rolled onto his side. Blood pooled beneath him. The guard in the chokehold began to struggle again, bellowing something in defiance.

The leader didn't like whatever it was. With a gesture, the Rats on all sides fell on the remaining four men with a sudden roar. Allan saw the one holding the chokehold wrench the man's head around, snapping his neck. The other three screamed, one cut off in a wet gurgle. The leader and his two betas turned and walked away as the rest of the Rats picked the bodies up and hauled them to the roof's edge. One of the Temerites was still alive, although he'd been gutted. They tossed all five of them over the side, the bodies hitting the Tiana with a silent splash, the current taking them instantly.

On the rooftop, the Rats broke into a chant, the sound almost tribal. As they began to celebrate, Allan drew back from the edge of the tower and climbed down to the slanted roof. Being careful not to draw attention to himself, he eased the trapdoor open and descended back down to the street.

He ran from the River Rats' island silently, his neck prickling as if he were being pursued, although he never caught sight of anyone following him. Nausea finally forced him to stop. He took refuge in a small apartment, crouching down with his head between his knees, breathing in deep. When the urge to vomit passed, he raised his head and leaned back against a wall, sliding down to his butt. He let his hands dangle over his knees.

"They're only kids. The leader couldn't have been more than fifteen."

He hadn't been much older when he'd joined the Dogs, he realized.

He pushed away from the wall and stood, searching the street outside before leaving. He almost headed back to the safe house, to report what he'd seen and to warn everyone they'd have to be more careful and avoid the River Rats completely. But only Gaven, Aaron, and a few Dogs would be there; the rest wouldn't have returned yet.

Mentally cursing, he hesitated at an intersection, then cut left, moving toward the distortion. He may as well check out some shards, work his way toward where the others were going to practice. Maybe he'd run into them before they were done.

He crossed the Tiana at a section where it had diverted itself into one of the unused ley channels, the bridges for the main streets that had once arched over the ley still intact. He kept himself in shadow as much as possible, and kept his ears open for the slightest sound, but all he heard was the roil of the river and the general background noise of the ruined city at night.

At the edge of the distortion, he hesitated again, glancing behind one more time. Nothing moved, so he stepped up to the distortion's face, and then stepped through.

It resisted at first, as it had before, something compressing his chest, as if he were underwater, but then he slid out of the face and into the shard. He sucked in a breath and immediately began coughing, one arm rising automatically to cover his mouth. The air was thick with the stench of putrescence and something else, something toxic that burned his throat. Taking in air through his mouth in shallow gulps, he ran for the nearest adjacent shard. The street was filled with stone debris and dropped trunks, clothes and other possessions spilled out onto the road. He tripped over a pile, but caught himself—

Except it wasn't a heap of clothing, as he'd first assumed. It was a body. A woman, fallen face-first to the ground, her cheeks sunken and hollow with decomposition.

Allan backed away, then scanned the street again. There were bodies strewn everywhere, sprawled as if they'd been fleeing the city and had dropped dead in their tracks. Based on the decay, they'd died only a week before.

Time must be moving slower in this shard. They had to have been caught when the distortion quickened.

Mouth still covered with his arm, he stumbled back, then turned and pushed into the next shard, gasping as he passed through the wall. The air here was fresh, and he leaned over and sucked it in, trying to rid himself of the stench.

When he'd stopped trembling, he began to explore the

shard, looking for anything they could use in the Hollow to survive, anything like the apothecary they'd raided the night before. He moved swiftly, entering buildings, taking stock, then passing on. The first shard had little to nothing, mostly a park. In the second, it was raining, so he didn't linger. The results varied after that. In one, he found a small mercantile, the shelves already raided, but there was a hidden trapdoor with steps down into a storage basement that hadn't been disturbed. The food on the shelf was still good, time frozen here. In another, a fabric shop had survived the blast, colorful bolts lining the walls. The candlemaker next door had thousands of candles in a back room. Before the Shattering, the candles would have been oddities, since everyone used ley globes. Now, candles were more precious than erens.

He traveled through ten shards, marking out locations on a makeshift map using a scavenged piece of paper and some charcoal. He tried to indicate where the fractures cut through the streets and buildings as he went, but it was difficult, since the planes of reality were skewed in all directions and intersected at odd points.

He had nearly decided to return to the safe house when he stepped through a plane into the next shard and halted abruptly. A breeze brushed past his face, chilling after the summer warmth of the last shard. Something was wrong, though. Something he couldn't quite—

He gasped and reached a hand up to empty air. He'd stepped out of the distortion. Except that wasn't possible. He was nowhere near its edge.

Unless—

"Kara?"

His voice sounded too loud and hollow in the space. No one answered.

He stepped forward, out into the middle of the street he'd been following, turning as he did so. The windows of the surrounding buildings, only two stories high, were all empty.

His hand settled on his sword as he edged further down the street. "Dylan? Cutter?"

The street emptied onto a marketplace. Allan halted at

its edge, staring up to where the facets of the distortion loomed directly overhead, to where the distortion ended three blocks distant beyond the square.

Kara and the others would never have been able to heal this much of the distortion in one night. Which meant—

"Someone else has been here. Someone else is healing the distortion."

# Six

"WHAT DO YOU MEAN someone else has been healing the distortion?"

Allan ignored Dylan and Kara, who had both leaped to their feet at his announcement upon returning to the safe house. Instead, he motioned to Glenn and Adder, and they stepped into the hallway and headed up the stairs. Allan halted at the door, one hand raised toward Kara, who had moved to follow them.

"Stay here. I'll tell you all about it once I deal with this."

The stairwell was dark, but Allan was familiar enough with it that he trotted up to where Glenn and Adder had paused inside the door leading to the roof. They didn't step outside.

"We may have a problem."

"I'd say so," Glenn said, "if someone else is messing around with the distortion."

"It's not that. It's the Rats." He told them what he'd seen from the roof—the Rats' leader, the prisoners, their deaths. "Whoever the pup is—and he's just a pup, no more than fifteen—he's managed to organize the Rats into something deadlier than they were before. They aren't cowering in the darkness and seizing opportunity when it appears safe any-more."

"What can we do about it?"

"Make certain we don't run into any of them. I want to move farther away from their island. We're more vulnerable than the Temerites, and they managed to grab five of their guardsmen."

"They were probably scouts."

"I don't care. They still managed to snatch five of them, hold them prisoner until they returned to their nest, and then slaughter them. The Temerites aren't going to sit back and let that slide. We need to move."

"We don't have a safe house farther west than this." Realization dawned and Glenn's shoulders sagged. "You want us to scout one out."

"As fast as you can. I want to be out of here within two days."

"Why not leave Erenthrall altogether?"

"I'm going to try to convince Kara and the Wielders to do that, but we came here for supplies, and right now we have almost nothing. The raid on the apothecary's shard barely filled the back of our cart. What I found looking tonight will help a little, but it's mostly cloth and some food. We need seed for planting, if we're going to feed everyone in the Hollow this coming winter, and raw metals for weapons, if we're going to try defending ourselves against those brigands on the plains."

Both Glenn and Adder considered this in silence.

Then Glenn scrubbed at his face, the sound scratchy. He hadn't shaved since they'd reached Erenthrall, nor slept much with their rotating watches. None of them had. His eyes looked bruised. "We'll start looking today, while the rest of you sleep."

Allan patted his shoulder, then turned and headed back down the stairs, the other two following. When they reached the main room, both of them wasted no time gathering up their supplies and heading out.

The Wielders, Gaven, and Aaron watched in silence. Allan didn't think Kara had moved since he left.

"What was that all about?"

"Nothing to be concerned about right now."

"Who's healing the distortion?"

"I don't know."

"Are you certain it wasn't what we healed earlier tonight?" Artras asked. "We did clear a significant section, but we ended a little early after a minor scare."

"Did you clear away a few blocks?"

All of the Wielders looked startled. Kara looked sick. "No, we didn't."

Allan turned to Kara. "We need to get out of Erenthrall altogether. The situation here is changing. We have no idea who is healing the distortion, and it's obvious that the tension between the rival groups here is escalating."

Kara held his gaze, but he couldn't read her expression. The other Wielders were watching her.

"It has to be other Wielders," Artras said. "Or Primes. It's stupid to think that we're the only ones who survived."

"But Allan's right. We don't know who these other Wielders are, or what their purpose is. Until we do, we should back off."

"No!" Carter threw up his arms in disgust. "Are we going to return to the Hollow with practically nothing and tell them we ran because someone had already started healing the distortion? Who knows when they freed that section. It could have been months ago. For all we know, they got what they wanted and are now gone."

Kara turned at that. "Do you really think they've left Erenthrall with only a few blocks released from the distortion? Don't forget the node. Someone placed those barriers around Tinker, cut that node off from the network. Someone is already messing around with the ley system here, and I don't think they're finished."

"Don't forget those people trapped in the shard today. Are we going to abandon them?"

"No. We aren't going to abandon them. We can't."

Allan stepped forward. "Why haven't you freed them already? And what do you mean someone cut off Tinker from the network? I didn't think there was a network left in Erenthrall."

"There is a network here, it's simply chaotic at the moment. We were going to heal the distortion and then try to stabilize the network, once all of the old nodes were free.

The main reason it's so chaotic now is that the ley keeps trying to reestablish its old lines and can't, because the distortion is cutting it off. So the ley gets backed up, creates the pools, the geysers, or simply gouges out new ley lines where it can. But from what we've seen so far—"

She halted, brow creasing in concern.

"What?"

"This Wielder—or group of Wielders—is trying to stabilize the ley by working around the distortion, bypassing the old nodes. They sealed off Tinker so that the ley would be forced to flow into new lines. One in particular, out toward the west."

"Don't forget the old node in that town we passed on the way here," Artras added, "in that abandoned town."

Kara's eyes widened.

"What old node?"

She looked at Allan. "Remember? We passed an active ley line on our way here, in one of the towns before we hit the city. It was attached to an old node, a stone formation near the town. At the time, I assumed the ley had reached out toward some of its old nodes naturally. But maybe it didn't. Maybe someone reactivated that node." She spun back toward Artras. "And that old node was funneling the ley toward the west as well."

"Not quite the same direction."

"No, it was angled farther south than this one. But that would make sense if—"

"If they were funneling the ley toward the same location."

Behind them all, Carter's eyes were following the conversation, although he was frowning in confusion. "What are you saying?"

"Someone is trying to create a new focal point for the ley. A new Nexus."

The young Wielder's eyes opened in shock. "After what happened with Erenthrall? Are they insane?"

"They may simply be trying to end all of the chaos in the ley. I doubt they plan on causing another Shattering."

"Augustus thought he had the Nexus in Erenthrall under control, and look what happened."

No one responded, all of them no doubt thinking about

those horrifying moments trapped beneath the broken Amber Tower, or wherever they'd been when the Nexus had exploded.

A rustle snatched Allan from his own grisly reverie and he found Gaven holding up a flask of water. Aaron was putting together a small plate of food behind him. He'd forgotten the Hollowers were even there.

"You should eat something, and drink. You didn't stop for anything once you returned."

Allan's stomach growled and everyone nearby smiled. He reached for the flask and took a long swig, Aaron ready with the plate when he was done. A hard biscuit and a hunk of meat from what looked like a rabbit, along with an apple.

He took a huge bite out of the meat, then glanced toward the Wielders again. "You never said why you didn't release those people caught in the shard."

"Because of the Wolves. Also, the edges of the shards cut right through some of the people in the wagon, so we couldn't open a face without killing one or all of them. The only way to release them is to heal the entire section all at once, but if we do that, then we release the Wolves as well. There are three of them."

Allan paused in his chewing, then swallowed. "We might be able to handle them, with all of us there."

Kara caught his arm before he could take another bite. "Could you go inside and pull them out? Like you did with those of us caught after the distortion quickened?"

"I could. But you know more than anyone how long that took. We don't have that much time."

Kara's arm dropped. "Then we'll have to face the Wolves."

"Not right away." Allan forged on as Kara drew breath to protest. "We should get all of our supplies first, then free those people right before we leave. There's no reason to free them now and have them hanging around the safe house the entire time. They've been trapped in the distortion for months, a few more days won't matter."

"Is that how long we'll stay? A few more days?"

"I don't want to stay much longer." Allan took another bite, rising so that he could wash the plate using the small barrel they'd rigged to collect rain.

Kara suddenly appeared at his side. "What were you discussing with Glenn and Aaron?"

"I should have known you wouldn't let that drop." He kept his voice low, like Kara's, although he could hear the other Wielders arguing behind them and didn't think they'd overhear regardless. "Before scouting out some of the shards, I checked up on the River Rats. They're more organized now, and more dangerous. I saw them kill five Temerite guards after interrogating them."

"What were they trying to find out?"

"Do you think I was close enough to hear? I have no idea."

Kara considered in silence, turning so she could lean up against the wall.

"I didn't think the others needed to know. I've sent Glenn and Aaron out to find us another safe house, somewhere farther west, away from whatever's happening between the River Rats and the Temerites."

"I'll tell the Wielders that we're moving."

"I'll have Gaven and Aaron begin packing up the wagon. Then we should all get some rest. It will be a long night."

Grant stalked forward through the bright sunlight toward the chunk of distortion that remained in the center of the street. Two of his Wolves padded along beside him. He halted in front of the shards, stared in at the Wolves trapped inside chasing after the cart. He reached forward and set his hand flat against the nearest facet, his fingers stained with the blood of those they'd hunted the night before. The group had encroached on their territory, had set traps in the streets to the northwest. His scouts had scented them two days before. They'd smelled of blood and fur and rendered fat, carried pelts of rabbit and fox from the plains.

But they'd wanted something more.

He and his pack had watched them settle into a burned-out husk of a building near West Forks and Tannery Row, but had hung back, wary of their blades and skinning knives. But when they'd begun setting the wire traps with the steel jaws—

Grant's lip curled, revealing an enlarged canine. The fur

along one cheek bristled. He did not tolerate hunters, especially those that reeked of the White Cloaks.

One of his Wolves—Drayden—whined in query, picking up on his tension. He pushed back from the shard, leaving a bloody handprint, and glanced around the surrounding street and park. A stiff breeze ruffled his fur, rustled in the newly released trees of the nearby park.

"They released this entire area from the distortion?"

Drayden huffed in answer, then nosed the distortion where their brethren were trapped.

"But they left these shards intact."

A curt bark, followed by another questioning whine.

Grant didn't respond. He didn't know why the shards had been left. The White Cloaks would have collapsed them, killing the Wolves inside. But that would have killed the family as well. Perhaps they'd hesitated because of that.

Or perhaps they weren't White Cloaks after all, even though they could open the shards. They did not carry their stench.

He glanced around one more time, still uncertain. A howl rose in the distance, and both of his Wolves' ears perked up. Grant snarled. "Rats." They'd grown bolder in the last month, craftier.

He placed a hand on Drayden's head. "Stay and watch."

Drayden sighed in complaint.

Grant ignored him, setting off to the east with a piercing whistle, three other Wolves joining him as he crossed the square.

Time to root some Rats out of their tunnels.

As soon as Glenn and Adder stepped into the room an hour or so before dusk, Allan asked, "Did you find something?"

Glenn and Adder reached gratefully for the hot mugs Gaven and Aaron provided.

"I found something on the far side of Tinker, close to where the fire from West Forks spread." Glenn described the location in greater detail between taking sips, so that the others could find the area if necessary. "It's not as secure as our other safe houses, but it's farther away from the

Rats, and we'll be able to see anyone approaching through the burned-out section of the city easily."

"Run into anyone while you were out?"

"No. Although we heard the Wolves hunting. I would have sworn we were being watched."

Artras snorted. "No matter where we go, I feel like I'm being watched."

Allan motioned toward Gaven and the others. "We're ready. Lead the way."

Gaven and Aaron toted the last of the supplies down to the wagon, Gaven climbing into the driver's seat. Glenn joined him, while Adder crawled into the back and lay down, pulling a blanket over himself. Within twenty minutes, they edged out of the alley leading to the safe house and onto the main street.

In daylight, the city appeared more desolate than at night. They cut through Tinker, heading west for ten blocks before Glenn motioned toward the south again. Cutter and Jack ranged to either side, one or the other reporting back to Gaven about obstructions in the streets or where buildings had collapsed, making it easier for the Rats to see them. They cut through a few side streets to stay hidden as they neared the open area surrounding the ley station.

As they drew closer, Kara approached Allan's position ahead of the wagon, the Wielders grouped behind. He turned when he heard her footfalls on the cobbles. "What is it?"

Kara's attention was fixed on the ley station a block away, as they passed an alley and it became visible for a brief moment. "Something's different. We came this way last night, to investigate the node. We passed through this neighborhood. But it felt deserted then, completely empty. Now it feels like someone's here."

"Watching us?"

"I don't know. But it's not empty anymore."

Before Allan could answer, a sharp whistle cut through the quiet. Allan's head jerked upward, to where Jack leaned over the rooftop of an adjacent building, frantically motioning toward the east. Allan brought his hand up, halting the wagon. Behind, the Wielders began to murmur, stepping to either side in search of Kara. Adder's head popped up out of the back, the blanket slipping off his shoulders, already reaching for his sword.

They'd halted at the mouth of another side street looking out on the ley station. The prickle on Allan's neck became a crawling sensation.

He spun toward Gaven and Kara. "Find someplace to hide. Now!"

"What is it?" Kara began to frantically search the street they were on.

Allan didn't answer. Jack suddenly appeared on the street, racing down the short stairs of one of the three-story brownstones that lined either side. None of them had entrances at street level large enough to fit the horses and wagon through. The alleys they'd passed were narrow, with no access to inner rooms like the loading dock they'd used last night.

Allan swore as Adder dropped to the ground from the back of the wagon and Jack ran up to Allan's side. "Report."

"A large group of Rats, headed this way."

"Did they see us?"

"I can't tell. But they're moving fast."

Allan swore.

"What in hells—"

Everyone turned at Glenn's shocked exclamation.

He pointed toward the ley station. "Where did they come from?"

Allan expected to see Wolves, perhaps even the Temerites—

But instead, an entirely new group poured from the doors of the ley station, whooping and hollering as they charged out into the surrounding open area carrying bows and spears and other assorted weapons, all lit with the eerie half-light thrown by the distortion and the dusky sunlight. A flock of birds took sudden flight from the station's colonnaded portico, a shifting mass of black rising into the darkening sky. More and more of the new group filled the wide stairs, spilling out onto the surrounding streets.

"Where are they coming from?"

Kara looked shocked. "The tunnels. The barge tunnels that connected the ley stations between the districts. They're coming up from underground."

"But the ley—"

"There is no ley! Tinker has been sealed off!"

Allan cut off any of the others' responses. "It doesn't matter. They haven't seen us yet. Gaven, Aaron, get the wagon into that alley, as far back as you can, then unhitch the horses and drag them inside the building. If you get the chance, grab some of the supplies as well, in case someone notices the wagon."

Gaven was already moving, Aaron leaping ahead to clear anything blocking the alley. Allan turned toward the rest. "Everyone else, cover the wagon, make it look like debris, then get inside as well. Dogs, secure the building. Jack, to the roof. Where the hell is Cutter?"

No one answered, everyone scrambling as the cacophony from the square rose even higher. Allan glanced toward the rooftops but didn't see Cutter anywhere. Gaze falling to the ley station, he noticed some of the group were beginning to erect barricades.

He helped push the wagon over some obstacle in the alley—a small heap of stones and a clutter of garbage—then guarded the entrance, keeping his eye on the distortion-lit street to either side, searching the thrown shadows. The Dogs snapped calls to each other in the building to the left as they passed from room to room. Behind, the Wielders were helping Gaven and Aaron with the supplies, the Hollowers working frantically to unhitch the horses. One of the animals whinnied in protest, and Allan glared at the street leading toward the station. His hand fell to the pommel of his sword, but no one appeared. The bellows from those at the station must have drowned out the horse.

He flinched when someone charged out of a building on the opposite side of the street four doors down, and had his sword half-drawn before he recognized Cutter. The tracker angled toward Allan's position, running flat out, making hand gestures Allan couldn't interpret, not in the half-light.

Then he realized they were frantic attempts to get Allan and the rest out of sight.

He spun toward the Wielders and the wagon. "Get inside now." When Kara reached for another pack, he grabbed her by the arm and shoved her toward the building. "Leave it! Go, go, go!"

He herded everyone toward a side entrance, grateful that the horses were already inside. Cutter skidded to a halt beside him.

"The Rats are almost here. They're going to pour down this street in a matter of moments. We're caught in some kind of territorial dispute."

Allan scanned the wagon. The Wielders had piled some scattered debris over its back end, but it still stood out. Too clean, too whole.

A raucous shout went up, echoing down the street behind them, taunting and vicious.

"Time's up." He pushed Cutter toward the side entrance, then ducked through the door with a last glance down the alley. River Rats began flooding the street, racing past, their attention on the buildings facing the station. They leaped up the steps of the brownstones, through the doors. Moments later, he caught sight of them on the roofs above and hoped Jack was keeping out of sight. Even more rushed into the street leading to the open area around the ley station.

Then Allan closed the door.

Everyone but Jack and two of the Dogs had crammed into a storage area, including the horses. Allan scanned the group in the darkness broken only by the window in the door, then worked his way toward Adder, Cutter following behind.

"Where's Glenn?"

"Watching the front."

"What's the situation?"

"We've holed up in some rich bastard's house. We're in the servant quarters right now. Nothing much is left in the rest of the house, mostly empty rooms. Jack's on the roof. Kent's watching the back, which leads to some kind of walled-in garden."

"Can we get to the adjacent buildings? Through the garden to the houses on the next street over?"

"There's no gate in the garden, but we could climb the walls. We'd have to abandon the horses and the wagon."

"I'm not ready to do that yet. Can we spread out into the other rooms?"

"I don't see why not."

"Good. Stay here and watch the horses and the door."

"I'll go check on Jack," Cutter said, slipping away.

Allan found Kara next.

"What's happening?" The rest of the Wielders crowded her.

"We've stumbled into some kind of war between the Rats and these Tunnelers. I'm hoping they keep each other distracted enough we aren't noticed. If they find us, we're going out the back."

"What about the wagon and the rest of the supplies?"

"We leave it all behind. The horses, too."

Glances were shared, but no one said anything.

"I made certain we grabbed most of the medicine." Kara patted a satchel. "But we didn't get much of the food."

"We'll worry about that later. For now, settle in, but be ready to move if the Rats find us."

They began gathering up what packs they'd pulled from the wagon. Allan hesitated a moment, then stepped out of the pantry and into the rest of the house.

Even in the darkness, Allan could tell it would once have been considered opulent, with hardwood floors, elegant woodworking along the moldings at the ceiling and floor and along the banister of the stairs, fine glass in the windows. Now it was covered in dust and dirt, the furniture gone, a few tapestries torn and crumpled on the floor among broken statuettes, pottery, and a few smaller nightstands or pedestals. Glass shards littered one hallway, crunching beneath Allan's feet as he made his way toward the front in search of Glenn.

He found the Dog hovering beside a large bay window. Outside, the street roiled with Rats, the scraggly and ragged group amassing in the alley leading toward the ley station. Stragglers, armed with rough weapons like cudgels and staves, tried to shove forward through the ranks, all of them yelling out inarticulate battle cries. All of those who had serious weapons, like spears or bows, were at the front of the pack and out of sight. Those Allan could see were younger as well, maybe ten years old. He assumed the older Rats kept the better weapons.

"They haven't noticed us yet." Glenn glanced back. "But they will. Once they're done fighting. It's too much to hope they won't."

"Maybe the fighting will draw them away from this street."

Glenn merely grunted.

"Keep watch. Yell if there's trouble."

"There's already trouble."

Allan retreated to the back of the house, found Kent watching the walled-in gardens beyond with sword drawn. Allan had expected an actual garden, with vegetables and herbs, like what he'd seen behind nearly every row of flats and apartment buildings in Erenthrall before the Shattering. But this was an ornamental garden, stone paths weaving among benches, small ponds, a dry stone waterfall. A few trees still remained, survivors of the blast that had destroyed the central part of the city, but they'd taken a beating. Branches had snapped off, but leaves had budded out on the skeletal remains. Some of the bushes beneath were already full, their leaves rustling in a breeze.

He scanned the walls. A few trellises were placed against the back, the latticework reaching all the way to the top, interlaced with vines and foliage. He didn't see a door.

Beyond the wall, the backs of more brownstone houses cut off the view, their details obscured by shadows.

"Why would they not have a door? Even if only for the servants."

"At least there are trellises."

From the street out front, a roar rose. Both men turned.

"The fighting has started," Kent muttered.

Allan placed a hand on his shoulder. "I'm going to start sending the rest back here. We need to be ready in case they discover us. If they do, send them over the wall and try to keep them all together."

"Where should we head?"

"To the new safe house, if you can manage it. Otherwise, back out onto the plains toward the Hollow."

Allan found Kara and the others huddled in the large dining room, the massive table still filling up the center of the room, the crystal chandelier a shattered heap of ley globes and twisted metal where it had fallen in one of the quakes. Kara and the rest were rooting through what supplies they'd managed to pull from the wagon before the Rats arrived.

"Get everything together. I want everyone to move toward the back of the house, near Kent's position."

"I thought we were hunkering down until the Rats left."

"I don't like how this is playing out. I want you all ready to run."

Fear flashed across all of their faces, but they began gathering up the supplies again.

Kara shifted toward him and said under her breath, "We have a problem. We didn't grab as much food as I thought we did."

"We can't do anything about that."

"We can grab what's left in the wagon."

"No, we can't. Not with the Rats out there."

"But—"

"No! If even one of them sees us, it's over. Our only chance is to sneak away and hope that the Rats don't notice the wagon. We can come back for the food later."

Kara sucked in a breath to protest, but Adder suddenly appeared. "We have a new problem."

"What?"

He motioned them out into the hall, then toward the front room where Glenn stood guard. The Dog gestured toward the far side of the large window looking out onto the street. "To the left."

Allan circled around the room, Kara on his heels, both keeping to the shadows. Glenn waved at Adder, who nodded and disappeared back in the direction of the dining room.

Allan halted when he saw the group of Rats on the street, one hand behind to warn Kara to stay back. Then he eased forward, the wooden floor creaking beneath his weight. The street was nearly empty, although he could hear the sounds of the battle being waged in the ley station's square from here. But a large group of Rats had been left behind, mostly the younger children. An older boy was giving out orders, pointing and motioning in different directions, Rats breaking away from the group in pairs or triples. All of them carried weapons, although they were mostly cudgels and knives.

"What's happening?" Kara's voice was no more than a puff of air at his back.

"They're sending out scouts." He glanced upward, close enough to the window he could see the rooftops of the buildings across the way. A few shadowy figures were looking down at the group below.

When he looked back down, the Rat's leader waved toward their section of the street and three of the Rats broke toward them—two older girls, one Morrell's age, and a boy. Their eyes were startlingly white in their dirt-smeared faces beneath scraggly hair. Their expressions were feral.

"Go tell the others to get to the back of the house. Take whatever they can grab, nothing more. Tell Kent to start sending people up over the wall."

Kara backed away. Allan turned back to the street, but the pack of Rats had completely dispersed. He didn't see the group headed toward their location, but he caught Glenn motioning toward the left. The Dog mouthed, "Three doors down."

Allan eased back from the window and moved to Glenn's side.

"I sent Adder to the roof to get Jack and Cutter. Tim's still in the pantry with the horses."

"I'll get him. We're going out the back. I'm not waiting for them to find us."

"Better hurry. The Rats aren't wasting any time."

Outside, they could see one of the groups trotting past them, headed farther down the street, well beyond their position. The two Dogs watched them in silence until they'd vanished, both tense.

"Let's hope they aren't headed for the rooftops."

He snagged Tim from the pantry, the horses restless, sensing the rising tension. They found the others gathered around the back door, Kent shoving them through. Adder already stood near the trellises. Allan caught Cutter's body slipping over the top of the wall, Jack a few seconds behind, and two of the Wielders were running toward Adder's position, shoulders hunched as if they expected to be attacked any second. The rest fidgeted as they waited, as nervous as the horses. Gaven and Aaron went next, packs jouncing on their backs as they hustled to where Artras and Dylan were climbing the walls. Allan shoved Tim forward, he and Carter waiting for the Hollowers to start climbing.

Glenn suddenly appeared.

"We need to move it! That patrol is moving to this house now!"

Allan spun to find Tim and Carter gone, racing toward the trellises. "Kara and Kent, you're next. Go!"

Neither one hesitated, dodging out into the distortion-lit night, ignoring the garden paths and shoving through brush to reach the wall. Adder practically flung Carter onto the trellis, the young Wielder crying out. Allan flinched, then hissed in warning as he heard the door to the brownstone burst inward. He and Glenn crouched down, both with hands on their swords, as they heard footsteps on the creaking floorboards. Two of the Rats were arguing with each other.

Allan glanced out into the garden, noticed Kara and Kent near the top of the trellises. He motioned Glenn toward the door, had shifted to follow when one of the Rats—the older girl, he guessed, the one that reminded him of Morrell—suddenly barked, "Quiet! Look. Someone's been here."

Allan's gaze shot to the floor, to the dust riddled with scuffed footprints.

He pushed Glenn out the door, hard on his heels. Glenn leaped for the wall, Adder already halfway up, behind Kara. Allan paused, glanced back toward the house, his skin tingling as he imagined the Rats scurrying through the brownstone's rooms, following the tracks, discovering the horses in the pantry, the cart in the alley, heading for the back door.

His breath quickened. His hand tightened on the pommel of his sword in anticipation, slicked with sweat, but he didn't draw. He clenched his teeth, tried to calm himself.

He wasn't certain he could kill a girl only twelve years old, even if she did carry a knife. Except all of their lives depended on it.

At the same moment he started to draw, someone barked in surprise.

He jerked in the direction of the shout, saw a Rat standing on the rooftop two houses down, arm pointing, the distortion a vibrant backdrop behind. Another Rat suddenly appeared at his side.

The second carried a bow.

Allan jumped for the trellis, a harsh whistle piercing the muted rumble of the battle being fought mere blocks away. The sound skated down his spine as he scrambled up the wall, his fingers grabbing for handholds in the trellis and vines. He hauled himself upward, heedless of the splinters. The point of an arrow cracked into the stone to his left, followed by another, closer, on his right. Behind, the Rats inside the house shouted and poured out of the door; he caught their movement out of the corner of his eye.

Then he reached for another handhold and his arm slammed over the top of the wall. He heaved himself up and over, another arrow whistling overhead.

He fell to the ground on the far side, hitting hard, Adder reaching down to help him up, Glenn shouting orders. Pain shot through his leg, but he ignored it. They were in another garden, this one not as immaculately laid out as the last. Half of the group was already inside the house, the rest charging across the ground between. Arrows hit the earth, the house, the wall behind, but they were sporadic. The Rats only had two, maybe three archers nearby.

"Go! Get inside before they hit one of us!"

They raced across the open ground, all three of them hunched down, trying to stick to the protection of the few trees and the shadows. Kara and Kent ducked through the open door and vanished in the darkness beyond. A second later, Adder, Glenn, and Allan joined them.

Inside, he found the group arguing, frantic, but he plowed through them, headed toward the front of the house. "Keep moving! They'll be on us in a moment."

His voice spurred them all back into motion. The entire group plunged through the house, past broken furniture and cracked walls, then spilled out onto the street beyond. Everyone ducked, expecting arrows, but a quick look proved the rooftops were empty.

"Where do we go?" Glenn asked.

"Can we still make your new safe house?"

"Yes. But it won't be that safe if we lead them right to it."

"We'll have to lose them." Allan turned to the group. "Wielders and Hollowers, stay in the middle. Dogs, protect the flanks. Move!"

Glenn sprinted down the street, the Wielders and

Hollowers on their heels, the rest of the Dogs taking up positions to either side and behind. Cutter and Jack did the same, bows set with arrows. Allan drew his sword, bringing up the rear.

They'd reached the end of the block when Rats began spilling out of the house they'd vacated. Allan swore as the leaders of the group pointed toward them and yelled. The entire group broke out into shrieks and bellows, like they had on the rooftop the night before, when Allan had watched them slaughter their Temerite captives. Most of the Rats' forces were back in the ley station plaza, fighting the Tunnelers, but there were still at least thirty Rats on the street here.

And he knew there'd be more.

He spun around. "Run!"

Adder tore around the corner at the end of the block, the Wielders and Hollowers close behind, everyone at a dead run, most nearly lost in the darkness. Allan's feet thudded into the gritty street as he dodged debris—dead ley carts, a few wagons and carriages, damaged beyond easy repair. His own blood pounded in his ears. His lungs ached. He kept his attention on his pack ahead, on the Dogs and trackers. When the Dogs turned the corner, the trackers at their heels, he saw the archers skid to a halt, bows rising automatically.

Then he could see around the corner and spotted the group of ragtag fighters loping toward them. Those at the front had been brought up short by the appearance of Glenn, Adder, and the Wielders and Hollowers, but their startled looks immediately set into grim expressions at the appearance of the trackers and the bows.

They raised their makeshift weapons and charged.

Glenn and the others turned back, to retreat, but Allan motioned to his right. "Into the buildings!"

Glenn and Adder veered to their left immediately, each one grabbing one of the panicked Wielders and steering them in the same direction. Gaven and Aaron stumbled to a halt, then followed. Kara hesitated only a moment, Carter catching on a second later. Only Dylan faltered and fell. Adder caught his arm and dragged him toward the buildings to the right. The Dogs and trackers before Allan angled toward the rest of the group, Allan doing the same as the new group bore down on them from farther up the street. He could hear the Rats coming in from behind. Too close. They weren't going to make it. Not as a single group.

"Split up! Head to different houses!"

Glenn barked something Allan didn't hear, but Adder suddenly banked to the right, heading toward the steps of a different house, Gaven, Kara, and Dylan breaking away with him. Kent followed, Tim sticking with Glenn, Artras, Aaron, and Carter.

Glenn vaulted up the few steps to the door, reared back, and kicked it in. It splintered as it came away from the frame, but Artras was already ducking through, Carter practically crawling over her back. Glenn shoved them both inside, then snagged Tim and Aaron and hurled them through. Cutter slid by before he could touch him. Adder already had the door open—Allan hadn't seen how—shouting for the others to get inside. Jack leaped up the stairs behind them.

On the street, the Rats had rounded the corner, brought up short by the second group.

Allan abruptly realized the second group wasn't part of the Rats.

The Tunnelers had sent a force around to flank them.

A quick scan told him that the two forces were about the same size. But the Rats could easily bring in reinforcements.

He had no more time than that. With a roar of hatred, the two forces converged in the middle of the street.

But not all of the attackers were focused on each other. At least two dozen broke away from the main group toward the buildings where Allan's pack had fled.

He spun and climbed the steps to where Glenn held the cracked door open. As he stepped through, the Dog said, "Where to? We can't hold them here."

He considered, the others standing just inside the foyer. "The roof. The houses are all nearly the same size."

"Not all of them."

"No, but we can throw them off by moving a few buildings down first before descending back to street level."

Tim and Aaron had already begun climbing the stairs. The rest followed, their footsteps pounding on the landing as they disappeared out of sight. Allan pressed his back into the door, planted his feet against the floor, sword raised before him.

Neither Glenn nor Cutter moved.

"Go!"

"What about you?"

Allan swore and glanced at Cutter. "We need to block the door somehow."

At the same time, the group outside slammed into the door, pushing it inward a foot. Allan braced himself and shoved back, slamming it closed on an arm and foot attempting to slide through. Someone screamed and Allan saw blood as the door rattled and then closed with a solid thud as the arm and leg retracted. The Tunnelers outside— it had to be Tunnelers; they'd been closer—began pounding on the door, the already splintered wood shaking in its frame.

"Cutter!"

The tracker had vanished.

A heartbeat later, Cutter reappeared, dragging a heavy table behind him. He and Glenn tilted it up as he neared.

When they were ready, Allan barked, "Now!"

He dodged out of the way as they slammed the table into the door. In that split second, the Tunnelers managed to open it a hand's span and there were more screams and cries of pain as it snapped shut on questing fingers. Cutter and Glenn held the table as Allan yanked its base around against the banister at the bottom of the stairs with his free hand, bracing it, although it wouldn't hold for long. Then he tapped Cutter's shoulder and all three released the table and charged up the steps. The Tunnelers shoved the door inward, cracking the table's base into the banister, but it held. They rounded the landing and could no longer see what was happening. But by the time the stairs ended on the third floor, a gut-wrenching splintering of wood echoed up as the banister gave and they heard the Tunnelers flooding the first floor below.

Allan slowed, trying to move swiftly but silently, as they began searching the hallway above, looking for access to the roof. Cutter noticed the footprints in the dust first, leading to the trapdoor. After that, the tracks led to the back, where a folding ladder led up to the roof.

Cutter and Glenn scrambled up the ladder. Allan followed, not as nimble. As soon as he hit the roof, he turned and grabbed the ladder, yanking it upward. It clattered as it folded up on itself, nearly catching his fingers.

Cutter and Glenn were already halfway across the roof. Allan took off after them, caught movement in the space between this set of the buildings and the one a street over, and glanced down. Adder, Kara, and the rest were crawling over walls in the remains of the gardens below. Allan saw them ducking into another building on the opposite side, and then he was at the roof's wall.

He jumped it, landed hard on the roof on the far side, and sprinted after the others, now two roofs away.

He began to think they'd escape.

But then a group of attackers spilled out of a trapdoor twenty paces ahead of Tim. Before the young Dog could react, there were a dozen of the scruffy adolescents on the roof, all with weapons, spread out and ready. Artras, Carter, and Aaron drew up short behind Tim. Farther behind, Cutter slowed, nocked an arrow and drew.

Allan slowed to a trot, then halted, as he heard the trapdoor they'd just left behind open and clatter down into the building. Without turning, he knew more of the Tunnelers were filling the rooftop behind him.

Cutter looked back, a question in his eyes. Attack or stand down?

Allan lowered his sword.

# Seven

KARA'S STOMACH SCRAPED OVER THE TOP of another garden wall, her body already sore, then she dropped to the ground on the far side.

Dylan grabbed her arm and hauled her upright. "Move. They're right behind us."

She allowed him to lead her diagonally across the garden in a half crouch, to where Adder and Kent were ushering the rest of their group through a side door that led into a servant's alley between two buildings. Gaven and Jack were already running ahead of them, barely discernible in the darkness. None of the distortion's light made it into this crevice. Behind, she heard the alley's door clatter shut, followed by the Dogs' heavy tread. And behind that she could hear a sudden uproar from the Rats and Tunnelers. The raw viciousness of the sound made her chest ache.

Then they were at the street, Gaven and Jack holding them back in the shadows.

"I don't think they saw us duck into this alley. Can we stay hidden once we're out there?"

"Not really."

The street was angled so that it was almost completely lit by the light thrown by the distortion. Kara expected to see another section of houses, but the landscape changed from row houses to three- and four-story tenements that spanned entire blocks, separated from each other by parks. The buildings had distinct architectural styles, to differentiate each from the other. A few surrounded their own court-yards, one or two with gates.

She glanced toward the distortion. They were closer now. "Where are the others? I thought they'd be right behind us."

"It doesn't matter. Allan said to get to the new safe house if we could, without being followed." Adder had shifted forward through the group. He scanned the empty street before them, then back at the alley. The sounds of the pursuing Rats—or maybe they were Tunnelers—grew louder. "Head for the building there, with the courtyard As fast as you can go."

He tapped Jack's shoulder, the tracker sprinting across the debris-strewn street. There were chunks of stone litter-ing the street here, not just ley carts and abandoned wagons and other possessions. She wondered if they were the re-mains of one of Grass' towers.

Adder sent Kent, Gaven, and Dylan next, bringing up the rear himself, Kara just before him. His footfalls behind her were light at first, then drowned out by her own breath-ing. Those ahead of her made it to the gates to the court-yard, the wrought iron screeching as Jack shoved it open to get inside. Adder cursed behind her—at the noise or at whatever was behind them, Kara couldn't tell. She picked up her pace anyway, aiming for the gate as Kent and Dylan twisted through the small opening. Dylan held the gate back for her as she slowed and ducked inside, his face lifting and registering fear a moment before she slid past him. Ad-der's hand shoved her out of the way and she stumbled to the interior walkway, biting back a cry as her hands scraped on the stone path.

Then Adder grabbed her around the waist and flung her to one side. She gasped in astonishment, before a hand clamped over her mouth.

They glared at each other. Then Kara noticed everyone in the group pressed up against the stone wall that housed the gate. Adder held her against his body, turned away slightly so that he could peer through the wrought iron into the street beyond. Kara forced herself to relax, then struggled lightly, until Adder looked back and let her go.

She pressed against the stone wall like the others. Outside the courtyard, their pursuers shouted, a few older voices giving out orders. Feet tramped back and forth, across the street at first, but then closer. Shadows bolted past the front of the gates. They tore up the street, calling out to other groups Kara couldn't see.

"What have you got?" someone shouted, so close Kara jerked back against the wall. Pebbles rattled down from the top of the wall, bouncing off Kara's head and clattering on the stone path of the courtyard. Adder shot everyone a harsh look, held his hand out and signaled them all back against the wall as he stepped deeper into the shadows.

Silence from outside the gate, where before there had been the noise of pacing feet and movement. A listening silence, broken only by the sounds of other groups searching farther away.

A shadow appeared in the gate opening again and paused. Kara could only see the top of the head, close to her feet, distorted by the wrought iron's shadow. Adder's hand shifted, grip tightening on his sword.

"Richten!"

The shadow shifted, head turned, then moved away.

Kara exhaled slowly.

"What?"

"The Underearthers have caught someone on the roof."

Allan? The others? Did they get all of them or only some?

And then her skin prickled with horror. If they were reporting on the Tunnelers, that meant they were Rats.

Their leader cursed. "How did you let this happen?" A fist slammed into flesh and someone cried out. A scuffle followed, punctuated by whimpers, as if someone were being beaten or kicked.

The beating stopped, someone gasping from the effort, another moaning.

"Fletch isn't going to be happy."

"No shit."

"What are we going to do about it?"

A considered silence, along with the crunch of grit as someone moved about. A street away, the battle between the Rats and Tunnelers escalated for a moment, then faded again.

The shadow reappeared, one arm rising to clutch at the iron before dropping.

"Mouse, head back to the main group and report." The leader moved away again. "Vole, I want you to . . ." Richten's voice dropped too low for Kara to make out.

A moment later, a group of at least three or four broke away. Kara shifted, but Adder held up a hand in warning, still listening.

"What do we do about him?"

"Pick him up and drag him back with us."

More feet scuffling, followed by a groan and the sound of someone being dragged away. Richten shouted more orders to those still combing the street beyond, but the sounds of the search were fading.

Kara leaned her head back against the stone behind her, eyes closed.

After ten minutes, Adder finally moved, stepping away from the wall. Kara opened her eyes, but said nothing as he leaned toward the gate and checked the street. Kara hadn't heard anyone for over five minutes, only the muted sounds of the fighting a street or more away.

A few of the others moved up to Kara's side.

"Are they gone?" Dylan asked.

Adder shot him a glare, but straightened. "I think so."

"Then let's get out of here."

"What about Allan and the others? You heard them. The group from the ley station caught them. We have to help them."

"We don't even know if that's true. Or how many they caught."

"Kent's right. We need to regroup back at the new safe house, as Allan ordered, see if anyone from the other group shows up."

"What if no one else shows?"

"We'll deal with that later."

The group considered this in silence, Kara thinking of Allan and Artras.

"Where's the new safe house then? I don't know where we are."

"This way. We're at the edge of the Clay District now."

Adder shifted toward the gates, peered out into the street as he spoke, Kara moving up behind him. She couldn't see anything except debris, although her gaze fell to a section of the nearest rubble where a dark blotch of blood now stained the cobbles.

As he stepped carefully through the twisted opening of the gate, Kara asked, "How far is it?"

"About three blocks down. We'll stay in Clay for a while, bypass the Rats and Tunnelers, then cut back in—"

"Well, well, well. I was right."

Adder spun, sinking into a crouch, as a Rat rose from behind a toppled ley cart twenty paces distant. Kara's hand reached for the knife in her belt. Behind her, Kent tried to squeeze between the iron gate and got caught, cloth ripping as he yanked himself free. Gaven, Jack, and Dylan were still in the courtyard.

The Rat smiled, his teeth surprisingly white in the dirt-smear of his face. He was tall and thin, his face narrow, like a real rat's, his hair mussed and wild. His eyes were pinched and cruel.

He motioned with one hand and more than two dozen Rats rose from their positions behind the scattered debris, all with weapons. All except the leader, Richten.

"Adder!"

Kara turned at Jack's shout to see more Rats dropping from the lower windows of the building that framed the rest of the courtyard.

They were surrounded.

Cory hunched down in the dense foliage of the forest and cursed beneath his breath. He thought for certain that the group of men and women traipsing through the trees on either side of the spot where he and two other guards from the Hollow were hunkered would hear it. Sweat trickled down his forehead and he dashed it away with one hand, his other resting on the handle of the sword sheathed at his waist. He'd become more comfortable with the weapon in the long practices, enough that he'd been chosen to help with the patrols surrounding the Hollow, but it still felt foreign to him when he was wielding it. Others in the training group were naturals; he was only passable. But they were younger than him, and most had been trained for more strenuous physical labor. Cory had been a candlemaker's son, then a student at the University. Everything about the sword felt unnatural.

But the Hollow needed guardsmen. These intruders were proof.

Reiss, crouched ten paces away, hissed to catch Cory's attention, then signaled with a flash of his fingers, almost too fast for Cory to follow.

*How many?*

Cory scanned the group, raising his head tentatively above the brush to do a quick count.

*Five south, seven north.*

*Weapons?*

*Bows. Swords.*

Reiss shifted his weight so that he could converse with Joss, bow across his knees. Reiss was Cory's age, Joss a few years older, but Reiss had taken control of the patrol without saying a word. He knew the woods better than any of them.

Cory turned back to the intruders. The men were all rough, fitted out in bits and pieces of armor, most of it matching, but not all. They picked their way through the forested hillside, staying clear of the dense brush beneath the trees, following deer trails or staying near the narrow stream that trickled between the hills to either side. Cory, Reiss, and Joss were on the southern hill just above the stream, the five intruders on their side on the bank above them, where a ridge of land made it easier to climb. The other seven were on the far side, scattered, all of them moving steadily to the west. None of them looked comfortable, cursing when a booted foot slipped in the matted leaves or earth. Most were sporting full beards, one or two with the narrow faces of Temerites. Two were women.

Cory startled when someone touched his shoulder, twisted to find both Reiss and Joss beside him. He hadn't heard them approach.

"They're following the stream." Reiss' voice was barely

audible. The others were making so much noise moving through the trees they couldn't possibly hear it. Reiss' eyes shifted constantly, both forward, where the intruders had passed them, and back the way they'd come. "Do you recognize them?"

"No, but I wasn't on any of the expeditions to the plains."

"They come from the plains, though. Look at how they're moving through the woods." Joss motioned toward those on the northern bank.

"I'd bet they're part of the group that attacked Bryce's wagon a few months back. The ones that killed Terrim and nearly got Claye."

"What are they doing here?"

"Looking for us."

"What should we do? Go back and warn the Hollow?"

Reiss considered, then shook his head. "We'll follow them. See where they go. The Hollow is far enough south there's no chance they'll find it the way they're headed. But if there are more of them, Bryce will want to know."

They waited until the last of the group had been gone ten minutes, then followed, Reiss scouting ahead. Cory and Joss stuck close to the stream, where the sounds of the running water would help mask their movements.

An hour later, the sound of a starling cut through the natural sounds of the wood and both Joss and Cory halted and dropped into a crouch.

Reiss trotted toward their position. "They've halted near a small waterfall ahead of us. They're arguing about what to do next. I think they're going to cut back this way. Joss, I want you to head back to the Hollow. Warn Bryce and the patrols."

"What are you and Cory going to do?"

"Continue following them. I want to see where their camp is."

Reiss gripped Joss' shoulder before he took off in a low crouch, weaving his way up over the top of the southern hill between the trees.

Ten minutes later, once again hunkered down in a stand of thick brush, Cory and Reiss watched the dozen bandits backtrack, many of them grumbling. One of them—a hard man, face scarred with pox, beard rangy—passed within five paces of them. He reeked, the stench assaulting Cory's nostrils, making him gag.

As soon as they passed by, Reiss and Cory followed, Reiss skipping across submerged stones in the stream to track them on the far side. Cory knew little to nothing about tracking, but skill wasn't necessary. The bandits were being less cautious on their way out than in.

The sun had begun to set, casting a significant portion of the valley in shadow, when Reiss raised a hand in warning. Cory dropped immediately onto his heels, then shifted toward a split-bole tree for cover. Between the break, he watched Reiss edge forward, then sidle left and draw up behind a ridge of granite jutting up from the soil. He peered over the boulder's edge, then drew back and motioned Cory forward.

Cory skirted a stand of reeds, splashed through the stream as silently as possible, then came up behind Reiss, settling down next to him, both using the boulder as cover.

"They're camped below. Take a look."

Cory raised his head high enough that he could see the camp. There were at least forty men in the hollow, including the group of twelve they'd been following. They'd set up tents to either side of the stream, near where the running water had formed a large pool. Based on the number of tents, Cory guessed there were at least a dozen others missing from the camp; another party like the one that had led them here. Horses were hobbled in a group east of the camp, not enough for all of those present. A firepit had been set up near a larger tent at the center, and a few men stood cooking food over the flames, another off to one side, gutting and cleaning game.

The group they'd followed broke up as soon as they reached the camp, most ducking into tents or greeting the others with backslaps or grins. Two—a man and a woman—headed toward the main tent, pausing outside and speaking through the flap before entering.

Movement much closer to their hiding place forced Cory to drop down. Reiss gave him a questioning look and he mouthed, "Patrol."

Reiss nodded, glanced over the boulder once, then brought a finger to his lips. He nocked an arrow, but didn't draw, leaning back into the lichen-covered stone.

Cory heard a twig snap. Ears straining, he picked out footfalls, coming closer. His hand fell to the sword strapped to his side.

The footsteps halted on the far side of the boulder. Cory glanced toward Reiss, the tracker perfectly still, head lowered, eyes squinted in concentration. He didn't appear nervous at all, merely tense. His fingers tightened to either side of the arrow, the bowstring taut. Muscles flexed in his upper arm—

And then the guard grunted and the footsteps retreated.

Cory let out the breath he'd been holding.

They waited another ten minutes, then pulled back to the stream, Reiss picking up the pace as soon as they were beyond the camp's patrols.

"Where are we going?" Cory asked as they ran through the trees, sunlight slanted through the foliage at a sharp angle overhead.

"The Hollow. Bryce needs to know they've moved into the hills."

It was dark when they reached the outer edge of the Hollow. When they passed over the patrol line Bryce had set up after the attack on the plains and weren't challenged, Reiss broke into a half sprint, slowed only by the terrain.

The buildings of the Hollow were quiet, nearly everyone retired for the night. Candlelight glowed in a few windows— Sophia's and Logan's most notably. Figures near the barns were settling in the last of the livestock. A few dogs barked as they passed. Cory didn't see any of Bryce's Dogs, or the alpha himself anywhere.

Reiss bolted for the refugee camp, racing through the trees.

They burst from the trees to find the refugee camp as sedate as the Hollow. Men were still working on the cabins by lantern light, and Reiss headed straight for them.

"Bryce. Where is he?"

"His tent, I think."

Reiss spun and trotted carefully through the cluster of tents, moving as fast as possible without tripping over ties and stakes.

Two of the Dogs and one of those in training huddled over a small firepit, chatting. One of them, the oldest, lurched upright as Reiss and Cory emerged from the shadows into the firelight, sword half-drawn before recognition hit.

He spat to one side, letting his blade snick back into its sheath. "Gods above, Reiss, you startled me." He began to sit back down.

Reiss crossed the distance between them and grabbed the front of his shirt, hauling him back up. "Where's Joss, Braddon? Did he check in?"

The other two men glanced toward each other, eyebrows raised, as Braddon's hands automatically gripped Reiss' wrists. "Let go, or I'll break your wrists."

Reiss had already released him, wresting his wrists free with a curse. He stalked toward Bryce's tent, the other two men jumping up in protest as he flung back the flap. "Bryce! Wake up, damn you. We have a problem."

"What in hells—?"

"We have a problem!"

"Give me a second."

Reiss let the tent flap fall back and turned again to Braddon. "No one has heard from Joss? He didn't report in?"

Braddon wiped his mouth. "We've heard nothing from Joss. You're the first to report back."

"What about Joss?" Bryce asked as he emerged from the tent, belting his sword. He'd obviously dressed quickly, but he appeared alert.

"We ran into a group of the bandits, as you predicted. They're searching the hills. I sent Joss back to report while Cory and I followed them to their camp. He should have checked in an hour ago."

Bryce eyed Reiss, then Cory, before turning to Braddon. "We haven't heard anything?"

"Nothing from any of the trackers."

"Wake the others. Everyone, even the trainees. Get them geared up and ready. Have them meet in the center of the village. Send a runner to the patrols, have them pull back, tighten up. Do it as quietly as possible. If the bandits are out there, I don't want them knowing we're onto them."

Braddon motioned toward the other two, all three of them trotting out into the darkness in different directions.

Within moments, Cory could feel the nearest part of the refugee camp stirring.

Bryce focused on Reiss. "What did you see?"

"A group of twelve, out scouting. We followed them halfway up the Kipsy stream, but they turned back. We let them pass us, which is when I sent Joss back to report. Cory and I followed them to a base camp. The group had been there a while. They had tents, a campfire, hitching posts, patrols. They were settled in."

"How many?"

"Thirty-eight."

Bryce glanced to Cory for confirmation.

"There were signs that at least a dozen others were missing."

"Out searching, no doubt."

"Maybe they ran into Joss." Cory realized Bryce and Reiss had already thought of it, were already ten steps ahead of him.

Both of them ignored the statement.

"How much time do you think we have?"

"Depends on whether they know exactly where we are."

"If they have Joss, they know. It wouldn't take much to break him." Bryce glanced around at the mostly sleeping camp. "Warn Sophia and Paul. Tell them to wake whoever they think can help defend us."

Reiss acknowledged the order by vanishing into the darkness, leaving Cory with Bryce.

"What about everyone else? Should we send them to the caves?" While planning the defense of the Hollow, one of the Hollowers had mentioned caves to the northwest. They weren't easily accessible, the two main entrances covered by growth and some deadfall, but the interiors were large enough to hold everyone in the Hollow and the refugees combined, with a pool of fresh water in a deeper chamber and room for storage. After protesting that the caves had never crossed their minds, both Paul and Sophia had organized the Hollowers and started sending supplies to the caves for storage, in case they were forced to retreat to them at some point.

"We don't know enough yet. I don't want to give away the caves' location."

A few of Bryce's chosen betas raced up, Bryce giving them orders. Cory hung back, feeling out of place, wondering where Hernande was, as well as the other Wielders and University survivors like Sovaan and Jerrain. Someone should warn them. They might not wield weapons, but maybe they could help in the defense in other ways.

He was about to slip away when Bryce glanced up. "Cory, come with me."

The Dog headed toward the patch of forest between the refugee camp and the center of the Hollow. Cory hustled after the Dogs' leader.

More men joined them, calling out orders in gruff voices. The refugee camp was waking up around them, the unusual movement too loud even with everyone trying to remain silent. Cory saw Sovaan crawl from a tent; he'd obviously dressed hastily. Cory tried to catch the University mentor's attention, but they passed by too quickly.

By the time they reached the edge of camp, Bryce was trailed by nearly forty men, others still fighting to get into their gear. A small crowd of the rest of the refugees had gathered behind them. Some were calling out questions, unease and panic growing.

Just before he stepped into the woods, Jerrain snagged Cory's arm.

"What's going on?"

Cory shot a look toward Bryce, but the alpha was already lost in the trees.

He grabbed Jerrain's thin shoulders. "We ran into the bandits during one of our patrols. Now Joss is missing. Bryce thinks the bandits have captured him and may be on their way here." The last of the armed men were entering the forest. "Get Hernande. Tell him to find me at the Hollow."

Jerrain harrumphed, but Cory stepped backward. "Get Hernande!" Then he entered the woods at a trot—fast enough to catch up to Bryce before he noticed Cory was gone.

He came out behind Logan's cabin, where the healer stood in his front doorway watching the growing crowd of men in the center of town. Claye stood beside him, one hand clutching his wounded side, the other holding a crutch tucked into his armpit. Bryce was calling out orders, men and women breaking away in pairs or groups of three, heading out toward the inner boundary of the village, one that Bryce had established after the initial attack. Nothing more than a series of stone walls the Hollowers had set up long before the Shattering, the defenses could be overrun easily with enough men. They hadn't had enough time to build them up into anything better.

Cory edged through the throng of men and women until he was close to Bryce. Sophia and Paul stood behind the alpha, looking concerned. Only then did Cory notice that many of the Hollowers had joined them, the farmers and herders mixed in with the Dogs and the other refugees.

"Braddon, take your men to the inner perimeter, northeast corner. Alex, your group's got the post west of Braddon. I've already sent Reiss and the others to the outer perimeter there, since that's the most likely direction the bandits will come from. The rest of you, split into groups of five and spread yourself around the perimeter. Concentrate on the northeastern corner, but make certain there are people on all sides, that you're not spaced too far apart."

People began moving, conversations breaking out as they began dividing up as directed, until someone shouted over the increasing activity, "What about our families?"

Nearly everyone halted, looking back at Bryce, the concern they'd been suppressing stark on their faces.

Bryce hesitated, drew breath to answer—

But Sophia suddenly stepped forward. "Leave your families for now. Let them sleep. We aren't certain if the bandits even know where we are yet. But if there is an attack, someone will ring the bell in the meeting hall, as we planned. Your wives, husbands, and children will know to retreat to the caves then."

Sophia fell back. Some of the men began to grumble in uncertainty, but Bryce caught their attention. "We've prepared for this. Your families know what to do. If you hear the bell, stay at your posts! We won't know how many of the bandits there are and they could be attacking at more than one location. Abandoning your post won't protect your families."

Most of the grumbles quieted. Braddon clapped his hands together to get things moving.

Bryce stepped up to Cory. "You're with me again. Stay close this time."

"I spoke to Jerrain—"

"I don't need to hear it. All I need is for you to follow my orders."

Cory clamped his mouth shut.

"You're my gods-damned runner, Cory. If we do get attacked, you're to head back here and make certain the bell is rung and the rest of these people get to the caves."

"I sent Jerrain to find the University students and mentors."

"Why in hells would you do that?"

"Because we didn't just read books at the University. We work with the Tapestry. There's got to be something we can do besides flail around with a sword or cower in a cave!"

Bryce flicked a hand in dismissal and turned his back. Half of those gathered had already headed off into the darkness carrying torches or lanterns. Cory glanced back toward the trees and the refugee camp, but he didn't see Hernande or any of the others.

They ran into the hills to the northeast of the village, the rest of the group shadowy figures to either side. Cory kept to the back. They slowed when they reached the steepest part of the hill, forced to ascend in a switchback pattern, the ground slippery. Cory slid two or three times, catching himself with one hand, before they reached the top.

Once there, they ran into another group, already settled in. Bryce spoke with the leader briefly, then headed east along the ridge, the group they left behind dousing their lantern as soon as they'd left. They passed four more groups before Bryce finally reached the location he'd chosen earlier.

"Spread out and settle in. And shutter that lantern. But don't lose sight of each other."

As the others complied, Bryce snagged Cory's arm. "I meant what I said earlier. If we're attacked, race back to the village and make certain that bell is rung. There are other runners besides you, but don't count on one of them making it."

Cory scanned the area, choosing the shadows of a fallen tree toward the back of the line, ten paces from where Bryce crouched down behind a large boulder.

The faint light of their lantern cut off abruptly, plunging Cory's spot into complete darkness. He heard rustling as the rest of the group adjusted their positions, one or two coughing quietly.

Then silence settled. Or what passed for silence in the woods. A breeze rustled in the leaves of the branches overhead. The boles of the trees creaked. Somewhere close, an owl hooted and the undergrowth crackled as smaller night creatures roamed the forest floor; they were too close to the village for larger game. Cory shifted as his leg began to cramp, resting his head back. Overhead, the sky was black, thick clouds obscuring the moon and stars. He could taste rain on the wind.

An hour later, a runner passed through, reporting to Bryce that no one had seen anything or anyone. Shortly after that, the rain started, a faint misty drizzle that strengthened into a chilling downpour. Someone groaned and another cursed, until Bryce muttered a curt warning. The group fell silent again, the sigh of the rain hitting the leaves above overriding all of the other night noises.

The adrenaline had long worn off when the birdcall came faintly from the northeast. Cory had nearly fallen asleep a dozen times, head jerking upward after his chin had sagged onto his chest. The call barely registered.

But Bryce shifted behind his rock and hissed a warning. Cory's hand fell to his sword as he twisted into a crouch, the earth wet and squishy beneath him. The rain hadn't slackened and water ran down his face, dripped from his chin. He shivered with the cold. To either side, the others shifted into ready positions as well. Cory glanced toward Bryce, who shook his head slightly, then focused on the darkness beyond their location.

He heard nothing but the rain for nearly ten minutes, then the unmistakable snap of a branch underfoot. His hand jerked involuntarily and he swallowed back a bitter taste coating his tongue.

Figures edged out of the darkness—three, then four ... no, five. Bryce pulled back further behind his stone, letting the shrouded men creep closer. He signaled to the others, none of whom Cory could see through the rain, then ordered Cory to stay put.

When the bandits had come flush with Bryce's position, the Dog moved.

His dagger cut into the side of the nearest man as he drew his sword, the bandit dropping without a sound. He cut another man's throat as the bandit jerked back in surprise and began to shout, the warning ending in a gurgle. The others had attacked as well, figures dropping on all sides with only grunts or gasps of shock. It was over in moments, Cory's held breath expelled in a huff. He'd clutched the hilt of his sword so hard his fingers were cramping. His entire body trembled in aftershock.

He hadn't even moved from behind his fallen tree.

Bryce straightened from examining one of the bandits when someone shouted to the west, a roar breaking the odd rain-soaked night, followed by the sudden sharp clash of steel on steel. The sounds escalated, the fight spreading. More shouts broke the stillness, coming from the north.

Bryce spat a curse. "Rex, stay here with Cory. The rest of you, come with me!"

They charged out along the ridge in the direction of the fight. Cory lurched upright. "What about the village? Do I ring the bell?"

But they were gone. He turned to Rex—

And saw two more figures emerging from the darkness, directly behind the Hollower.

"Rex!"

He lurched toward the swineherd.

Rex twisted as the lead figure reached him. He cried out, one arm snapping up to protect himself as the other lashed out with his sword in an unwieldy slash. The bandit's blade clanged into the makeshift armor Rex wore on his forearm, slid down to the joint and cut into flesh. Rex screamed, his own blade finding the bandit's gut and slicing across it. Blood gushed from both wounds, black in the darkness, the bandit roaring as his hand clamped down over his stomach. Larger than Rex, he sagged to his knees as he yanked his sword out of Rex's arm and tried to stab the Hollower again.

But his blade met Cory's. Cory didn't remember drawing it, didn't even remember moving. As the swineherd fell back, arm cradled to his chest, Cory shunted the bandit's sword to the ground, staggering as the bandit collapsed forward onto his stomach and groaned. The second bandit grinned, his teeth startlingly white in the darkness, face streaked with rivulets of rain, beard matted to his chest.

"Not much of a fighter, are ya?" He blew the rain from his mouth in a spray. His voice was thick and cracked at the edges. "None of ya are. Easy pickins, then."

He lunged.

Cory dodged, slid in the slick muck on the ground as he scrambled aside. The bandit's blade snagged his pant leg and cut deep into the earth, the bandit cursing. Cory's leg twinged as he pulled himself into a crouch, back hunched, his entire left arm and side covered in chunky muck. But he still gripped his sword.

The bandit jerked his blade from the ground and glowered at him. "Quick bastard." All of his light-hearted, malicious humor had died.

He struck quick and without forewarning, Cory barely bringing his sword up in time. The clang of metal on metal shivered up Cory's arm, throbbed in his shoulder. But he didn't have time to recover, the bandit's next blow coming in hard from the opposite direction.

Cory stepped back, his feet hitting one of the already fallen bodies. He pitched backward. His back slammed hard into the squelching earth, jarring the breath from him, and his sword snapped out of his grip.

He rolled to the side, grasping for his blade, but the bandit kicked him hard in the gut. Pain exploded outward from his stomach and he gagged, heaving in a torn gasp of air, coughed it back out as he curled around his gut. He reached toward the sword again.

The bandit's feet appeared before him, one settling on his outstretched hand, pressing down hard. If not for the softened earth, Cory knew his wrist or the bones in his hand would have snapped. The pain made him yelp and he cocked his head so that he could look up into the bandit's eyes.

The bandit grinned again, as he ground his foot down harder.

Cory moaned.

Something inside him tore, and a white-hot anger poured forth.

He looked up through the scraggly tendrils of hair plastered to his face and reached for the Tapestry. He twisted it, pulled it tight and knotted it before the bandit's chest.

Then he punched it forward and released it.

The bandit reeled back, a startled look crossing his face as he tripped over another body, sprawling back. Cory snatched up his sword, the bones of his hand screaming in agony, then staggered to the bandit's side. Before the man could recover, he sank the blade into his chest. It slid in with surprising ease, one edge grating against bone, the sensation traveling up through his hand and into his arm and chest. The bandit bucked up and gasped, mouth opening as if to scream, but all that came out was a bloody cough, the fluid black. He coughed again, heels digging into the earth as he tried to push himself away, arms flailing. He'd dropped his sword.

Then he sank back to the earth, hands reaching for the blade jutting from his chest, his eyes searching out Cory's. Before he could grab the steel, he collapsed back, as if all of his strings had been cut.

Cory let go of the hilt and staggered back a step. He leaned forward, his bruised abdomen aching. The anger that had suffused him as the bandit stepped on his hand had died, leaving him hollow and shaky. He sank down to his knees, hunched forward.

The ferric scent of blood slammed into him.

He retched, his gut screaming at the new abuse, but he couldn't stop, even after his stomach had emptied. When it finally ended, he sank to one side and spat.

He had only experienced terror like this once before, outside the walls of the University, after the Shattering, when everyone had loaded up into wagons to escape the quickening of the distortion. They'd been attacked by the Wolves.

But this was different. He and Hernande had protected one of the wagons loaded with supplies and children. The Wolves had gone after the Dogs and fighters, like Bryce. He hadn't needed to use the knife he'd held.

Here, he'd killed. And not a Wolf.

Another human being.

His stomach heaved again, and he rolled back to his hands and knees.

"Cory?"

The voice was barely discernible through the rain, ragged with pain.

Rex.

Cory jerked upright, stumbled toward where he thought Rex had fallen, but it was the bandit the swineherd had gutted. Slipping on to the next dark shape, he found Rex shivering, arm clutched to his chest, his face shockingly pale in the dark.

"C-Cory." Relief flooded the herder's face.

"Let me check it."

Rex withdrew the hand holding his arm to his chest.

Cory's stomach lurched again at the sight of bone, a sizeable chunk of Rex's arm near the elbow simply gone. "Stay there." He crawled to the nearest body, removing the man's belt. Distantly, he heard fighting, but it was difficult to place through the hissing rain. Cursing, he scrambled back to Rex and hastily cinched the belt as tight as possible around Rex's upper arm, the herder moaning. Rex's eyes fluttered, and Cory slapped him to keep him conscious.

"Stay awake. I can't carry you."

Then he wrapped his arm beneath Rex's neck and hauled him up into a sitting position. He tucked his shoulder into Rex's armpit, beneath his good arm, and with Rex's help managed to stand.

Through the pouring rain, they began making their way down the side of the ridge.

"Where . . . going?"

"Back to the Hollow. You need to get to Logan. And I need to make certain someone rings that damn bell."

# Eight

CORY STAGGERED INTO THE Hollow's central area, Rex's body a dead weight hanging on his shoulders. The swineherd had nearly made it to the village, then passed out within a hundred yards of the outlying cottages. Cory had dragged him the rest of the way, but now his strength gave out. He let the Hollower sag to the ground.

"Logan! Over here!"

In the center of the village, a small group of those left behind suddenly turned. They'd been focused on the ridge to the north, although they couldn't see or hear anything through the pounding rain.

"It's Cory!"

Cory settled Rex's body as carefully as he could as nearly the entire group raced toward him, Hernande and Logan in the lead.

"He took a sword to the arm. It's bad. It cut deep."

Logan knelt on the ground, hands flying over Rex's body, looking for damage. Morrell threw herself down next to him.

Paul stepped forward, the others gathering around. "What's happening?"

Cory thrust himself up from Rex's side and pushed

through the crowd. "The bandits attacked. Bryce and the others are fighting them off now. We need to get everyone to the caves."

Paul grabbed his arm and halted him. "Are you certain that's necessary? We haven't seen or heard anyone."

"Let go of my arm." When Paul's grip merely tightened, Cory jerked his arm free. "We need to sound the alarm. Now."

He spun, everyone stepping out of his way, and broke into a trot toward the meeting hall and the medium-sized bell on a stand erected before it. Reaching beneath its mouth, he grabbed the rope hanging down from the clapper and began hauling it back and forth.

The sound was loud and higher-pitched than he expected, but he continued clanging away as everyone scattered on the square. Someone grabbed a nearby handcart, dumped out the wood already loaded, and dragged it toward Logan, who carefully picked up Rex and laid him down inside. Morrell raced for Logan's cottage. Everyone else headed toward the nearby cottages, pounding on doors or rushing inside to grab what little possessions they'd prepared for the caves. A smaller group raced toward the refugee camp, although they should be able to hear the alarm even with the rain. Sophia was arguing with Paul, heatedly.

Hernande made his way toward Cory after sending a small cluster of the Wielders and University mentors and students off toward the refugee camp.

"What are they arguing about?"

"Retreating to the caves. Paul thinks we should stay and defend the village."

"He's stupid."

"He's afraid."

People were emerging from the cottages now, satchels and bags thrown over their shoulders. Mothers herded children toward the distant paths, at least one man in each group carrying a weapon. Some of the children and a few of the adults were sobbing. Cory saw Janis emerge from Morrell's cottage, figure hunched, lantern swinging from one hand. She settled a pack on her back and joined another group, helping to keep the children in line. They faded into the downpour, the lantern light dying quickly, as if smothered. More groups emerged from the screening forest between the refugee camp and the village, all of them headed northwest, most being led by Wielders or those from the University. Cory recognized Sovaan and Jerrain. Mareane, one of the younger Wielders, was carrying a struggling, yipping Max.

Cory started when Hernande's hand gripped his shoulder. "I think you can stop now."

Cory relented and began massaging his shoulder, only now feeling the ache. He suddenly realized he hadn't been ringing the bell so much as beating it, his motions frantic, barely in control. His entire body felt stiff with tension, locked under rigid control.

But as the adrenaline rush of getting Rex help and sounding the alarm faded, he began to tremble.

Hernande squeezed his shoulder. "What happened?"

"The bandits attacked!" But that wasn't what Hernande meant.

He looked toward the ridge. "I . . . I killed someone."

"Ah. Killing someone is a hard thing, isn't it? It isn't as simple as thrusting a sword and walking away. It's much more personal than that, even when you don't know the man or woman you have killed. Even if that man or woman was attempting to kill you."

Cory looked down at his hand, the one the bandit had crushed into the mud with his boot. It still ached—a deep, internal pain. He flexed his fingers, making and unmaking a fist, telling himself it was to loosen it up.

"It was so easy."

"Death is always easy." Hernande let his hand drop from Cory's shoulder. "Dealing with the consequences is hard."

"How would you know?"

"I wasn't always a mentor at the University."

"What happened?"

"It was a long time ago, in the Demesnes. Right now, we need to get you and the others to the caves."

He tugged on Cory's arm, but Cory resisted. "There's something else. I did something during the fight. I used the Tapestry."

Hernande's eyebrows shot upward. "How?"

"I knotted it up and punched it into the bandit's chest.

It's what knocked him over, made him lose his sword. It's what gave me the chance to kill him. Otherwise I'd be dead."

Hernande considered him in silence, eyebrows lowered, knit together in thought.

"I was thinking, even before the attack, that those of us from the University—and even the Wielders—could do more than just hold swords. We can help in the defenses in other ways. But after what I did, maybe we can actually fight."

"Perhaps. You'll have to show me what you did. But later." He tugged on Cory's arm again, more insistent. "We need to go."

Cory didn't resist this time. They trotted across the commons, toward the last of the people making their way in groups toward the caves. Joining Sophia and Paul and a few of the Hollowers who'd stayed behind with weapons, they herded the last of the people through the paddocks and fields in the widest part of the valley into the trees beyond, abandoning the worn tracks and trails made by the herders and animals. Some of the stock brayed or bleated as they passed the barns, sensing the turmoil outside. Then they were in the forest, somewhat sheltered, rain dripping down from above. Lanterns trailed away ahead of them, flickering as the groups passed through the trees. Someone handed Cory another sword, which he accepted hesitantly. He took position at the back of the group with Paul and two others, watching their retreat.

Thirty minutes later they were at the entrances to the caves, people bunched up outside as they hauled the cart carrying Rex up over the steep slope leading to the mouth. The screen of vines and brush that had hidden the entrance had been ripped aside, the two openings—one significantly larger than the other—lit from within by lantern light. People were shouting, the sounds muted by the rain, punctuated by curses as the cart slipped in the slick mud. Others were filing past the group dealing with the cart, another group forming a chain into the smaller opening, handing up the smaller children and passing along whatever supplies or packs people had grabbed and brought with them as they fled.

Rex and the cart made it inside, Logan already shouting for people to get out of his way, his bellowing voice echoing out from the opening. The remaining men and women grabbed the last of the children and ducked through, leaving only Sophia, Hernande, and the rest of those with weapons outside.

To Cory's right, Paul spat a curse. "We'll never hide the entrances now. They've destroyed the cover."

Hernande had been staring at the shredded vines and brush with a frown. He would have been chewing on the end of his beard, if it hadn't been soaked with rain. "I believe the mentors of the University can help with that."

"How?"

Hernande moved toward the smaller entrance and Cory felt him reaching out for the Tapestry. As he'd seen his mentor do a thousand times in the practice rooms at the University grounds in Erenthrall, Hernande gathered up folds, plied them like cloth, careful not to stretch them too tight or tear them, and then layered them over the opening. He tied one side off with a knot that could be easily removed, if you knew what to look for. As he did so, the mouth of the cave shimmered, and a curtain that looked like rock appeared over it. Except that the lantern light from within glowed through, as if the rock were sheer fabric.

"It needs some work."

Paul's eyes widened and he looked toward Sophia. But she didn't object.

Hernande released the knot with a sharp tug and began refolding the Tapestry, this time in a slightly different shape. Cory moved up to see if he could help, letting the others better suited to wielding swords watch the surrounding woods.

"What do we do now?" one of them asked as he passed.

"We wait."

Bryce ripped his sword out of another bandit's side, thrusting the gagging woman away from him as he did so. She landed in the muck and rolled, one arm clutching at the wound, then shuddered and stilled.

Bryce staggered back a step, exhaustion passing through

him in a wave, but he gripped the slick handle of his blade and scanned the area. Bodies littered the ground between the trees, some of them Hollowers, most of them attackers. He watched Braddon cut another one down, the rest of those in sight either being finished off or fleeing back into the night.

"They're running!" someone shouted, and those nearest let out a triumphant roar, swords raised overhead. A few of them took off in pursuit, but Braddon called them back.

"Shouldn't we follow them?" someone asked. "Hunt them down?"

"In the dark? In the rain?"

"But they know where we are."

"We'll send Reiss and the others after them. They'll have better luck tracking them in this mess."

Bryce doubted Reiss and the trackers would have much chance of finding them all, not with the rain coming down this hard, but Braddon passed on the order.

Bryce turned to the rest. "Check all of the bodies. Get our wounded back to the Hollow, and if any of the attackers are alive, find me." Suiting action to words, he knelt down, sword at the ready, and rolled the woman's body toward him. She was dead, pale face streaked with tendrils of her hair, mouth open, the rain already washing away the blood and mud. He wiped his blade clean on her clothing, noting her makeshift armor. He spent a moment searching through her pockets.

Braddon joined him a moment later. "They aren't trained. And look at their armor, what few had any armor at all. They're thieves."

"They're more organized than most. How many do you think attacked tonight?"

"No more than fifty."

"Which is about how many Reiss and Cory reported seeing at their camp." Bryce stood, staring off into the distance, blinking away the rain that dribbled down his face. "This wasn't their main force. I don't think they expected to meet any resistance. They thought they'd catch us by surprise, overwhelm us."

"With fifty men and women?"

"They think we're just a rogue group, like those we've

seen from a distance on the plains. They haven't realized how many of us there are yet, that we aren't a bunch of refugees with a few wagons and a desperate grasp on hope."

"What happens when they figure out we have an entire town here?"

Bryce didn't answer. He glanced down at the dead woman at his feet. "Someone's not going to be happy. Send runners to the rest of the groups, the village, and the caves. Make certain there wasn't another group attacking on a different front. If not, tell everyone it's over for now."

"Already done."

"Then let's find Sophia, Paul, and the others. We need to talk."

⁂

Kara bit back a curse as the Rats who had dragged her from the Clay District shoved her down, hard, onto the roof of one of their island buildings in the middle of the Tiana. Her hands burned where the grit had taken the skin off in a thin layer. To the side, Dylan cried out as they kicked his knees out from under him. He landed on his side, both hands clutching at his left leg. Adder, Kent, Gaven, and Jack fumed as they were all pushed down into kneeling positions. Their weapons had been seized back in the courtyard in Clay. Both Adder and Kent bore the bruises from the minor scuffle that had followed after the Rats surrounded them. It had been a hopeless attempt. Jack hadn't even drawn an arrow, handing his bow over with a glare that promised retribution.

They'd been herded through the city, skirting the fight that had continued between the Rats and the Tunnelers, the excitement of the group escalating into a near frenzy until Richten, the Rats' leader, had shouted out orders and punctuated them with a few punches and kicks. Subdued, the group had left the battle behind, most of the Rats sullen and disgruntled.

That hadn't lasted long. Their excitement grew as they drew closer to their home base and they began anticipating the reaction from Fletch. Their speculations as they shoved their prisoners forward grew steadily more gruesome and graphic, turning Kara's stomach and terrifying Dylan.

Kara recalled what Allan had said the Rats had done to the Temerites they'd captured. He hadn't provided any details, but if even half of what the Rats had gleefully imagined on the way here were possibilities—

Richten gave a half-hearted kick to Dylan's kidney, eliciting a choked cry from the Wielder, before stepping over him and moving toward an empty chair. He turned to face the Rats that surrounded them—at least fifty more than the three dozen or so that had dragged them here from Clay. When he raised his hands, a knife glinting in the firelight, the already riled Rats roared, stamping their feet and clanging weapons against bits of metal armor or the stone firewalls that protruded a few feet above the rooftop. Three bonfires burned in stone firepits, one of them off to one side of the chair. At least a dozen torches were scattered throughout the group. To the right, the shattered outer edge of the distortion glowed a feral orange-pink, rising into the night sky. Kara couldn't see the river from their position, but she knew it was below. She'd seen it as the Rats extended the bridge to the adjacent rooftop and marched them across it to their lair. The water came up to the edge of the building on the sides that she'd seen. She didn't know how deep it was, but maybe she could make it to the edge of the building and leap off.

She scanned the nearest Rats, practically climbing over each other, like their namesakes. There were too many of them, and more appearing from the depths of the building every moment. How many of them were there? She'd say at least a hundred here on the roof. How many were still in Tinker battling the Tunnelers?

"We come from the battlefield!" Kara's attention snapped back to Richten as the Rats in attendance roared again. Someone began beating on a drum, the sound low and hollow, joined a few moments later by two others. "And we bring prisoners!"

Someone rushed to Richten's side with a water skin, and he drank as the Rats flew into a steel-edged frenzy layered with anticipatory violence. Many of them were yelling out suggestions. Kara could practically taste the bloodlust.

But Richten raised his hands again. The frenzy quieted, but didn't die.

"I brought them back for Fletch." A tide of barked disdain and hisses of disapproval washed over the rooftop. Richten pointed his knife at the Rats, circling so he caught everyone watching. "You know Fletch is searching for something. For someone. Would you deny him? You know his wrath. You've witnessed it here many times! The Temerites refuse to answer and they die. The Underearthers spit at our feet and they die. The White Cloaks . . . well, the White Cloaks elude us for now. But not for long."

Kara shot a questioning glance toward Adder and the others as the Rats hooted and gloated in response. Adder met her gaze, but shrugged.

Richten turned back to face them. "No, the White Cloaks won't escape us for long. Fletch will take care of that. And Fletch will take care of these as well." He sidled forward, toward Kara, knife pointed at her face. He halted a few paces away, locked gazes with her. His eyes were a dark, muddy brown. His hair was a wild mess that, if cleaned, would be a light brown. He had a scar along one cheek, near his left ear, the lobe missing, as if it had been torn off. Beneath the scrim of dirt were freckles.

He was probably fifteen, but the hatred in his eyes was far older.

"Who are you?" He held the knife steady. "Where did you come from?"

Kara swallowed, trying not to look at the point of the blade, keeping her eyes on Richten's. She didn't answer.

Richten shifted his gaze to Dylan, who watched in horror where he lay. He flinched as Richten passed by him, hunched forward, eyes closed. Richten sneered, but left him, halting in front of Gaven. The wagonmaster raised his chin in defiance.

"What about you? Will you answer me? What group are you with? Where are they hiding?"

Gaven ground his teeth together, didn't respond. The shouts of the Rats surrounding them turned derisive, many laughing at Richten, others calling out suggestions. Richten didn't look toward them, but the needling jests were getting to him.

He flicked the blade forward, Gaven sucking in a sharp breath as the edge settled against the skin of his throat, just beneath his jaw. The Rats on all sides went eerily silent and still.

Richten bared his teeth. "No answer? Afraid we'll slaughter your friends if we find them?" He twisted the knife and Gaven stiffened, head tilted away from the blade. Blood trickled down the wagonmaster's neck, stained the collar of his shirt.

Richten laughed and pulled the knife away, the Rats breaking into another roar, half encouragement, half disappointment. Richten displayed the blood on the blade and the roar escalated.

Then he spun toward the Dogs and Jack. "I think they all believe they're safe without Fletch here." He twirled the knife in his fingers. "But they're wrong."

With two quick steps, he reached Kent's side and plunged the knife into his throat.

The Rats erupted into a frenzy, the sound smothering Kara as nausea rose with a hot bubble of bile. She swallowed it down as Kent arched back, Richten twisting the knife in his neck viciously before jerking it free and shoving the Dog's body backward into the hands of the waiting Rats. They swarmed over him with a howl, not heeding the arterial splash of the Dog's blood as they surged over him, spears and blades sinking into flesh even as they lifted his body up and began parading it around the rooftop. Kent bellowed in belated pain and rage, began to buck, but they were too strong. The Rats began to chant. Kara was too stunned to make out the words. Beside her, Dylan rolled to one side and vomited onto the roof, the stench slamming into Kara's senses, overriding the metallic scent of Kent's blood. She wanted to reach out to Dylan, drag him to his feet and flee, but she couldn't see any way through the Rats, not to the roof's edge, not even to the numerous rat holes that led down into the building.

Her gaze skimmed over the chaos of faces surrounding them. Something struck her shoulder, the pain sharp, and she whirled, faces leering down at her, taunting, screaming, laughing. She jerked back, one hand landing on the roof for support. She'd half climbed to her feet when she caught sight of Adder.

He shook his head, flicked his eyes to the right.

She glanced in that direction, saw Richten standing still, watching her with a hunter's look, muscles tensed, anticipatory, waiting patiently for the prey to bolt so he could pounce and savor the kill.

She choked on a gasp, a wave of dizziness passing over her. She was hyperventilating, her breath too short, her chest tight.

Bowing her head, she sank back down to her knees and sucked in a large lungful of air to steady herself. Disappointment crossed Richten's face before he turned away to watch the rest of the Rats parading Kent's body around the roof. The Dog was still bellowing in rage, although it sounded weaker. Kara blocked it out, crawled forward to Dylan's side, and rolled him gently toward her. His eyes were glazed, mouth slack. Bile smeared one side of his chin, its acidic reek sickening, but she reached out and slapped his face.

"Come on. Wake up. You don't stand a chance if you're catatonic."

She slapped him again and he jerked away from her, arms flailing in self-defense. Kara caught his wrists. "Dylan, it's me!"

He tried to pull away until her voice registered, his eyes latching on to her face. "Kara? What happened?" As if finally becoming aware of his surroundings again, his eyes widened. "Kent."

"You need to stay with us if you're going to make it out of here."

She helped him to hands and knees. He winced in pain, favoring his left leg.

The Rats had migrated to the edge of the roof. Kara watched as they hoisted Kent's body up for display, the Dog limp now, covered in blood from a hundred cuts, the most garishly visible the one Richten had made in his neck. Then they tossed him over the side.

She didn't hear the body hit the water of the river below. The roar from the Rats was too loud, the drums beating in a rapid rhythm that thrummed in Kara's skin.

"Now." Kara's head snapped back in Richten's direction. He'd moved closer, still held the knife, Kent's blood on the blade. "Who are you and where do you come from?"

Allan signaled to the Dogs and Cutter to remain silent as their weapons were taken and their hands were bound. The two Wielders and Aaron followed suit, no one protesting. They were forced to kneel on the rooftop where they were captured, a group of the Tunnelers guarding them, most clustered near the edge of the roof where they could see the fight still going on below. He was certain these were from the group beneath the ley station now. They were older—maybe fifteen to twenty-five—and now that he'd had time to study them, he realized they were dressed better. The clothes were cleaner, had been patched and repaired, and most of them wore shoes or boots. The Rats went mostly barefoot. And they'd bathed recently.

Glenn caught his eye and nodded toward the open trapdoor on the rooftop where the Tunnelers had cut them off. Only three of their captors stood guard there, one of them the youngest of the group. They could probably knock all three off their feet and be down the stairs inside before those gazing down at the street below even realized they'd moved.

But then what? There were bound to be more of the Tunnelers on guard inside the building, and even if they made the street, where would they run with the fight raging just below? He doubted they could wade through that without drawing attention, especially with their hands still tied.

He shook his head at Glenn. Artras had noticed the exchange. She appeared to be trying to tell him something with her eyes, but he couldn't figure out what it was.

Then the sounds from the street below shifted, drawing away, and the oldest of those on guard—a young woman, maybe twenty-two, who Allan had heard one of them call Sorelle—drew back from the roofline. She had long, dark hair, nearly black, and her expression was hard.

"Jaimes, Laura, get the rest. We're moving."

Laura headed for the stairs and disappeared below. Jaimes' group surrounded Allan and the others.

Sorelle came to stand in front of Allan. She carried a sword in one hand, loosely, her stance casual, unthreatening, but he could see the alertness in her muscles. She could kill him within a heartbeat if he made a move.

Allan found himself reassessing the group. Especially this woman.

"Stand up." Sorelle emphasized the order with a twitch of the blade.

He climbed to his feet, wincing as muscles in his leg and back that had been strained by their flight twinged. "What are you going to do?"

"Take you below."

Jaimes grabbed his arm from the side and shoved him toward the trapdoor, the other Tunnelers closing in on the Dogs and Wielders. Carter jerked out of the grip of the boy holding him, then stumbled and fell face-first to the rough stone of the roof. A few of their captors snickered as he moaned and rolled himself to his knees, his face now scraped and bloody, but they were cut off with a sharp word from Sorelle. The Dogs had all tried to move to protect the Wielder, but were held back.

Jaimes hauled Carter to his feet, and then they were all hustled toward the trapdoor and maneuvered down through the building and out into the street. As soon as he ducked through the battered door, Allun glanced east toward the distortion, muscles tensed, but the fight had carried the Tunnelers and Rats in that direction, and the thoroughfare was clogged with the melee. The street outside was littered with bodies, splashed with blood, a group of Tunnelers younger than the fighters methodically looting whatever they could. Wagons had been pulled up and were being loaded with weapons, armor, and even some clothing and food as the children raced back and forth along the street, going body to body.

Sorelle paused outside the door, staring in the direction of the fight, then shook herself and pointed with her sword back toward the ley station. "Walk."

They wound through Tinker, past the house where they'd holed up when the Rats arrived, then into the wide plaza before the ley station. The barricades the Tunnelers had hastily erected were still up, the bodies of Rats being removed from the stakes where they'd been impaled and stacked to one side, more children scavenging here. Sorelle was challenged by a slew of fighters on guard, but she gave a curt password at each post and they moved on without stopping.

They mounted the wide stone steps of the ley station and passed through the crowded doors, Tunnelers dashing in and out all around them. Inside, the cavernous mezzanine roared with voices, the volume doubled by the echoes. A statue of a man and his family surrounding a covered cart, like a cottage on wagon wheels, filled the center of the room, pots and pans dangling from the cart's roof, parcels and barrels latched to nearly every available space on its sides. It was carved from a bluish-white granite streaked with green and black.

"What in hells is that?"

"A tinker's wagon. They used to come to Canter all the time." At Glenn's befuddled look, Allan added, "It's how the villages too far from Erenthrall received new materials and the latest gossip."

They picked their way across the mezzanine, the floor covered with wounded being tended by a flurry of healers. Quite a few of those they passed were dead.

When they reached the tunnel mouth that had once led down to the ley barge system that connected the districts throughout Erenthrall, the ground began to shake. Sorelle paused, hand up, but the tremor only lasted a moment, dust sifting down from overhead. Healers leaned over those they were working on to shield their bodies, and others broke into sobs, but after a moment of anticipatory silence, activity resumed.

Sorelle led them down a walkway, past quiescent ley globes and standing torches, into the underground series of barge tunnels. They were challenged twice more, then passed through to one of the station's docks. Allan shuddered at the strangeness of it all, the room lit with lanterns, the ditch that cut through along one side dark and empty. Before the Shattering, it would have been flooded with the white light of the ley, a river connecting this station to over a dozen others. Even with the ley line so obviously dead, Allan kept expecting to hear the warning bell that a barge was approaching, or the whistles of the station masters as they directed flow off and on a new arrival. The sounds echoed in his ears, mocking him.

The platform was obviously a staging ground for the activity above, a figure—the oldest person Allan had seen yet, at thirty—at the center of the room at a desk, receiving and handing out orders from runners. Sorelle approached him, Jaimes and Laura keeping the Hollowers in check. The Tunneler leader spoke to the man. His gaze raked over them all, settling back on Allan, before he waved one hand dismissively and said something. Sorelle spun on her heels and stalked toward them.

As soon as she was close enough, Jaimes asked, "What are we to do with them?"

"Take them below. To Cason."

"You knew that's what Ren would want. Why'd you even bother asking?"

"Because I don't like being a guard."

Jaimes rolled his eyes and tugged on Allan's arm, leading them closer to the ley line's bed. Half of their guards scrambled down a ladder leaning against the channel's wall, then waited while the Dogs and Wielders were untied, allowed to climb down, and bound up again.

They proceeded down the line's bed, the bottom made from river stones, which made walking awkward. Allan found himself next to Artras, the Wielder staring around them avidly as they passed into the main tunnel heading east, toward the distortion.

"What were you trying to tell me earlier, on the roof?" Allan kept his voice low while he watched the guards for a reaction.

"I was trying to warn you that these weren't Rats. They seemed more organized than that." She turned to him, her face lit briefly as they came upon another torch. "But you've figured that out already."

"I still don't trust them."

"I think we're safer with them than with the Rats."

Allan said nothing, Sorelle glancing back.

Then they passed out onto a ledge and into an open chamber. Artras gasped.

"What is it?" Allan scanned the domed roof overhead

and the dozen or so tunnels that branched off from this one room, all of various sizes. Those that belonged to the ley barges were the largest, one directly opposite them, another to its left at an angle, another pointing southward. Beneath their ledge, the bed opened up into a pit, with smaller openings scattered around the stone walls.

"It's a junction. No one has ever been inside one as far as I know, except while on a barge. Certainly not a Wielder." She dropped her gaze. "It's normally filled with ley, only the barge tunnels and this dome above the surface. Everything beneath is usually submerged. If the ley were to return, this room would be flooded in moments. We'd all be annihilated."

Allan recalled what they'd seen after emerging from the broken Amber Tower. The ley had consumed every living thing it had touched, nothing left behind but buckles and buttons and clasps. "What's holding the ley back?"

"Someone sealed off Tinker. Whatever ley was here has been diverted."

They edged along the ledge until they reached another ladder, repeating the earlier process as they made their way down to the bottom of the pit, passing multiple sets of guards, all in their twenties or thirties. Sorelle entered one of the smaller tunnels, but they weren't inside long before it spilled out into another pit, this one smaller and without the larger ley barge openings up above.

The room was bustling with people, most of them focused on a firepit in the center, large pots and rotating spits over the flames, the scent of roasting meat permeating the chamber. Allan started salivating, but Jaimes dragged him along to the left, circling the pit toward a group off to one side. As they passed the openings of some of the other tunnels, he saw makeshift tents within stretching as far as he could see, with people sleeping on pallets and others mere shadows of activity as they worked by lantern light behind obscuring sheets.

"They live here."

"Better than living up above with the Rats and Wolves at your door. Here you can defend yourself, if anyone even risks coming after you through the tunnels."

"They could lay ambushes at every intersection. You may take the tunnels in time, but it would cost you."

Allan agreed with his Dogs' assessment, but his attention was now fixed on the group they'd drawn up to. Jaimes tugged him to a halt as Sorelle continued forward, waiting for a man to finish speaking to a woman who was at least forty-five, if not older. Her face was scarred, her stance solid, her hair graying near the temples. She wore no armor, but her clothes were cut and shaped as precisely as a uniform. A sword hung sheathed at her side, two knives visible on the other side, and Allan suspected there were at least two other weapons hidden discreetly in a boot or sleeve.

When she turned to face them, her eyes first locking on Allan, then Glenn and Tim, Allan's hackles rose. Beside him, Glenn stiffened. "She's a Dog."

Her eyes narrowed as she took in the rest of their group, then she spoke to Sorelle, turning away as if dismissing them.

Sorelle stormed toward them, angrier than after speaking to Ren.

"Follow me." She swept past them and crossed the central part of the pit, skirting the kitchen. Allan's stomach growled as they passed close enough to the fires that he could hear the fat sizzling in the coals beneath the spits. Smoke wafted into his face, acrid but with a hint of herbs and spice. He glanced upward to see it venting out through one of the smaller openings above, but then the yeasty smell of baking bread brought his attention back to the firepit, where loaves of some type of flatbread were being pulled from a roughly constructed oven.

They passed on, until Sorelle reached a wide opening with a large metal grate placed over the front. Allan and the others were forced to wait while Sorelle's group emptied the room beyond of a surprising number of crates and barrels and sacks. The markings indicated they were all stocks of food—grains, salted fish and pork, even a crate of oranges.

Sorelle pointed toward the tunnel with her sword. "Inside!"

Allan gestured with his head. "You first, Glenn."

The Dog took his meaning, stepping up into the tunnel and shifting back into the darkness. But Sorelle wasn't inclined to give him time to investigate. She ordered Jaimes and the rest forward with their prisoners, shoving them all into the opening before slamming the grate closed and latching it from the outside.

Jaimes sidled up to Sorelle. "Now what?"

"We watch them. Cason's orders. I thought we were going up above to *fight*." She caught Allan watching her. "Settle in. I don't know how long it will take before she finds time to talk to you."

Sorelle turned away, and after a brief pause, Jaimes edged closer. "She doesn't hate you, she'd just rather be killing Rats." Then he stepped away hastily, before Sorelle could notice.

Allan scanned the chamber before edging farther back into the shadows. There were no torches or lanterns in here, the back of the tunnel nearly pitch black. Glenn's broad-shouldered frame was barely visible as he shifted around, feet scraping along the floor. Stones skittered, followed by a curse, then what sounded like dirt and pebbles cascading down in a small avalanche.

Glenn reappeared.

"What did you find?"

"The ceiling has caved in twenty or thirty paces back, probably from the quakes. I don't see a way out."

Allan twisted his hands, the rope that had been used to bind them cutting into his wrists. "Untie me."

They stood back to back. The others saw what they were doing and did the same. Within minutes, all of them were untied and massaging their wrists. Allan worked the feeling back into his numbed fingers, but noticed that the abrasions on his skin were less serious than he'd thought. Tim and Carter hadn't fared as well; both of them had struggled to free themselves during the long walk here from the rooftop.

"What do we do now?" Artras asked.

Allan sank down and sat, leaning his back up against one curved wall. The position was awkward, but he settled in and closed his eyes. "Wait for Cason."

The others hesitated a moment, then followed suit. Allan cracked an eyelid to watch, noting that Glenn was still too anxious to rest. The Dog began pacing in the depths of their prison.

He must have dozed off. The screech of the grate opening up again jerked him out of sleep. His hand fell toward the empty sheath at his side before he remembered that Sorelle and the others had taken all of their weapons. Glenn stepped forward as Allan stood, the rest of the group watching warily or rousing themselves from their own naps. Allan couldn't tell how much time had passed, but his mouth tasted awful, so he'd slept more than an hour. He desperately wanted a drink.

Sorelle held the grate open as Cason stepped into the tunnel. Jaimes closed the bars behind them, and Allan heard the latch falling back into place.

He and Cason stared at each other, the Dog's hand resting on the pommel of the sword strapped to her side. Her back was stiff, her broad shoulders tensed, her bearing confident. She bore all the markings of a Dog—scars on her face, harshness in her gaze. If she had been male, Allan would have described her as grizzled. Instead, her age lent her an air of brutal competence.

"Sorelle says she captured you fleeing from the Rats." Her voice was softer than Allan had expected, though brusque. "You aren't Temerite, and you certainly aren't with the Wolves. Where do you come from?"

"The plains."

Cason's gaze flicked toward the others, lingering on Artras, Carter, and Aaron, before returning. "You don't look like Aurek's men. Did you escape from the Baron's camp?"

Allan thought of the group that had attacked their wagon on their last trip, and the wagon train they'd seen slaughtered on their way here. So the leader of that group called himself a Baron? He could see the resemblance to Baron Arent in the way the man had carried himself. A cold aloofness. But also a dangerous intelligence.

And since there were no other true Barons left to challenge him as far as Allan knew, who was to say he didn't deserve the title?

"We escaped Baron Aurek, if that's what he calls himself. We didn't stick around long enough to find out."

Cason's eyes narrowed. "How did it happen?"

It was a test, Allan realized. Cason already knew about the Baron, about how he operated, probably more than Allan knew himself.

"We were traveling across the plains, a small band of us, three wagons. We'd survived the winter, but were running out of supplies. We thought we might find something in Erenthrall. But then Aurek's men hit us. They came out of nowhere, surrounded the wagons, killed a few of our group until the rest were cowed. Most of us here weren't with the wagons, scouting ahead. But we came back in time to see Aurek slaughter everyone else with the wagons, after they'd looted and burned them. We waited until they were gone, then buried our dead and headed here."

Cason's chin rose. "All of you were out scouting? A strange scouting party." She motioned toward Artras and Aaron. "An old woman and a boy?"

Cutter said smoothly, "I was training the boy. There is no such thing as young anymore. Look at the Rats."

"And what of her?"

Artras snorted. "I was with the wagons. They found me beneath some of the bodies. Terrim fell on top of me when he died and I played dead until this Baron and his men left."

Cason stared at Artras, perfectly still.

Then her gaze shifted back toward Allan. "A believable lie, I'll give you that. You've certainly run into the Baron and his men. That's exactly what he would have done. But you forgot to factor in the others."

"Others?"

"The others that were with you when you fled into the building. Sorelle saw it all. You split. Sorelle caught you on the roof."

"What happened to them?"

"The Rats caught them."

Allan clenched his fist. "We have to help them. The Rats will kill them."

Cason's eyebrows rose. "And why would we risk ourselves to do that? They're already back at the Rats' lair, likely already dead." When no one answered, she bristled. "You'd better start telling me the truth about where you come from, why you're here, and why the others are so important."

"Or what?"

"Or I'll hand you over to the Rats myself."

Glenn's urge to leap forward and grab Cason by the throat rippled through his shoulders. Tim edged forward as well. Cutter remained quiet, but Allan knew he was coiled and ready.

But even if Allan unleashed them on Cason and Sorelle, the grate behind them was closed. They might kill these two, but then what? These Tunnelers could have killed them at any point since their capture on the roof.

"We're from the foothills west of the plains. We came here for supplies, like I said, and we did run into this Baron. We know of the Rats and the Wolves and the Temerites, but we didn't know about you Tunnelers."

Cason's lip twitched at the name, "And the others with you? Why are they so important?"

"Besides the fact that they're part of our group?"

Cason didn't answer, eyes fixed on Allan.

"We need them."

"Why?"

"Because resources are getting short, out there and here in Erenthrall. And two of them are Wielders."

A shocked silence settled. Allan didn't need to turn to see Artras' disapproving frown.

Cason's fingers had tightened around the hilt of her sword. "Wielders?"

"It's how we've been getting supplies."

Cason's lips pressed into a thin line. "You've been releasing the shards of the distortion."

"There's not much left outside the distortion now."

Cason said nothing for a long moment. But her sword remained sheathed.

"We'll have to save them."

Unease crawled across Allan's shoulders. Something wasn't right. "Why?"

"Because we've barely held the Rats in check up until now. We can't allow them to have access to any of the shards." Cason turned toward Sorelle. "Tell Ren. We'll have to plan an attack on the Rats' lair, or hope to catch them outside at some point. Tell him about the Wielders, so he knows it's urgent."

Glenn stepped forward, hands fisted. "What about us?"

"You're a Dog. You fight with us."

"No! We can't trust them—"

Cason cut Sorelle off with a look as Jaimes opened up the grate behind her. "Arm them! And watch them. They're your responsibility now."

As she stepped out of the tunnel and stalked away, she shouted back at them, "The only thing keeping the Rats subdued is a lack of sufficient supplies. They've been searching for a Wielder for months now, taking down Temerites, Gorrani, my own people—whoever they can get their hands on—to find one. You've just made all of our lives a lot more difficult. And Erenthrall a hell of a lot more dangerous."

# *Nine*

MORRELL PUSHED THE SWEATY HAIR out of her eyes with one trembling, bloody hand, then returned to suturing the cut across Sara's upper arm. The woman moaned as she tugged the needle through for the last stitch, pulled the gut tight, tied it, then snipped the rest free. She cleaned the wound with a damp cloth, washing the blood away and checking her work, before packing the needle, cloth, and thin gut into her makeshift kit.

As she folded the leather satchel in half, Sara's good arm caught her and held her in place. Morrell halted, staring down into the woman's gray eyes. She recalled that this was Terrim's wife, the man who'd been killed on the return from Erenthrall. Her face looked haggard and haunted, and her fingers bit painfully into Morrell's flesh.

"Is it going to be all right?"

"It wasn't very deep. You might have a scar, but you'll be fine."

"Good. Thank you." She collapsed back onto the pallet in the meeting hall and began to cry, the tears leaking out of her eyes and coursing down her dirt-smeared face and into her scraggly hair.

Morrell glanced away, down the line of pallets, where the

wounded had been brought after the end of the fighting on the ridge. Logan stood at the far side of the meeting hall, watching her. Janis knelt about halfway between them, cleaning up as best she could. It looked as if all of the wounded had been taken care of, although there were a few pallets that had been occupied that were now empty.

Logan caught her gaze and held it. Morrell dropped her eyes first and grabbed her rolled up satchel, noting that Sara had stopped sobbing and slipped into sleep. She checked the woman's arm again, then stood.

A wave of exhaustion washed over her and she nearly passed out, holding on by sheer force of will. Logan took an inadvertent step forward, one hand rising, but then he stopped himself. He turned and headed out of the meeting hall.

Morrell waited until the dizzy spell passed, then picked her way through the bodies toward Janis. As she went, those who she'd helped earlier and were still conscious thanked her. The attention made her uncomfortable, the expressions of gratitude a little too fervent.

Janis looked up as she approached. "Has everyone been seen to?"

"I think so. Sam and Karen?"

Janis shook her head grimly.

Morrell sucked in a steadying breath, held it, then let it out slowly. "What's wrong with Logan? What did I do wrong?"

Janis struggled to her feet. "Nothing, Morrell. It's just . . ."

"What?"

"Everyone's heard about what you did to heal Claye, even though we said nothing. It's all rumor. They think you're not just a healer, but a Healer. A true Healer."

"But I didn't do anything. Not here. All I did was bind some wounds, stitch people up."

"I know that. Logan knows it, too, although he's too hurt at the moment to admit it."

"Hurt?"

Janis tousled Morrell's hair. "Let's go clean you up."

They made their way out of the meeting hall, Morrell setting her healing tools to one side before leaving. Outside, some of those at the cave had returned and activity had picked up near the barns, the shepherds herding the sheep out toward the meadows, others slopping the pigs. Paul, Sophia, and Bryce were deep in conversation with a few others near the church. The dead that had been set down outside the meeting hall had been taken away somewhere. Morrell wondered where, and how many had died.

Janis guided her away from the activity, toward the creek. "You weren't there to see it, but nearly every person who Logan tried to help asked about you, where you were, why you weren't there to help them. A few even had the temerity to ask if he could fetch you to have you work on them instead. He's been the healer in the Hollow for years."

"But I didn't ask them to ask for me! And I don't even know what I did with Claye."

"It doesn't matter. Logan's pride is bruised, and it will take him a while to get over it."

They picked their way down the bank to the creek's edge. As she splashed the water over her arms, scrubbing at the blood and dirt and grime, she thought about Logan, about the intensity of the faces of the wounded as they gazed up at her when she first knelt down. It had troubled her at the time, but she thought it was normal. They hadn't ever dealt with anything like this before. Mostly, they were fixing cuts and scrapes from farming accidents or maybe burns from the forge. Those came in ones or twos. Five years ago, some kind of disease had spread through the Hollow—people vomiting, a red spidery rash spreading across the neck and onto the chest. That had laid up nearly a dozen people. Morrell hadn't been helping Logan back then, but she knew everyone was relieved when the sickness didn't spread to the entire community.

But now they had the refugees from Erenthrall here. Over twice as many people to care for.

"Maybe I shouldn't help Logan anymore." Her stomach gave a strange little tug.

"Lean down and let me wash your hair." Morrell complied, shuddering as her old nursemaid poured cold water over her head before continuing. "You can't quit, especially now. It won't help Logan and it won't help the Hollow. They need you."

"But—"

"Logan isn't angry with you, Morrell. And even if he is, he'll get over it." She pulled Morrell upright again, water trickling down Morrell's neck and beneath her shirt. Her clothes were a mess, but having her hands and hair clean made her feel infinitely better. Janis grabbed her shoulders, turned her and held her gaze, eyebrows lifted. "Give him time? Before you do anything rash?"

"I still don't know how they found out about Claye." Except she did. There were no secrets in the Hollow. Not with so few people.

Shouts suddenly arose from the direction of the cottages, men barking orders, at least one woman crying out in a shrill tone.

"What now?" They scrambled up the bank again, Morrell reaching the top before Janis was even halfway up. The older nursemaid motioned her on. "Go. I'll catch up."

Morrell dashed through the screen of trees and out into the Hollow to see three men hauling someone else toward the meeting hall. Logan raced from his cottage followed by two others. Bryce, Sophia, and Paul were running from the church. One of the men stumbled and dropped the man's legs, and the man screamed in agony. Morrell saw his leg was twisted, bent at an odd angle, and his breeches were soaked in blood. Then Logan and the others blocked her view, Logan's harsh voice ordering them to carry the man inside the meeting hall and set him down. The group vanished.

Morrell halted at the door to the hall, steadying herself. But then Logan bellowed, "Morrell! Where are you?"

"Here!"

She dove through the door, shoving through those circling Logan where he knelt at the man's side. She gasped as she recognized Harper, then her gaze fell to his leg.

The bone jutted out of his thigh through a long gash, blood gushing too fast for those trying to stanch the wound to keep up. Logan was cursing beneath his breath. He tossed the blanket he'd been using aside. It landed with a sickening wet slap on the floor as someone handed him another. He used it to press the heel of his hand hard into Harper's inner thigh, cutting off the artery there. "A belt. Someone get me a gods-damned belt!"

Morrell grabbed one from one of the gawkers and knelt down next to Harper, reaching to wrap the belt around Harper's leg, fumbling as she worked around Logan's arms. She cinched it tight, pulling with all of her strength, then pulled again when Logan said, "Tighter." The healer released the pressure and leaned back, already examining the wound now that the blood flow was temporarily stemmed.

Behind them, one of the fighters was babbling. "We were checking the ridge. Harper slipped and fell over a ledge. He didn't fall far. He must have landed wrong. His leg just snapped, like a twig, and the sound! Not a crunch, but a tearing snap, and then he screamed!"

"Shut up!" Logan focused on Morrell. "We have to reset the bone, if it isn't too badly splintered." He glanced back down and grimaced. The end of the bone was jagged.

"My kit."

She leaped up, grabbed her satchel from near the door, and skidded to her knees again at Harper's side. Logan had placed another man's leather belt between Harper's teeth, murmured something to him that Morrell didn't catch. Harper nodded, his face slicked with sweat, already pale, his blond hair matted and wild.

Logan patted his face, then turned to Morrell. "Hold the leg steady. I need to see if there are any pieces of bone in there."

Morrell grabbed hold of Harper's lower leg, leaning her weight over it. Two of those watching crowded down to help, one across Harper's torso, the other beside Morrell, stretching over both of Harper's legs below the knee. Logan crouched down to examine Harper's wound more carefully. He grabbed a few tools from his own satchel, dabbing at the continued blood flow, sluggish with the tourniquet in place, while poking around the torn muscle and shattered bone with a thin rod. Harper writhed and moaned through his gag, his leg shifting beneath Morrell's body. Logan's hand halted abruptly and, setting the cloth aside, he grabbed a pair of tweezers and plucked a sliver of bone from the mess, as long as the tip of Morrell's finger. Some of those watching gasped and gagged, stepping back, but Logan simply set the sliver aside and resumed his search.

He pulled three more slivers out, Morrell entranced. The

muscles, the tendons and ligaments—even the blood—absorbed her attention. She could feel Harper's pulse where she held him, noted his struggles weakening.

The healer sat back. "I think I've found the largest pieces. I'd look for more, but he's fading." He caught Morrell's gaze. "We have to push the bone back into place."

She nodded.

"It's going to hurt." Setting what he'd need within reach, he shoved everything else out of the way. "Whoever can squeeze in here and help hold him down, do it. Morrell, I'll need you to help. Let someone else take your place."

She released her grip and knelt close to Logan's side.

"We have to try to get the ends of the bones together. I need you to hold here and here, while I push down. The end of the bone is sharp, so be careful. I'll work it through the torn muscle as best I can. Ready?"

"Yes." Her hands were already in place.

Logan began pushing down on the bone.

Harper screamed, the sound muffled by the leather stuffed into his mouth. He thrashed as Logan cursed and pushed harder. Morrell's fingers were slick with blood from holding the wound open. The muscle and flesh was oddly supple and stringy to the touch, twitching and throbbing with every move Harper made.

Then she felt the bone slipping into place, everything beneath her hands suddenly *right*. Morrell could feel the ends of the bone scraping against each other. Logan pulled back as Harper lapsed into unconsciousness.

Morrell's fingers began to prickle, as they had when she'd been inspecting Claye's wound in Logan's cottage. The commotion of those around her faded and she felt herself sinking into the flesh and blood rhythms of Harper's leg. She could *see* the sharp edges of the bone where they touched, could feel those edges cutting the sinew and muscle around them as Harper's body was jostled by movement. The torn ligaments and gaping wound throbbed in her vision, all of the blood vessels and severed tissue a pulsating mass of damage.

She could also see how it was all meant to knit together, even with pieces of it missing, like the removed splinters of bone.

The prickling in her fingers intensified. She closed her eyes. Her hands grew warm. Someone gasped and the commotion that swirled around her died out. She breathed in once, the flesh and bone beneath her fingers flooded with sudden heat, then exhaled.

When she opened her eyes, she caught a blue-green glow of fading auroral lights, and then she withdrew her hands.

Harper's thigh was still covered in blood, but the gaping wound was closed. All of the torn muscle was hidden beneath a mottled scarring of stitched-together flesh, the skin raw and new. Except Morrell knew the muscle underneath wasn't torn anymore, and the bone had knit back together.

"What—" Sophia's voice broke. She hadn't been holding Harper down, but she'd been close. "What did you do?"

"I saw how it was supposed to be. And fixed it."

A few of those watching flicked their fingers as if to ward off evil.

"She healed him." Logan wiped the back of one arm across his sweat-sheened forehead. His hands were covered in Harper's blood. "She healed him. Better than I could have." He waved those nearest back, then began examining Harper's thigh, carefully at first, then more thoroughly. "As far as I can tell, the bone's been reset, as near to never having been broken as is possible. The flesh is hardened and he'll likely be stiff for days, but aside from the possibility of some scarring and weakness, Harper should be fine. If you'd asked me, I'd have said we'd lose him for certain, even if I did manage to get the bone set and his leg splinted. He'd lost too much blood."

Morrell glanced around at everyone else. Their expressions ranged from awe to fear.

Morrell dropped her head and stood abruptly. "I just healed him. That's all." Then she backed up, stumbling slightly, and fled.

"Morrell." Janis reached for her arm as she swept by, but Morrell evaded the grasp and rushed outside. She paused in the sunlight, blinking at its harshness, but ducked and cut right. Her eyes burned with unshed tears and her chest ached with a liquid amalgam of uncertainty, fear, and anger.

She burst through the door to her father's cottage—her cottage—and slammed the door behind her, leaning up against it as the tears broke. She stayed there, sobbing, head lowered, until the ache in her chest faded, then pushed away and made her way to the table, where a heap of small potatoes had been left, the peeling knife discarded to one side. Janis must have been working on them when the warning bell sounded.

Morrell sat down and began methodically slicing the skins off, tossing them into the slop bucket and setting the raw potatoes aside. She had thought the incident with Claye could be forgotten, that if she simply left well enough alone that it would fade.

That wouldn't happen now. The actions of those wounded in the fighting told her that it wouldn't have faded away even without Harper injuring himself.

A short time later, Janis opened the door and stepped inside. She hesitated on the threshold, eyeing Morrell at the table, before entering and moving toward the small hearth to set up a fire. She gathered a few chunks of wood from the stack close by, then straightened.

"How are you feeling?"

Morrell stopped her peeling. She felt numb inside. Lost. She didn't know who she was anymore. "They won't stop looking at me like that ever, will they?"

"Like what, Morrell?"

"Like I'm different. Like I'm dangerous. Or like I'm special, like one of the Wielders."

"No. Not now that they know for certain you can do these things."

"I didn't think so." Morrell picked the knife back up and began peeling again.

Janis hesitated again, then moved to the fire, lighting the dried moss beneath it until the flames caught.

She grabbed a pitcher and poured water into a pot. "It's nothing to be ashamed of, Morrell. Yes, there will be some like Paul who will hate you for it. He doesn't trust anything that he can't do himself. Others will revere you, even if you don't think you deserve it. But most of the people here in the Hollow and elsewhere will fall somewhere in between."

She hung the pot of water on the iron arm beside the fire, then swung it out over the flames, coming to the table to grab up the potatoes that were already peeled. "Just remember that you *can* do these things, and be careful how you use the power. Like the Wielders. And like your father."

Morrell gave a start that Janis didn't see as she turned to plop the potatoes into the warming water. She'd forgotten about her father and what he could do, because here in the Hollow there were no distortions and little ley to affect. He'd saved Kara and the others after the distortion quickened in Erenthrall.

And yet no one in the Hollow mentioned it. They'd accepted him after he'd fled here.

Perhaps they'd accept her too.

Baron Aurek watched the approaching group on horseback through the spyglass. At his side, the lookout who had spotted them earlier shifted nervously. The man had probably already noticed what had set Aurek on edge and was fearful of how his liege lord would react.

Lowering the spyglass, Aurek handed it back to the watcher. "Keep an eye on them, and the woods beyond. Make certain no one follows them."

The lookout nodded. Aurek turned and walked back into the central part of his camp.

His men were already well situated, their routines settled. Smoke rose from a dozen fires, meat roasting on some of them. A group was butchering a bison to one side, downwind of the camp, three other hides already stretched out for tanning. A trench had been dug for the offal and as a latrine.

In the camp proper, over twenty tents had been raised, with Aurek's near the center, three times as large as any other. He wove through the guy wires, nodding to those who greeted him, but his focus was on his second in command, Devin Baldurs.

Devin saw his approach and stood. "What word?"

Aurek motioned him toward his own tent, away from the ears of the others scattered about. They passed between the two guards outside and ducked beneath the tent flap. "Verrent is returning, with less than half of his men."

"Less than half? What happened?"

"I'd say he found someone."

"The group we're looking for?"

Aurek settled into one of the seats around the portable table in the center of the room. The tent gusted around him, the canvas wuffling as if inhaling and exhaling with the breeze from the plains. "We won't know until Verrent reports, but if he's lost half his men, then whoever he ran into must have fighters and be of significant size. Larger than any of the groups of wanderers we've hit so far."

"And if they've survived this long, they must have food and supplies."

"Even if they aren't these White Cloaks, we can take what they have and find out what they know. But Verrent was a good half hour away. Tell me what our scouts have found elsewhere while we wait."

Devin straightened and began in a more formal tone. "The scouts have ranged as far as the escarpment at the base of the Reaches to the north, this side of the Tiana. They report scattered enclaves in some of the towns and villages between here and there, mostly bands of survivors. They're struggling because some of the supplies they're used to getting from the cities have run out, and they haven't gotten organized enough yet to start trading with each other."

"Perhaps those from Haven can help with that."

"They also report three of the burning lights above the Steppe and the Reaches, one each above the cities of Dunmara, Severen, and Ikanth, which would make sense given what happened in Erenthrall, Tumbor, and Farrade. The locals call them the Three Sisters. The auroral lights that occasionally appear on the plains were seen all over the Reaches. There's some kind of dark cloud cover over the mountains that the scouts report is unnatural."

"Unnatural? In what way?"

Devin fidgeted. "The scouts say that it rarely breaks, so the mountains beneath are nearly always in shadow, broken only by blue-white and purple lightning. What sunlight does get through shows a landscape that's distorted. And—"

Aurek met Devin's eye balefully. "What?"

"They claim there are monsters in the mountains. The locals avoid the higher reaches, what with the auroral lights, the cloud cover, and the strange noises. A few of the scouts entered the forest to investigate, but only one of them returned. He claimed he was attacked by a creature at least twice the size of a bear, and he had claw marks across his back to prove it."

Aurek had leaned forward as Devin delivered the report, but now he settled back, the chair creaking beneath him. Once, before the Shattering, when he'd been nothing but a minor lord with a small area of land surrounding Haven—land titled to his father before him for service to the Baron of Erenthrall—he would have dismissed such accounts out of hand as nonsense and superstition.

But since the Shattering, the world had changed. He'd seen the Wolves in Erenthrall himself, after venturing there to determine what had happened and whether the Baron or any of the lords above him remained. He'd seen the destruction, the city laid waste, the towers shattered, the heart of the city caught in the center of the massive distortion.

It was then he realized the opportunity he'd been given, the chance to become more than a petty lord groveling at the Baron's feet. The plains were in turmoil, without direction, without a leader. His father had been content with the lands of Haven, but he needed more. He could be the next Baron.

And he wouldn't base his power on something as obviously volatile and fragile as the ley.

Outside, shouts and sudden activity heralded the arrival of Verrent and the others.

"Given what we saw in Erenthrall, I find it hard to dismiss the possibility of monsters in the forests of the Reaches."

"Yes, sir, although this sounds worse."

"And it's all the damned Primes' fault." Outside, the commotion approached their tent. "Anything else to report?"

"We haven't heard recently from the scouts that headed east, beyond the Urate toward Temerite lands. But they have farther to travel since we've moved west."

"We won't hear from them for at least another week." Aurek reached for a decanter of wine set to one side, poured himself a glass, then motioned for Devin to shift behind him, his mood darkening. Devin positioned himself clear of the table and rested one hand on the pommel of his blade, the gesture casual, but Aurek noted with approval that the sword's ties were already loosened, the blade ready to be drawn.

His men were not yet as trained, nor as vicious, as Baron Arent's Dogs before the Shattering, but they were getting there.

As soon as he heard the men outside challenge Verrent and the man's gruff response, he stood, fingers pitched lightly on the table. He schooled his expression as one of the guards pushed back the flap and entered, followed by Verrent and another, both of them looking coarse and unkempt compared to Aurek, Devin, and even the guard. But that was to be expected. Verrent and his unit were merely soldiers. Their makeshift armor was dirty and nicked, their clothing matted and stained with blood. Their faces were unshaven and gritty. Aurek could smell their sweat and fear as soon as they entered the tent.

This was what he had to work with. He had not found any surviving Dogs to lead his forces, had been stuck with those in Haven who had not immediately run in fear or killed themselves in despair. His own house guard had been minimally trained, coming mostly from the city watch. They'd begun training whoever remained as soon as he'd returned from his journey to Erenthrall. They were rough and wild, but they were slowly learning discipline.

Verrent's gaze flicked toward Devin, then back to Aurek, before he stepped into the room and knelt. "Baron Aurek."

Belatedly, the man who accompanied him followed suit, head bowed.

"Report."

Verrent rose. "We scouted the western hills as you requested. The first few days, we found nothing. But on the fourth day we captured a tracker. He was headed southwest of our position when we took him. He revealed that he came from a village hidden in the hills. We thought to catch them by surprise, so I gathered the group and we stole up on the village that night."

"Let me guess. They were waiting for you."

"He said there were only fifty in the village!"

"And it never crossed your mind that this prisoner would lie to you?"

Verrent didn't answer.

"Go on."

"They took us on the ridge, cut us down like grain. Some of them were villagers, but not all. I'd swear there were Dogs fighting us. And there were more than fifty."

Aurek's eyebrows rose. "Dogs?"

"Yes, Lord Baron. At least, they fought like Dogs."

"How do you know there were more than fifty? Did you see the village?"

Verrent's teeth ground together. "No. It was dark and it was raining."

Aurek shifted around the table until he was standing directly in front of Verrent. The would-be guardsman's nostrils flared, but he didn't step back.

"Are you telling me that you attacked a location you hadn't scouted out, at night, in the rain, based on the word of a prisoner you'd captured and, I assume, tortured for information?"

"Yes, Lord Baron. We thought it was what you'd want."

Aurek pressed forward, Verrent unconsciously leaning farther back. "You thought— "

"We brought you the prisoner, my lord. He's outside. He's still alive. His name is Joss."

Aurek hesitated, then backed off. "Perhaps something can be salvaged from this mess then. Dismissed."

Verrent shoved his second out of the tent before him in his haste to retreat. Aurek watched him go, then waved the guard back outside.

As soon as they departed, Aurek turned to Devin. "Interrogate the prisoner. Break him. We'll get nothing more of substance from Verrent or his men. They will have seen nothing, attacking at night and in such weather. Find out who this group is, how many of them there are, and what they might be hiding."

"Is it the White Cloaks?"

Aurek rapped one hand against the table in thought. "I don't think so, but make certain. We don't want to attack them blindly, as Verrent did. We need information. And they may have something of use to us."

Devin moved toward the door. Aurek waited until he had reached for the tent flap before saying, "And Devin? Make certain Verrent realizes his mistake. His many mistakes."

"Yes, Lord Baron."

Light flared through the door into the cell where Kara had been thrown as someone thrust it open a crack. Kara blinked into the harshness of the torch, raising one hand to shield her face. Her eyes were gritty with lack of sleep, her entire body coated with a tacky sheen of sweat and blood and grime. Her clothes scraped against her body with every movement, every cut and bruise inflicted by Richten and the Rats the night before aching or itching. Or was it two nights before? She couldn't tell. She'd managed not to scratch herself and make things worse by curling up into a huddle against one wall, arms around her knees, eyes wide in the pitch black of the cell. It had once been a closet or storage room deep in the heart of the building, no more than her body length on each side. Now, the floor was covered in patchy, softened straw that reeked of piss and offal and a strong undercurrent of mold.

She lifted her head from the floor as someone shuffled in. Backlit by the torch, the figure was nothing more than a shadow, reaching out to set a rounded tin on the floor two feet in front of Kara's face.

"Eat. Fletch will return tonight. You'll need your strength."

"What will he do to us?" After Richten's tortuous questioning last night, she was too angry to be afraid. He'd toyed with them, malicious and sadistic, but he hadn't killed anyone else after Kent. The Dog had been a sacrifice to placate the rest of the Rats, although Kara had no doubts that Richten had enjoyed every minute of his death.

"Eat."

Outside, someone barked, "Hurry up!"

The figure flinched. As it retreated, Kara caught the profile of a young girl, long hair, maybe ten years old, although

it was hard to tell. One of the ruffians from the roof caught
the girl's shoulder and shoved her behind him, glaring into
the room before shutting the door. The scrape of a heavy
object being pushed in front of the door followed. There
was no latch. Kara had checked.

She listened to the shuffling of feet out in the hall as the
pinpricks of faint light seeping around the edges of the door
faded. Farther away, muted laughter broke the silence. A
dog barked excitedly. Someone cursed, the words too distant and muffled to make out, but the intention was clear. It
was followed by a harsh slap, a cry, and then sobbing.

Kara levered herself into a seated position, back against
the wall, and reached for the tin of food. Her questing fingers found a ragged chunk of bread, obviously a day or two
old, and a thick soup or stew. Her stomach knotted in hunger as she brought the tin close to her face and sniffed it.
She couldn't tell what it was, but as soon as she scooped
some of the stew into her mouth with the bread it didn't
matter. The food vanished, the last of the bread stuffed into
her mouth before she'd had a chance to taste any of it. She
set the tin aside, leaning her head back against the wall behind her.

"How did we get into this mess?"

She closed her eyes, a vision of Kent rising unbidden,
Richten's blade jutting from his neck. She hadn't known
Kent well, but the shocking abruptness of his death, the
cruelty of it —

She shook herself, thrust the images from the rooftop
aside, and winced as the various cuts and bruises were re-
awakened. She brought her fingers to her face, prodded the
edges of where Richten had punched her, then touched the
split in her lip. Swollen and raw, it had finally stopped bleeding.

The cuts on her arms burned as she traced them, worrying about infection, then she barked out mocking laughter.
The sound was loud in the confined space and she flinched.
They were all going to be killed, like Kent. Infection should
be the least of her worries.

She let her hands fall into her lap and stared at the door.
She'd gotten off lightly. Adder had received the worst of the
treatment, to the point where Kara had been convinced

they were going to kill him, too. They'd kicked him into unconsciousness, then turned their attentions to Jack, Gaven, and Dylan. Richten had wanted Kara to watch, nicking her when she'd turned away. One of the other Rats had wanted to start breaking fingers, but Richten had refused, threatening and then punching the Rat until he'd submitted. That was when Kara realized Richten was only toying with them. He didn't dare mess with them much more than he already had, not until Fletch arrived.

Shortly after that, as if Richten had realized he'd done everything he could, he'd ordered them brought below. They'd been separated almost instantly once below roof level and into the maze of corridors and rooms. Kara had lost all sense of direction and caught only glimpses of the Rats' living conditions: rooms with cots and hammocks strung haphazardly everywhere, like a crew in the underbelly of a ship; Rats roughhousing in what looked like a banquet hall, half of the floor caved in; a kitchen area that was surprisingly clean and orderly, with an older girl overseeing those cutting up carcasses and vegetables. All of it lit with sporadic torches, the halls and rooms more shadowed than not, walls cracked, plaster pocked and smeared with more and more dirt and grime the deeper into the building they went. The stench grew thicker as well, cut only by the rising smell of dampness and river water.

The last of their group that she'd seen had been Dylan, her fellow Wielder crying out as they shoved him around a corner, twisting his already wrenched knee.

She began knocking her head against the wall behind her. "We have to get out of here. But how? How?"

Dylan and Adder were likely in no condition to resist, much less flee. Gaven and Jack weren't much better. She had no idea what had happened to the rest. They hadn't been paraded onto the rooftop with them, so there was hope that they'd escaped. But would Allan and the rest figure out what had happened to them in time to help? Probably not.

Which left her.

"Think, Kara, think."

No weapons. Nothing to bargain with. No way to plan and coordinate with the others. She had nothing.

Her head snapped up. "The ley."

They weren't in Tinker anymore. And while the ley system in Erenthrall was in chaos, in parts of the city it was still there.

She reached out, a gesture that had once been habit, and cried out in triumph when she felt the ley respond, stronger than she expected. She sat forward, halfway to her feet, before she realized she didn't know what she could do with it yet. She sank back down and tested it.

A strong line ran beneath the building. It cut diagonally beneath the water, deep, in what must once have been one of the main lines of the city. Its flow was steady, skirting the edge of the distortion. Kara guessed it was one of the only lines that hadn't been interrupted by the destruction of the Nexus and the resulting quickening. It brushed up against Tinker, angled southwest. Its other end headed northeast, in the direction of the Temerite enclave.

Kara traced out its pathway, then let herself sink into its comforting embrace as she considered her options. She could call it upward, as she'd done when trying to heal the massive distortion over Erenthrall, but could she control it? That was the mentors' job. When there wasn't already an established line, those from the University used the Tapestry to create channels that the Primes and the Wielders could route the ley through for whatever purpose they needed. She'd used well-established tunnels beneath the Nexus to control the ley when healing the distortion after the Shattering. She had no such tunnels here. She'd be calling the ley up through the earth. A Prime might have been able to handle the ley without a University mentor's help, but Kara was no Prime. She'd barely even begun her training. If she tried to call the ley up now, she might end up killing herself and the rest of her group along with the Rats.

She settled back down again, back against the wall. She needed to be patient. The Rats would never expect an attack from the ley. An opportunity would arise. She just had to wait.

And if not, she could always call the ley at the end, burn herself and the Rats to less than ash, like those who had been too close and too exposed to the Nexus when it shattered.

Outside her door, the tread of multiple feet approached. She tensed as they drew nearer, jumped when something thudded to the floor outside. A heartbeat later, her door slammed inward and two Rats poured into the room, more outside. The two in the room snatched up her arms and hauled her to her feet, thrusting her out into the corridor. One of them stumbled on the tin tray her food had been in, the metal clattering.

Kara was brought to an abrupt halt before Richten.

"Fletch is back, and he wants to see you."

He grabbed her upper arm and propelled her along at his side, the rest of the Rats before and after them whooping and hollering. She wondered if she'd been collected first, or if the others had already been taken to see Fletch.

She got her answer when they emerged onto the roof, the sun setting in a blaze of orange and copper on the horizon. Adder, Gaven, and Jack were kneeling, a Rat Kara assumed to be Fletch standing over them. She didn't see Dylan. Had they killed him already? Or was he still below?

Fletch turned and saw her, and something flickered through his eyes. "Bring her here."

Richten hauled her forward, twisting her arm. She hissed in pain as she was forced to her knees beside Jack, the tracker not looking at her. One side of his face had swollen up so much he couldn't see out of that eye, the skin a purplish-yellow. The other two didn't look much better.

Fletch shifted toward her, his motions casual. She almost missed the knife he held in one hand. The Rats gathered around them, their anticipation high.

Then Fletch said softly, "I know you." He laughed, the sound loud, the Rats quieting in surprise. Their leader threw up his arms and shouted as he slowly spun, looking at them all. "I know her!"

Adder and Gaven stared at her. She met both of their gazes in consternation.

The leader of the Rats had completed his spin. In a move too fast for Kara to see, he stepped forward, his free hand wrapping around her throat. He hauled her upright, the muscles in his arm rigid as he squeezed. Her hands seized his wrist of their own volition as she choked. It felt as if her windpipe were being crushed.

Fletch dragged her close, until they were eye to eye. "I know you from before. You worked in Tallow for a while." His grip on her throat tightened. "You're exactly what we've been looking for. A Wielder.

"And you're going to do exactly what I say."

# Ten

FLETCH TIGHTENED HIS GRIP on her throat, then released her. Kara dropped to her knees and gagged, aware that Adder had lurched toward her but had been brought up short by the Rats. She heard him being beaten as she leaned forward onto one hand, the other not quite touching her throat as she heaved in huge gulps of air. Her windpipe felt bruised, the muscles in her neck throbbing from the abuse, but as her lungs filled the ache receded. She hung her head and lowered her other hand to the roof for support, reduced to coughing as she regained control. The Rats roared, the sound pulsing with her blood. To her other side, Fletch barked orders, and Adder's beating stopped. The Rats began to chant, scrambling into motion, and then Fletch turned back to her. She didn't raise her head, but she could feel his eyes on her.

"Watch her, Richten. And have Vole bring up the other one, with the busted knee. We'll take them all."

"Why?"

"Because we may need them to force her to help."

Kara choked on phlegm, spat it out onto the rough rooftop, then sat back, wiping the tendril of drool from her lips with the back of her arm. The Rats were snatching up weapons, another group bounding toward the metal contraption they used as a bridge.

Richten lunged forward, grabbed an arm, and wrenched her to her feet. "Get up." Two other Rats did the same to Adder, but Gaven and Jack were forced to support him. He couldn't keep his feet. Blood and drool dropped from a cracked lip and his breath came in a ragged wheeze. Yet when he caught Kara's attention, she realized he was overplaying his injuries. He tried to communicate something, but she couldn't figure out what.

Richten thrust her toward the others. "Stay with them. Move or I'll kill you, no matter what Fletch wants."

They were herded toward the bridge, Rats with spears and knives on either side, prodding them with shoves and glancing blows. A large group ran across to the far building, making the makeshift span bounce with each step. As she reached the edge, Kara glanced down toward the black water she knew ran far below, hidden in the shadows. She contemplated throwing herself over, but as soon as they reached the bridge, Richten called a halt and ordered their hands tied. They tied another rope around their waists. Even if she jumped now, the rope would pull her up short, and they'd haul her back to the roof again.

When they jabbed the butt of a spear into her back, she went, resigned. They untied her on the far side. The rest of her group followed, even Dylan, brought by one Rat, his arm flung over a shoulder. He limped unsteadily, his face sheened with effort.

With the Rats swarming around her, she scanned the surrounding rooftops, searching for Allan, for any of the others, while praying that they'd managed to escape both the Rats and the Tunnelers and had left the rest of them behind.

"I haven't seen anyone." Gaven still had Adder's arm over his shoulder, although the Dog was standing up straighter now.

"I doubt Allan knows where we are." Adder's voice was barely audible. "And even if he did know, he should leave us and head back to the Hollow."

"Why?"

"Because he's a Dog."

Kara wanted to point out that Allan had abandoned the Dogs long before the Shattering, but the Rat carrying Dylan finished crossing and approached. He shoved the Wielder toward them. "You carry him." Kara caught him, managed to get one of his arms over her neck, and heaved him up again.

"Where are they taking us?" Dylan asked.

"I don't know. But keep quiet, no matter what happens. They know I'm a Wielder, but they don't know about you. How bad is your leg?"

"I can put some weight on it, maybe walk on my own a ways. But I can't run."

Fletch and Richten crossed after speaking to the Rats who remained on the roof of their lair. As soon as the two leaders were safely on the far side, hand signals were passed and the bridge was withdrawn. Scouts raced out ahead of them, scrambling down into the holes and crevices in the roof they stood on, half of which Kara hadn't even noticed. A second wave was sent out ahead, and then they were moving.

They descended through the main entrance, down three floors, then through a maze of corridors and rooms. Rats raced out ahead at intervals, others rejoining them to report back before being sent out again, Fletch and Richten never halting. Kara watched them carefully, as did Adder. The group that guarded them fluctuated between twelve and twenty, one or two of them trotting ahead or falling behind on occasion, checking doorways or niches of shadow. The boisterous shouting they'd seen on the rooftops had died away into an efficient, eerie silence, broken only by curt commands from Fletch or Richten, hissed warnings, scuffing feet, and the clatter of weapons.

At one point, they passed from one building to another, three floors above ground, over another bridge. Part of one building had collapsed inward, and they skirted the debris-laden interior. At another collapse, they ascended two floors up, then down again on the far side, the entire western face of the building gone, rubble puddled like a mud-slide in the street below. The next window showed that they had moved closer to the distortion, its curved edge reaching up over their heads. The Tiana's waters flowed beside them, but ahead, it poured through a block of shorter buildings, their rooftops a bridge.

Kara glanced over her shoulder, searching the buildings behind. She saw nothing but the Rats. She shrugged Dylan into a new position and mentally bolstered herself at the same time. She couldn't count on anyone rescuing them. They'd have to find their own way out.

She focused on Fletch and Richten and where they were headed, at the same time reaching for the ley again, feeling for its conduits as they passed from the rooftops over the river back into buildings. Now they were steadily descending, the Rats more on edge. The buildings changed architecture as they entered a new district. The ley lines became more erratic as they neared the distortion. She could feel it, like a vibration on the air. Fletch had said he needed a Wielder. But why? What would he—?

Kara halted in her tracks.

"Keep moving," one of the Rats behind them snapped.

Kara shot a look toward Adder. He nodded. He already knew. He'd been trying to tell her back on the rooftop of the Rats' lair.

"I said, keep moving!" The Rat jammed the butt of his spear into her back and Kara stumbled forward.

"What is it?" Dylan's words were broken by gasps of exertion.

"I know what they need a Wielder for. They want something from the distortion. They must have seen that some of the shards were healed."

"But that wasn't you. Not until two nights ago anyway."

"It doesn't matter." She scanned to see if any of the Rats had been close enough to hear them, but none of them were paying attention.

"What do they want?"

"I don't know. But it looks like we're about to find out."

Ahead, Fletch and Richten emerged into a back alley, cut left down the narrow passage, and then right into the rear entrance of a large stone building. The back rooms were full of tables, desks, and shelves piled high with books. Most looked as if they were in the process of being transcribed, old tomes spread open on tiny easels, fresh paper in stacks to one side. A few had been stopped in the middle of being copied, text and illuminations only partially filling a new page. Kara was given only a brief glimpse, then they were passing through a set of large doors into the main part of the building. Shelves upon shelves of books were revealed in the Rats' torchlight, the stacks brushing Kara's shoulder on one side. They barely fit three abreast in the main corridor; those branching off to either side were narrower. All of the tomes were old, bound with string with covers in leather or wood. The room smelled of dust and death. Then another set of doors, and they entered the main part of the library.

The cramped inner stacks opened up into aisles, the shelving taller, ceilings higher. The books were newer as well, bindings made with glue, the paper thinner, covers a heavier stock. A few leatherbound editions were mixed in. But the Rats paid no attention to the books, stepping over heaps that had been disgorged during the quakes and lay scattered about the aisles. When they reached the center of the library—a circular open area filled with tables and chairs for study and a large central desk for the librarians— Fletch and Richten slowed. Nearly half of the Rats were ordered out through the foyer, scampering over the cracked marble floor and through the huge doors that rested partially open. Dust and litter glittered in the amber light that leaked through the entrance, thrown by the distortion.

"No one should be out there." Kara's escort drew the Hollowers to a halt a few paces behind Fletch. Richten sounded annoyed. "I don't think anyone else knows what's here."

"I won't risk it. Not when we're this close."

The leader of the Rats turned to look back at Kara. In the light of the distortion, he looked crazed.

"We have to figure out a way out of here," Adder muttered.

"How? The Rats are everywhere. And we have no weapons."

"I can still use the ley." All of them turned to face her. "It's erratic here, but there's power."

"We'll follow your lead then. Everyone pay attention. We may have to move quickly."

No one had a chance to respond. A flurry of Rats came

seething back through the door, rushing to report. Richten listened, then turned back to those that had waited inside the building. "It's clear."

The Rats poured out of the library into the area beyond. A plaza of multicolored flagstone in a diamond pattern spread outward from the library's wide steps and thick columns until it was interrupted by the distortion, the fractured faces rising up and out overhead. Only a small corner near the library remained free. Through the distortion's edges, Kara could see another massive stone building, almost a mirror image of the library, except this building had ironbound, studded double doors and its few windows were narrow and high up. It had a solid weight to it, like a fortress.

Beside her, Adder stiffened in recognition.

"What is it?"

"It's the city watch's armory. It will be jammed with swords, spears, knives — weapons of every kind. Maybe even black powder. We can't let the Rats get their hands on it."

Fletch had paused at the top of the library's stairs to gaze at the entombed armory. Now he glanced back.

"Heal these shards and free the armory," he said, "or all of your friends die."

---

Allan drew to an irritated halt when Sorelle's hand rose in warning. He and the rest of the Hollowers were surrounded by Sorelle, Jaimes, and the rest of their band, all keeping a careful watch. The other Tunnelers, including Cason, were farther ahead. Sorelle was taking her guard duties seriously. Too seriously. Allan couldn't see anything; they were too far back. The sword he'd been given was useless. He flexed and tightened his grip on the hilt in frustration.

When he took a few steps forward, coming up on Sorelle from behind, she spun, her own blade half-raised. "What are you doing?"

Allan raised his free hand, palm out. "I can't see a damned thing. How do you expect us to help you if we're this far back? By the time we know the fighting has started it will already be over."

Sorelle let the tip of her blade drop. "I don't trust you."

"You've made that perfectly clear. But we can't help if we can't see what's going on."

Sorelle relented, motioning them forward. Glenn and Cutter joined Allan at the edge of the roof next to Sorelle and two of her group. Artras, Tim, and Carter remained behind with Jaimes, Laura, and the others.

The roof looked out over a slew of random rooftops, each building of different architecture, of varied heights, but all only two or three stories tall. Allan recognized the house he'd used to watch the Rats a few nights before, and beyond it, the Rats' lair. Scattered over the buildings below, the shadows of the Tunnelers crept forward, taking advantage of the broken rooflines as cover. Cason and Ren each led a small group of twenty. The rest of the Tunnelers must have remained behind.

He shifted his attention to the Rats' domain, squinting at the distance. "There's not much activity. Not like before."

"Maybe your friends are already dead. The Rats don't keep prisoners alive for long."

"Or maybe they aren't there any longer."

"We'll know soon enough. We have watchers on the lair. Cason will check in with them."

Allan settled in. His gaze darted across the Rats' rooftop, then below to where Cason and Ren converged and conferred. The Rats were too quiet. He couldn't shake the feeling that the lair was mostly empty, only a token force left behind. He counted at most twenty people visible, half of them on sentry duty, the others scattered around the few fires. There had been many more the night he'd watched them slaughter the Temerites.

Finally, Cason and Ren retreated. Someone signaled, and Sorelle pulled back from their vantage. "Come on. Cason wants to talk."

They descended through the building down the central stairwell, doors opening up onto apartments on either side. It had once been a high-end apartment complex, the banister made of solid oak, with chandeliers overhead and windows with stained-glass panels above and to either side. Cason and Ren were waiting for them on the second-floor landing, Cason with a helmet tucked in the crook of her arm.

"They're gone. The Rats left nearly an hour ago, your friends with them. My watchers report that at least one of them was killed."

"Which one?"

"One of the Dogs."

"Adder or Kent then. The others?"

"Alive. The remaining Dog has been beaten badly. The man about your age has a ruined knee. The others are helping both of them walk. The focus of the Rats' leader seems to be on the woman."

"They must know Kara's a Wielder."

"Which is why we need to stop them. Now. Before they force her to do something we'll all regret."

"Like what?"

Cason ignored him. "My watchers have been following them. They've headed across the river, to the edge of the distortion. But they're a good hour ahead of us. We need to move quickly." She twisted the helmet up in a smooth gesture and slammed it onto her head. The nose guard, eye slits, and cheek protectors blunted her features, made her look fiercer. "Once we're beyond sight of the Rats' lair, we'll abandon the buildings, use the streets. We need speed more than secrecy now."

The Tunnelers surrounding them were already in motion. Cason and Ren led the group out through a gaping hole in the wall to the next building.

Sorelle grumbled something under her breath, then sighed and motioned Jaimes, Laura, and the rest of them forward.

Kara turned her attention back to the distortion. She knew Fletch's threat was real. Kent's death proved that. She had no doubts that Richten itched to inflict more pain on them. He'd barely controlled himself on the roof the night they'd been captured.

"Don't do it, Kara. Forget about us. Don't let them ha—"

The sentence ended in a choked off cry of pain and the thud of a body sprawling to the ground. She spun to find one of the Rats with an arm wrapped around Gaven's throat, the wagonmaster's back arched, the blade of a knife an inch from his left eye. Adder was already pushing himself back up to his knees, one arm holding his midsection where he'd been kicked earlier.

Fletch hadn't moved. "Should he be first? Or one of the others? Which one do you care about most?"

Kara swung back toward the Rats' leader. "I care about all of them." Then she stepped forward, descending the stairs. Fletch's eyes widened slightly in surprise as she passed, but he said nothing. Richten shouted orders as the group shifted down to the plaza, closer to the distortion. She glanced back once to make certain the others were being brought forward as well, then focused on the shards ahead of her. At the same time, she reached for the ley, tapped into the potential lines around them.

There were three. Two thin lines were nothing more than the remnants from a disrupted node. Before the Shattering, they would have channeled at least five times as much power, and the node itself would have branched off in more directions. But the distortion had interrupted that configuration, so only two lines remained. They shot off toward the northeast and west.

The third line contained more ley, but was deeper beneath the city, harder to reach.

She tapped into the two smaller lines as she halted a few paces away from the distortion. The shard's face before her was amber in color, the plaza beyond tinted a dull orange. Like the shards she'd seen before, it was littered with abandoned carts, luggage, and assorted odds and ends thrown aside as people fled. She didn't see anything living—horses, animals, or people—but the yarn hair on a dust-covered doll tossed to the ground a few feet inside the distortion moved as if tugged by an occasional gust of wind. So time inside this distortion wasn't halted. The shard didn't reach all the way to the armory. There were five other shards visible along its edges, and she suspected at least one more underground. Two of those intersected the armory, with most of the building caught in one of them. Of the other three, one was adjacent to her and appeared to be filled with smoke or fog. Another was deeper inside the distortion—

And was filled with ley.

She shot a glance toward Fletch, but the Rats' leader was staring hungrily at the armory. He sensed her look and turned toward her.

"Do you need a demonstration?"

"Richten already provided one."

"Then get on with it."

Kara motioned toward the shard. "Healing a shard of this size isn't easy. I'll need help."

"From who?"

"Him." Kara pointed to Dylan, standing on his own now. "He's a Wielder as well."

Dylan's look of betrayed shock could not have been faked. His mouth hung open, eyes wide. Adder began searching the distortion. He stilled when he noticed the shard full of ley, eyes dropping to Kara.

"Do it."

Richten shoved Dylan forward, following a few paces behind.

"What are you doing?" Dylan's voice was panicked. "I thought I was supposed to keep my mouth shut."

"You were. But I need your help. You need to hold the edges of the shard stable while I work, or the whole distortion might collapse." She tried to indicate the ley-filled shard with her eyes, but Dylan was too distracted to notice. "I'm going to need *even more* help once this first shard is down."

Dylan still seemed oblivious, but behind them Jack perked up. She didn't think he'd noted the ley-filled shard yet, but at least the tracker was paying attention.

She grabbed Dylan's arm. "Just hold the edges, like before."

She turned toward the shard, pulling the ley toward her as she did so. Dylan reached out as well, but his hold trembled. She wasn't certain he'd be able to maintain the edges, but she said nothing. Instead, she formed the needle as she'd done before. "Ready?"

Dylan's hold on the shard solidified.

She pierced the face of the shard, controlling the collapse as the hole widened. Behind her, Richten let out a whoop of triumph, the Rats beyond following suit. The air released from the shard gusted into her face, smelling like rain. The ground beyond was damp, as if a light shower had passed by a short time before.

When the face was healed, Kara stepped forward and picked up the doll. It was wet, but not so soaked as to keep the breeze from ruffling the light blue dress.

"Now the next one."

Kara lifted her eyes to find Fletch standing close, his body unnaturally still.

Kara dropped the doll. "We need to wait." She motioned toward Dylan. "He needs to recover. You've beaten him so badly he doesn't have much strength."

Fletch took one small step closer. They were almost nose-to-nose now. "Heal the next shard, or he dies."

"I don't know if—"

Fletch gestured with one hand, and before Kara could protest Richten had snapped a knife from a wrist sheath into his free hand and jerked Dylan to his side. No one moved. The Rats had quieted, the air throbbing with anticipation.

"Do it."

Kara moved into the healed shard, the scent of rain sharpening. Overhead, a layer of the shard filled with smoke passed by. To the left, the face of the shard that contained the ley pulsed a bright white, almost blue. She could feel the energy trapped there, seeking a release. The shard was engorged, ready to burst. Another face ran beneath the ley's shard, angled upward at a steep pitch. She dared not look at it or the ley, kept her attention focused on the slanted wall of the shard that cut toward the left side of the armory and the trees at the far end of the plaza. As she moved, the Rats and their captives followed, a few stationed outside as guards. She caught Adder's attention and tilted her head toward the right, away from the ley. He edged in that direction. A few of the Rats did as well, but mostly they spread out, filling up the opened area of the plaza.

Fletch stayed behind her, wary, just out of reach.

Standing before the next shard, Kara raised her hands, clenched her teeth, and closed her eyes so that she could focus. "I've never done this by myself." She reached for the shard's face and split her attention, half of it surrounding the edges, trying to hold them stable, the rest intent on forming the needle needed to pierce the barrier. "If I can't control it, it may set off a chain reaction. The entire distortion could collapse."

She thrust the needle home. The tension holding the face stable snapped, and she tried to control the resultant collapse. But it was too taut, her attention too divided. It slid from her grip, and with a cry she braced the edges. The face cut through the air, sliced through the limbs of the trees, then slammed into the edges. The force sent tremors through all of the distortion's surrounding structure, but it held. She didn't think it would have without her assistance. The severed tree limbs crashed to the ground, the thickest as wide as Kara's thigh. One of them split with a resounding crack.

Then silence, for a single breath, two.

The Rats erupted into another cheer that dissolved into a carousing chant. Kara exhaled harshly as she lowered her arms, then opened her eyes. The left side of the armory sat feet away, but still locked inside the distortion, beyond reach.

Fletch's hand wrapped around Kara's upper arm, the grip painfully tight. "One more to go."

"Are you mad! I barely controlled that collapse. Didn't you feel the distortion shudder?"

Fletch jerked her close again. "I need what's in that armory. Release it now, or I will kill you and wait for this other Wielder to regain his strength so that he can do it himself."

He'd drawn his own knife, she noted, the blade poised near her stomach. "No. I'll do it."

She shook free of his grasp and faced the remaining shard. She raised her hands, closed her eyes.

But instead of reaching forward and preparing the armory's shard before her, she stretched back with her senses and seized hold of the shard containing the ley. At the same time, she nudged Dylan with the Tapestry, felt the Wielder start in surprise, then tentatively reach out and join her. He hadn't picked up on her earlier hints or warnings; she hoped he was paying attention now.

She formed the needle and bolstered the ley shard's boundaries. Drawing in a deep breath, she centered herself and tensed.

Then, from the direction of the library, outside the distortion, someone screamed—a high-pitched cry of agony—followed by a bellowed warning and the clash of weapons.

Kara's eyes snapped open and she turned, arms still raised. At her side, Fletch took a step toward the open plaza, the rest of the Rats, including Richten, doing the same.

On the library steps, two bodies lay sprawled, arrows jutting up from their backs. A third girl—the one letting out the blood-curdling scream—had fallen to her knees, her left arm held out before her, an arrow pierced through her bicep, sticking a good four inches out the other side. Blood dripped from the tip. She tried to struggle to her feet, but another arrow took her in the throat.

As she fell forward, people swarmed out of the library doors and into the plaza. The Rat who had bellowed the alarm lurched forward, and as if it were a signal, the rest of the Rats outside the distortion surged after him in a wave. The leader of the attacking force—wearing a helmet that hid the majority of the face—raised a long sword and met them, the two forces grinding together in a melee.

"Underearthers!" Richten spun toward Fletch. "What are they doing here? We're far outside their territory."

Fletch didn't answer. "Mouse, head back to the lair and warn the others. Richten, get everyone else out there now!"

The Rats' leader turned on Kara, but she didn't wait to see what he'd do.

Arms still raised, she drove the needle into the ley's shard.

The barrier between the ley and the world outside the distortion flashed with a ripple and then burst like a soap bubble. The trapped ley cascaded down from the opening, the white light behaving like water. Fletch jerked around in time to see it slam into the canted shard beneath it and pour down the funnel toward them. Kara tensed as she held the edges of the shard, aware that the ley was bearing down on her—

But then an invisible wall formed before her.

The released ley roared down on them like a flood and engulfed the nearest Rats, their screams cut off as the intense raw power of the ley annihilated them. It slammed up against the shards on either side in spumes, more and more of it pouring out from above. Dylan roared in defiance as it slammed into the shield he'd thrown up, sloshing up over and around Kara, Fletch, Dylan, Richten, Gaven, Adder, Jack, and six other Rats. All of the rest of the Rats inside the distortion turned to run, most of them caught by the ley as it surged out through the opening and into the plaza beyond.

No one else had moved.

Except Adder.

He threw off Gaven's supposed support, jabbed a Rat's throat with stiffened fingers, seized the choking body with his other arm, and disarmed him. Sword bared, he threw the writhing body toward the two near Jack, already moving toward the next Rat, the boy unaware of his approach until the blade sank into his chest. He coughed up blood, the red-black liquid staining the front of his shirt. One of the Rats near Jack caught his fellow Rat's body. Jack twisted in a move Kara didn't quite catch. Something cracked and the second Rat fell to the ground cradling a broken arm. Jack disarmed him and spun, but Adder had already moved on to the two Rats farthest from them. Both of them attempted to defend themselves with their spears, but Adder was too quick. One fell with a hand severed at the wrist, his shrieks echoing oddly inside Dylan's shield, the other defending herself for two ringing deflections before Adder drove his sword into her side.

Both Adder and Jack turned toward Richten and Fletch. Richten had twisted Dylan around to face them and placed the edge of his knife at Dylan's throat.

Fletch still hadn't moved. His mouth had thinned in disapproval, his eyes following Adder's movements. He didn't seem aware of the danger of the ley only a few paces away, although he must have seen what it had done to the Rats who'd been in its path.

"Don't come closer, or I'll kill him."

"Don't be stupid, Richten. If you kill the Wielder, we all die. He's the one keeping the ley at bay." Fletch looked to Kara. "Now what?"

Kara released the edges of the ley's shard and lowered her arms. "You let us go."

Before he could answer, Dylan said tightly, "Kara."

Fletch's eyes narrowed. "And if I don't?"

"Kara, I can't hold it." Dylan was sweating, his face pale.

"Then Dylan loses his grip on the shield and we all die."

The muscles in Fletch's jaw tensed as he ground his teeth together. "Richten, let him go."

The Rat practically threw Dylan from him. Gaven caught him.

At the same time, Kara reached out and erected her own shield beneath Dylan's, a moment before his collapsed. The ley surged a foot closer, but again Fletch didn't move. Kara mentally cursed. If she'd had more time, she could have thrown up a shield around only those from the Hollow.

"You don't want to go with the Underearthers."

"Why not?"

Fletch didn't answer.

Kara edged around him, then switched places with Richten. Behind them, she noticed that the ley pouring from the healed shard had thinned and abated. It still lapped up against the shield, but in another few minutes it wouldn't be high enough or intense enough to harm them. She could feel what remained already seeping into the ground, seeking out the new ley lines created by the Shattering.

When Adder touched her shoulder, she started. He and Jack flanked her as they backed away from the two Rats.

"We don't have much time."

"I can see that."

As if he'd heard them, Fletch glanced back.

Kara let the shield go. "Run!"

Her last glimpse of Fletch and Richten was of both of them throwing their arms up to protect themselves as they flinched back from the cascade of ley. Richten screamed in terror as it struck them.

"Are they dead?"

"No! The ley isn't concentrated enough anymore."

Adder cursed. A moment later, the ley struck them, washing about their feet, rising almost to their hips. It tingled against Kara's legs, the hair on her arms standing on end in reaction. Adder and the others plowed forward, Gaven supporting Dylan.

They emerged from the hole inside the distortion onto the plaza and were brought up short. The scene before the library was utter chaos, Rats fighting Tunnelers on all sides except for a wide area before them where the ley flowed out onto the plaza. It spread like a pool, now only ankle deep and receding fast. Both the Rats and the Tunnelers avoided it.

"This way." Adder grabbed Kara's arm and tugged her away from the fight. They edged along the distortion to the left, heading toward the nearest building, diagonally across the plaza, the white-hot lightning of the distortion overhead. Adder led, Jack behind, swords raised. But the majority of the fighting was at the base of the library steps.

They'd almost reached the edge of the plaza when Kara heard someone shout, the voice familiar.

She halted and glanced back, Gaven and Dylan bumping into her from behind.

"Keep moving! We're almost there!"

Kara shook her head, still scanning the fight, searching faces. "I would have sworn I heard—" Her eyes opened wide and she spun back to Adder. "It's Allan! He's fighting with the Tunnelers!"

"What?" Adder trotted back to them. "Where?"

"There, toward the back, at the top of the library steps. I can see Allan, Glenn, and Cutter."

"I see them. What about the others?"

"Inside the library?"

"Possibly. We can't get to Allan and the others directly. We'd have to fight our way through the Rats." Adder motioned back toward the street. "Jack, take the lead. Gaven and Dylan next. Kara and I will follow. Head down a block or two, then circle back to the library."

Jack took off, Gaven and Dylan limping along behind him. Adder and Kara followed at a slower pace.

"Something's not quite right."

"What do you mean?" Kara glanced back toward Allan. "It looks like they're fighting with the Tunnelers."

"They are. But look at the Tunnelers around them. They're not just fighting the Rats. They're keeping a close eye on Allan, Glenn, and Cutter as well."

Now that he'd pointed it out, Kara could see it. At least

five of the Tunnelers near them were staying close, even when there were obvious openings for them to advance down the stairs. The Hollowers were hemmed in. "We won't know what's going on until we find them."

They'd reached the street. As they passed behind the building, their view of the plaza and the fighting cut off, Kara thought she saw Cutter look in their direction.

# Eleven

"T HEY'VE ESCAPED!"

Allan swept a Rat's sword out from the boy's clumsy thrust and sliced across his chest, pulling the swing a little so the cut wasn't as deep. As the boy gaped at him in shock, then collapsed—blood blooming in a thin line across his chest, his clothing sagging away from the cut—Allan stepped back, aware of Sorelle and the rest of her guard on either side. He scanned the fight. "I don't see them."

Cutter slashed the Rat before him, the girl curling forward over her cut arm with a silent scream. The tracker pointed with his sword. "They just vanished behind that building."

Allan saw nothing, but he turned toward Sorelle. "Sorelle!"

"I heard." She thrust her own blade through her opponent's chest. "I'll inform Cason we can retreat." She turned and, bringing fingers to lips, sounded a piercing whistle.

Those in the plaza began to fall back, fighting as they went. The Rats harassed them the entire way. Sorelle's group surrounded Allan, Glenn, and Cutter and herded them back inside the library, where Artras, Carter, and

Aaron waited with Tim watching over them. They all carried weapons in case the Rats broke through, but it was obvious that Carter and Aaron wouldn't have contributed much to the fight. Artras appeared surprisingly comfortable with hers, although its length looked unwieldy in her grip.

As they passed inside the shadows of the library, two Rats emerged from the gaping hole in the distortion where a shard had once been. The taller of the two glanced over the fighting, then said something to the other, who began bellowing orders.

Then Allan's sightline was cut off, Sorelle and the rest of the Tunnelers surging through the library's double doors. The inside study area was filling fast, Sorelle directing everyone back into the stacks.

Allan bumped into Artras, who grabbed his shirt. "Kara? Is she safe?"

"I didn't see her. But Cutter said she escaped."

"Good. After what I've seen here in Erenthrall, we need her more than ever."

Allan was going to ask her what she meant, but Cason appeared. With a roar, she thrust the Rats clinging to her like their namesake vermin back outside, a slew of Tunnelers closing the doors to keep them out. Others dragged tables to brace them, and then Cason searched the room until her gaze fell on Sorelle.

"Where are they?"

Sorelle motioned toward Cutter. "He saw them flee the distortion."

"Where did they go?"

"They came out of the distortion and turned right. They entered the first street, but they saw Allan and the rest of us fighting on the steps."

"You're certain?"

"Yes."

Ren turned to Cason. "Then they'll likely try to circle around to find us."

"The Rats aren't going to just sit there in the plaza and let us get away." She turned to Sorelle and Allan. "We'll have to pick them up on the run. I'll leave that up to your two groups. We'll focus on protecting our backside."

They moved, the Tunnelers spilling back through the

stacks of the library, into the back room, then out into the alley and streets beyond. Scouts fanned out ahead, scattering as soon as they hit the street. Sorelle, Jaimes, Laura, and the rest loosely circled Allan and the Hollowers as they cut left, heading in the direction Cutter said Kara and the others had run. Sorelle and the others kept their attention forward, one of the scouts appearing occasionally in a doorway or window or rooftop, flashing a wordless signal before disappearing again. Allan recognized the hand gestures from the Dogs; Cason must have taught them. Allan kept his gaze roving, both ahead and behind.

Glancing back, he thought he saw a figure standing on a roofline, outlined against clouds backlit by the moon. At the figure's feet were the silhouettes of two Wolves. When he blinked to focus, the black shapes were gone. He scanned the nearest buildings, but saw nothing.

Then Sorelle barked a warning. He spun back to see the Tunnelers fanning out on the street. Ahead, Adder and Kara stood in front of Jack, Dylan, and Gaven. Gaven was supporting Dylan, the Wielder keeping the weight off of one leg. All of them had dark bruises on their faces, Adder in particular, although he still held his sword with cold confidence. Kara's throat was bruised in the shape of a hand, as if someone had choked her.

He didn't see Kent at all.

"Stand down! We're here to help!"

Adder glanced toward Allan. "How can we be sure of that?"

Sorelle spat and cursed under her breath, locking gazes with Allan. "We don't have time for this."

Allan thought about the figure and his attendant Wolves and agreed.

He stepped forward, sword lowered. "We came to get you the hell out of here. The Rats will be on us any minute now."

Behind him, he heard fighting spill out into the street. The Rats had made it through the library. More of them would be circling around the buildings, like Adder and Kara.

Kara muttered something to Adder, who nodded, his shoulders relaxing. "Dylan can barely walk. Kent's dead."

"We heard." Then, to Sorelle: "Whenever you're ready."

Sorelle turned and sounded another harsh whistle before pointing toward a secondary street beyond Adder and the others. "That way."

Both groups took off for the street. Allan edged close to Kara as they ran.

"Are you all right?"

"No, we're not. None of us are."

Sorelle shouted, "Into the ley station." They hustled up the steps to another ley station, Sorelle holding open the still-intact door and shoving them through as fast as possible. "Take the right tunnel down to the platform, then right into the barge line."

They skirted the stone statue of a flock of birds in flight, the petrified creatures exploding toward the shattered glass ceiling, then crossed the mezzanine and entered the tunnel. Jaimes and Laura were ahead of them, racing down the slanted corridor until they reached the platform. They headed directly toward the right edge, where the barge line shot off to the southwest. Jaimes and Laura didn't even pause, just leapt into the channel. Jaimes turned around and motioned Artras and Glenn down. "Come on!"

Glenn jumped. Artras turned and levered herself over the side. Allan halted just behind Carter, Adder, and Cutter, all of them scrambling to get down.

Beside him, Kara sucked in a wavering breath.

"What's wrong?"

"There's still ley running through that line."

"I don't see anything."

"It's not concentrated enough to be visible, but it's there."

More of Sorelle's group entered the platform, trailed by Sorelle herself.

"They seem to know what they're doing regarding these tunnels." Allan grabbed hold of Kara's upper arm. "We're going to have to trust them."

Together they dropped down into the stone-lined bed then ducked into the deeper shadows of the channel beyond. Twenty paces inside, Sorelle called a halt and ordered everyone silent. She listened, head canted to one side, her shape barely visible as an outline against the rounded mouth of the tunnel behind them.

Finally, she turned and motioned to Jaimes, who pulled a lantern from a small niche in the wall and lit it. Allan wasn't thrilled to see that the niche was really a huge crack in the tunnel wall that ran all the way up to the ceiling and down the other side. A result of the Shattering, he assumed. Or the quakes that had followed.

"We weren't seen." Sorelle's gaze raked over Kara and the other new additions. "Which of you are Wielders?"

"I am. And Dylan over there, the one injured."

"Did you free that armory for them?"

"No."

"Good. Then we won't have to kill you."

Allan couldn't tell if Sorelle was serious until he caught Jaimes' eyeroll off to one side. Even then, he wasn't reassured. His old Dog instincts prickled; he'd learned long ago not to ignore them.

Sorelle motioned them all into the tunnel, Jaimes leading the way with the lantern, the Tunnelers both ahead and behind, hemming them in. The old barge channel branched right, then left, but they didn't diverge from the main path until they reached another left branch.

Kara tugged on his sleeve as they moved through the dark and mouthed, silently, "We've left the ley," as soon as they cut left.

They passed a few junctions, dropping down to deeper levels or climbing up to higher ones using ladders obviously set there by the Tunnelers. At one point, they crossed a series of makeshift bridges, like those the Rats used, where the channels once filled by the ley were flooded with running water. The sound of water cascading down in a thin waterfall was deafening after the silence of the tunnels, but the fine spray thrown up provided some cooling relief.

By the time they emerged again into the Tunnelers' home base, people rushing forward to help Sorelle and the others deal with weapons and wounds, Allan's arms were weak and shaking from exhaustion. He didn't protest when Sorelle ordered them back to the same grated tunnel they'd been held in before. The Tunnelers took Dylan away to see to his leg. Allan watched silently, standing protectively before their assigned prison, but no one moved to herd them inside and close the grate behind them.

He ducked into the tunnel and found Artras and Kara conversing, the rest sprawled out in as comfortable a position as they could find, massaging bruised arms or legs, nursing wounds. Gaven was methodically going over Adder's body, the Dog wincing whenever he touched a sensitive spot, Aaron acting as an assistant. Adder had obviously been beaten worse than the others.

All of them looked up as he entered. He met each of their gazes, ending with Adder. "What happened to Kent?"

"The Rats killed him."

"What for?"

"To intimidate us."

"What did they want?"

"Wielders, so they could free up the armory trapped inside the distortion."

Someone coughed, and Allan turned to see Sorelle standing at the entrance to the tunnel.

"I came to tell you that your other Wielder—"

"Dylan. His name is Dylan."

"Dylan, then. He's fine. His knee was sprained. We bound it up. He'll be limping for a while yet, but he'll heal."

She turned to go, but Glenn stepped forward. "What are you going to do with us now?"

"You'll have to ask Cason about that."

After she'd moved a short distance away, Glenn murmured, "Somehow I don't find that reassuring."

Allan caught the Dog's eyes. "So I'm not the only one feeling unsettled?"

"My hackles have been up since we left the Hollow. But there's something not quite right about these Tunnelers."

"They rescued us from the Rats."

"Only because they wanted to make certain our Wielders didn't hand the armory over to their enemies. But now that they've stopped that, what are they going to do with us?"

Allan let the question hang unanswered, then cut into the uneasiness. "There's no reason to create trouble. They haven't locked us up since we returned—even let us keep our weapons—so we give them the benefit of the doubt, but keep our eyes open." He noted Glenn's disapproval. "I'm on edge as well, but can you say it's because of the Tunnelers specifically, or is it everything that's happened since we entered what's left of Erenthrall?"

"It's the Tunnelers, Sorelle in particular."

"Jalmes and Laura haven't treated us badly. And Sorelle may be prickly, but it's obvious her hatred is focused on the Rats, not us. We're just easy targets. She didn't have to come back to report on Dylan, but she did."

Glenn remained unconvinced.

Behind, the Tunnelers' main chamber erupted in a roar of triumph. Allan and Glenn shifted toward the entrance, Kara and Artras coming up behind.

"What is it?"

"Cason, their leader, has returned."

Everyone inside the Tunnelers' main chamber converged on the leader as she entered with Ren and the fighters behind her. Sorelle must have told everyone they'd succeeded, for they were all trying to congratulate the returning heroes at once. Cason ignored the adulation, tossing her helmet to a waiting youth while others rushed forward to tend to wounds. They began removing her armor piece by piece. She grimaced as they drew her arm free, blood pouring out of the metal sleeve and pooling on the ground. At least three healers swept in, bodies hunched as they bound the cut.

She glanced toward Allan and the others as they worked, saw them watching.

Allan's uneasiness grew.

"You have a report, Devin?" Aurek didn't take his eyes off of the message the latest courier had brought in.

"Yes, Lord Baron. We've broken the prisoner Joss, from the western foothills."

Aurek glanced up, eyebrow raised. "The one Verrent captured, before his foolhardy attack on that settlement?" He sat back, tossing the message to the small portable table that served as his desk. "Are they White Cloaks?"

"No, sir. He doesn't know anything about the White Cloaks. As far as I can tell, he's never even heard of them."

If it wasn't the White Cloaks, and they knew nothing of them, then perhaps he should shift his attention back to the east. His men were spread thin enough as it was.

And yet, Verrent had mentioned the group contained Dogs. Real Dogs, from before the fall.

"Bring the prisoner here."

"I don't think that's wise, sir. He might not survive the walk. Even if we carried him."

"I see." Devin could interrogate him alone and simply report back, but the resistance Verrent had met was unprecedented. No one had fought back so successfully since Aurek had first started expanding outward from Haven into the surrounding territory. A few of the nearby villages had balked at first, but Aurek and his men had cowed them within the first few months. Others had joined them willingly after that. Nearly everyone else they'd run into on the plains since then had been in groups too small to be considered a threat.

This group had defeated Verrent and his pack, pushed them back, killed over half of them. Granted, Verrent had attacked without a clear understanding of who he faced, but even then he wouldn't have expected his own men to be defeated so resoundingly.

"Is the prisoner ready?"

"Of course."

"Then take me to him."

Devin led him out of the tent, into the center of a hub of activity. One of the packs had returned with the courier early that morning, the men already assembling their tents, feeding their horses, and catching up with those who'd stayed behind. Many of those they passed brought their fist to their chest in salute, Aurek nodding in return. They'd come from the northwestern foothills, closer to the Steppe, verifying the reports of the unnatural cloud cover over the mountains and mysterious aurora and purplish-blue lightning within. But they hadn't traveled far enough north to encounter any of the strange creatures reported in that area. In fact, they'd found nothing except small villages, a few of them so remote the people knew nothing of the Shattering, only that something had happened to the south and east. They'd witnessed the blinding flash of light and heard the roar of the explosion, but they hadn't bothered to find out what had caused it, even after the earth began shaking in spasms afterward. It had nothing to do with them. According to the pack leader's report, they'd said it was "Barons' business" and shrugged it off before returning to their spring planting and shearing.

It was Barons' business, Aurek thought dryly. But it would be their business soon enough. Let the villagers plant and shear and tend to their animals. He'd be by soon enough to collect his due.

They passed Verrent, the man on his knees, arms outstretched and lashed tight to a makeshift railing, body hunched forward. The marks of a lash stood out on his bared back, his skin crusted with dried blood and burned by the sun. Flies buzzed around him, clustered around the cuts. Verrent raised his head as they passed, his face mottled with bruises, his lip split, nose broken.

Aurek paused, Devin taking a few more steps before realizing he'd stopped. Aurek didn't answer his beta's questioning look, merely moved to stand before Verrent. His nose wrinkled at the reek of shit and piss, with an overlying sweetness of rot.

"Why are you here?"

Verrent tried to look up, but could only tilt his head enough to catch Aurek out of one eye. "Because I led my men into an ambush." His voice was a husky, dry croak.

"That was the result of your actions. That's not why you're here."

Verrent sagged forward. The temporary fence he was tied to creaked with his weight. "I should never have attacked them."

"Why not?"

Verrent rocked back slightly, a few of the flies rising to hover, disturbed, before settling again. Aurek noted a few of the whip marks had begun to fester. "Because I should have interrogated the prisoner longer, found out more, before I attacked."

Aurek sank to one knee, caught Verrent's chin in one hand, and raised his face so he could look him in the eye. The man sucked in a breath through his teeth at the pain.

"You had the resource at hand, and in your haste to gain my favor you reacted too quickly, trusted your prisoner, and didn't stop to consider the consequences. If you intend to remain one of my alphas, remember this the next time you find yourself acting on your own."

"Yes, Lord Baron."

Aurek searched Verrent's eyes, saw humility, shame, but no fear. Anger, but focused internally, on himself, not outward, toward Aurek or Devin.

Aurek released him. Devin had come up behind him.

"Cut him down and clean him up. Make certain those cuts are seen to by our healers."

"Yes, Lord Baron. What should we do with him after that?"

"Return him to his men."

Devin called a few of the nearer men over and gave them orders before trotting to catch up to Aurek.

His second simmered for twenty steps before finally breaking. "He let over twenty men die!"

"He attacked before he was ready. Would you have done any different when I first sent you out?"

"I wouldn't have attacked at night in the middle of a storm without any idea of who I was facing."

"You would have done the same as he did with half the men. You forget that I've known you since you were a brash youth in my guard, much like myself. We both would have attacked back then, especially if we knew my father was waiting back home. I doubt we would have asked the prisoner any more than Verrent did. He was cocksure and he's been punished for it, harshly. He's learned his lesson."

"Perhaps."

"Isn't this how the Dogs in Erenthrall were trained? Mistakes held brutal consequences. Every Dog I ever saw in the city before the Shattering bore the marks."

"He should still be watched."

"Oh, he will be."

They'd reached the tent where the prisoner Verrent had

captured was kept. Devin held back the flap as Aurek ducked inside, then followed.

Aurek was struck immediately by the scent of blood, shit, and terror. It clung to the air like a mist, so heavy and thick his eyes watered. Aurek stood for a moment to allow himself to adjust, blinking at the dimness after the brightness of the sun outside. At the far back of the tent, the prisoner lay spread-eagled on the ground, hands and feet bound with rope to stakes set into the grass. Two tables, one to either side, bore instruments of torture—hammers and knives mostly.

As Aurek stepped forward, he noted the instruments were still slick with blood not yet dried. The grass beneath the body was stained dark. He knelt down carefully, sitting back onto his heels, and scanned the man's body. He'd been stripped naked. His upper torso was covered in thin cuts, bruises, and burns. His legs were covered in blood. Two of his fingers were mangled and pointing in odd directions.

Aurek looked into the man's eyes. His face was surprisingly normal, left intact so that he could talk. His gaze shot back and forth between Aurek and Devin.

"He held out longer than I expected. He broke only when we began snapping his fingers. His name is—"

Aurek held up a hand. He leaned forward. "What's your name?"

"J-Joss."

Aurek had already known that from Verrent's initial report, but it was good to know Joss hadn't lied. "And where did you come from?"

Joss' gaze flicked toward Devin, then back again. "The Hollow."

"I've never heard of the Hollow." Joss' eyes widened in terror, as if he expected more torture because Aurek didn't believe him. "Do you know who I am?"

Joss shook his head.

"Before the Shattering, I was a lord, keeper of a small section of land around Haven, on an offshoot of the main ley line between Erenthrall and Dunmara. Baron Arent would likely not have even known my name, though I attended most of the events in the Amber Tower. I was there for the sowing of the Flyers' Tower, and its activation. I was there for the last Baronial Meeting, when the Kormanley attacked. But thankfully, I was at home when the Nexus shattered. I saw the pulse of ley as it traveled down the ley line from Erenthrall to Dunmara, witnessed the explosion of light over the Reaches from my window when it hit, and stumbled through all of the aftershocks. I knew every village of consequence on the plains and the surrounding lands. And yet, I've never heard of the Hollow."

"Tell me about it."

"It's just a village." Joss licked his lips. They were cracked and dry. "Just a village. We only wanted to be left alone, free from the Baron, free from the ley. We wanted nothing to do with any of it. I was just a shepherd. All I wanted to do was tend sheep. But then the Nexus shattered and the refugees came."

"Refugees?" Aurek reached out to slap Joss' cheeks, to keep him focused. "What refugees?"

"From Erenthrall. Survivors of the explosion. Allan brought them. Dogs, men from the University, people they collected in the streets, Wielders."

"Wielders?" Aurek glanced up toward Devin. His second had bristled, hand falling to the sword hanging at his waist. "How many?"

"I don't know. Seven. Eight. From the city." His voice had thickened, began to slur. "I just wanted to herd sheep," he muttered to himself. "I didn't want to scout." The shepherd's eyes grew unfocused and his head tilted to one side.

Aurek considered forcing him to talk more, to tell him about the layout of the village, how many people were in it, what its defenses were, but he'd obviously slipped away. Devin could gather those details from him later, if he hadn't already.

He stood and motioned for Devin to follow him.

"He didn't mention Wielders before. And I swear he knows nothing of the White Cloaks."

Aurek waved Devin's concern aside. "I don't think these Wielders are White Cloaks. There aren't enough of them. I was considering heading back to Haven. The reports coming from the east say there are plenty of towns and villages ready to be raided, minimal defenses, multiple types of supplies. But we'll have to alter those plans.

"Find out as much as you can from our shepherd—about this Hollow, its people, its defenses, and these Wielders. We'll take the entire camp with us."

"The objective?"

"The Wielders nearly destroyed us once with the Icy. We can't let them do it again. We're going to attack this Hollow, root them out, and kill them all."

# Twelve

"NO, NO," Sovaan snapped, waving Cory back from the edge of the rough field of rock and scrabble before them. "Like this."

Keeping himself focused on the Tapestry, Cory concentrated as Sovaan took his place. To either side of him, he felt Jerrain and Jasom's presences, with three other undergraduate students at the University at the time of the Shattering behind them, hovering a good distance away. Based on what had happened so far with their experiments, Cory didn't blame them. But he'd been a graduate student, and he'd be damned if he'd show how nervous he was with Sovaan's attempts so far.

The Tapestry flexed beneath Sovaan's pressure on a spot about twenty paces across the rock-strewn slope.

"There, see? See how I twisted the fabric? That's what we need to do if we want to hurt these people."

"I don't see how that's going to—" Jerrain began.

Sovaan released the tension with a triumphant look, which might have been appropriate if something more than a sharp pop of sound had come from his knot.

Jerrain was at least a decade older than Sovaan, half the pompous University mentor's size, and spindly. Cory had assumed he was frail as well, but the elderly mentor was surprisingly spry.

"As I was saying, I don't see how that's going to do what you want."

"It should have cracked and sundered the earth!"

Jerrain muttered something under his breath about administrators that Cory didn't quite catch, then stepped forward. "Let me try."

"You haven't practiced with the Tapestry since you retired, but by all means, have at it!"

Sovaan stomped out of Jerrain's way, the older mentor shuffling forward and raising one hand. He cocked his head, squinted one eye, and Cory felt the Tapestry twitch, tuck, fold, then release—

Twenty paces out, earth exploded upward in a fanned spume with a clap of thunder. The undergraduates yelped as rock debris rained down. Cory ducked, ears ringing, one arm raised to protect his head, while Jerrain cackled and pranced, oblivious to the hail. Behind him, dust from the explosion drifted off to the right, chunks of larger stone settling near a small pit.

Sovaan lay flat against the ground where he'd thrown himself. Jerrain halted his dancing and pointed at him. "That's how you cause an explosion, boy."

"You could have killed us!"

"But I didn't. I think that showed surprising restraint."

Cory stood and brushed himself off as the patter of pebbles from above stopped. "How did you do it? You twisted the Tapestry so fast I couldn't see."

"It's all in the twist. And you have to tie the knot *beneath* the ground, not above it. That way when you release the tension, it's fighting against something more solid than air. That's what creates the explosion."

"But I still don't know what kind of knot you formed," one of the undergraduates said carefully. Of the three, Cory thought she had the most potential.

Jerrain waved a hand in dismissal. "It's just a Cormaven cincture, with a Jervollan gnarl inside."

All three undergraduates looked confused, one mouthing, "Cormaven cincture?" to another, who shrugged.

Cory ignored them, concentrating on what Jerrain had

said. "So the gnarl is in the center and you cinch it. Then, when you release the cinch—"

"The gnarl snaps open, yes. It's trivial."

"I wonder if any gnarl will work. Or even a coil. A coil might be more controlled."

Jerrain's eyes lit up. "Let's find out!"

"Wait!" Sovaan held out a hand to halt the mentor. He'd dragged himself up off the ground. "We should find better cover before you try anything else."

"Better cover before he tries what?"

All of them turned at the new voice. Hernande and Bryce were picking their way up through the trees.

Bryce was in the lead, sword drawn, eyes scanning the clearing. "Where did that thunder come from?"

"Not thunder. A knot."

Hernande halted near Cory. "A knot caused that noise?"

"A Cormaven cincture, with a Jervollan gnarl wrapped inside it." Jerrain rubbed his hands together. "We were just about to try a coil instead of a gnarl. What do you think? Should we try a Klein or an Alexander? I think the Klein would have more oomph."

"You're not trying anything at the moment," Sovaan said sternly.

Bryce had lowered his sword. "I'd like to see this knot."

Sovaan heaved a sigh. "At least place the knot farther away this time."

Hernande and Bryce moved to stand near Jerrain, the elderly mentor talking rapidly to Hernande, who nodded occasionally as he chewed on the end of his beard. Bryce listened in, but kept quiet, his sword now sheathed.

Sovaan herded Cory and the others farther back among the trees so they could use the nearest boles as a screen. The mentor kept up a running dialogue to himself about the folly of his brethren.

Ahead, Bryce said something and pointed to the scattering of rock. Jerrain raised his hand—

And thunder clapped, dirt and stone thrown up into the air at least a hundred paces out in the direction Bryce had pointed. The Dog looked impressed, hands on hips, as Hernande and Jerrain spoke again. Cory itched to know what they were discussing.

Then Hernande turned and motioned to him. Cory trotted forward. He heard one of the other students swearing behind him.

"What do you need?"

"Jerrain is going to do his gnarl again, but I want to compare it with the Klein and Alexander coils. I'll do the Klein. You do the Alexander. We'll space them apart across the ground beneath the ledge there. See it?"

Cory tried frantically to recall the Alexander coil. He didn't have much time, since Jerrain and Hernande were already forming their knots along the base of the ledge.

Reaching out, he pulled the Tapestry taut, coiled it in what he hoped was the appropriate form, then wrapped the cincture around it. He had to concentrate to hold the tension. These forms were more complicated than the base form he'd used to punch into the bandit on the ridge. That had been desperation and instinct, more brute force than anything else. This was delicate and subtle. Not to mention that all three mentors were probably judging his technique. He didn't care what Sovaan's opinion might be, but what Hernande thought of him mattered more than anyone else except Kara.

The thought of Kara nearly made him lose his hold on the knot. He wondered where she was, what had happened to her, whether he'd ever see her again.

Hernande glanced to one side as if sensing the tremor in his hold. "Ready? Release on my mark. Three, two, one, mark."

Cory let the cincture go, felt it snap open and the coil inside release. He felt the ripples on the Tapestry from the other two knots at the same time. Ahead, the earth fountained upward in three distinct showers of dirt. The thunderclap shuddered on the air, accompanied by two smaller cracks, the three blending almost like a chord strummed on a fiddle, although far more discordant. The three plumes were different as well. Jerrain's was the most violent, rising twice as high as Hernande's. Cory's was the shortest.

Jerrain let out a whoop of delight.

Hernande stroked his beard. "The knots reacted as expected, the Alexander the weakest, the gnarl the strongest. I expected the Klein to produce a larger plume."

"The one on the left—"

"Cory's."

"Cory's then—it may have been the weakest, but it covered more area."

"Bryce is right," Jerrain said.

Hernande waved toward the ledge. "Let's see."

They climbed up the slope, to where three small craters pocked the ground. Bryce knelt down, pointed with one hand as he spoke.

"See the differences? Cory's is much wider, covers more ground. These two are only half the size. If we're going to use this against the bandits, we'll likely want the explosions to go wider, so that it can kill or maim more of the attackers. We'll want to stop them before they reach us."

Jerrain suddenly sobered. "I won't use this to kill someone."

Bryce stood. "This isn't an experiment. This isn't research. If the raiders attack, the people of the Hollow will need you to help stop them, or we'll all die. We aren't protected by stone walls, isolated so that we can read books and talk ourselves to death over theories and made-up problems. This is the real world, and you'd better start living in it."

He stalked away, across the stone slope and into the trees, Sovaan and the undergraduates stepping out of his way.

No one spoke, staring after him.

Cory shifted uncomfortably. "He's right." Both Hernande and Jerrain looked toward him. "The raiders won't hesitate to kill us. They didn't on the ridge."

"And we should stoop to their level?" Jerrain gestured toward the cratered ground. "We're scholars, not fighters."

"If I'd hesitated on the ridge, I'd be dead now."

"So you're willing to use the Tapestry to kill? Look at what we've done with some simple knots tucked into the ground. What if we put them into something living, like a tree? What if we stuck one inside one of these bandits? What do you think that would look like?"

Hernande's hand fell gently onto Cory's back. "You weren't there, Jerrain. Who knows what you would have done? Don't judge someone until you've suffered through their circumstances yourself."

"The fact remains that we aren't fighters."

Cory shrugged Hernande's hand off. "We weren't fighters, back at the University. But out here? We have to fight back."

"And you'll use your talents to do it? You'll use the Tapestry?"

"I'll be more useful using the Tapestry than a sword."

Jerrain's gaze shifted toward Hernande. "And you?"

Cory's mentor straightened. "There is a difference between killing and fighting for survival. I will fight to keep us alive."

"You are perverting the Tapestry, just as the Primes perverted the ley. Look what came of that."

Jerrain's words hit too close to the many discussions he and Kara had had about the Wielders, the ley, and the Shattering. "I don't intend to use the Tapestry to kill indiscriminately. But I won't let these raiders kill us indiscriminately either. Not when I can stop them."

"Easy words to say, young man." Jerrain waved a hand toward Sovaan and the others, still waiting at the tree line. "And what will you do with them? Will you teach them how to kill as well? They're undergraduates. They haven't even passed their final examinations yet."

"We'll have to. Cory and I can't defend everyone alone."

"Let them choose whether they want to learn or not. It's a burden they'll have to carry the rest of their lives."

Then Jerrain walked away, back toward Sovaan. He spoke to the University administrator briefly, then both turned their backs and stalked away. The three younger students watched silently, then glanced toward Hernande. Cory's mentor's motioned the three to join them.

Before they could reach them, one of the Wielders—Raven—emerged from the trees. She paused to speak to Jerrain and Sovaan, both pointing toward the stone slope where Hernande and Cory stood. She caught up to the students and passed them, coming to a halt before Hernande, breathing hard, face sheened with sweat. She was over forty, her long black hair streaked with gray that was only noticeable when she was close. Her skin tone was southern, her cheeks and eyes holding hints of the Archipelago.

As soon as she caught her breath, she waved toward the

direction of the caves. "I don't know what you did up here, but whatever it was, it collapsed a wall in the caves. There's a chamber behind it that can hold damn near everyone in the Hollow."

"You didn't need to come all the way up here to tell us that."

"That's not why I'm here. It's the stones we found inside the cavern. They're node stones. For the ley."

Hernande and Cory shared a look.

"Show us."

"We weren't certain we'd be able to house everyone here, even with the extended caves beyond the first few chambers." Raven led Cory, Hernande, and the three other students through the outer chambers and into the corridors beyond. The tunnels were narrow and shaped oddly, more like crevices than hallways. The floor was uneven, Raven picking her way carefully ahead of Cory, both hands out to either side to steady herself. Lanterns were placed at odd intervals, the light casting the corridor in strange contrasting shadows and flickering flame. They'd passed a few people in the outer chamber, sorting and stacking supplies, but they hadn't seen anyone since entering the tunnel. "Then we heard these thumping sounds, distant, like far-off thunder. The ground shook slightly, nothing more than a shiver, with some dirt falling down from overhead. We thought it was a quake and were headed back out from the farthest room when a much louder crack sounded and the ground shook worse than before. The crack was muted, but it was followed by a sudden rolling growl of collapsing stone and a puff of dust and debris from the tunnel. I thought for certain the roof had collapsed and we were trapped down here, but when we rushed forward, we found this."

She halted and pointed to the side wall. Except it wasn't a wall of stone any more. It had caved inward, stone debris cascading down from the new opening into the chamber beyond in a shallow scree. The chamber's floor lay at least twenty feet below, the ceiling the same height above, stalactites and stalagmites sticking out of both. Most were only a foot long or shorter. The chamber stretched out beyond the edge of the lantern light, but just within range Cory could see two plinths of stone that were obviously handmade.

"Stellae." Hernande stood next to Cory. The three students crowded up behind them.

"Yes. Like Oberian's Finger or those in Halliel's Park."

"Or any of a hundred others scattered across the plains." Everyone turned to face the newcomer.

"Mareane, you shouldn't sneak up on people like that, especially not down here. Where are the other Wielders?"

"They went to fetch more lanterns. Or are too afraid the tunnels are going to collapse completely."

"Useless. They do realize we're going to be living down here shortly?" Raven flicked her fingers in dismissal. "Never mind. Grab the lantern farther down the tunnel and bring it back here."

As Mareane hurried off, Cory asked, "How do you know they're stellae? We can barely see them from here."

"Because Mareane climbed down the rockfall as soon as we found the opening. She's seen them up close. I can also feel the ley. It's not that strong at the moment— probably because of the Shattering—but this used to be a significant node. Before Prime Augustus created the Nexus anyway."

Mareane returned with the lantern, handing it off to Cory as she started down the scree. "Be careful. The rockfall is still settling."

Hernande and Raven followed her, moving slowly. Cory waited until they'd made it a quarter of the way down before he started, testing each rock before putting his full weight on it. Holding the lantern made it more difficult. The stones in the fall were mostly the size of his head, with hard edges and flat faces. He was nearly halfway down when one gave out beneath him, starting a small avalanche of stone as his sharp cry of warning echoed through the cavern. He caught himself with his free hand, the one carrying the lantern held high. The light swung erratically as, below, Hernande grabbed Raven's arm and pulled her to one side. Mareane was already on the floor, scrambling out of the way as the sea of shifting rock hit the bottom and slowed, stones bouncing away from its edge.

They all reached the floor of the cavern without further incident. The light reached up to the ceiling, the far wall still too distant to make out. But the stellae in the center of the room were now clear—seven stone pillars rising up from the level floor. Mareane, Hernande, and Raven were already walking among them, Cory's mentor reaching out to touch their faces. They were all of the same shape and height: rectangular, with a slight taper toward the top. As Cory moved closer, he noted carvings in the stone, symbols that looked vaguely like archaic letters. He traced one with a finger.

"Old Amanskrit." Here in the middle of the room, Hernande's voice was muted, as if being absorbed by the shadows. "From before the Baronies claimed the plains."

"This looks more like it came from the Archipelago."

Hernande shifted closer to Raven, eyes squinting at where she indicated. He leaned back. "It's still Amanskrit, but there are definite hints of the Shattered Isles in the accents and placements of the flourishes. Many believe those from the Archipelago originated elsewhere, even though the current rulers vehemently deny it." He scanned the surrounding stellae. "These definitely predate the Baronies."

"There are paintings on the walls!"

The students rushed to Mareane's side, Cory, Hernande, and Raven following at a slower pace. Cory kicked stones out of the way, frowning down at the cavern's floor, then up at the ceiling.

"That's a bison. And that's a horned deer."

"It's called a gaezel."

"Which is a horned deer."

"What's that?"

"It looks like an elephant, but it's too big. And I don't remember the ones I saw having so much hair, or such long tusks."

"The paintings are kind of crude, don't you think?"

"That's because they're old." The students looked back as Raven joined the conversation. "But like the stellae, they're definitely made by man."

Cory had barely paid attention to the art on the wall. "The entire cavern is manmade. Look at the floor and ceiling. They're too flat to be natural. The stalactites and stalagmites aren't that old either, that's why they're so small. They must have started forming after the cavern was abandoned."

Hernande looked around at what they could see of the chamber. "It won't be abandoned much longer." He met Cory's gaze, then Raven's. "You're right, Raven. We can fit most of the Hollow in this room. We need to let Sophia and Paul know what you've found."

"What do you think is going on?"

Kara stood at the entrance to their blocked-off tunnel, the grate standing open against the wall to one side. In the cavernous junction before them, the majority of the Tunnelers were going about their usual activities—cooking, cleaning utensils, washing and repairing clothes, and taking care of the needs of the warriors and scavengers who typically left early and returned late, although it was difficult to tell whether the sun was up or not here. Cason and Ren directed the ragged groups of fighters, each group typically led by someone like Sorelle, who appeared to have been placed on permanent Hollower watch. When she wasn't out on patrol—or whatever the groups were doing when they left the cavern—she, Jaimes, Laura, and the rest of her group were camped out near the opening, someone always awake. Neither Cason nor Ren had spoken to them since they'd returned from where the Rats had wanted Kara to release the armory—not to find out about the Hollow, nor to question them about being Wielders. They'd been ignored, except by those guarding them. Jaimes and Laura brought them food and chatted with them on occasion, usually when Cason and Ren weren't around.

Today, they weren't following their usual pattern.

"Cason trained them using the same system as the Dogs. They're divided up into packs, each pack with its own alpha. She sends some packs out on patrol or as guards for the scavengers. The rest stay here for training. When the packs return, they report to Ren or directly to Cason. It's a simple system, but it worked well in Erenthrall before the Shattering, and we had more people to watch and protect."

"I wouldn't call what the Dogs did 'protecting.'"

"No, often it wasn't. That's one of the reasons I left."

Kara jutted her chin out toward the chamber. "So what are they doing now?"

"Something more significant than a patrol."

On the far side of the chamber, Cason stood on a chunk of broken stone three times her size that had fallen from the ceiling. Ren was organizing the rest of the alphas around her. Cason waited as they gathered, hand resting on the pommel of her sword. Her gaze settled on where Kara and Allan stood watching, but Kara couldn't tell what she was thinking. Eventually, she looked down at the alphas and the rest of the Tunnelers arrayed behind them. When she finally spoke, she was too distant for the words to carry, although they could see her gestures clearly.

"Can you tell what she's saying?"

"I don't read lips. But it's something about the Rats. And some other group."

"The Temerites?"

"No, I don't believe so."

"Then who? The Wolves?"

Allan gave her a steady look. "I think the Wolves have been following us."

Kara couldn't speak for a moment. "For how long?"

"Since we entered Erenthrall, or at least their territory. You thought you saw them when we were crossing the river. I've caught glimpses of them a few times since then, most recently when we were all fleeing the Rats. But they're staying in the shadows. Every time I think I see them, when I look again they're gone. It's happened too often to be a coincidence."

Kara glanced around the chamber, as if she expected to see the Wolves hiding in every corner or crevice. "Why didn't they attack?"

"Too many people around? We've been moving in groups since we arrived."

"Not with *that* many people, though. The Wolves attacked everyone who fled the University while we were trying to reach the Nexus, and there were many more in the group then."

"That was when Hagger led them. He's dead now."

"So whoever is leading them now is more cautious?"

"There's no need. They could have taken all of us out at any time before we ran into the Rats and the Tunnelers. I'd wager they could have taken us even after that."

"You have an idea why they haven't attacked, right?"

He looked at her again, then away. "I have no proof."

"But?"

He rolled his eyes. "I caught the leader's interest when I escaped them by going through the distortion. I could see it in his eyes. Maybe he hasn't attacked because he's watching us, to see what we can do, what I can do. Or maybe he's waiting because he wants to know what we're doing here in Erenthrall. He must know we haven't been living in the city since the Shattering. The Wolves are excellent trackers."

Kara considered what he'd said for a quiet moment, while Cason began pointing to specific alphas to give them their orders. She watched, but her thoughts were on the Wolves, on what their actions could mean.

"All of that makes sense, but only if they intend to take you alive. Otherwise, they could have taken you out any number of times since you returned."

"Or they haven't decided yet. If they think I'm too much of a threat, then they'll attack to kill. And don't forget, they know we have Wielders now, after what the Rats had you do. Although I don't see any reason the Wolves would need Wielders."

Kara couldn't think of any reason either.

On the floor, the Tunnelers broke into a chant that echoed oddly throughout the chamber, all of those not in one of the packs halting whatever they were doing to watch. The chant escalated, then broke into ragged cheering as the group began to stream out of the chamber into three separate tunnels, branching in three different directions. The largest group poured through the widest opening to the south.

"That's the tunnel they brought us through after we ran into them near the ley station."

Cason jumped down from her makeshift dais and spoke to Ren, the strategist nodding and trotting out after the last of the packs. Kara picked Sorelle and her pack out of the group headed into one of the smaller tunnels. It appeared nearly every one of their fighters was on the move, except those set to guard the tunnels.

At her side, Allan closed his hands into fists, knuckles popping, then purposely relaxed them, massaging one palm with the fingers of the other. His eyes were on Cason, who Kara noted was staring at them.

As if reaching a decision, she headed toward them.

Allan straightened, hands dropping to his sides. Kara heard someone approaching from behind and turned to see Glenn, Adder, and Artras taking up positions a few paces back. The others in their group weren't much farther behind. All of them were tired of being confined to the narrow tunnel, even though they'd been provided pallets, blankets, and food. Only Dylan remained at the back end of the tunnel, near the rubble of the collapsed section. After he'd been returned, his leg bound and braced, he'd remained as immobile as possible so that his knee could heal. But even he shifted onto his side and raised himself onto one elbow as Cason reached them.

"What's happening, Cason? And before you say it's none of our business, know that we're getting tired of being trapped in this tunnel. We appreciate the food and protection, but we need to get back to our people. They're waiting for us."

"We kept you here for your own safety. The Rats have been searching for you. We've been watching them for the past few days. The location of this junction has been kept secret from them since we found it and claimed it after the Shattering. The closest they've come to finding us is the ley station in Tinker. They've been focused on that station for months now, attacking it on a regular basis. But helping you retrieve your Wielders has exposed us. They know we aren't only at that station."

"What's changed? How come they didn't figure this out earlier?"

"Because we've only let them see us entering the barge tunnel system from that station. But when we rescued your group, we had to slip into the tunnels through other access points. They noticed. Whatever fear of the ley kept them from investigating the tunnels before has vanished. We were lucky in that their first few attempts to get down in the tunnels were along routes where the ley is still active and deadly. They lost a few of their people there, which made them more cautious. Some of them refused to try after that.

But they've managed to find a few other access points where the ley is either too weak or nonexistent."

"So you're going to attack them directly, before they find your true location."

"We can't kill the scouts without revealing our own access points. So we're going to try to divert them."

"Let us help." All of the Dogs with them shifted, as if anticipating the fight. "You've seen us fight. We're better than a good portion of your own men and women. We're more experienced."

Cason hesitated.

"The Wielders can help as well," Kara said. "If you get us close to the battle, trap the Rats in one of the ley line tunnels, we can channel the ley into that tunnel and burn them out. No one's at risk then."

Cason raised an eyebrow. "You could do that?"

"It's similar to what I did at the armory. Except that was desperation. I wasn't certain any of us would survive. Here, we could draw the Rats into an ambush. But we'd have to choose a place close to where the ley was active, so I could manipulate whatever is blocking it and redirect it down a different path."

Artras edged forward. "Any of the Wielders could do that, not just Kara. If they're attacking on multiple fronts, we could hit them in at least three locations."

Cason's lips pressed together in a thin line, her gaze flicking from Kara to Artras to Dylan farther back. Kara found herself unconsciously holding her breath.

But when the Dog's eyes returned to hers, she saw the answer before she spoke. "No. No to any of you helping."

"Why not?" Glenn asked in frustration. "What the Wielders are saying sounds like good strategy. And we're fellow Dogs. I recognize the training in you."

"Because I can't trust you. How do I know your Wielders won't release the ley on us?"

"That's stupid. We've done nothing but follow your lead since you found us. We haven't even tried to escape this prison!" Glenn slammed his fist into the wall of the tunnel for emphasis. "You have strong fighters here. Use them."

"No! I can see you're Dogs, and yes, I know you're strong

fighters. But what your Wielder suggests would require too much planning. We'd have to find appropriate sections of the ley lines, lure the Rats there, and then hope that she managed to release the ley in time to catch them inside. And what if she makes a mistake? What if the ley escapes her control and she floods this junction? Then we all die! She admitted that what she did at the armory was a desperate move. No, I won't risk it. We can handle the Rats without you. And when we're done with this battle, we'll escort all of you out of our tunnels. I want you all gone. And I don't want to see any of your faces again."

She spun away, marching across the chamber toward the main tunnel, where a small pack of Tunnelers had apparently been waiting for her to join them. They mounted the steps to the tunnel's mouth and vanished, the rest of the Tunnelers in view returning to their own work as soon as she was gone. Those posted as guards around the junction stared at Kara and Allan, then focused again on their tasks. The pack leader spoke to a few of his men, who surreptitiously shifted position so they were closer to the Hollowers. Not enough of them to keep Kara and the rest contained, but enough to make their point: they didn't want Allan and the others going anywhere.

"Do they think we're just going to sit here and wait for the Rats to catch us?"

"That's exactly what we're going to do." Allan faced Glenn. "You heard her. They don't want our help. And they're willing to let us go as soon as they finish with the Rats. So we're going to sit here and wait for them to return, and then we're getting the hells out of here."

They waited, Kara settling in near Dylan while the rest found small tasks to keep them occupied. Glenn paced in the back of the tunnel like an animal, his constant movement grating on Kara's nerves. Adder and Allan remained at the mouth of the tunnel, watching the activity beyond. From her position near Dylan, Kara could see the Tunneler guardsmen as they shifted positions, their body language also tense. From that alone, she knew that whatever Cason and the rest of the Tunnelers were doing wasn't the norm for this group. The guards watching the entrances to the junction were more alert, and while they kept watch on Allan and the others, their attention was focused more outward than in. Even the men, women, and children working in the junction were anxious. One of them dropped a wooden paddle used to slide bread into the back of the makeshift oven, the clap as it landed sharp and startling. At least half of those in the cavern cried out, the guards leaping up, weapons drawn. It took long moments before everyone calmed down, and even then Kara saw one woman sobbing silently into another's shoulder.

Then, from outside, in the junction, the guards barked a warning, and everyone working on the floor scrambled for cover, the men and women left behind to keep watch racing into positions around the chamber. Those who'd been stationed near the Hollowers joined them, and Allan and Adder stepped out into the room, both drawing their swords. Glenn stalked forward, motioning Tim to his side with a curt gesture. Cutter and Jack followed. Kara stood, listening intently, then moved toward Artras and Gaven, all of them standing just inside the mouth of their prison. Aaron and Carter stayed with Dylan.

"Someone's coming."

A moment later, Kara heard it as well. A faint scramble of footsteps that escalated as the group approached, echoes bouncing around the chamber. The guards snapped out a few more orders, everyone shifting their attention to one of the main tunnels, but then someone shouted from inside that tunnel's mouth and the guards in position relaxed. Three of the younger Tunnelers emerged from the opening, drawing to a halt before the guards' leader. He listened intently, then signaled to the rest to stand down.

The main force streamed into the chamber, jumping down from ledges to the floor below while others descended the ladders already in place. Family members rushed out to greet them, everyone milling around. Allan and the other Dogs and trackers relaxed, but they didn't move back into their tunnel.

Behind the first wave came another, this one moving slower, with walking wounded and others bearing makeshift litters or carrying their bloodied fellow Tunnelers in their arms. Those who'd been left behind immediately broke away from their reunions and set up a section of the floor as a hospital, the healers ordering everyone around and seeing to the wounded. The number of people clutching bloodied arms or sides, or collapsing to waiting pallets, was staggering. A few had faces covered in blood from scalp wounds. Others were vomiting off to one side as their wounds overcame them. One or two crawled onto bedrolls and then grew still before the healers could get to them.

A third wave came through the tunnel, obviously the rearguard, protecting their retreat. Cason led this group, and the entire chamber erupted into cheers as she arrived. She raised her sword above her head, her helm tucked under her other arm, but said nothing. Behind her, Ren doubled the guard on the junction's entrances, then descended with Cason to the floor.

Kara had begun to relax when she noticed that Cason was headed straight toward their prison, followed by Ren, Sorelle, and the rest of Sorelle's pack. Allan and the Dogs and trackers tensed again.

Cason halted a few paces away, her gaze sweeping them all. "Pack up everything you want to take with you. We're getting you out of here. Right now."

# Thirteen

"**C**AN WE TRUST THEM?"

Kara and the others were frantically packing up what few possessions they had in the Tunnelers' junction, which amounted to almost nothing. At Cason's brusque command, Sorelle and her pack had run off to find them satchels and some food. Jaimes and Laura had returned with a litter so they could carry Dylan. It had obviously been used to carry someone from the Tunnelers' recent fight with the Rats, with one side stained nearly black with blood. No one protested. Glenn and Adder hefted Dylan onto it, then positioned themselves at its front and back. They'd volunteered to carry him, although Kara wasn't certain who else could have done it; certainly not Gaven and Aaron, or Artras or herself—at least, not for long. Perhaps Cutter and Jack, but Allan had ordered them to take point and rear. The Tunnelers had reluctantly provided them with bows and a few arrows, and the two were testing the pull as the others finished organizing the last of their meager supplies. Cason had given them far more than they'd had when captured. It had taken no more than ten minutes to pack, and most of that had been arguing over who would carry Dylan.

Kara hefted her satchel onto one shoulder and stared at Allan expectantly.

"As I said before, we have no choice. But they could have killed us at any time over the last few days."

"Why give us food and supplies if they intended to kill us?" Artras asked. "And why give us a litter to carry Dylan?"

"It still doesn't feel right."

"Then stay alert. Cutter and Jack are front and behind. Tim and I will flank if possible, and Glenn and Adder have orders to drop Dylan and fight at the first sign of trouble. He'll be your responsibility after that."

"We'll watch over him."

Allan's attention was already focused on the activity in the junction. Most of the fighters that had returned from the confrontation with the Rats were settling back into what passed for daily routine or were working with the healers. But Cason and Ren had pulled those who'd guarded the entrances while they were gone down into a small group that included Sorelle's pack. A moment later, the group broke apart, Sorelle heading back toward them, Cason and the rest gathering up their own supplies. A few of the fighters shot Kara and the rest odd looks.

"We're ready."

"Good." Sorelle's gaze raked everyone. She noted Glenn and Adder standing at either end of Dylan's litter. "They're going to carry the Wielder?"

"He can barely walk on his own, and they're the strongest of our group. It's a long way back to the Hollow."

Sorelle's attention flicked back to Allan. "Cason is going to lead the group. We'll take you to the southern edge of our territory, through Tinker and Clay, but that's as far as we'll go."

"What happened with the Rats?"

"We beat them back, trapped a few in the tunnels while the others ran away. They won't be entering our territory for a while."

Kara thought about Fletch and Richten, the conviction in their eyes, and doubted they were as beaten as Sorelle pretended.

Someone whistled. Sorelle glanced back, then motioned them forward. "Time to go."

Glenn and Adder grabbed the handles of the litter and hefted it upward. Dylan snatched at the sides, Glenn muttering a curt apology.

They climbed out of the tunnel, Cutter and Allan first, followed by the rest of the Hollowers, with Dylan and his two handlers in the middle. Sorelle's pack surrounded them as they headed across the junction, skirting the healers and their charges. They joined Cason and the rest of the guards she'd selected for their escort. Kara counted twenty altogether, not including Cason and Sorelle's pack, and she noted Ren had stayed behind. Enough fighters to keep them under control if they tried anything, but not an overwhelming force.

Maybe Cason did intend to let them go.

They left through one of the smaller tunnels, angled southwest, narrow enough that only two people could walk side by side, Cason in the lead. Most of them split into singles, trotting along as fast as Glenn and Adder could move carrying the litter. Those in front spread out ahead, their shouts echoing back to Kara's position just behind Glenn. Someone had given Gaven and Aaron lanterns, Aaron ahead and Gaven just behind Kara. The lanterns threw odd shadows against the walls as they moved, but since the tunnel had a lower ceiling, Kara was grateful for the light. She followed Glenn with her shoulders unconsciously hunched, even though the curved ceiling was at least a foot above the top of her head.

They emerged in another much smaller junction, chose a second tunnel a level above that angled farther west. Fewer tunnels branched off this chamber. They were slowed as Adder and Glenn set the litter down, heaved Dylan up high enough that Allan and Cutter could grip him beneath the shoulders and pull him to the next tunnel, then passed up the litter. They resumed with the same formation on the far side, this tunnel wider, but now only a half a foot over Kara's head. She reached up at one point and let her hands trail across the granite that had been molded by the Wielders and Mentors into its current shape. One of the newer tunnels then, since the oldest in the city had been constructed using river stones.

The tunnel branched, the Tunnelers taking the southern

or western forks every time. At one such intersection, Kara felt the presence of the ley return as she stepped across the new tunnel's opening. It shivered through her skin, tingling with its energy. She immediately called out, "Artras!" her voice loud in the confines of the tunnel.

"I feel it."

"Feel what?" Gaven kept his voice low, so that only Kara likely heard.

"The ley. It's flowing through this tunnel. No need to worry, it isn't strong enough to harm us. But it's there, which means we've left Tinker behind. We must be beneath Clay."

The farther south and west they moved, the stronger the ley's current. The faint tingling became a prickle, until the hairs on Kara's arms began to stand on end, but before the ley reached a level where Kara knew she'd have to warn everyone, they spilled out into another junction. Except this one wasn't empty.

As she emerged, Kara's eyes were drawn first to the upper left. Part of the distortion sliced through the dome overhead, cutting out a thin but wide chunk of the ceiling before merging back into the stone wall. It glowed a vibrant blue, like the arm that had swept over Kara when the distortion formed. She could see the rest of the ceiling through the shard's face, but it looked pitted and crumbled, as if it were a thousand years older than the section of the dome outside the shard. If they healed the shard now, that entire section of the ceiling would cave in, likely bringing the rest of the dome down with it.

But the section of the distortion wasn't the only part of the junction that made it different. There were active ley lines here, strong enough that the ley flowing through them could be seen. The white paths cut through the air above, emerging from two separate tunnels a level above them, one from the northwest and the other more northerly. They merged into one line over the center of the chamber and shot off to the west, the line thicker, pulsing slightly at the merging point.

Kara realized that she and the other Wielders were staring. None of them had seen an active junction before.

She met Artras' gaze and saw the astonishment she felt mirrored in the older Wielder's eyes, along with the sudden understanding that the ley system within Erenthrall had been immensely more complicated than she'd originally thought. Not even the maps that Hernande and Cory had created had covered this. Only three of the tunnels in this junction were visibly active, but there were at least a dozen of varying sizes inactive. All of them had once carried ley lines, and they'd all merged and interacted here.

There were dozens of junctions throughout Erenthrall, if not hundreds. All active at one point, all channeling ley, all of it being directed by the Primes and the Nexus.

Kara's mouth went dry at the enormity of it. "No wonder it was so destructive when it failed."

The leading Tunnelers were already halfway across the chamber. They had lived here for months, had obviously already grown used to seeing the active ley lines.

Behind her and Gaven, Jaimes motioned toward the rest of the group. "Keep moving. But be careful. There's another ley line up ahead, near the edge of the chamber."

They began moving again, Gaven and Aaron requiring a bit of prodding.

The ley line Jaimes had mentioned wasn't hovering in midair. Instead, it flowed through a physical channel in the floor, like the ley barge lines throughout the city. The Tunnelers had used a large piece of stone debris to bridge the narrow channel. They crossed single file, then entered another larger tunnel running almost directly beneath the active ley above them. This tunnel showed signs of the quakes, the walls crazed with cracks, chunks of the ceiling the size of Kara's head littering the curved floor. They slowed because of the awkward footing, but not by much. At one point, they passed a section where the left wall had collapsed, nearly blocking their route. A short time later, the ceiling had partially fallen in, forcing them to climb up over the rockfall. Occasionally, dust and small pebbles shifted down from above, disturbed by their passage.

Then Kara noticed a subtle change in the Tunnelers guiding them. They tensed, bunched up closer to their charges, their eyes cutting left and right, even though they were still in the tunnel. Jaimes came up to walk beside Kara and Gaven.

Ahead, someone shouted. Kara could see the end of the

tunnel. As they drew closer, she realized it ended in the pit of a node, like the one in Tinker.

"Almost there."

"And where is that?"

Jaimes didn't answer.

They emerged in the pit, Kara shuddering at the familiarity of it, even though she'd never been here. The well of river stone rose around them, the stairs curving up one side toward the closed doors. Cason, Sorelle, and a few of the others were at the top of the steps, removing a thick wooden slat from the braces used to keep the heavy doors from being opened from the outside. The crude mechanism had obviously been added after the Shattering; none of the nodes Kara knew of had needed to be locked from the inside. With effort, the Tunnelers pulled the door open, the hinges grinding. Four of the Tunnelers slipped through and into the dark outer room.

Cason motioned them up from the pit. "This is where we part ways."

The clump of Hollowers headed for the stairs, Allan first, followed by the rest, Dylan hanging onto the edges of the litter as Adder and Glenn hoisted him up, both trying to keep it as level as possible. They passed Cason. Sorelle stood by her side, head bowed, eyes locked on the floor. Her body twitched, as if she wanted to say something or do something, but she held herself in check. When Kara looked behind to make certain Gaven and the others were following, Jaimes caught her gaze and muttered, "I'm sorry."

She jerked around, not certain what she expected to see. The four Tunnelers who'd entered the room before them killing Allan and the others? The Tunnelers they'd left behind waiting for them with knives drawn? But the node's main chamber was exactly as Kara had imagined it. Desks were scattered throughout the room, bookshelves against the walls, chairs set up here and there for conversations. Everything was covered with a film of dust, abandoned. One desk was tipped over, some papers and books scattered around where it had fallen, a chair on its side. Other than that, it could have been the node at Eld or Stone, absent of all of its Wielders.

Kara flexed her hands, wishing she had a knife, even

though she barely knew how to use one. She reached for the ley instead, knowing some flowed through the node below, but was surprised to find much more of it all around them. Unlike in Tinker, the ley here was abundant, at least three major lines coursing beneath them, all flowing to the west.

She drew it toward her as the group crossed the room and exited through the front doors, already open. The node looked down on a small square, the buildings that surrounded the square three or four stories high, the upper floors extending out over the walks and streets below, with the yellow plaster siding and crossed wooden slats of the eastern Temerite style of architecture. The roofs were slanted and covered in slate, with gables and narrow windows protruding from them. The square was cobbled in stone in some kind of pattern, although its details were lost in the harsh glow of the distortion off to their right. The sun was a blazing halo of orange and red to the west above the rooftops, sunset an hour or two away.

Allan, Cutter, Artras, and those carrying the litter had already descended the steps to the square. The Tunnelers had emerged from the doorway and were fanning out. Gaven and Aaron passed Kara as she turned to thank Cason, Jack and Tim behind them, but the words caught in her throat.

Cason was scanning the far edge of the square. "Where are they? They should have been here by now."

Beside her, looking troubled, Sorelle silently mouthed, "Run."

Kara jerked around. "Allan! Wait!"

The ex-Dog turned, hand falling to the handle of his sword. Adder and Glenn reacted as well, both glancing back over their shoulders, but Cutter and Jack acted the swiftest. Both trackers slid into crouches, bows up, an arrow appearing in their hands, nocked, and ready to aim in the space of a breath.

At the same time, archers appeared across the rooftops around the entire square and in the windows of the higher stories of the buildings, all of them ready to fire. Glenn swore, he and Adder dropping Dylan unceremoniously to the ground, hands going to swords. Every Dog in the group drew blades at nearly the same moment, crouching down, although there was no cover in the square at all—no debris, no abandoned carts or wagons, nothing. That should have been their first clue. Kara hadn't seen anyplace in Erenthrall without some kind of debris since they'd entered the city. They were pinned down, their only option the streets leading out of the square.

But as she scanned those, she noted that at least three of them were blocked off, probably using whatever had been cleaned out of the square. The two on either side of the node were covered by the Tunnelers. Only two other streets remained open, both on the side opposite the node. Four figures dressed in white cloaks with hoods drawn and a forked symbol embroidered in black on the chest stepped into the square from one of those streets. They were surrounded by at least ten others in guard uniforms with red shirts and black pants, all with swords drawn. The archers wore the same uniform. Another set of guards escorted a horse-drawn wagon out of the second street, but halted once they'd entered the edge of the square.

Both Cutter and Jack swung their bows toward those in the white cloaks. The Dogs faced them as well, since they couldn't do anything about the archers. Artras had pulled her knife.

"What's going on, Cason?" Allan's voice carried through the stillness of the square. "Who are these people?"

"We're called the White Cloaks," the leading figure in white said, then calmly raised a hand, two fingers extended. He gestured—

And arrows shot down from the rooftops.

Kara cried out involuntarily. Jack and Cutter both lurched, Cutter biting off a curse as he fell, his arrow releasing and slamming into the side of one of the houses. He clutched at his upper arm, a shaft protruding from the muscle there. He tried to raise the arm, but winced and settled into a lower crouch instead. Kara could see blood already soaking into his shirt.

Jack's body merely slumped, his arrow firing harmlessly into the stone of the square and skittering away. Artras, closest to him, leaped to his side and rolled him onto his back.

The elder Wielder looked toward Kara, stricken. "He's dead."

Kara had known the moment Artras rolled him over. An arrow shaft jutted from his eye.

Glenn started forward, but Adder grabbed onto the Dog's shirt, hand fisted in the cloth, and halted him before he could take two steps.

The White Cloak's arm was still raised.

"No one move." Allan lowered his sword, but didn't drop it. The rest of the Dogs followed his lead.

Behind, Cason descended the steps, four of the Tunnelers flanking her, including Sorelle. They bypassed those from the Hollow, heading toward the White Cloaks, but stopped well away from the group.

"We brought you the Wielders. Where are our supplies?"

"Which ones are the Wielders?" One of the others had spoken, not the one holding his hand up. The voice was female. Authoritative.

Cason turned. "The one on the litter, named Dylan, and Kara, the female standing closest to the node. I suspect the older woman is as well. I'm not certain about the others."

"We'll test them as soon as we return to the Needle. In the meantime . . . Iscivius?"

The man lowered his arm. "Bring out the wagons!"

On the far side of the square, the single wagon rolled to one side. Behind, four more wagons appeared, angling across the square toward where Cason and the others waited. Cason signaled, and Sorelle and the others with her trotted forward while the guards with the wagons jumped down and backed off. The Tunnelers searched the wagons, calling out to Sorelle in lowered voices. Sorelle flung the tarp covering her wagon back, then grinned. "It's all here."

Cason turned back to the White Cloaks. "Then they're all yours."

A stricken look crossed Sorelle's face, but she climbed up into the seat of the first wagon, taking up the reins. The White Cloak guards on the ground began to move toward Kara and the others, everyone tensing—

A howl cut through the square, cold and forlorn and incredibly close.

The hackles on Kara's neck prickled and her arms shivered with gooseflesh. "It can't be." As the howl began to fade, visions of Hagger's attack after the Shattering flooded her mind.

Someone screamed, the sound torn apart by a vicious growl.

Everyone twisted toward the sounds, the guards near the second street crying out then turning to flee as five Wolves tore into their rear ranks with snarls. Kara saw one of them snap its jaws on a man's throat and twist, tearing it out as it continued on, already tackling another man to the ground and seizing a flailing arm, ripping it from the man's shoulder. The others fell on the guards with the same abandon, clawing and tearing at whatever came within range. The street slicked with blood.

The nearest horse screamed, the sound raking down Kara's back, but howls broke out behind her and she spun. The Tunnelers who'd been keeping Kara and the rest from retreating back to the node were being overwhelmed. Wolves streamed out of open windows and doors on the lower levels of the buildings, leaped over the barricades at the end of the blocked streets. Everywhere she looked, men and women were falling beneath their teeth and claws.

Glenn grabbed her arm and hauled her to one side. "Get to the wagons! Stay behind them!"

She didn't understand why until an arrow snapped past her head, shattering against the stone of the square. The White Cloak archers on the roofs were firing at anything in the square that moved. Glenn pushed her from behind as they headed toward the four supply wagons in a low crouch, but the horses hitched to the wagons were already prancing, eyes rolled back in fear. Sorelle fought to control hers, but it reared, nostrils flared as it scented the Wolves, and then bolted. Sorelle was jerked back, reins lost, and fell down into the footwell. Arrows thunked into the wood where she'd sat. The horse tore across the square then veered sharply left as more Wolves appeared in its path, hounding the Tunnelers. It careened back toward the White Cloaks, who scattered as it raced through their ranks. The Wolves hadn't appeared at that corner yet. Sorelle's wagon vanished down the street, supplies spilling from its back.

"Left!" Glenn hauled Kara toward one of the remaining wagons. None of the other horses had bolted, but they were fighting the hitches. Allan and most of Kara's group were racing for cover ahead of them, Adder hauling Dylan along using only one side of the litter, the other handles scraping along the ground. He made it halfway to the nearest wagon before Dylan jounced and spilled out onto the ground, yelping as his bad leg twisted beneath him. Adder tossed the litter aside and hauled Dylan up over his shoulder like a grain sack, skittering to a halt and dumping the Wielder to the ground near a wagon wheel next to Artras and Aaron. The Dog barked an order to Artras, who leaped up and started cutting the horse's ties.

Kara reached the wagon next to Artras', ducking down as arrows spat across the air above her, Glenn at her side. Allan, Gaven, and Cutter had taken shelter at the last wagon. She didn't see Tim or Carter anywhere.

"What do we do now?"

"You do nothing. They're after you, so stay put unless you're attacked." Then Glenn took off at a crouch along the edge of the wagon.

"Wait! Where are you going?"

Glenn skirted the wagon next to them, then dodged to Allan's wagon. Kara leaned back against the wheel behind her, but it lurched as the horse thrashed side to side. Someone cried out in the footwell, and she realized the Tunneler that had taken charge of the wagon had ducked down into the space for cover. She edged up beneath where the driver sat and peered inside.

The Tunneler wasn't one she recognized.

"Give me your sword. Or your knife. Some kind of blade."

The boy hesitated.

"Now!"

Cursing, he scrambled for a knife sheathed at his waist, pulled it, held it out—

And an arrow thunked into the wood straight through the back of his hand.

He screamed, dropped the knife, and jerked his hand instinctively. The shaft of the arrow slid through the wound partway, then snapped off. He reared up, hand held before him, the arrow jutting out from one side, but two more arrows struck him in the back. His scream cut off and he slumped forward into the footwell, head hanging out the side, facing Kara.

She pulled down and back, head cracking into the sideboard. She swallowed, mouth dry, the entire square full of screams, grunts, and growls. The Tunnelers were fighting back against the Wolves, the stairs at the node a scene of turmoil. Cason had retreated to their edge, her blade swinging in wide arcs, slicing into animal flesh in a broad circle around her and two others. Most of the rest of the Tunnelers still alive were ranged up the stairs, keeping the Wolves at bay. Bodies lay everywhere, including one Wolf. Cason and the Tunnelers were slowly pulling back to the node's doors, one side already closed.

The wagon lurched again. Kara steeled herself, then reached into the footwell, fingers scrambling to find the knife the Tunneler had dropped. Another arrow thudded into the wagon seat above her and she yelled, "Target the damn Wolves!" as her fingers closed over a steel handle, too large to be a knife. She gripped the sword and yanked, but it wouldn't budge, lodged beneath the Tunneler's body. Swearing, she let it go and continued to search until she found the knife in the center of a pool of blood. She snatched it out of the footwell.

The entire cart suddenly heaved, the horse rearing, feet kicking. It landed hard enough that Kara felt the jolt through the stone at her feet, then it charged off, cracking something inside the wagon.

It left Kara exposed.

"Kara!"

She spun toward Adder's voice, noted Artras and Aaron had freed their own horse, the animal racing toward the only opening available—the corner street where the four wagons had come from. It charged through the dead bodies there, trampling a few.

"The street!" Kara pointed. "It's clear!"

Adder jerked around, then called to Allan. Aaron and Artras had moved to the far side of the wagon, closer to Glenn's position, supporting Dylan between them.

Kara had taken a step toward them when someone tackled her from the side, bearing her to the ground.

She struck the stone pavement hard, but she held on to

the knife. She struggled, kicking and stabbing, but whoever it was had wrapped their arms around her torso. Her attacker lay on top of her, crushing her. She couldn't breathe.

"You," the person ground out through clenched teeth, "aren't going anywhere."

She recognized the folds of scuffed white cloth of the man's cloak—

And then the square erupted in a surge of white ley light.

"What do we do now?"

Allan turned at the question, Glenn hunkered down beside him in the lee of the wagon. Gaven and Cutter were huddled at the front wheel, Cutter's arm hanging limply, its entire length sheathed in blood. The tracker's face was pale.

Allan glanced toward the other two wagons: Artras and Aaron working to free their horse, Kara sliding toward the footwell. "We get Kara and the other Wielders out of here."

"And how do we do that?"

Artras suddenly stumbled backward, Aaron catching her, as their horse charged away.

"We steal a wagon." Allan motioned toward the first wagon that had showed up in the square, still off to one side. The Wolves had ripped through the White Cloak guards that had escorted it, so it sat by itself, unattended, its horse's sides lathered in fear sweat, its legs trembling. But it hadn't bolted yet.

From behind, Adder shouted, "Kara says the street in the corner is clear!"

Allan and Glenn both turned, then edged up to the end of the wagon and peered around it.

"She's right." Glenn patted the wagon they were hiding next to. "Why not take this one?"

"It's full of supplies. That one's empty. We need room to hold Cutter and Dylan."

"Go for the reins. I'll protect Gaven and Cutter."

Allan didn't wait, sheathing his sword and charging the short distance between their refuge and the other wagon. Arrows cracked into the stone near his feet, but he ignored them, skimming around the back of the wagon to the side nearest the buildings. Protected on two sides now, he worked his way to the front of the wagon, the horse snorting and growing more agitated as he neared it. He tried to calm it with words as he scrambled into the footwell, hunched down, and snatched the reins up in one hand.

The wagon lurched, and he twisted to see Gaven helping Cutter climb into the back, Glenn behind them with sword drawn.

"Glenn, get the others! Did anyone see what happened to Tim or Carter?"

"I saw Tim grab Carter and head toward the node's stairs." Gaven practically threw Cutter up into the empty bed of the wagon. Cutter groaned in agony as he landed, rolling to one side. Gaven climbed in after him.

Allan spun toward the node, caught sight of Tim and Carter hunched down in a niche at the steps' base.

And then the square erupted in white ley light. Gouts of it poured directly out of the stone across its length, fountaining up just as Allan had seen it do during his time as a Dog at the sowing of the Flyers' Tower. He flinched back from it, arm raised protectively, remembering how it had killed some of the lords and ladies who'd been stupid enough to be out on exposed balconies. But this ley light wasn't nearly as turbulent or active as that had been, rising only twice the height of a man. It was enough to spook the horse, though, which lurched forward against the wagon's brake. Allan pulled the reins, trying to calm it, as the surges of ley continued. Out of the corner of his eye, he saw the White Cloaks standing to one side of the plaza, arms raised, and realized they were Wielders. But then the horse reared and jerked forward. The brake released with a groan, and suddenly the wagon was shuddering forward.

He hauled back on the reins again, but the animal ignored him, cutting sharply left as a wall of ley light spurted up in front of it. Allan slid to the edge of the seat, catching himself with one hand, heard Gaven and Cutter being thrown around the bed, and then the entire wagon jumped as it ran over the bodies scattered over the square. Allan gave up on the reins and clung to the seat as the horse continued to turn. The node's stairs swung into view, and Tim, lurching up as if to try for the wagon, but the burning ley light separated them. Carter dragged him back down into hiding. Then they were rounding back toward the other wagons. Kara was struggling with one of the White Cloaks on the ground, also separated by a wall of ley. She slashed the White Cloak across the face with her knife, blood splattering his cloak, and then he snatched her wrist and drove it into the ground until the blade tumbled from her grip. Beyond her, the others cowered against their wagon, Adder standing over Dylan with Aaron at his side, Glenn at the end of the last wagon holding tight to Artras' arm.

Glenn's intent hit Allan a second before the horse finished the turn and shot straight for the open street beyond.

At the same time, to the far left, the Wolves broke through the White Cloak guards' resistance. Three of the Wolves charged Allan's wagon from that side.

Beyond them, behind the roil of guards and Wolves, Allan saw the pack's leader, standing in the middle of the street, watching. Except he wasn't focused on where his Wolves were ripping the guards to shreds, nor where the White Cloaks were controlling the ley.

His attention was fixed on Allan.

"Watch out for the Wolves!" Allan pointed as the wagon rocketed past Glenn and Artras and the others. Glenn shoved Artras before him, but she was already running, Glenn on her heels. They fell in behind the wagon, Allan reaching for the reins and pulling back on them hard to slow the horse. He glanced over his shoulder, saw Artras snatching at the bed of the wagon with one hand, almost there. The Wolves leaped over a wall of ley, one getting caught. It yelped as it tumbled to one side, part of its leg and haunch missing where it had been touched, but the others left it behind, snarling after Glenn and Artras, teeth snapping at the air.

Artras put on a burst of speed and vaulted onto the back of the bed, almost slipping off before Glenn shoved her hard, rolling her forward into Cutter and Gaven. They grabbed her and hauled her deeper into the bed as Glenn scrambled to follow. He jumped, caught hold of one side, feet dragging behind him, then hauled himself up, the cords sticking out in his neck at the effort.

He'd barely managed to collapse to the bed when Artras yelled, "Look out!"

Allan shifted in time to see the two Wolves leap. The first landed on top of Glenn, who'd rolled onto his back at the warning and raised one arm in defense. The Wolf's jaw snapped shut on his forearm and shook, Glenn roaring in pain. The second Wolf scrabbled for a hold, claws digging gouges in the bed of the wagon, but lost its footing and tumbled out of the back of the wagon to the road.

Allan faced forward, reins still held uselessly in one hand, then dropped them, turning to leap over the seat to help Glenn. But Artras had already crawled forward, over Cutter's body. With Glenn struggling beneath the Wolf, she drew her dagger back and sank it into the beast's shoulder—once, twice, then again, farther down its side, as it released Glenn and snapped at her. Glenn had managed to draw his own knife and stabbed the Wolf. It snarled and thrashed, blood pouring from the wounds, and collapsed to one side.

Glenn and Artras sank back, both breathing heavily, Glenn holding his arm close to his chest. Gaven and Cutter huddled against one corner of the wagon behind them. The Wolf lay stretched out on the other side, its odd-shaped limbs limp, blood matting its fur. Allan settled back into the wagon's driver's seat and noted that the horse had slowed, whether exhausted or simply calmed, he didn't care.

Behind them, far down the street, they could see the white ley light glowing in the square, and beyond that, the multicolored shards of the distortion.

Kara's knife sliced across Iscivius' face, but the White Cloak snatched at her hand. Blood dripped down and pattered against her cheek as he slammed the fingers clutching the blade into the stone of the square. She gripped the hilt tighter, but on the fourth attempt pain tingled up her arm and her fingers went numb. The knife clattered to the ground.

Kara reached for the ley, but it was riled up all around her, the other four White Cloaks keeping it in turmoil. She felt their presences working the ley, calling it upward. They were trying to hit the Wolves, but it couldn't be controlled that precisely, not with moving targets that were weaving in and out among their own men, and not without the aid of the mentors from the University.

Wielders were trained to smooth out disruptions in the ley, not cause them.

She reached for it nonetheless, intending to wield it against Iscivius and the other White Cloaks. But Iscivius slammed her wrist into the ground once more, the pain stabbing into her shoulder like a dagger. He had both her arms now, straddling her. His hood had been knocked askew and she could see a neatly trimmed beard, marred by the shallow cut she'd given him, and half-shadowed eyes.

"Stop it! Stop or the rest of your group will be burned from this earth!"

She fought a moment more, then relented. "Let us go. We only want to leave Erenthrall."

"We can't. We need you."

"Iscivius!"

Kara recognized the White Cloak woman's voice from before.

"I have her!" He glanced toward the remaining wagons. "And some of the others. At least four of them escaped. One of them was the suspected Wielder."

The woman cursed. "We're contained. Cason and her group have retreated into the node and sealed the doors."

"What about the Wolves?"

"They're trapped behind the ley for now. Our enforcers have pushed them back."

Iscivius' grip on her wrists had slackened, enough that Kara's hand now tingled as the blood returned. It still throbbed from being struck into the stone.

Iscivius gazed down at her. "Are you going to cause any more trouble?"

"Yes."

"At least you're truthful."

He released her suddenly, rolling to one side. He picked up Kara's knife before she had a chance to react. "Don't try anything. You and those still here are surrounded by ley."

Kara sat up, wiping at her sweaty face. Her fingers came away smeared with blood. Her wrist throbbed and multiple parts of her body felt bruised.

But Iscivius was right. She and those of her group still in

the square were surrounded by a wall of ley boiling up from the flagstone. Adder, Aaron, and Dylan were still at the side of one of the wagons, twenty paces away. Tim and Carter were at the base of the stairs leading up to the node. The White Cloaks and their original escort of guards held the far corner of the square, but closer in, so that the ley shielded them. The only others within the wall were a group of twenty guards in the opposite corner, standing ready, facing the street beyond, where at least ten Wolves paced back and forth, snarling and snapping at the ley but keeping a respectful distance. Upright in the middle of them stood another man, although Kara realized he wasn't completely human. He'd been transformed by the auroral lights, like Hagger after the Shattering—half wolf, half human. Unlike Hagger, his transformation appeared to be closer to human. He wore a tan jacket with gold buttons and black embroidery, like what a lord would wear.

As she watched, the pack's leader snarled an order, literally, the command more growl than words. A few of the Wolves backed off immediately, only turning to lope off into the distortion-lit dusk when they were over twenty paces distant. More stayed behind, their growls increasing in intensity, the ruff on the back of their necks raised, lips drawn back from wicked teeth. The pack leader spoke again, his tone harsher, and they pulled back as well, but not without a bout of plaintive howls echoing up into the descending night.

The pack leader gazed at them all, eyes fixed on the White Cloaks in unabashed hatred before falling to meet Kara's gaze. He held it a long moment, long enough that Kara felt oddly disconcerted, and then he turned and stalked off after his pack.

Kara exhaled, unaware she'd been holding her breath. Her gaze strayed to the bodies that littered the square. Some of the Tunneler dead had been left behind on the steps of the node, two Wolves mixed in with them. More of the White Cloak guards lay scattered in the corner streets to Kara's left. They'd taken the brunt of the attack. Kara counted at least twenty dead, and she knew some of the bodies must have been consumed by the ley. But they'd killed more of the Wolves—at least five. One of them was whimpering and struggling to rise, part of its leg and haunch burned away. The red-shirted guards that had kept watch while the Wolves were still present turned to rejoin the White Cloaks, two of them using their swords to kill the wounded Wolf on their way back.

Except they didn't rejoin the White Cloaks. They surrounded Adder and the others at the wagon, a smaller group heading toward Tim and Carter.

Adder looked toward Kara, eyebrows raised, sword tipped slightly up in a ready position, but Kara shook her head. There was no reason to fight, not when they were hemmed in by the ley with no chance of escape.

Adder lowered his blade. The guards disarmed him. They searched the rest, taking away swords and knives and anything else that could be used as a weapon.

The other White Cloaks arrived.

"Why didn't you use the ley to kill them all?" It took Kara a moment to realize Iscivius meant kill the Wolves, not those from the Hollow.

"We were barely controlling the ley as it was. If we'd tried to burn them all out once we had the square under control, we may have lost control completely and killed everyone. Father wouldn't be happy with that now, would he?"

"No." Iscivius had been staring at Kara, thoughtful, but now he turned toward the wagons. "Send out some guards to see if they can round up the missing horse. We aren't leaving any of these supplies behind."

"What about our deal with Cason?"

"They must have led the Wolves to us. I feel no urge to compensate them for that. Besides, they made off with at least one wagon, while half of this group they'd captured managed to escape. I consider that fair enough trade. We'll take these three wagons back with us, if possible. Begin loading in the Wielder that's wounded. Transfer supplies to another wagon if necessary."

They scrambled, three small groups heading out into the southern streets once the other three White Cloaks killed the gouts of ley protecting them in that direction. The rest either watched to make certain the Hollowers didn't escape or began to shift supplies around to make room for Dylan.

Kara watched silently, then climbed to her feet, brushing

grit and dust from her hands. The blood on her skin had dried and now prickled unpleasantly, but the tingling in her wrist had faded. Tim and Carter were herded toward her, followed by Adder and Aaron. Someone had retrieved Dylan's litter where it had fallen and the guards hoisted him back onto it. The horse had obviously not run far, because the guards were already returning with it. The others had calmed and the guards were checking hitches, bridles, and traces.

As soon as the others joined her, Kara asked, "What are you going to do with us?"

Iscivius turned to face her again. "We're going to take you all to the Needle."

"What's the Needle?"

"You'll see."

"Why are you taking us there?"

"Because Father needs you."

"What for?"

"He'll have to explain. It would be meaningless coming from me."

Kara fisted her hands in frustration. "Who is this Father? Who are you?"

One hand rose to touch the symbol stitched in black on Iscivius' chest—a single vertical line with a second lancing down at an angle to join the first. It was splattered with dried blood from where Kara had cut him, but he didn't seem to notice. He hadn't even tended to the wound; it had stopped bleeding on its own.

"We're the Kormanley."

# PART II

## The Needle

# *Fourteen*

"**D**AMN, DAMN, DAMN," Artras muttered, frantically ripping another band of cloth from the bottom of her shirt and wrapping it around Cutter's upper arm. She'd already yanked the end of the arrow out, but the wound was deep and continued to bleed.

She wound the makeshift bandage tight, then tied it off as the wagon jounced over more debris. She knew Allan couldn't slow, not until they were safely away from the White Cloaks and Wolves in the square, even with night falling. She didn't think the Tunnelers were an issue any longer.

Something hard worked its way up from her chest into her throat and she paused to glance out the back of the wagon, down the street to where the distortion rose above the buildings, all of it receding. Glenn held on at the back of the wagon on the right, his mangled arm tucked close to his chest, Gaven beside him, allowing Artras and Cutter the more protected space at the front nearest Allan. The body of the Wolf still filled the left side. They hadn't had a chance to dispose of it yet.

But her thoughts were of Kara and the others, caught by the White Cloaks. Tears pricked the corners of her eyes as she thought of Jack, his body left behind. She wondered if any of the others had been killed. Jack's death had been merciless. She doubted the White Cloaks would treat the others any differently.

She shook herself and focused on Cutter, examining the bandage. Her shoulders relaxed when she realized it hadn't been soaked through with blood yet.

"How bad is it?"

"It's hard to tell. I haven't had a chance to really look, but the bleeding appears to have slowed."

Cutter had barely flinched when she'd jerked the arrow free, and had suffered stoically as she'd cinched the bandages as tight as possible. "It's not good. I can feel it. I can barely move my arm. The muscle is damaged enough I don't think I'll be drawing a bow any time soon."

Artras placed a hand on his shoulder, forced him to meet her eyes. "It's too soon to tell."

He held her gaze a long moment, lips pressed thin, but nodded.

"Is anyone following us?" Allan couldn't even spare a glance over his shoulder. "I need to slow down. There's too much stone and debris in the road."

The wagon jolted again, throwing Artras back against the wagon's side, then began to judder, as if it were rolling over a washboard. Gaven steadied her.

"I think we're safe for now."

A moment later, the breakneck pace of the wagon slowed, the clattering of the wheels eased. The ride was still rough, but manageable. Artras pulled herself upright and glanced around.

The style of the surrounding buildings had changed. This district had suffered worse than the Temerite-inspired one surrounding the square. Many of the larger buildings had collapsed inward on themselves and were now nothing more than heaps of rubble, glass, and wooden supports. The cobbles in the road had been shaken loose by the quakes. Sections of walls had fallen out into the street, partially blocking their path, but not all of the buildings had been destroyed. Every now and then one rose from the debris, sometimes with only a wall or small section fallen in, the interior rooms exposed, sometimes standing untouched and forlorn, with only broken windows or a few cracks in the facade. Most had been built with mudbrick, not forged by the Wielders and mentors of the University.

"Gaven, keep watch." Glenn switched places with the Hollower, then worked his way up to the front of the wagon.

"Someone needs to see to your arm." Artras pointed to where blood matted his forearm, the shirtsleeve shredded and stuck to the wound.

"Later. We don't have time now."

She'd known that's what he'd say. Artras shifted out of his way, ending up next to the Wolf's head. Its tongue lolled out of the muzzle, wet and glistening, and black blood matted its fur near the wounds in its shoulders and side. The wagon bed was stained with it, a stream running down its slope, dripping from the back.

Artras' brows drew together in consternation. A moment later, she shifted forward and placed her hands on the Wolf's side.

"We need to find a place to hide," Glenn said to Allan. "We can't outrun those White Cloaks or the Wolves if they decide to come after us."

"We can't hide from the Wolves at all. Not for long. They'll find us because they're hunters. They'll sniff us out."

"So we just keep running? Leave Kara and the others to the White Cloaks?"

"Of course not!"

"We have to stop," Artras shouted over both of them.

They both turned toward her.

"Cutter's wounded. We have to stop long enough for me to properly dress the wound or Cutter's going to die. Not to mention Glenn's arm. It needs to be seen to. I've noticed how you're holding it." Artras hesitated, then straightened. "And we have another problem. The Wolf isn't dead."

Both of them started, then shifted their attention to the Wolf. Artras' hand was still resting on its chest, which rose and fell in long, labored breaths. The fur was warm beneath her touch.

Glenn pushed away from the headboard and reached into the side of his boot, pulling out a long knife. "That's easy enough to fix." He sank to his knees beside Artras, reaching for the Wolf's throat, but Artras caught his forearm.

Glenn tensed. "Let go."

"No. It's one thing to kill them when they're attacking, another when they're unconscious and defenseless."

"They're animals. It would kill us in an instant if it woke up!"

"You forget. They weren't always animals. It used to be human. Maybe it—maybe *he* still is, somewhere inside, beneath the pelt and teeth."

Glenn hesitated, then hardened, twisting toward Allan.

The ex-Dog shrugged.

Glenn jerked out of Artras' grip. "If it so much as twitches before we get a chance to tie it up, it's dead."

Artras' eyes narrowed.

Allan slowed the wagon to a halt. "Glenn, Gaven, see if you can find a place for us to hole up."

Both of them hopped out of the wagon and split, each heading to a different side of the street to search the buildings. Artras watched Glenn, concerned about his arm, but she didn't see any other option. Cutter couldn't help, not in his condition, and Artras knew nothing about scouting.

"How much time do you think we have?" She turned to frown down at the Wolf.

"The White Cloaks won't wait long once they break away from the Wolves."

"Maybe the Wolves will take them down."

"The White Cloaks were already regaining control when we careened out of there. The ley had the Wolves pinned down and their guards were rallying."

Artras reached up and caught his arm in hope. "Then maybe Kara and the others are alive."

Allan squeezed her hand in reassurance. "The last I saw of Kara, she was still fighting."

"We need her, Allan. She's the strongest among us Wielders. If we have any hope of repairing the damage that's been done to Erenthrall, starting anew, she's the one that will do it."

"Then we're in trouble."

"Why? You just said the White Cloaks would survive the fight with the Wolves, and they're the ones that have Kara."

"Did you notice the symbol they had stitched onto their

cloaks? The two black lines? I've seen it before. It stands for convergence, or a return to the natural order. It was used by the Kormanley before the Shattering."

"The Kormanley? But how?"

Allan released her hand and climbed down from the seat into the back of the wagon. "We survived the Shattering, why not them?"

He moved to check on Cutter, inspecting the bandages on the tracker's arm, then shifting his attention to the Wolf, wincing at the raw, open wounds and the trail of blood running down the back of the wagon. "Glenn's right. We should kill it."

"It's still human. *He's* still human. Look at their pack leader. The auroral lights changed them, but they still follow a mostly human alpha. And don't forget Devitt, back in the Hollow. The lights caught and changed him, and he's still human."

"Devitt was barely touched by the aurora. And you shouldn't forget Hagger. He was one of their pack leaders at one point."

"From what you told us, Hagger was always a monster."

"True. But I still don't understand why you stopped Glenn." He motioned to the Wolf. "It will kill us all the moment it comes to."

Artras reached out and ran her hands over the Wolf's back, where the fur wasn't soaked with blood. "Can't you see it? There's humanity still in him. Here along the lines of the torso, and especially in the legs. Even in the creature's face. It was a man once. It *is* a man now, trapped in an animal's body."

"Are you certain? At what point do those lights change the person completely? What if those are simply vestiges of his humanity, and there's nothing but animal left inside? Can we take that risk?"

Artras crossed her arms over her chest, stubborn but troubled.

"Maybe we can use him somehow," Cutter said, his words strained, edged with pain.

"How?"

Cutter shifted position so his injured arm rested more comfortably against his side. "I don't know. We both know the Wolves have been following us, but they haven't attacked until now. Why?"

"I spoke to Kara about it. Their pack leader saw me enter the distortion. Afterward, he seemed far too interested in me. Not as prey, as something else. When they started following us after we reached Erenthrall, I assumed it was because of me, so he could see what I could do."

"That doesn't make sense. He may have been watching you, but he could have taken you alone numerous times—when you went in search of provisions, or while you were watching the Rats."

"What are you saying?"

"The Wolves must be interested in more than just you."

"The only other people they could be interested in are the Wielders, but I don't see why. Kara couldn't come up with a reason either."

"That doesn't mean they don't have one." Artras considered for a moment. "They may have wanted to see what you and the rest of us could do, but waited too long. Then the Rats and Tunnelers had us, a group too large for them to attack with any success."

"There were as many White Cloaks, guards, and Tunnelers in the square just now as there were when we attacked the Rats to save the others. And the Wolves were there then. I saw them as we fled."

"Then there must be something else, some difference between that time and now."

Allan and Cutter glanced at each other. "The White Cloaks."

"They must not have wanted us handed over to the White Cloaks. But why?"

Artras stared down at the Wolf. "Maybe we can find out from him."

"If we're going to keep him alive, we need to stanch his wounds or he'll bleed out. And even the White Cloaks can follow a trail of blood. He needs to be trussed up so if he does wake, he can't attack us." Allan turned to Artras. "He's your problem for now."

Artras noted Allan was now calling the Wolf "he" rather than "it." She began tearing another strip from the bottom of her shirt, but Cutter reached out and stopped her. "Use mine. You won't have anything left but your undershirt shortly."

She worked on binding the Wolf's wounds, moving carefully, drawing back any time the Wolf appeared to twitch or struggle. But he was out cold from blood loss, any movement more Artras' imagination than anything real. Her hands were sticky with blood by the time she was finished, her arms coated. She couldn't tell how much the creature had lost, but knew it was significant.

"Whether we keep him or kill him is probably moot. He'll likely be dead before dawn."

Allan dropped a bundle of leather straps over the side of the wagon, startling her. "This was all I could find for rope. Make certain he can't get free. Gaven found a place in a building a block or so up the street. Let's get both of you settled in there and then we'll see if we can find out what happened to Kara and the others."

Allan moved to the front of the wagon, and a moment later it lurched into motion, much slower than before. Artras reached for the straps and realized they were the reins from the horse's bridle. They'd be stronger than rope, and more durable.

She trussed the Wolf's front legs together, then the back, cinching them tight to restrict his movement. Then she bound his muzzle.

"Efficient. You've done that before."

"Not on a Wolf. But I worked in the slaughterhouses of Butcher's Block before the Wielders found me."

"So you didn't save him because you're averse to killing animals."

"Not killing animals, no. Nor people. I can kill when necessary. I've done it before."

Cutter's eyes widened at her blunt tone, which didn't invite further questions.

"Can you walk?" Allan had leaned over the wagon's side again.

Cutter looked up. "I can walk."

"Then come on, both of you. Gaven's getting us set up in a room on the third floor."

Artras hopped down out of the back of the wagon, then helped Cutter down. Allan had pulled the wagon as close to a half-collapsed building as he could. A quarter of the left facade had crumbled, revealing the shadowed room within, but the rest of it appeared intact, only the windows broken. Both buildings on either side had fallen down, the mud-brick on the left scorched, as if part of it had caught fire. Trails of soot blackened the side of their refuge, creating an eerie mural of char and ash.

As they began picking their way over the rubble covering the street and the front steps leading up to the door, Allan returned to the cart, crying out in triumph a moment later.

Both Artras and Cutter halted, turning back. "What?"

Allan held up a satchel, then slung it over a shoulder, reached into a compartment he'd found under the seat bench, and pulled out a small trunk. "I don't know what's in it, but let's hope that it contains some food and water."

"I'm getting tired of being chased, getting captured, and going hungry." Artras tugged Cutter toward the building.

The door creaked as they stepped into the interior. Like most of Erenthrall, it was covered with a thick layer of grit, but most of the furniture remained where it had been abandoned. Artras and Cutter ascended the stairs, dust and silt sifting down from above as the steps shifted. Cutter was sweating with effort by the time they made it to the third floor, Allan urging them toward one of the front rooms.

Gaven looked up as they entered, pointing to a rough space already cleared for them in the corner farthest from the windows overlooking the street. Artras settled Cutter against one wall and wiped the sweat from his face with her sleeve, frowning at how pale he appeared. But she said nothing.

Allan set the trunk down with a thunk in the center of the room and flipped it open. He scanned the contents, pulling out a wicked-looking hunting knife. He opened the satchel as well, then tossed it to Gaven as he stood. "See what else is useful here. I'm going to move the wagon."

"Where's Glenn?" Artras asked.

"Scouting the area around this building and the far side of the street."

She moved toward Gaven. "Anything for Cutter? Bandages? Salve? Medicine?"

Gaven pulled out a rolled length of white cloth, then a small leather pouch. It held needles and thread for stitches. "There are a bunch of small vials and paper pouches as well."

"Let me see."

He handed a few of them over and Artras squinted at the writing on the pouches, hard to read in the dim light. "Feverfew, for headaches. Rosemary—not sure what that's for."

"If we had some hare or pheasant . . ."

"Yarrow!"

"What's that good for?" At Artras' disapproving look, Gaven shrugged. "Logan handles the healing in the Hollow. I take care of the hogs."

"Yarrow helps wounds clot and cleans them as well. And this valerian root should help with the pain."

"What about the vials?"

"I don't know what's in them. They aren't labeled." She worked the small cork out of the top of one with a brown tint to it and sniffed, wrinkling her nose. "It smells like some kind of tea."

Gaven had begun rummaging through the trunk. "The satchel is obviously a medicinal kit. And this looks like it's full of everyday things, like flint, a small lantern." He set these on the floor next to him, then pulled out an urn the size of his hand. He broke the wax on the stopper and sniffed, mimicking Artras. "Oil for the lantern."

"Any water? Food?"

"Nothing."

"We'll have to make do." She moved back to Cutter, checking the torn scraps of cloth she'd used earlier. They were soaked through with blood. She gently began removing them, Cutter cringing as she tugged the cloth away from the wound, then began applying what she could of the herbs. She could have used some water to flush the dried blood away, but there was obviously nothing in the apartment that could help.

She began to bind Cutter's arm again with the new bandages, fretting about infection as she wound the cloth around the hole in his arm. But her thoughts drifted to the square. The Wolves, the sudden surge of ley prickling along her skin, Kara being attacked, and the White Cloaks. Or rather, the Kormanley.

Cutter hissed, his free hand clamping down on Artras, halting her. "It's a little tight."

Artras stared at him, uncomprehending, then realized he meant the bandage. "Sorry." Cutter released her hand and she carefully loosened it. Her fingers were shaking and tears burned at the corners of her eyes. She fought them back but knew her cheeks were flushed with the effort, her lips pressed tight to keep them from trembling.

Cutter placed his hand over hers again, and she glanced back up. "She'll be fine. They all will."

She didn't trust her voice. To distract herself, she continued unrolling the bandage, but she could no longer see what she was doing; she was shaking too hard. "I don't know what's wrong."

Cutter squeezed her hand. "It's all right. It's a delayed reaction from the attack in the square. Gaven, take her. I can finish the bandage."

Gaven drew her up and held her as her last wall gave out. She pressed herself into him as she sobbed, seeking the support as a wave of weakness coursed through her from head to toe. The choked sobs lasted for no more than a few minutes, but they left her drained and hollow. As they faded—her breathing returning to normal, her face aching as if bruised—she pulled back from the Hollower, gripping his shoulders. "Thank you."

"It's nothing. Just . . ."

"What?"

"You're usually so tense and in control. Nothing ever appears to affect you. This is a little unexpected."

Artras' eyes narrowed. "I've seen blood before. Plenty of it. And not just in the slaughterhouses."

"Of course, of course. I didn't think the blood set you off at all."

She turned to look at Cutter, who shrugged and finished tying off his bandage with one hand, his teeth holding the cloth taut. He spat it out. "Don't look at me. I've seen the hardiest men cry over the death of a calf at birth."

"It wasn't the blood."

Neither man said anything, simply stared at her.

She huffed and retrieved the healer's bag, then scrounged until she found a pair of scissors. She knelt at Cutter's side, trimming the bandage and rolling up what remained again, thrusting it into the sack with everything else she'd removed. Her movements were clipped. Then she stalked to one of the windows overlooking the street below and drew in a deep breath, letting it out with a shuddering sigh.

"It wasn't the blood." Except that, in a sense, it was. That and Allan mentioning the Kormanley. She crossed her arms over her chest, watching the street, but saw another square in her mind's eye, hearing the screams. "I was there in Pickett's Garden during the Purge, when the Dogs arrived and began killing everyone, claiming the Kormanley were there. They were targeting anyone who moved, overturning carts, setting tents on fire with the owners and their patrons huddled inside in fear. I saw them slaughter children as they tried to flee, stabbing them in the back."

In a shard of glass that remained in the window, she saw Gaven and Cutter exchange a confused glance. Then she remembered: they were both from the Hollow. They hadn't been in the city during the Purge, didn't know of the bloodbath that was Pickett's Garden, or any of the other hundred atrocities the citizens had suffered through then. Only those who had been in the city at that time would remember, would understand.

She straightened her shoulders, stiffened her back. "They killed hundreds, and carted off a dozen or more to the Amber Tower, saying they were Kormanley. And perhaps some of them were. I survived Pickett's Garden because, as I tried to flee, one of the carts landed on top of me, pinning my legs and covering me with bolts of silk. I was a Wielder, but I knew that wouldn't protect me from the Dogs. So I pretended to be dead. And all of it happened because of the Kormanley." On the street below, her attention fixed on a figure—Glenn—dodging between the debris, running hard toward their building.

"And now they're back," she finished under her breath.

Someone came pounding up the stairs outside and burst into the room. Cutter jerked up into a seated position, and Gaven stepped back toward Artras as if to protect her.

"They're coming." Allan ran across the room toward the

window next to Artras'. "Everyone, get back from the windows and stay down."

Gaven grabbed the trunk and pulled back to Cutter's position as Glenn charged up the stairs below and entered the room. As soon as he saw all of them were there, he halted, then crept across the room to join Artras.

"Where's the wagon?"

"Around back. The Wolf is tied and gagged, still unconscious. Which way are they coming from?"

"The main street we came down. They're moving slow. It looks like they have the wagons from the square."

"What about Kara and the others?"

"I couldn't see. They're too far away. But they should pass beneath us."

Everyone fell silent, waiting. The world collapsed down to Artras' breath and the steady beat of her heart thudding in her ears.

She jerked when the first of the White Cloak guards appeared—three scouts, sprinting out ahead of the main force. They crawled over the debris, arrows nocked, searching the surrounding heaps of stone and still-standing buildings for any sign of movement. Artras drew back from the window slightly, hands dropping to her sides, her palms itching for the feel of a knife or dagger. But she'd left it next to Cutter, had set it aside while she worked on his wound.

Outside, the scouts moved on past their building, followed by a larger group of twenty guards and a few of the White Cloaks. They moved slowly, allowing the wagons behind them time to pick their way through the rubble, some of them carrying torches. Artras leaned forward so she could scan the beds of the wagons, drawing a sharp breath of relief when she saw Dylan lying flat in one, surrounded by stacked supplies, one of the White Cloaks and another guard seated with him. Kara and the others trudged behind the wagon, penned in by another set of guards and the wagon behind them. The third wagon, the rest of the guards, and the last two White Cloaks brought up the rear.

It took more than twenty minutes for the entire group to drift past. Even after the last of the guards faded from view, Artras remained hidden behind the edge of the window, afraid there might be scouts keeping watch. But eventually

Glenn stirred, motioning toward Allan. They pulled back from the windows toward Cutter and Gaven, crouching down. Artras joined them, after a swift glance outside to see the White Cloaks' wagons nothing but a vague shimmer of torchlight in the distance.

"Are they alive?" Gaven asked Glenn.

"They're alive. All of them. I'm not certain why."

"What do you mean?"

"Keeping prisoners is difficult. Moving prisoners is worse. I'd have killed those I didn't need and left the bodies behind."

Artras' eyes narrowed. "You truly were a Dog."

"It's practical."

"And it also answers your question." Allan tapped his knuckles against the floor in thought. "They don't know which ones in the group are Wielders, aside from Kara and Dylan. You heard them talking about testing them once they reached the Needle. Any idea how they'll do that, Artras?"

"They must have a Prime."

"Why?"

"Everyone is tested in school when they reach the age of fourteen by a Prime. He or she simply touches your head. If a child has talent, he knows. I'm not sure how."

"I wasn't raised in the city," Allan said, "but I've heard of the testing."

Cutter lifted his injured arm. "Obviously, they decided that those of us with bows weren't Wielders."

"They probably made the same assumption about everyone with weapons. Kara and Carter carried at most a knife, not even a dagger. I don't know about Dylan."

"He had a knife, but nothing like what I usually carry." Artras gestured toward the hilt of her own dagger.

"Why do you carry that? It's not something I would expect."

"I grew up in East End and Shadow. No one goes around without a weapon of some kind there. Not if you want to survive."

Allan waved a hand to bring them back on track. "All that matters is that, for now, it appears everyone is safe until they get tested."

"I wouldn't count on that. They were willing to kill Jack and Cutter based on a guess that they weren't Wielders. If circumstances change between here and this Needle, I don't think any of the others are safe except Kara and Dylan."

"Which raises another question: What is this Needle they spoke of? And where is it?" Artras glanced among all four of them. "No one has any idea?"

"We'll have to follow them, find out where it is in the city."

"Who? Cutter and Glenn are both hurt. Gaven and I don't know the first thing about tracking. Allan, you're the only one fit enough for that."

"Then I'll do it myself."

"Like hell. You'll take me with you." Glenn motioned with his bloodied arm, trying unsuccessfully to hide his wince of pain. "This is nothing. The Wolf barely tore the flesh."

"Fools." Artras reached out and snatched his arm, jerking it close. Glenn yelped, but Artras had already yanked the bloodied sleeve back, exposing the mangled flesh beneath.

She glanced up as Glenn, Gaven, and Allan sucked in horrified breaths. "This is more than 'barely torn.' Allan, we need water. This has to be cleaned before I can do anything. He's left it exposed too long. Gaven, start a fire and find more cloth for bandages."

Allan slid out the door. Gaven started a small fire not far from where Cutter lay. He also found the remains of a bed in one of the other rooms, and they hauled the metal frame and disintegrating stuffed mattress into the corner, setting Cutter up on it. The tracker promptly fell asleep. Glenn sat next to the bed, leaning against the wall, muttering to himself. Artras checked him for fever, but his forehead was cool and his skin wasn't flushed.

An hour later, Allan returned bearing three skins and a stoppered urn filled with water. Artras didn't ask where he'd found the containers or the water, taking the clay jug, pulling its cork with her teeth, and immediately dousing Glenn's arm. He roared in pain, thrashing until his free hand closed down on the edge of Cutter's bed, jerking the tracker awake. Artras ignored his cursing. The Wolf's teeth had punctured Glenn's forearm in two distinct ridges, one on top and the other below. But he'd thrashed back and forth once he'd taken hold. Glenn's skin was shredded, a few flaps hanging loose.

"It's going to require stitches."

"Do what you have to."

At some point during the stitching, Allan slipped out again. He still hadn't returned when she finished, and Gaven didn't know where he'd gone. She cleaned Glenn's arm once more, then bound it, the sweat-slicked Dog leaning back against the wall. He shifted into a more comfortable position and then dropped to sleep almost as fast as Cutter had.

Artras packed up the healer's bag. She'd used up most of the valerian root and all of the yarrow. One or more of the vials may have been helpful, but she didn't dare apply any of them without knowing what they held. Once finished, she sat in front of the fire, staring blankly into its flames. Her shoulders ached. The joints of her fingers throbbed with arthritis. She massaged them without thought. Gaven had stationed himself near one of the windows, watching the street below. Neither one of them spoke, the silence calming.

Artras must have dozed off, for her head snapped up when sounds came from the stairwell. Gaven rose from his crouched position at the window, sword raised awkwardly in one hand, but he relaxed as Allan reappeared, carrying two hares tied together by the feet.

"I followed the White Cloaks." He set the hares down near the door, retrieved the hunting knife from the trunk they'd found in the wagon, and began to skin them. "They followed the street until they reached the burned-out section of Erenthrall to the southwest. Then they turned directly west."

"But there isn't anything to the west. The fire that started in West Forks burned uncontrolled all the way to the edge of the city in that direction."

"I know."

"That means they aren't from the city."

All three of them turned toward Glenn. Artras rose, grimacing as the muscles in her legs protested. "Then the Needle isn't in the city either." She knelt down next to Glenn, one hand pressed to his forehead, the other raising his arm so she could inspect the bandages. "That's likely why none of us have heard of it. And that changes everything."

"No, it doesn't. We still need to follow them." Glenn pulled his arm from her grip and shifted into a better position. "We need to find out where this Needle is, or get Kara and the rest away from them before they reach it."

"You aren't going anywhere." Artras glanced toward Allan. "He's burning up with fever."

"What about Cutter?"

Artras shifted to the tracker's side, laid the back of her hand to his forehead and frowned. "No fever yet. But now that we have water, I should change the dressing, see if there's sign of an infection."

"Get both of them ready for travel. We'll take the wagon and head west, then north, back toward the Hollow."

"What?" Glenn lurched forward as if to rise. Before he'd made it halfway up, he faltered, wavering as if dizzy. Artras caught his shoulder and lowered him back to his seated position. "We can't. We have to get Kara and the others. We can't leave them with the Kormanley!"

"I don't want to leave Kara and the others with the Kormanley any more than you do, but look at us. Both you and Cutter are wounded, which means if we have to leave the city, we either leave you behind or split our group."

"So split the group!"

"How? You and Cutter need a healer. The closest we've got is Artras, which means she'd have to stay behind with both of you. But she can't protect you and care for you at the same time. Gaven is a fine wagonmaster, but he's a lousy fighter."

Glenn refused to look at any of them. A stricken look crossed his face, but then he hardened, turning back to Allan. "Then leave us behind. Take Artras and Gaven and go."

"We aren't leaving either of you behind." When he made to protest again, Artras cut him off with a jerk of her hand. "No! We're taking both of you and heading back to the Hollow and that's final! We can get Bryce and some of the others, track where these Kormanley have taken Kara and the rest, and figure out what to do then."

She stormed away from Glenn and Cutter, past Allan,

and into the room across the hall, beyond the stairs. It was another flat, with the same layout as the one they'd occupied, but with different furniture. Whoever had lived here before had had children. There were signs of them in the tiny chairs around a small table in one corner and a few scattered wooden toys. Artras' heart lurched when she thought of what might have happened to them, but she brushed the pain aside as useless as she crossed to the shattered window and looked down on the street below.

She stiffened when she heard someone pause at the door behind her, the floor creaking beneath his feet. It had to be Allan.

"It's the right decision."

"I know. But it still hurts to give up on them."

"We aren't giving up on them. I'll keep an eye on them for as long as I can as we head toward the Hollow. Once we regroup, I'll go back out, find them, and get them out of the Kormanley's hands."

Kara looked back as the wagons of the White Cloaks ground their way through the remnants of the western part of Erenthrall. The multicolored lights of the distortion rose against the eastern night sky, surrounded by a band of darkness where its light washed out the stars. To either side, the darkness was broken by scattered fires within the outer city, both to the north and south. She knew the Temerites were the likely source of the northern fires, but wasn't sure who controlled the southern parts of the city. Probably the Gorrani, based on what Allan and the others had reported.

Here, at the western edge, no one ruled the streets. The buildings had been reduced to ash and piles of charred rubble. The street they were following had obviously been cleared for easy access to Erenthrall's interior, which meant the White Cloaks had been operating in the city for a while.

She searched the surrounding darkness as their captors produced more torches.

"I haven't seen anything." Adder kept his voice low, his eyes ahead on the wagon where Dylan lay among the supplies.

"You said they escaped?"

"Glenn and Artras made it into the wagon with Gaven and Cutter. The White Cloaks were dealing with the Wolves. I didn't see any of their guards going after them, and the Tunnelers retreated back into the node. I think they escaped."

The guards kept them penned between the wagons. They'd taken all of their weapons and supplies, tossing them into one of the wagons behind them. But even though the guards watched their group, their attention was focused more on the darkness beyond the wagon train. "Are they worried the Wolves will return? Or is it something else?"

"We don't know much about this part of the city. We didn't even know about the Tunnelers in the northern section, and we thought we'd scouted that part out rather well. I'm beginning to think we should have approached the Temerites. At least started talks with them. Maybe none of this would have been necessary."

"What do you mean?"

He sidled closer, watching the White Cloak in the wagon ahead, but neither he nor the guards appeared to care that they were talking to one another. "Instead of trying to find the supplies on our own, maybe we should have negotiated with the Temerites. They seem to have control over their part of the city and are capable of defending it against outside forces like the Rats."

"Why would they give us supplies? What do we have to offer them in return?"

Adder looked at her. "You."

"Me?"

"Not you specifically. But the Wielders. The Temerites must be running short of supplies like everyone else. We could have traded access to the shards in the distortion for a portion of the supplies inside and protection for ourselves while we were inside the city."

"Why didn't anyone think of this earlier?"

"None of us realized there were so many groups in play. We knew of the Rats, the Wolves, and the Temerites, at least in the northern parts of the city. No one knew of the Tunnelers or the White Cloaks. If I had to choose an ally from any of those groups, I'd certainly rather work with the Temerites than the Kormanley."

Kara came to a dead stop. Adder took two steps more before realizing she'd halted. The wagons continued forward at the slow, steady pace. Carter, Aaron, and Tim hesitated, slowing their pace, not certain what was happening.

"The Kormanley." Her throat didn't seem to want to work.

Understanding dawned on Adder's face. He snatched her arm and hauled her back into motion, her body jerky and unresponsive. Her hands ached and she clenched them into fists. She'd been too stunned earlier to react, then too focused on the White Cloaks as they herded them to the wagons and headed out. She'd nearly forgotten what Iscivius had said.

"It doesn't make any sense."

"Quiet. They're watching."

They'd caught the attention of both the guard and the White Cloak riding with Dylan. It wasn't Iscivius or the woman who'd spoken to the Tunnelers in the square. This White Cloak was younger, perhaps thirty, with darker skin, like that of the Gorrani, a bound beard jutting out from his chin. The beard made the Gorrani's typically thin face appear even narrower.

Kara forced herself to look down at the ground. Her fists slowly released as she focused on placing one foot in front of the other. Adder's grip on her arm tightened in warning at first, then relaxed, his hand finally dropping away.

Kara looked up then to see the White Cloak and guard chatting, their attention diverted.

Carter and the others were shooting both her and Adder questioning looks. At a signal from Adder, Tim drifted closer, the others following suit.

When they were all within listening distance, Adder said, "What doesn't make sense?"

"The White Cloaks are Wielders. They can't be Wielders."

"Why not?"

"The Kormanley wanted the ley system destroyed. They wanted the ley returned to its natural order."

"How better to do that than with Wielders?"

Kara drew breath to respond, then stopped herself. She had a difficult time separating the deaths of her parents and her mentor Ischua from the Kormanley's actions. They'd killed her parents in the bombing at the raising of the Fly-ers' Tower. Ischua had died protecting her and the others at the beginning of the Purge after the bombing in the Amber Tower. Every person she'd loved had been torn from her because of the actions of the Kormanley. How could any-one, let alone her fellow Wielders, be part of their group?

"Not only that, but they seem to be searching for Wield-ers. They traded supplies for all of us. Why?"

No one answered.

"Whatever the reason, we can't let them finish it. They've destroyed too much as it is."

Before anyone could respond, orders were issued from the front of the group. The wagons slowed, then halted. More torches were lit, and lanterns set up on hooks and posts on either side of the wagons. The landscape had changed subtly. The streets were still scarred and littered with debris blackened by the fire, but there were fewer heaps of stone. Most of the buildings in whatever district this had once been must have been built of wood and were completely destroyed by the flames. Based on the charred remains of support beams, the buildings were smaller as well, probably only two stories high at most. They were at the edge of Erenthrall, and would be passing out onto the plains to the west shortly.

Kara traded a surprised look with Adder. "We're leaving Erenthrall."

Around them, the White Cloaks' guards were forming up into new positions, more of them breaking out bows and grabbing quivers. The guard around Kara and the rest dou-bled. The White Cloaks checked the ties on the supplies, making certain nothing was loose.

Iscivius and the White Cloak woman appeared. Kara felt a twinge of satisfaction upon seeing the ragged cut across Iscivius' cheek.

"We're leaving Erenthrall. If you try to escape, my guards have orders to shoot you." Iscivius eyed all of them individually, ending with Adder. "Don't run."

Then he proceeded down the line, checking with the guard and speaking to the other White Cloaks.

The woman stayed behind, watching Kara. As soon as Iscivius was too distant to overhear, she said, "We need you.

But don't think for a second that we won't kill you if you cause us problems." Then she turned to follow Iscivius.

"She's a cold bitch."

"Her name is Irmona." They turned to see the Gorrani White Cloak towering over them, standing at the bottom of the wagon. The hilt of a Gorrani saber peeked from beneath the folds of his cloak. "She is Iscivius' sister. You would do well to take care in her presence. She is, indeed, a cold bitch."

He jumped down from the wagon and straightened, still a half a hand taller than Kara or Adder. He moved off toward the front of the wagons.

"We were talking about the Kormanley. How much of that do you think he overheard?"

"All of it."

Nothing could be done about it now. Kara peered into the darkness beyond the torches and lanterns. It appeared darker now, deeper. "Do you think Allan and the others are following us?"

"I don't know. Cutter was wounded. I don't know how bad. Let's hope. I'm more worried about being followed by the Wolves."

Grant watched the torchlight of the White Cloaks with their captives fade into the distance on the plains. Around him, the rest of his pack paced in agitation, huffing and grunting and nipping at each other. He'd lost a half dozen of the pack at the square. Many of the others had been wounded. And still the White Cloaks had captured the Wielders.

He spat a curse, the Wolves answering by breaking into howls around him.

He'd waited too long. He should have taken the Wielders when they were fleeing the Rats. They'd been vulnerable for a short while, before that other—the man who'd stepped into the distortion—had found them. He could have seized them and then forced them to release his brethren captured in the distortion—the three Wolves in the shard chasing the wagon first, then all the others he knew of.

Maybe even find and release his wife.

He quashed the errant thought and the grief that welled

up with it. It was pointless. He had no idea where his wife might be, only a vague hope that she'd remained home before the quickening, that she'd been caught in a shard where time had halted, where she'd be protected. He had no way of knowing what her fate had been, caught here on the outside.

But that man could find out. He could walk through the distortion, find her, lead the Wielders to her.

Except he'd lost track of him in the fight at the square, along with the other Wielders.

He growled in frustration, shoved his raw emotion aside, and turned to his remaining Wolves.

"Follow the White Cloaks. Don't attack them, there are too many. But track them. We need to know where they're being taken."

Three of the Wolves broke off from the group and vanished into the darkness after the wagons. The rest gathered closer, sat on their haunches. One of them whined a question.

Grant faced the charred ruins of western Erenthrall. "We need to find the others from their group. We'll start back at the square."

# Fifteen

MORRELL HEAVED THE SACK OF FEED onto the stack at the side of the chamber that was going to serve as the stable for the livestock, then wiped the sweat from her forehead. Gritty chaff that had filtered through the burlap of the sacks made her skin itch. She wrinkled her nose in irritation, but turned to step out of the way as someone else threw down another sack.

The chamber had already been modified with some stalls for the horses and pens for the hogs and sheep and cattle. Carpenters were working on building additional fence, while those that could be spared from the fields were hauling in the feed and other supplies that could be brought up from the Hollow to the caves now rather than later. Some of the animals were already present, ewes bleating in a pen in the back corner. A few chickens that had escaped their cages before they could be released into the wire enclosure surrounding their new coop were scratching around the floor, pecking at pebbles. Goats were butting heads up against the stone wall on the opposite side, and a few cows were chewing their cuds beside them, unperturbed by the new location. Both would need to be milked soon, although Morrell didn't intend to be around for that.

She wanted to be studying the stone stellae in the interior chamber with Cory, the Wielders, and a few of the others from the University. Everyone in the Hollow had come to see the formation, even Paul, intrigued by how old it must be and how it had been buried and left undiscovered for so long. For most, the initial awe had died quickly. Bryce and the Dogs returned to training within the day, the rest drifted away over the next week. Sophia had kept everyone busy with preparations for the move to the caverns, including Morrell.

She turned back to join the line of people bringing in barrels and sacks from the wagons waiting just outside the cave entrances. But before she'd gone ten steps, she felt a shift in the air, as if someone had grabbed it and pulled.

She halted. No one else in the chamber had reacted, but the animals suddenly quieted. A single sheep *baaed* as if in question—

And then all of the livestock panicked. The goats raced to one edge of their pen and back, the younger ones kicking and lashing out with their hooves. The sheep rushed to the back wall, pressing up against each other, bleating as if they sensed a wolf nearby. The loose chickens took flight, those still trapped in their crates flapping and shrieking. Even the cows bawled in fear.

Everyone from the Hollow stopped and stared. "What in hells?"

Then the quake hit.

It wasn't a mild tremor, like what the refugees had experienced while fleeing Erenthrall after the Shattering. The ground lurched upward, throwing Morrell to her hands and knees, skin scraped raw and bloody on the stone floor. As she gasped in shock, rocks and pebbles pelted her back, dust and silt sifting down onto her neck. She cringed, shoulders hunched, as somewhere nearby in the stone tunnels something cracked, the sound overriding the deep-seated roar of the protesting earth and the terrified screams and shouts from the rest of the Hollowers in the chamber. The sounds were so chaotic—animals, people, the grinding earth—that she couldn't pick out any one voice. Instead, she cowered closer to the floor and prayed that the ceiling held, visions of being trapped in her cell in the Amber Tower immediately after the Shattering flooding her senses. Her breath seized in her chest, and for a horrifying moment she couldn't draw air, convinced she had never escaped that pitch-black room, that Kara had never found her and her father and released her.

The floor lurched again and she cried out. A chunk of the ceiling gave way, stone crashing to the floor within arm's reach, splintering and throwing shards up on impact. She scrambled sideways, coming up hard against the edge of the goats' pen. She clutched at the wood as if it would save her, a goat battering itself against the wood right next to her, then scanned the room. Men and women from the Hollow were scattering in all directions, seeking safety, as more and more stone fell from above. On the far side of the chamber, the sun shone out beyond the cavern's entrance, obscured occasionally by sheets of dust and silt. Nearby, a woman lay motionless, face turned toward Morrell, eyes blank as a pool of blood spread beneath her head. As the ground lurched a third time, less powerfully than the first two, the stacks of feed gave way, the grain crashing to the floor to Morrell's right. Men and women alike were hunched around the edges of the stalls and pens and the sides of the cavern, but as the third quake's rumble faded, the village's blacksmith staggered into the center of the room. "Everyone out! Now!"

He grabbed the woman next to him, pulled her up from where she hunkered as close to the floor as possible, and shoved her toward the opening. He did the same to two others, but by then everyone in the chamber was stumbling toward the entrance, and those who'd been outside were yelling for everyone to get out.

Morrell hauled herself to her feet using the pen's siding, drawing in a ragged breath that instantly turned into hacking coughs as she sucked in the dust and sediment that filled the chamber. Eyes tearing, she started toward the blurred light of the entrance, the silhouettes of people ahead of her blocking out the light. She paused to check for the fallen woman's pulse, although Morrell knew she was already dead, then continued, but as she passed the tunnel that led toward the deeper chambers, she heard distant, frantic barking.

Who would have a dog down here in the caves?

Then her eyes widened in recognition. "Max. Cory!"

She ducked into the tunnel and headed deeper. The path was littered with debris, and she quailed when a minor tremor shook the ground, but forged ahead immediately after. Shouts echoed up from below, urgent and frightened. Within twenty paces she ran across Paul, unconscious. A quick search found a knobby bump on his forehead, just within the hairline. The skin wasn't broken. As she prodded its outer edges, Paul flinched and pulled away, one hand rising to ward Morrell off. He blinked in the half-light from the few remaining lanterns. "Morrell?"

She reached down and grabbed his arm. "You were struck in the head. It might be a concussion." He didn't resist her efforts to get him to his feet. "You need to see Logan. Can you make it out yourself?"

Paul steadied himself against the tunnel's wall, one hand raised toward the lump on his head. He hesitated as he heard the frantic calls coming from deeper inside the cavern, then waved a hand for her to continue. "I'll be fine. Go and see if you can help. I'll send others down if I can. But be careful! We don't know if there will be any aftershocks."

Morrell slipped past him. She passed two others holding each other up as they stumbled out from below. Neither of them said anything. The ground shook twice more, sending more silt down from above, but the majority of the dust had begun to settle, making breathing easier. Only a third of the lanterns that lined the tunnel remained lit, but it was enough for Morrell to see the corridor ahead.

As she approached the side entrance to the cavern that contained the stellae, the barking became louder. Max leaped out of the opening in the side of the wall, his frantic bark escalating as he saw her. He raced toward her, hopping back and forth, then darted back toward the entrance, turning back to see if she was following. "I'm coming, I'm coming." She picked through the stones littering the tunnel's floor. There were more of them here. But then they'd known this part of the cavern wasn't as stable as the rest.

Slipping through the side entrance, she halted at the top of the scree of stone that led down to the floor and the stone monuments. Part of the cavern's roof had collapsed, near the wall with the ancient paintings and writing. Ten people were clustered around the rockfall, half of them tossing smaller stones or rolling boulders aside, where Cory sat on the floor. Two were holding Cory upright, his legs splayed out before him, one of them trapped beneath the fall. His face was twisted in pain, although he wasn't screaming. The other three were wringing their hands and fretting to one side, calling out orders.

In the center of the room, between the stone stellae, white ley light spouted up from the stone floor like a miniature fountain, splashing onto the stone and running down the stellae and across the floor like water, then submerging again beneath the rock before it reached the outer ring of stone plinths.

Max charged back up the scree, yapping wildly and breaking Morrell's momentary paralysis. She scrambled down to the floor, skirting the outside of the room as she trotted toward Cory and those trying to help him. As she approached, she realized most of those shifting rock or holding him up were the remaining Wielders in the Hollow and some of the University students.

But then Morrell's attention was caught by Cory, the contorted angle of his right leg, and how nothing from the calf down could be seen, caught beneath a boulder at least twice the size of Morrell herself.

She halted ten paces away, Max racing forward to place his paws on Cory's chest and lick his face. The small dog turned to look at Morrell, tongue lolling, eyes expectant. He was no longer barking, as if his job were finished.

"Morrell!" Raven, the senior Wielder now that Kara and Artras were gone, stepped up to her side and grabbed her arm, tugging her forward. "Morrell, you have to help us. We can't get the boulder off his leg. It's too large."

Morrell resisted. She didn't want to see how badly Cory's leg was crushed, didn't want to see the blood, the splintered bones. She didn't care what miracles everyone in the Hollow thought she could do now; there must be some wounds that even she couldn't heal.

"What do you think I can do?"

Raven's eyes narrowed. "You're a healer. You do whatever you can!"

Not allowing Morrell to protest further, she dragged her

forward, flinging her to the stone near Cory's legs. Morrell caught herself with her already bloodied hands, but bit back her anger when she caught the sheer anguish in Cory's eyes.

She straightened, wiping the dirt from her hands on her thighs. The calm she had often seen settle over Logan in front of the most serious wounds brought before him—a calm she had often thought cold and distant and unfeeling—enfolded her, like a shawl.

"Move aside." The University student who knelt next to her scrambled out of her way, and she shifted down closer to the boulder, steeling herself for what she'd see. But the pent-up breath she didn't realize she'd drawn exploded outward in relief as she noticed that the boulder hadn't completely crushed Cory's foot. There was a slight indentation in the stone, and the boulder had collapsed on top of other debris, keeping it somewhat elevated off the floor.

It was clearly pressing down on Cory's leg, though. The calf was twisted to one side, Cory on his hip to lessen the pain. His struggles had scraped the skin deep enough that blood coated the stone, pooling on the ground beneath. The amount of blood was small, but as Morrell leaned over and tried to peer into the crevice beneath the stone she realized that she couldn't see how badly damaged his ankle or foot was.

"How bad is it?" Raven crouched down on Cory's other side.

"Can you feel your foot, Cory? Wriggle your toes?"

"Yes. I think. It's started to go numb."

"The stone's cutting off circulation. But I can't tell if the foot has been crushed or if it can be salvaged, not without moving the stone."

"We've already tried. It's too large. We can't even get it to budge." Raven waved a hand over Cory's leg. "Can't you do something? Fix it somehow?"

"It doesn't work that way."

Raven grabbed her by the shoulders. "I know, I know. But do something. For Kara's sake."

Kara had saved her from the Amber Tower, had saved them all from the quickening of the distortion in Erenthrall. And the Wielder loved Cory. Everyone knew that. It would destroy her if she came back from Erenthrall to find Cory missing a leg or dead. If Morrell could stop it—

But how?

Cory had sunk back against the two students supporting him. As she watched, his eyelids fluttered, as if he were fighting unconsciousness, but then he gave in and slumped forward, the two students catching him.

Morrell shook off Raven's hold and dropped her hands to Cory's leg. She closed her eyes and tried to focus, tried to pull the tingling sensation she'd felt with both Claye and Harper into her fingertips.

"It's just a leg. Thigh, knee, kneecap, calf. Just like Harper." She'd worked from Cory's thigh down across the knee to the calf, squeezing the muscle, feeling the tension in the tendons, even through the cloth of Cory's breeches. As she neared the calf, where the stone held the leg tight, the flesh grew swollen, already bruised, but she still didn't feel the prickling sensation in her fingers that had accompanied her healing of Claye or Harper. "Swelling here, possible bruising. Nothing broken. The bone is still intact. But nothing's happening. Why isn't anything happening? Why can't I make it wor—?"

A surge of power shot down her arm into her fingers when her hand encountered blood. Her eyes snapped open as those around her gasped and began to whisper to one another. Morrell felt a few of them drawing back as if in fear, but she ignored them. Auroral light wove around her fingers, a pale blue streaked with yellow. It was barely visible, but it was there.

"Why did it start now? Why not earlier?"

"It started when you hit the blood."

Morrell shifted her hands further over the bloody portion of Cory's clothes and the auroral lights strengthened. "Rip his breeches down near his calf. I need to touch his skin, not his clothes."

Raven didn't hesitate, grabbing the breeches where they'd been torn by Cory's struggles and ripping the fabric. It tore up to his knee, Raven pulling back bloody hands as Morrell wrapped hers around Cory's calf above the worst part of the wound.

The reaction was instant. The auroral lights strengthened, flooding outward from her fingers and up along the stone in waves. As with Claye and Harper, she merged with the prickling sensation, closing her eyes as she visualized sinew and muscle and bone. She traveled down Cory's calf, beneath the stone, into his ankle and foot, flowing through it all as if she were Cory's own blood. She felt the stressed flesh, the broken skin, the compression on the bones as the rock pressed down with its immense weight. After the initial shock, she relaxed into the sensation, realized she had also merged with the boulder, the stones holding it up, and the granite of the floor beneath. The connection wasn't as intense as it was with Cory's flesh and blood, but it was there.

And as with Claye and Harper, she could sense what was wrong.

"Cory's foot has been compressed. None of the bones are broken. Everything's just been squeezed together. All of it's bruised. And the muscles are damaged. Some of the tendons are torn, especially in his ankle. His foot's been twisted too far to one side."

"Can you heal him?"

Morrell opened her eyes to look at the Wielder. Her connection to Cory's leg and the stone surrounding it lessened, but didn't break. "Not while the boulder is still on top of it."

"Then we have to move the boulder. Somehow." Raven lurched to her feet, using the boulder for support. "You three, get on either side of Cory and Morrell. The rest of you, fan out around them. I don't care if you think you're too weak, we need everyone we can get. All we have to do is lift it enough so that I can pull him free."

The others moved into position, someone brushing up against Morrell's back. She closed her eyes again, focused. The circulation had been cut off for long enough that parts of Cory's foot were dying. She felt it as a shadow, settling over the skin and beginning to seep into the muscle and tissue beneath.

"Hurry."

"On my mark, everyone push as hard as you can. One, two, three, mark!"

Feet scraped against the stone floor as everyone on either side of Morrell grunted with effort. Through the stone, Morrell felt them shoving back and upward, trying to force the boulder to roll. But it was too large, its bottom too flat.

"Again! One, two, three, mark!"

They all shoved again. Morrell mentally pushed hard at the stone surrounding Cory's leg, where it touched his foot.

"It moved! I felt it move!"

"One more time! One, two, three, mark!"

Morrell shoved as hard as she could through the strange prickling that spread from her hands through Cory to the stone around her. Something shifted, and then Cory's leg jerked beneath her hands as Raven hauled Cory free. Morrell lost contact with his leg, the auroral light around her hands flickering and dying. Everyone who'd been pushing against the stone released it, but it didn't seem to move at all as they did so. Morrell reached forward and wrapped her hands around Cory's calf again, connected with the wound, and began repairing it as best she could. As with Claye and Harper, she knew what was wrong, could sense how the flesh and muscle had been twisted out of true and where it should be if it were healthy and whole. Her hands grew warm, the skin beneath her touch shifting and re-forming in a way that sent shivers up her spine, but she didn't pull away. She worked from his knee downward, the worst damage at the ankle. The only time she spoke was to ask someone to tear away Cory's lower pant leg and to remove his shoe. Raven did so without a word, everyone around them silent.

And then it was done.

Morrell drew her hands away slowly and opened her eyes. Weariness washed through her entire body. She let her hands flop into her lap. Cory's foot was sheathed in blood, skin scraped off down to muscle in some spots, but it was no longer wrenched around at an unnatural angle nor flattened. Its entire length was a livid purplish-black from bruising, but Morrell knew that would fade with time. Besides, she didn't have the strength to heal it. Her entire body was drained. She could barely hold herself upright.

"That's the best I can do."

Raven knelt down beside her, rubbing her back. "You did fine. You did better than fine."

More people had shown up, standing back and watching silently. Behind her, someone whispered, "I don't think we moved the rock at all. I didn't feel it move. And look here. The hole's bigger, where his foot was. Isn't it?"

No one answered, and Morrell was too weary to care. Raven pulled her into a hug, rocked her back and forth, rested her chin on the top of Morrell's head. Someone ordered Cory to be taken up to Logan's cottage using one of the carts, the chamber suddenly full of activity as people began to vacate. Morrell let the sounds wash over her until finally Raven pulled back, still holding her shoulders.

"You did a great thing, Morrell. You should be proud."

"I am. I'm just tired."

"I'll get you back to your cottage. You can rest and Janis can take care of you."

Raven helped her stand, and they shuffled over to where the others were lifting Cory by the shoulders and legs and carrying him up the scree and out into the corridor. Raven and Morrell trailed behind them, Max trotting back and forth between his master and Morrell. The small dog occasionally licked Cory's dangling hand, as if coaxing him to wake up. The corridor was already jammed with people going back and forth, assessing the damage or starting to clean it up. The chamber housing the animals where Morrell had been when the quake struck swarmed with people, Paul at the center calling out orders.

As soon as they emerged into the sunlight, Morrell blinking and holding up one hand to shade her eyes, Raven commandeered a wagon, recently emptied, and they slid Cory inside. Raven steadied Morrell as she climbed in beside him, taking a seat near his head and shoulders, a few of the University students climbing in toward the back. Max jumped up and curled into Cory's arm, laying his head down on Cory's chest.

"Take him to Logan," Raven said to the wagon's driver. "Have him look over Cory and Morrell, then see that she gets handed over to Janis."

Before he could snap the reins, Hernande hurried up, grabbing onto the side of the wagon. His normally stolid, contemplative expression cracked with a deeper, stricken emotion that Morrell couldn't identify as his knuckles whitened.

"What happened? Was it the quake?"

"Part of the ceiling caved in inside the ley node's chamber. Cory was trapped under part of it, but we freed him, and Morrell healed him as best she could. We're taking both of them to Logan."

Hernande reached out to grip Cory's arm, squeezing once, then turned to Morrell. "Thank you."

Raven motioned to the driver, who flicked the reins. The wagon jerked into motion, Morrell slipping into a more stable position. Behind, Hernande made to follow, but Raven caught his shoulder.

"There's something you need to see."

When Hernande turned with a questioning look, she added more, but Morrell was too distant to hear her.

"We were working in the node chamber when the quake struck. The rest of the Wielders and University students are still down there."

Hernande almost ignored her, looking back at the wagon that carried his student as it jostled down the hillside in the ruts already worn into the ground from the recent activity. They were moving the supplies and animals to the caves first, and were nearly at the stage where they would begin shifting people, but the entire process would be worthless if the tracks from the wagons led the raiders right to the cavern entrances. He'd have to get the other students to work on cloaking the ruts in the ground, as well as hiding the entrances.

But the thought slid away as the wagon carrying Cory jolted out of view, Morrell holding onto the wagon with one hand, keeping Cory steady with the other.

"Why?" As the wagon vanished into the trees, he shifted toward Raven. "Why are they still there? Shouldn't they be helping with the quake?"

"They are. The quake woke the node. I haven't had time to take a look yet."

"Woke the node?"

"The ley is bubbling up through the center of the stellae."

"Visibly?"

"Visibly. Which means there's at least ten times as much ley passing through that node now, after the quake, than before."

Hernande began stroking his beard in contemplation. "Do you think the quake—"

"I don't know what to think yet. I haven't had time to deal with it."

"No, I suppose you haven't." He looked back toward where the wagon had disappeared. Cory was in good hands. Morrell would take care of him. There was nothing he could do but hover and distract Logan.

He motioned toward the cave and the rest of the men and women scattered about. "Lead the way."

As they trudged up through the remaining wagons, they ran across three bodies—a woman and two men—watched over by grim-faced Paul.

"Was anyone else hurt? Was there any additional damage?"

"I don't know. It didn't seem like it when we came up from the node cavern. I saw others injured, but none as seriously as Cory. His leg was crushed beneath one of the fallen stones. I honestly didn't think there was anything Morrell could do. I didn't even think we'd get Cory free. Not without cutting off his leg."

Hernande halted. "Cory's leg didn't look that bad."

"You should have seen it when we finally pulled him free. That girl is a miracle worker and she doesn't even know it."

"She knows it." Hernande started moving again. "She just doesn't know how to deal with it yet."

They passed through the jumble of activity in the outer chamber, down the long corridor, then picked their way to the bottom of the node chamber. The ley surged up from the ground between the circled stellae, shooting up to waist height before falling back down again. Hernande noted that none of the ley penetrated beyond the outer circle cut into the stone floor. It must be a barrier of some sort.

He was still fixated on the ley as Raven drew to a halt before the collapsed portion of the ceiling. She touched Hernande's arm and pointed to the rockfall. "That's the boulder Cory was trapped under."

The boulder was five times as large as Hernande had imagined, a significant chunk of the ceiling scattered around it in smaller pieces. But it was the sight of the blood that jolted him. The floor was covered with a dark stain around the boulder, a smaller pool a short distance away, where he assumed Cory had lain after being pulled free. He stepped forward, near where two students knelt, looking at an indentation in the stone's base.

One of them motioned toward it. "That's where Cory's leg was. Everyone else thinks we moved the boulder, but I don't think so."

"If we didn't move the boulder, then how did we get Cory out?" the girl protested.

"I think it was Morrell." The boy waved a hand at the small crack between the boulder and the floor. "I think she made the opening wider. Can she do that?"

"Of course not. She heals people. We've all seen her. She can't move stone. Right, Mentor?"

"I didn't say she *moved* it."

Hernande chewed on the end of his beard. "I don't know the extent of Morrell's powers, but she can certainly heal."

The girl sent a scathing look at her fellow student, as if Hernande had verified her claim.

Hernande knelt down beside them. He traced the outline of blood on the ground. It was already drying, tacky now. He turned his attention to the boulder and the crevice at its base.

He brushed the outside, the stone grainy and rough, then reached further into the hole.

Inside, the rock was smooth, as if eroded by water.

Or molded, like the stone of the buildings in Erenthrall created by the Wielders and mentors.

He pulled his hand free, scrubbed it on his breeches, then stood. The students were waiting expectantly, but he shifted his attention to the node. "What do we know about the appearance of the ley?"

"As I said before, nothing. We haven't had a chance to study it yet."

Hernande gave Raven a steady look.

She headed toward the circle of stellae in the center of the room. Hernande and the others trailed behind her. She halted outside the circle carved into the floor that Hernande had noted earlier. "Give me a moment. All of the Wielders—follow along, but stay out of my way."

The Wielders nodded. All of them tensed, eyes distracted and distant, signs that Hernande had learned long ago meant they were reaching for the ley.

A moment later, some of the Wielders gasped.

Hernande stepped forward. "What is it?"

"The ley is strong. Coming from the north, although I don't know from where. It's not the right angle to be from Dunmara or Severen. Perhaps Ikanth? But even then . . ." Raven trailed off.

"Where is it headed?"

Raven remained silent long enough that Hernande almost asked her again. "Southwest." The black-haired Wielder's shoulders hunched forward. She drew in a couple of deep breaths, steadying herself, while all around her the Wielders withdrew from the ley. Mareane stepped forward, one hand on Raven's back. She murmured something, too low for Hernande to hear.

"What happened? What did you do?"

Mareane answered. "She tried to follow the ley line to wherever it led, but she extended herself out too far. She could have lost herself." She met Hernande's gaze. "None of us are as strong as Kara, or even Artras. Raven has a hard time accepting that. That's why she's always so bitter."

Hernande didn't respond, watching as Raven's shoulders straightened. Hernande thought her eyes looked hollower than before, her skin sallow and haggard. But that could have been from the quake and Cory's rescue, not just tracing the ley line.

"I couldn't follow it to its end. The next node is too distant."

"I didn't expect you to. We may be able to find out where the line is coming from and where it's going using the sands." Hernande glanced at the ley. "The real question is, is it safe? Or do we need to abandon this cavern?"

"It's safe. Whoever built this node made certain they were protected. The stellae act as a shield, keeping the ley inside the circles here in the chamber."

"And can we use it? Kara said before there was only enough ley in the area to create a minimal network, enough for heating stones and some light to help us survive the winter."

"We can do more than that now. This isn't as powerful as the Nexus, nowhere near as strong, but it's ten times more than what we managed before. The entire ley structure in this area has shifted."

"Because of the quake."

"We don't know that."

Hernande tugged on his beard. "It does raise a curious question, though, doesn't it? Are the quakes causing the ley lines to shift, or are the shifting ley lines causing the quakes?"

"Or neither."

"Consider the fact that we have not had a quake in this area of any significance since we arrived. Now, we've had one worse than any of those we experienced in Erenthrall since the Shattering, and this node—one that was dead before this—has now been awakened. I think it's too strong a coincidence. The quakes and the shifting ley lines must be connected."

"Then how do we make it stop?"

"We have to stabilize the ley," Mareane cut in. "Which is what Kara has been saying since the beginning. But the only way to do that is by healing the distortion."

"So we're back where we started."

"No, we're not." Hernande motioned to the node. "Now we have ley to work with."

"Hernande!" All of them turned to where Paul stood at the top of the scree. "We're needed back at the Hollow. Bryce and Sophia want to talk."

Raven stepped closer to Hernande. "They're going to want to halt the move to the caverns. They're going to say they aren't safe because of the quake. And they're right."

"We can't abandon the caves. Not without getting slaughtered by the raiders. I'll make certain they realize that. You make certain you stabilize this node. We don't want to have another quake like the last one. And we don't want to lose our access to the ley now that we have it."

He began climbing up the scree, Paul waiting patiently at the top. The elder councilor grabbed Hernande's hand and helped him up the last, steepest section. "We need to get some stairs built here, either with stone or using lumber. We can't all be crawling over the fallen stone, especially once we're ready to shift the rest of the Hollow here."

Hernande dusted himself off. "You still intend to move the Hollow here?"

"The quake doesn't change the arguments for why we

need to move here. Unless there's more going on." He eyed the ley roiling inside the circle of stellae.

"There is, but I don't think it changes anything." Hernande moved past him, down the corridor. Paul hesitated, then followed. "I'll explain what we think happened—the ley and the quake—once we meet up with Bryce and Sophia."

Paul paused to pass on additional instructions and to put a group onto building stairs in the node cavern, then they hoofed it back to the Hollow, following the ruts created by the wagons. Hernande pointed to the worn ground and mentioned having the students from the University hide the tracks using the same technique they would use to cloak the entrances to the caverns. Paul agreed.

They entered the Hollow from the west, passing the meadows where the shepherds were grazing the sheep, then the fields where the corn, tomatoes, and other vegetables from the earliest spring planting were beginning to flower. It would be weeks before most of it started in earnest— months for some of it—but the plants looked healthy. A few of the Hollowers were working the fields. Behind the produce fields, stretches of hay, wheat, and barley, already knee-high, bowed gently before the gusting breeze.

The Hollow was bustling with activity, two wagons loaded down with supplies heading back up the path to the caverns, another three being filled, ready to follow them. Janis was in the garden outside the cottage with Morrell, Allan's daughter sitting on a small stool picking basil. The girl looked exhausted and distracted, not even glancing up as Hernande and Paul walked past, but Janis waved and motioned that Morrell would be fine at Hernande's questioning look.

They paused long enough at Logan's to look in on Cory. His student hadn't woken yet, but Logan appeared unconcerned.

"He's recovering. I don't know anything about this healing power of Morrell's, but I'd guess that it takes its toll on the patient as well as the healer. I've cleaned up his leg, but Morrell didn't leave me much to do. He needs time, that's all. Like her. I'll keep a watch over him."

"Find me when he wakes up."

Logan shooed them out of his cottage with assurances he would.

They walked across the center of the Hollow to the meeting hall. As soon as they entered and Hernande's eyes had adjusted to the shadow after the bright sunlight outside, he noted Sophia and Bryce at the far end of the hall in deep discussion with Claye, Braddon, and a tracker named Quinn.

"Now what?" Paul muttered.

"Let's find out."

Bryce broke off as he saw them approaching, the rest turning as they came to a halt.

"What happened at the caverns? We heard there were some collapses. And we saw what happened to Cory."

"Three deaths. Everyone else is shaken up, but we've already got groups cleaning up and others working on shoring up the corridors and ceiling in case there are any more quakes."

Sophia's eyes widened slightly in surprise. "You aren't advocating that we abandon the caves?"

"I don't think we can afford to. Where else would we go? You've convinced me that we can't stay here, not with any expectation of safety."

"And we may not need to concern ourselves with more quakes." Hernande settled in a chair. "We believe that the quake was caused by a shift in the ley system. The node we found earlier, which was inactive, has now been awakened. There is ley running through it, strong enough that it's visible. Raven and the other Wielders are attempting to stabilize it. If they can do that, and keep it stable, then we shouldn't have any more quakes of that magnitude here."

"So the quakes are the result of the ley system reorganizing itself?"

"We believe so, yes."

"Are we still able to use the cavern as a refuge?"

"Raven assures me that the ley is contained. I can also use the Tapestry to make certain of that, as long as it's not too strong. It's one of the ways the mentors at the University aided the Prime Wielders in Erenthrall before the Shattering."

"I won't be comfortable with the ley that close."

"Then you can sleep in the deeper cavern!" When Paul

bristled, Sophia raised a hand to forestall him. "Don't. You won't have any choice in the matter. Bryce?"

"She's right. Tell them what you saw on the plains, Quinn."

Quinn—a foot taller than Hernande, with a rugged, pocked complexion—stopped fiddling with his bow. "There's a force of about two hundred men headed our way. I spotted them during one of our sweeps of the plains. They were camped two days' ride from the edge of the hills yesterday."

Bryce took over. "This isn't a ragtag group of bandits. There's a core group of fighting men, with a few bands like the one that attacked us attached to them. They're organized, with a base camp that they're moving steadily in our direction. They have horses, swords, bows, and enough men to overwhelm this village within an hour, even if they act as stupidly as they did before. Based on what I've been told, they aren't going to behave that way. This group has a leader, and he's disciplined." His gaze fell on Hernande. "We may need your students and their knots sooner than expected."

"If they are needed, they'll be ready."

"Let's hope so."

"How long before this group gets here?"

"Our best estimate is a week. It depends on how fast they move. We've seen two groups join them since we started watching—one coming from the northwest, another from the east. Every time a group joins them, they slow down."

"A week." Paul looked at Sophia. "We'll have to speed up the move to the caverns."

"We'll manage. Keep a watch on this group. Let us know a day or so before they might arrive. We'll need to harvest whatever we can, even if we have to reap the hay early and let some of the vegetables ripen in the caves. I don't expect that they'll leave the fields untouched if they attack."

"No, they won't."

Sophia and Paul left, already discussing what work needed to be accelerated. Hernande waited until they'd exited the hall, even their shadows gone, before turning to Bryce.

"There may be something else we can do now to defend the Hollow."

"I thought we'd considered everything."

"We did. But we didn't have access to the ley before."

Allan crawled up to the edge of the low ridge, parting the grass before him so that he could see across the sunlit plains that stretched out toward the horizon to the west. Mountains rose in the distance, purple beneath the blue sky and above the yellow-green of the prairie. The road that the White Cloaks were following cut through the lightly rumpled land in a straight line heading slightly south of west. It had once been a caravan route, heavily traveled, until Baron Arent and Prime Augustus had created the Nexus and trade had switched from wagons and drivers to barges and pilots plying the ley lines between all of the major cities on the continent. Allan knew a little about the lands to the west of Erenthrall—the village of Canter, his home, lay in the foothills of the mountains—but not what lay to the south. The main ley line that connected Erenthrall to Tumbor ran along the river. He knew another ley line branched off from that toward the Demesnes and the Western Peninsula, But the ley lines were too dangerous to be used for transportation since the Shattering.

He tried to recall everything he knew about the old roads and exactly where they ran. The roads around Canter were as familiar as the wells and springs, creeks and streams that dotted and snaked through the grassland and the hills, at least close to his old village, but Allan couldn't remember anything of significance about the routes here.

A sudden barked command echoed up from the plains. His gaze snapped back to the White Cloaks and their small entourage of wagons and guardsmen. They'd reached a section of the road a good distance away, far enough that Allan had to squint to see one of the stone wayposts jutting up out of the ground there, old enough to be tilted to one side. The road must branch. It was difficult to tell from Allan's vantage.

The wagons slowed. He couldn't pick out individuals, but he knew based on the last few days of watching that Kara and the others would be at the center, surrounded by guards, a single wagon in front of them, two behind. Dylan would be in the front wagon. At dusk, the group would halt and make camp, Dylan forced to stand and walk or hobble around the wagons, the others tied up near one of the fires built by the White Cloaks. Watchers were placed around the circled wagons, close enough they could see each other, attentive enough that Allan knew he couldn't risk sneaking past them. Everyone would be fed then, and the captured group given pallets to rest on. They slept in the darkness, beneath the stars.

But it was far too early for a halt today. The sky was clear, although storm clouds roiled to the south, lit occasionally from within by lightning. Much farther west, hints of an auroral front glittered, although it could have just been heat waves. Almost directly south, the white light of the distortion over Tumbor burned, still threatening to quicken like the one in Erenthrall.

Allan fidgeted as the group continued to hesitate at the waypost. If they continued on a mostly western track, he'd be able to follow them for another day or two without losing track of Artras, Glenn, and the others. But if they turned farther south—

He spat a curse as the group below began angling southwest, then watched in frustration as they faded into the distance. They were moving almost directly away from Artras and the wagon headed toward the Hollow.

He hesitated, then stood and trotted down the back end of the ridge, breaking into a ground-eating stride as he reached flatter land, heading toward Glenn and the others.

He needed to tell them that the White Cloaks had angled farther south.

And that he still had no idea where they were headed, or how to save Kara and the others.

# Sixteen

"**H**AVE YOU SEEN ANYTHING?"

Kara scraped her spoon across the bottom of the plate in an attempt to pick up the last few dregs of gravy without looking up at Adder. He'd spoken in barely a whisper, so that the White Cloak enforcers who stood no more than ten paces behind them, near the edges of the circled wagons, couldn't overhear. They'd learned to keep certain conversations quiet and tried to be as circumspect as possible when they talked. She knew if she glanced up she'd find Adder half turned away, washing their dishes in the small bucket they were provided for the task.

"Nothing." She shoved the gravy into her mouth. She regretted eating the bread so quickly. Gravy was always better soaked into bread, even the passable but dry biscuits the White Cloaks provided them.

She contemplated licking the plate.

"Tim and Carter haven't seen anything either."

She handed her plate to Adder with a broken smile, then sank back onto her pallet.

Adder finished washing the plates, handing the crude clay disks back to the enforcer who'd brought them their food, along with the bucket of now-dirty water. Kara listened to the familiar sounds of Adder settling onto his pallet, situated close enough to Kara's so they could speak, but not so close as to arouse suspicion.

"They would have attacked by now, before we turned south."

The words were too close to what Kara had been thinking.

Adder remained silent, shifting his position on the pallet a few times before sitting up. He felt around the ground for a moment, only half-visible in the firelight, then held something up in one hand before tossing it over his shoulder and settling back down.

"Stupid stones."

Kara snorted. She rolled onto her side, her back to the fire, head resting on an outstretched arm, her face in shadow. She could see beneath the wagon behind their group. One enforcer stood at the end of the wagon on their side, but beyond, at least twenty paces into the night, she knew there were at least two enforcers watching the plains.

"Why didn't they come get us?"

"There are only five of them, if all of them survived. We're being held by five White Cloaks and nearly forty enforcers. They're outnumbered. And we have no allies in Erenthrall."

"I thought the Tunnelers were allies."

"So did I."

"We should never have trusted them."

"We had no choice."

She let her anger churn for a while, but slowly her thoughts returned to the White Cloaks. They hadn't spoken to them except to give orders to halt, rest, or move since Erenthrall. "Where are they taking us?"

"The Needle. Still no idea what it is?"

"I thought it might be something in Tumbor, but if it were, we should have turned directly south at that waypost. We're still heading west."

Adder shifted position, settling into what Kara now recognized as his sleeping position. "I noticed. Whatever it is, it's related to the Wielders. They're the ones that talk about it the most. The enforcers barely speak of it, except as a destination."

Kara scoured her memory for anything she had learned

at the Wielders' college or during her tenure at the various nodes in Erenthrall that dealt with something called the Needle, but she couldn't recall anything. Near her, Adder's breath evened out. Mind restless, she cursed the Primes for their damn secrecy while worry nagged at her over the fate of Allan and the others. She hoped they were safely on their way back to the Hollow, if they weren't still attempting to rescue them.

But if they couldn't count on Allan to save them, how were they going to save themselves?

⟡

When Kara's eyes popped open the next morning, the question leaped forward, still unanswered. She listened to the camp being taken apart, the enforcers calling out orders as the spits and supplies were packed up and shoved back onto the wagons. Three of the White Cloaks were arguing tersely at the back of the lead wagon, Iscivius listening with a stern face while Okata gestured at Irmona to make his point. None of them looked happy.

"No!" Okata barked, loud enough to be heard by nearly everyone. Enforcers paused all around them. "He will take credit for what we've done. You know him."

"Father will know."

"How? By divine intervention?"

"He'll know because I'll inform him! I, at least, have his ear."

"Enough." Iscivius glanced around, and the enforcers who'd paused to listen in hastily picked up where they'd left off. His gaze ended on Okata. "Father will not care who found them, or how. He will only be concerned with what they can do and how they can further our cause. That should be your only concern as well. The others will intercept us—"

His words were lost as he turned, his back to Kara, and began walking toward the front of the wagon, Okata at his side, Irmona trailing behind.

Kara remained still, searching for an opportunity.

Nothing presented itself. Within minutes, one of the enforcers nudged her with a foot from behind. "Wake up. Time to get moving."

She rolled over as he moved on to wake Tim and Carter.

Another enforcer was already helping Aaron walk Dylan around the small camp. The Wielder still limped, but each day he could walk farther and put more weight on his knee.

Kara sat up, Adder suddenly standing before her. He reached down and helped pull her to her feet, handing her a biscuit. She took it gratefully and bit into it.

"Are these getting harder?"

"Definitely drier."

Kara stretched. "I need a bath and a change of clothes. These reek."

"Don't get too personal now." Someone shouted from the opposite side of the wagons and his expression sobered. "They're on edge this morning."

"Did you overhear the White Cloaks this morning? They don't trust each other, or the enforcers. It sounds like there are some rivalries in their ranks."

"They trust the enforcers, they just don't want them to overhear their arguments. But I agree that not all of the White Cloaks are friends with each other."

"It sounded like they expect to run into someone today, or at least soon. We need to escape before that happens, whether Allan and the others are out there to help us or not."

"We can't. Dylan can barely walk. We'd never make it."

"We should leave Dylan behind."

Adder met her steady gaze and she realized he'd already considered the option, had probably thought of it as soon as they'd left Erenthrall, but had kept quiet.

"You already agree."

"If we hope to have any chance at all, then yes, we need to leave Dylan behind."

Kara found she couldn't look Adder in the eyes any longer. She stared out at the rolling grasslands around them, its details slowly emerging as the sun rose higher above the eastern horizon.

"I'll talk to him, explain it—"

"No! I'll explain it. He deserves that much at least."

She scrubbed at her eyes with her free hand as she broke away from Adder without looking at him. He didn't attempt to follow her. She halted abruptly in front of Aaron, the younger Hollower boy helping Dylan climb up into the back of the wagon.

"Let me watch over Dylan today, Aaron."

Aaron glanced toward the enforcer watching them, then nodded, pulling away. Kara swallowed the last of her biscuit, the bread a leaden lump at the base of her throat, then cupped her hands so that Dylan could use them as a step up into the wagon.

"Ready?"

"Whenever you are."

He heaved his ass up into the wagon with her help and shoved himself toward the back, situating himself against a crate as Kara hoisted herself up after him. The enforcer eyed both of them, but one of the White Cloaks strode by, catching his attention. The White Cloak—Okata, Kara saw when he turned—checked the other two wagons, then waved a hand toward the front of the group. "Ready!"

The wagon jolted up onto the smoother stone of the caravan route and the enforcer stepped to one side, out of sight.

Dylan said immediately, "You have to chance it."

"Chance what?"

"Escape! You have to try. You and the others."

"But—"

"You'll have to leave me behind. I know that." He gestured toward his knee in anger. "The damn Rats made certain of that, didn't they? It didn't help when I twisted it again falling from the litter when the Wolves attacked." He slumped back against his crate. "I realized I'd have to stay behind days ago."

"We thought maybe Allan was following us, that he and the others would get all of us out, but we're running out of time."

"I heard them talking about meeting up with another group of White Cloaks. They expect to run into them before nightfall."

"You overheard more than I did." She reached out and grabbed his forearm, squeezed it. "If at all possible, we'll come back for you."

He placed his free hand over hers. "Don't. If you get a chance to run, take it, and don't look back. Save the Hollow. They need you more than they need me."

"I wish everyone would stop saying that! The Hollow

needs everyone—every last person—if it's going to survive. No one is more important than any other. I know I'm some sort of Prime Wielder in Artras' eyes, but she's wrong. I may have been headed toward the black jacket, may have eventually even received one, but it didn't happen. The Nexus shattered, which meant I never got trained. So I'm only as good as the rest of you."

Dylan gripped her hand tighter. "No, you're not. You're stronger. And not just in manipulating the ley."

Kara pulled her hand free. The enforcer returned and she choked back her response. She leaned back into the crates again instead. But even with her anger over Dylan's unshakable belief in her—a belief she knew had been reinforced by Artras—she couldn't come up with a way to escape that would save Dylan as well.

Two hours later, when Iscivius called for a rest, she still had nothing. As she slid toward the back of the wagon, Dylan caught her arm and even with two enforcers watching said, "You have to chance it. For me."

She couldn't respond.

She hopped from the back of the wagon and let the enforcers lead her to where a stream passed beneath the road. The bridge had been shoved askew by flooding waters in the past, not quite lining up perfectly with the road. To either side, stone steps led down to the edges of the stream, the water clear and cold and refreshing. It dribbled down Kara's chin, and she shivered as it slid beneath her sweat-stained shirt. She sluiced water over her head, let it soak into her hair, her clothes, getting in three large handfuls of it before the enforcers watching protested and dragged her from the water's edge. They shoved her toward the back of the wagon, where Adder stood.

"Was that necessary?"

"You have no idea."

Adder's gaze flicked toward their guards. "They're not watching. Have you talked to Dylan?"

"He'd already figured out he'd have to be left behind if we tried to escape."

"Good."

"I still don't like it."

"It's necessary. We'll do what we can to get him back. As

soon as I see an opportunity, Tim and I will distract them. That's when you, Carter, and Aaron make a break for it. Head out onto the plains to the west if you can. If we get separated, meet back at the waypost we passed a few days ago. I've already told Aaron and Carter."

"I'll be ready."

Adder started to turn, then halted. "Can you help distract them, using the ley? Like they did in Erenthrall with the Wolves?"

She stretched out her senses, reaching for the ley lines that might be present near them. "I might be able to wield the ley like that, but not here. It isn't that strong."

"Then it will be up to Tim and me."

Adder drifted away slightly. When Tim caught her eye, he nodded, once, before turning to one side. Tim, the youngest of the Dogs, didn't seem as young to her now as he had before they'd left the Hollow.

Iscivius ordered the wagons back into motion. Kara headed toward Dylan's wagon, but before she could jump up onto its bed, Adder caught her arm and shook his head. Dylan motioned with one hand for her to stay back, the gesture hidden from the enforcers.

Kara fell back to join the others.

They followed the road the rest of the morning, the enforcers and White Cloaks never giving them any decent opportunity for Adder to seize upon, not even when they halted for a midday meal of cured meat, cheese, and the ubiquitous biscuits. It felt as if there were even more enforcers watching over them for this meal than in the past, all of them tense, but then she realized that their tension was focused outward, as if they were expecting an attack from outside the group. They were closing their ranks. She recalled what Dylan had overheard between Iscivius, Irmona, and Okata, that another group would be joining up with them, perhaps that evening.

They were running out of time.

After the wagons trundled into motion again, the group plodding along behind, Carter approached her, walking beside her for a long stretch in silence. A few times he drew a breath, as if about to ask her something, but he'd hold it a few moments, then exhale slowly.

Eventually, he shook his head and drifted away, looking angry and miserable.

Confused, Kara nearly called him back.

But then suddenly Adder dodged left. One moment, he was walking along behind Dylan's wagon a few paces in front of her, the next he took two steps to the side, body hunched down, and slammed into one of the enforcers. The man grunted as Adder drove him to the ground, those nearby, including Kara, brought up short, startled. Dust churned upward as they grappled with each other, rolling to one side, and then Adder landed two hard punches to the man's face, crushing his nose. He cried out as blood spurted, hands flying upward—

And then Adder had hold of the man's sword. He drew it with a snick as he spun into a crouch over the enforcer's body. It had all happened in an eerie silence punctuated only by grunts of effort and the scrapes and huffs of the scuffle.

Then Iscivius roared, "Get him!"

Adder lunged toward the enforcers closest to him. "The Kormanley must die!"

Kara jerked back as he drove the blade through another enforcer's chest and pulled it free. The man staggered, a look of surprise crossing his face as he fell, but Adder was already moving. He struck another man in the arm, slicing deep, the enforcer screaming. He caught another across the chest as Tim dove for the enforcer already dead from the chest wound. The younger Dog drew the man's sword and stepped into position at Adder's back, the two settling in and circling as if they'd practiced the move before.

But the enforcers had had enough time to shake off their shock and react. Swords had been drawn on all sides.

The nearest enforcers charged forward.

At the first clang of sword against sword, Kara spun, searching out Carter and Aaron. The younger Hollower stood paralyzed, mouth open, two steps behind her. Carter had one hand gripping the back of Dylan's wagon, knuckles white.

Kara bolted for the plains, grabbing onto Aaron's arm as she passed. "Come on." She didn't dare shout. It might draw the enforcers' attention. But Carter didn't move. Not even when he saw them charging straight for him. His entire body stiffened as Kara halted in front of him, shoving Aaron out onto the plains. "Run!"

Aaron sprinted into the grassland.

Swords clashing behind her, Kara seized Carter's arm. "Come on. We don't have much time."

Carter stared into her face, expression lost, mouth working.

But then he hardened, straightened. His hand refused to let go of the wagon. "I'm not coming."

"What?"

"I'm not coming! I'm staying with the White Cloaks. They need Wielders. They need me. No one in the Hollow cares about any of us. They only care about you."

Kara gripped both of his shoulders, aghast. "Carter, listen to me. We do care about you. The Hollow needs you. You don't know the Kormanley. You don't know what they're capable of. You need to come with us now. This is our only chance!"

She glanced over her shoulder. Adder and Tim were holding their own, Tim bloodied, but they were surrounded by the enforcers. None of the White Cloaks or the guards were paying any attention to them. But it wouldn't last long.

She spun back to the Wielder. "Carter, they will destroy you!"

"I'm staying."

He meant it. Kara could see it in his eyes.

She dropped her hands from his shoulders and ran onto the plains. The stone of the road changed to the softer pounding of earth as stalks of grass slapped against her thighs. She ran without a destination, pushed as hard as she could, her legs already protesting after the long, exhausting days of walking behind the wagons. Air burned in her lungs and sweat broke out on her forehead. Her still-damp clothing scraped at her skin, but she shoved all of the discomfort aside, her mind boiling with images of what the Kormanley had done to Erenthrall since she was young. The explosion in Seeley's Park that had killed her parents. The bombing of the Barons' Meeting that had set off the Purge that had killed Ischua. The riots that had rocked Erenthrall for years afterward.

She didn't want anything to do with the Kormanley or the White Cloaks or whatever they'd decided to call themselves now. This was her only chance to escape. They hadn't been given an opportunity before, but Adder and Tim had created one—

Adder.

She halted, so abruptly that she nearly pitched forward into the grass, and looked back. She'd made it maybe three hundred feet onto the plains. Adder and Tim were still fighting, and she suddenly realized they had no intention of breaking away to follow her and Aaron. They were fighting solely to give them the chance to flee. But by the wagon, Carter was calling out to the enforcer who'd remained with Dylan on the wagon and motioning toward her position.

The enforcer stood up and pointed.

Then he reached over into the seat of the wagon driver and pulled up a bow, already strung. He grabbed an arrow, nocked it, drew.

A moment before he released, Dylan leaped up and swung a water skin at his back. The arrow launched, shot harmlessly to Kara's left, as the archer tumbled from the wagon to the ground, Dylan clinging to the headboard between the bed and the seat. He shouted something to Kara that she couldn't hear through the pounding of her own blood in her ears, but she knew what he'd said.

The wagon's driver clubbed Dylan on the back of the head as she spun and lurched back into a run, thoughts of the Kormanley now threaded with a sickening nausea over what Adder and Tim had done. Tears blurred her eyes and she wiped at them furiously. Her mouth and throat were dry. She was choking on her own breath. Ahead, Aaron's figure outpaced her, at least five hundred feet away, a dark blot on the green-yellow grass.

Then he disappeared behind a ridge, dropping out of sight suddenly.

Kara continued, not slowing, her legs tiring, her chest aching. All she could think of was Adder and Tim, Dylan slumping into unconsciousness, Carter's betrayal. She and Aaron would have to return to the Hollow, get Bryce and some of the other Dogs, and return to save them. If they were still alive.

And then a figure rose up before her, a fist flying in to land a mind-numbing blow across her face.

Her last thought, before she slammed into the ground on her back and darkness claimed her, was that they'd forgotten about the enforcer scouts.

~~~

She woke abruptly with a cry of pain as someone tied her hands behind her back, the ropes cutting into her flesh. The cry was muffled by the gag in her mouth. It tasted of someone's sweat, salty and rank. As soon as the knots were finished, someone grabbed her by the back of the shirt and hauled her into a seated position.

She blinked, her head throbbing, her jaw swollen and aching. The sun hadn't moved. Dylan was still slumped over the headboard, the wagon driver standing over him. Adder lay prone, and Kara's heart skipped a beat in horror until one of the enforcers straddled his body, snatched up both limp arms, and began tying them as they'd done hers. They wouldn't be bothering if he was dead. Adder didn't stir. Behind him, Tim knelt, hunched forward with blood drooling from his mouth, his blond-brown hair hanging over his face. The front of his shirt was covered with blood as well, a flap hanging open where someone had cut him. He spat once, then lifted his head and met Kara's gaze.

"But I warned you!" Carter was thrown to the ground in front of Kara. "I stayed! I want to stay with you!"

An enforcer placed one knee on his back, and he could no longer breathe. He struggled, flailing, until another enforcer—the captain—grabbed his hands and trussed him with a few quick twists of the rope. Then they rolled him over and sat him up next to Aaron, the young Hollower hunched and dejected.

Iscivius, Irmona, and Okata stepped into view. Their white cloaks were stained with dirt, but they still hurt to look at in the bright sunlight. Or else Kara's vision had been screwed up from the fist to her face. She wondered where the other two White Cloaks were.

Iscivius moved to Adder's side, nudged him with one foot, hard, then knelt down to the unresponsive body. He rolled him over onto his side, slapped the Dog's face a few times, then let his body fall back as he stood.

He pointed to Tim. "Kill him."

Kara's eyes widened as one of the enforcers stepped forward, drawing a blade. She screamed, "No!" through the gag as the guard gripped Tim's head by the hair and slit his throat in one smooth motion. Blood sprayed outward onto the dusty road, Tim's eyes widening in mild shock as he choked and gurgled. Then the enforcer thrust him forward. His body slumped to the stone behind Adder, twitched, then stilled.

Kara swallowed back the urge to sob, her chest swollen with the effort. She wanted to scream, to let the cries rack her body, the accumulation of terror from all that had happened in Erenthrall seething inside her. But she bit down on the gag instead, breathed out forcefully through her nose, focused her anger and rage on Iscivius as he stepped forward. His cloak had been splattered with Tim's blood, but he didn't appear to have noticed. His attention was fixed solely on her.

He knelt down on one knee so that he was at eye level with her. "You shouldn't have tried to run. And they shouldn't have tried to fight." He motioned to Tim and Adder. "No Wielder from Erenthrall can fight like that. I suspected they were Dogs, but couldn't prove it. Now they've given themselves away."

He pointed to the unconscious Adder. "Kill him."

Kara bit down so hard on her scream of frustration she caught her tongue. The salty taste of blood flooded her mouth as two enforcers stepped forward, grabbed one arm each, and hauled Adder upright. The same enforcer that had killed Tim twisted his fingers into Adder's hair and yanked his head back. He raised the knife, still stained with Tim's blood, and placed it on the Dog's neck.

"Iscivius! Iscivius, someone's coming!"

Iscivius rose abruptly and turned toward the lead wagon, where one of the other White Cloaks now stood, pointing off toward the south. "Who?"

"It's the Son."

"How long do we have?"

"Not long. They're moving fast. It looks as if the Son and a small escort are outpacing the rest of the force."

Iscivius glanced around, gaze falling on Adder. "Release him. We'll have to let the Son deal with them now."

Okata merely stood to one side as Iscivius motioned for the enforcers to remove Tim's body. As they dragged the younger Dog off, Iscivius spoke with Irmona and Okata, their voices too low to make out, and then the White Cloak standing on the wagon warned them that the Son was near. Iscivius and the White Cloaks moved forward, to the far side of the wagon, along with the captain of the enforcers.

Adder was still unconscious. The man who'd killed Tim stood over him, knife still readied.

Kara's gag was soaked with saliva now and she realized it felt loose. She worked her jaw, managed to spit it out. "Who's this Son you're so afraid of?"

The man flicked a glance toward her.

Kara let her eyes wander over the rest of the enforcers. "So who is he? What has he done to make you fear him so? Why do the White Cloaks hate him?"

"You'll see soon enough," someone murmured.

"Quiet!" Tim's executioner dared someone else to speak, then wiped the blood from his knife using his sleeve.

Kara turned toward Aaron and Carter. "What about you two? Ever hear of this Son? Or this Father?"

Carter dropped his gaze, shoulders tense with defiance, but not fast enough that Kara didn't see the flicker of doubt. He pulled at the ties binding his hands as the muscles in his jaw clenched.

"Never heard of either of them," Aaron said.

One of the enforcers stepped forward and clouted him across the back of his head. The Hollower hissed in pain and hunched forward, but then caught sight of the pool of blood soaking into the ground where Tim had fallen. He carefully straightened, back stiff, stance rigid. A stoic defiance, in counterpoint to Carter's sulk.

On the other side of the wagon, the thunder of approaching hooves grew, then died as the horses slowed. She couldn't see anything and didn't dare move, not with the enforcers watching them so closely, especially Tim's killer.

But she heard the heavy thuds as the men who'd approached dismounted. Harnesses jangled, and one of the horses snorted.

"What did you find in Erenthrall?"

Kara stiffened. Iscivius answered, but his words were lost in the blood rush in Kara's ears. Aaron shot her a questioning look. She knew her face was likely white with shock, slack with denial, but she couldn't force any words out, her throat too tight.

Iscivius, Irmona, and Okata appeared from around the side of the wagon, followed by the enforcers and another man, head turned slightly away as he spoke to the White Cloaks. He was dressed like them, the white blazing even though he was as dusty as they were, if not as bloody.

As he rounded the corner of the wagon, he turned and caught sight of Kara. He stopped dead in his tracks, whatever he'd been saying cut off midsentence.

"Kara?" He laughed, the sound choked off by disbelief as he ran a hand through his thick, brown-blond, mussed hair. He hesitated, the other White Cloaks staring at him in confusion. He didn't appear to notice. Instead, he reached for her, another laugh breaking out, and asked, "Is it really you?"

Through teeth clenched so tight her jaw ached, she spat, "Marcus."

# Seventeen

MARCUS RECOILED FROM HER. The enforcers surrounding them tensed, the man who'd killed Tim stepping forward until Iscivius halted him with a wave of a hand. Marcus appeared oblivious to all of it, his focus on her. After his initial retreat, he stilled, hands falling to his sides.

"Kara?" Hope still touched his voice, although it had become curiously flat.

None of it affected Kara's rage.

"It was you, wasn't it? You were the one causing the blackouts. You were the one manipulating the Nexus. All for the Kormanley? You destroyed Erenthrall. You destroyed everything!"

"I knew you wouldn't understand. That's why I never told you." He noticed the tension in the guards, in his fellow White Cloaks, even the anger in the rest of those captured. He also noted the pool of blood soaking the earth where Tim had bled out, but his gaze returned to Kara. "You don't understand. But you will."

He gestured toward the blood on the ground. "What happened?"

"They tried to escape. Two of them attacked our

enforcers while the others tried to flee onto the plains. Our scouts stopped them."

"Not all of us tried to run," Carter grumbled. "I warned you. They might have escaped if not for me."

Iscivius gave the young Wielder a condescending look. "Our scouts would have found them regardless."

Marcus ignored the exchange. "So what happened? Was one of them killed during the attack?"

"No, we killed him afterward. He wasn't a Wielder. He fought too well for that."

Marcus' hands closed into fists. "You couldn't have known that. Not all Wielders are like us. Some of them know how to handle weapons. Have you forgotten about Chekla? She had no idea she could manipulate the ley, because those in the Archipelago aren't tested. Yet Lecrucius said she had more latent talent than even you. We need every Wielder we can find."

"He wasn't a Wielder."

"We'll never know now, will we?" Marcus swept his gaze over Kara and the rest. "Were these the only ones found in Erenthrall? I thought there were more."

Irmona stepped forward. "There were. The Underearthers brought twelve of them to the meeting place. Iscivius had one of their archers killed, but only wounded the second. We would have had them all if the damn Wolves hadn't attacked. The entire square erupted into chaos. We had to call up the ley in order to keep the Wolves at bay. But before that, they tore into our enforcers. Five of the ones the Underearthers brought us escaped with one of our wagons. We managed to subdue these and drive off the Wolves."

Marcus scanned the rest of those with Kara. "Aside from her, which of the others are confirmed Wielders?"

"The man in the wagon, named Dylan, and the snitch, Carter."

Carter focused on Marcus. "I want to join up with you. I want to become a White Cloak."

Marcus moved closer, until he stood over him. "Why?"

"Because they don't listen to me. They don't let me do anything. It's all about her." He jutted his chin out toward Kara. "I'm better than her, but they don't give anyone else a chance to do anything."

Marcus' eyebrow rose. "Better than her? Are you certain?"

Carter dropped his gaze to the dirt. He steadied himself, then raised his head, eyes narrowed and hard. "I know I can *be* better than her. You just have to give me a chance."

Kara didn't think they'd been ignoring him in the Hollow or on the excursion to Erenthrall, but obviously Carter had seen things differently. Resentment laced the pain in his eyes as he stared up at Marcus.

The tableau held for an uncomfortable moment, even the enforcers fidgeting in place. Irmona and Okata traded glances. Iscivius stiffened in affront.

Finally, Marcus reached out. The young Wielder flinched back at first, as if he expected Marcus to strike him, but when Marcus simply held his palm flat, arm extended, Carter shifted back.

Marcus rested his hand on the Wielder's head. "The Father accepts this young man's words as truth through me, his Son. He will be judged by the Father on our return." Then he dropped his hand and faced Iscivius. "Release him. He's one of us for the moment, until Father has had a chance to speak to him."

Iscivius drew a breath as if to protest, but Irmona cleared her throat behind him and, after a slight hesitation, he motioned the enforcer who'd killed Tim forward. The guard stepped behind Carter and cut the ropes that bound him. "What of the others?"

Marcus looked directly at Kara. "Keep them bound. Load them into the back of the wagons and join up with our group. Keep a watch on them at all times."

"Where are we headed?"

"Back to the Needle. The latest quakes to the north have rearranged the ley lines yet again. There are some new, stronger lines coming down from the north that we may be able to use to our advantage. We need to consult with Father."

Iscivius pointed to the guard who'd killed Tim. "Riley, get them into the wagon. Then secure it. I want at least half a dozen enforcers around it at all times. As soon as you're ready—"

He stilled, eyes going wide, then spun toward the

southeast, hands rising as if to ward off an attack. Everyone in the entire group halted where they stood, midmotion, the enforcers in bewilderment. Aaron gasped. Riley's hand flew toward his sword.

Then Kara felt it. Her skin crawled, as if covered in a thousand ants. Except these ants weren't prickling her flesh, they were seething underneath her skin. Her head snapped toward the southeast. At the same time, a spike of pain drove itself deep into her skull between her eyes. She groaned, mouth open as she bent forward. Someone near her—Okata she thought—cried out and collapsed to the ground. She could see him writhing in the dirt, shouting something in his own language, but a wash of jagged yellow light blinded her. Her forehead struck the earth, but the pressure continued. Her ears popped, and one of the horses screamed, shrill and panicked.

"What's going on?" Riley—who stood right beside Kara—sounded as if he were a thousand yards away, muted and distant. "What's happening?"

Kara ground her forehead into the dirt, trying to end the pain. Grit gouged into her flesh, a stone cutting into her skin. That pain was a breath of cool air compared to the white-hot ice pick inside her skull. It dug deeper, then deeper still—

And then it halted, as abrupt as Riley's slicing of Tim's throat.

She collapsed to one side. Something warm trickled down her forehead. Something else etched itself down her cheek and dripped off the bridge of her nose. She knew it was blood—her own blood. Moans surrounded her. It took her a moment to realize some of them were her own. Her chest ached. Her skull felt hollow. But the sensation of ants crawling beneath her skin had abated, ending as swiftly as the ice pick. All of it echoed through her body with a dull sense of familiarity, as if she'd experienced something similar before: an escalating sensation that cut off abruptly.

Except what she'd experienced before hadn't been physical. It had been a sound.

She rolled back onto her forehead and knees, then lurched upright. All around her, the Wielders lay on the ground in various stages of pain or recovery—Okata apparently unconscious, Irmona on her back, staring up at the sky, Carter staggering to his feet, Iscivius on his knees, back ramrod straight. Only Marcus remained standing, staring off toward the southeast. The enforcers hadn't been affected. Riley had stepped protectively to Marcus' side.

Kara took all of this in with a swift glance, her attention riveted in the direction Marcus and Iscivius were staring.

Toward the piercing light that hovered above Tumbor.

That light had intensified to an eye-straining white that forced Kara to flinch away as soon as she looked at it directly. She blinked, the image of it burned into her vision.

Then, face still averted, she caught the flare. The ground around her was bathed with the pulse, everything eerily silent, just as it had been in Erenthrall when the distortion there quickened. Her skin tingled with remembered terror— the growls of the Wolves as they bore down upon her and Allan, Artras and the rest, the helplessness of her own exhaustion, the fear of being trapped. All of it washed through her as the white flare bled the color from the world. But then it died and she snapped her attention back toward Tumbor.

The white light that had hovered over the city like a tiny, vibrant sun since the Shattering imploded down to nothing in utter silence, paused, then suddenly exploded in a sheath of vibrant color. Arms of gold, fiery red, and deep purple expanded outward, reaching for the heavens and the earth at the same time, a whirlpool of exquisite beauty. The distortion grew and grew, larger than the one that had engulfed Erenthrall. But of course it was larger. There was no one in Tumbor attempting to halt the quickening, no Wielders attempting to control it—to heal it—like Kara, Artras, Dylan, and Nathen had tried to do. This distortion was unfettered.

It engulfed the horizon, reaching toward them. Everyone stood silent. But when it didn't halt within a few breaths, some of the enforcers stepped back. One of them turned to Marcus and asked, "Will it stop? Should we run?"

"Where would you run to?"

But the distortion slowed and halted. A pulse of light coursed through the jagged threads of lightning that wove between the thick, colored bands of its arms, and then it set.

A sphere ten times as wide as the one in Erenthrall. Kara shuddered to think of how much land it had captured, how many people. Everyone who had remained in Tumbor, for certain. It must have encompassed the city within moments. She couldn't imagine why anyone would have stayed after what they'd seen happen to Erenthrall, but she knew after the initial shock of the Shattering, after they'd survived the winter, they would have drifted back into the familiar streets and buildings, even with the threat of the pulsing white light overhead. They would have convinced themselves that the danger had passed, that the distortion would have quickened by now if it were going to quicken at all. And some would have been driven to the streets in desperation, regardless of the danger.

All of them were trapped inside the fractured shards of the distortion now. Caught, like insects in amber.

Kara climbed to her feet, wincing as pain lanced through her skull when she bent her head forward. The world reeled for a moment, but she steadied herself. The tackiness of blood mixed with grit from the ground coated her forehead, but her hands were still bound behind her back, so she couldn't wipe it away.

When she could focus again, she found Riley between her and Marcus, a knife in one hand. "I can barely stand, and you think I'll attack someone?"

He began to respond, but Marcus put a restraining hand on his shoulder. "Do what Iscivius ordered before the quickening. I doubt any of the Wielders are in any shape to resist you now."

The enforcers loaded Aaron and Adder into the cart where Dylan's body still slumped. They ignored Carter, except to force him to one side as three of them hefted Adder's limp form into the wagon. Two others dragged Dylan down from the headboard. When they let him fall so that his head cracked into one of the crates, Aaron cried out in indignation and leaped into the back of the wagon, hunching over the Wielder protectively.

"Are you all right?"

"You didn't seem to be affected by the quickening, Marcus. Why is that?"

"It felt like my entire body had seized up. My muscles

were locked so tight I couldn't move. I was paralyzed. That's the only reason I didn't keel over or collapse like the rest of you. I didn't react that way when the distortion over Erenthrall quickened."

Weakness washed through Kara. She didn't know if it was from the effects of the distortion or simply weariness with Marcus. "None of us did. But Tumbor's distortion was significantly larger."

"That could be the reason." He was staring off into the distance, at where the orange-red-purple sphere cut off a significant chunk of their view to the south.

"Look at it! It's ten times the size of the one in Erenthrall!"

"No need to get exasperated. I'm only thinking out loud." He waved toward the distortion. "It's farther away than it looks. Distances on the plains are deceiving."

"And you think that makes a difference? It swallowed all that remained of Tumbor. It must have swallowed up ten miles or more in every direction outside of the city. If this is what happened in Tumbor after the distortion waited six months to quicken, what will happen in Farrade? In the cities to the north?" She staggered, Marcus reaching out to steady her without thought. "Gods, Marcus. We can't even figure out how to fix the distortion in Erenthrall. How are we going to repair the one in Tumbor?"

Marcus' face abruptly went blank. "Father will find a way."

Kara stared at him, then pulled her arm from his grasp even though she was still feeling weak. She stepped back. "What happened to you, Marcus? You weren't this deluded back in Erenthrall."

"Back before the Purge, you mean? Before the Baron killed Ischua and executed all of those supposed Kormanley insurgents in the marketplaces across the city?" Kara flinched at the mention of Ischua. Marcus saw it and visibly controlled himself. "I'm not the one who's deluded about what happened in Erenthrall. I haven't been deluded since the Purge."

"Since Deirdre, you mean."

"Since Deirdre, yes. Since she showed me what was really going on in Erenthrall with the Baron and the Prime Wielders, how they were controlling us with the ley."

"I'm certain she showed you more than that."

Marcus didn't answer. Instead, he spun around and stalked off. "Iscivius! Are we ready to depart yet?"

One of the enforcers came up to Kara's side and with a flick of his fingers motioned her toward the wagon where Aaron, Adder, and Dylan were already waiting, all but Aaron still unconscious. Kara allowed herself to be hefted up into the wagon beside Aaron, who now knelt next to Adder's body.

"How is he?"

"He's out cold. He probably has a concussion."

Kara nudged Adder's head to one side until she found the blood-matted hair where he'd been struck. A large lump had swollen up just beneath the base of his skull, the skin split. If they'd been in the Hollow, Logan would have likely already stitched it closed, but she couldn't do anything about it here.

She let his head roll back, then steadied herself as the wagon lurched forward. The White Cloaks were shouting back and forth, the enforcers spreading out, although a quick glance verified that Iscivius had kept twice as many of the guards on the wagon as usual. Up ahead, the riders who'd accompanied Marcus waited, Marcus himself riding out ahead of the wagons to return to them.

When she settled back down into the wagon, she noted Aaron's pale face.

"How are you doing?"

Aaron opened and closed his mouth a few times before any words escaped. "Everything happened so fast. The fight, running, Carter, and then Tim—"

She let Aaron lean into her for comfort, until he pulled back. He was staring at Carter.

"How could he do it? After everything that happened in Erenthrall, how could he turn on us?"

"He did what he felt he had to do."

"He got Tim killed."

"Yes, he did."

"He nearly got Adder killed. If the White Cloaks hadn't been interrupted—"

Kara nudged him, forced him to focus on her. "Yes, and he'll have to live with that. You need to focus on us, not him. He made his choice. Now, what about Dylan?"

"He's better off than Adder. They didn't hit him as hard."
Through the part in Dylan's hair, they could see the swelling
where he'd been clubbed. It was higher up and to one side
and the skin hadn't been split. But it was an ugly red-purple
in color.

Kara checked it as Aaron slumped back against the
crates in the wagon. Then she looked Adder and Dylan over
from head to toe as best she could while still bound. Aside
from a few cuts and scrapes on Adder from the fight, and
Dylan's knee, they both appeared to be in relatively good
shape.

She sat back, the wagon jostling beneath her as they continued down the roadway toward the Needle. Her mind
drifted, returning to Tim, to the stark horror of seeing his
throat slit in front of her. What had they done with him?
Had they just left his body behind, by the side of the road?

"Is it really him?"

It took a moment before Kara realized it was Aaron who'd
spoken, and then she couldn't figure out who he meant.

"Is it really Marcus? The one they say caused the Shattering?"

Kara couldn't answer for a long moment, the roiling mass
of emotion Marcus' name called up tightening her chest.

But finally she said, "Yes. It's really him."

Cory was limping toward the entrance to the caverns when
he felt the world around him shudder. It was like a hard
gust of wind coming from the south, rippling through reality
in a wave, except that it didn't bend the branches of the
trees forward, or even set the leaves fluttering. Yet it compressed his chest. He gasped and leaned his weight against
the makeshift walking stick he'd been using for the past two
days, even though he didn't really need it; his ankle was
nearly whole again.

Ahead, no one bustling around the mouth of the cavern
reacted to the strange shudder after it passed. They continued hauling supplies from the wagons into the rooms and
tunnels beyond—the last of the supplies, from what Sophia
said. All that was left was what remained to be harvested
from the fields.

If they were given enough time to do any reaping.

Cory had decided that the shudder had been nothing but an aftereffect of his injury—a wave of dizziness from exertion—when Paul suddenly charged from the cavern's entrance. "Where's Logan?"

Someone responded, and the elderly leader of the Hollow scowled through his panic. "Drop that sack and get into the village! Drag Logan back here if you have to. Tell him something's happened to the Wielders!"

Cory surged forward. He reached the cavern's entrance a moment later, Paul now surrounded by babbling villagers. Paul held his hands up to keep everyone back then motioned him forward. Cory waded through the throng to his side.

"Everyone, go back to work. You heard Bryce's last report. The raiders were last seen three days ago, and we haven't seen them since. We need to get the caverns secured now!"

The group grumbled, but most began hauling sacks and barrels again.

Paul watched them until he was satisfied they were working, then focused on Cory. "Come with me. Most of them are in the main cavern with the stellae—"

He cut off as a flare of light passed overhead, like lightning. But there wasn't a cloud in the sky, and this flare was brighter and held longer before dying. Everyone looked up, one or two shading their eyes, searching the heavens, including Paul.

"What in hells' flames was that?"

"I don't know." But Cory could think of only one thing that would produce a flare of light like that. "I'll investigate it later, if Bryce and Hernande haven't looked into it already. What happened to the Wielders?"

Paul let his hand drop. "Right. The Wielders. Whatever happened, it didn't affect them all the same way." They entered the cavern and he led Cory toward the deeper rooms. "Two of them just passed out, hitting the cavern floor like sacks of stone. Raven clutched her stomach like she'd been punched and then vomited. Mareane and another collapsed in some kind of seizure."

"Were only the Wielders affected?"

"One of the University students said he felt nauseous. But the others in the room only looked spooked. I thought it was because of what had happened to the Wielders."

They ducked through the doorway into the main chamber. The stellae remained unchanged, the white light of the ley bubbling up from the stone undisturbed. Whatever had happened, it hadn't affected the ley in any visible way here. The floor of the chamber had been cleared of all of the debris from the previous earthquake, except for the stones that were too heavy to move, like the one that had crushed Cory's leg. His eyes skimmed over that one as he scanned the rest of the room, Paul already beginning to descend the steps that they'd built over the scree. The outskirts of the chamber had been rigged with wooden frames and hung with blankets and sheets and tarps, so that each of the rooms had some small amount of privacy. The refugees from Erenthrall had adjusted to the bareness of the accommodations immediately—they'd been sleeping in tents and ruins since the Shattering—but those from the Hollow were finding it more difficult.

"Paul! Cory! Over here!"

Cory caught Raven waving both hands to the left of the stellae. He and Paul veered in that direction as Cory picked out bodies laid out on the stone floor to either side. Raven had dropped back down into a crouch near Mareane.

"What happened?"

"Mareane had a seizure. The others either seized or passed out." She ran the back of her arm across her forehead. Only then did Cory realize her skin was pale beneath the smudged dirt and drying blood.

"What about you?"

"It was as if someone had stabbed me in the stomach with a hot poker. It took me to my hands and knees, and then I—" She waved vaguely to where a puddle of vomit stood off to one side. "There was a pain in my head as well, right here." She pointed to the center of her forehead, between her eyebrows. "After I recovered, I realized I'd bled from the nose."

Cory glanced around at the others laid out on the floor. Mareane was quiet and appeared to be asleep, her hands folded primly over her chest.

Logan and Morrell appeared at the top of the scree. Paul waved and they began to descend. Logan knelt next to Mareane immediately, reaching to touch her forehead lightly with his fingertips as he motioned Morrell toward the others.

Cory watched silently, then turned to Raven. "What caused this?"

"I don't know." But she reached out to squeeze his hand. "Check Erenthrall."

Then Logan pushed him back from her, forcefully but not unkindly. "Let me take a look."

Cory retreated. He wanted to speak to the other University students, but they were all helping the healers.

Jerrain suddenly appeared, the elderly mentor straining up into Cory's face. "Did you feel it? Did you feel the Tapestry writhing?"

"Mentor! You startled me."

"The foundations of the Tapestry shuddered and somehow I startled you? What is the University system coming to?"

"What do you mean the foundations of the Tapestry shuddered?"

"Exactly what he said."

Cory turned as Hernande came up beside them. His mentor glanced toward where Logan and Morrell were working on the Wielders.

"The Tapestry . . . shuddered."

"Isn't that what it felt like to you?" Hernande caught Jerrain's attention and motioned them away from those gathered. "Or didn't you feel anything?"

"I felt it. I haven't spoken to the others yet, but Paul said that all of them here looked spooked, so they must have experienced something."

"I'm not surprised. They aren't as trained as you are. They don't know how to interpret what it is they see or feel yet." Jerrain dismissed them with a wave of his hand. "But it was definitely a systemic warping of the Tapestry. Something caused the entire structure to shake on a fundamental level."

"What?"

"Do I look like I have all the answers? It could have been anything!"

"I don't recall any mention of such an event in any of the readings at the University," Hernande said. "I'm not certain it's ever happened before."

"Practically none of what's happened since the Shattering has happened before."

"What about Sovaan and Jasom? Have you spoken to them yet? What did they think?"

"Sovaan panicked and rushed off to warn Sophia, although I don't know what he expects her to do. Jasom is still helping to move supplies. I don't think he's stopped."

They reached the stairs up the scree and began to ascend.

"Where are we going?" Cory asked.

"Outside, to see if we can't figure out what caused the shudder."

They wound through the tunnels to the outer chamber, everyone buzzing with the strange occurrences except for a few of the younger children racing about. Quite a few people paused to ask Hernande and Jerrain questions. One or two shouted from a distance. Jerrain ignored nearly everyone, waving a hand distractedly and mumbling something incomprehensible, but Hernande tried to be reassuring.

Once they were outside and clear of the main activity at the cavern entrance, Hernande looked toward the sky in thought. "Which direction did the disturbance come from, in your opinion, Cory?"

He thought back to his hike up the slope of the hill toward the cavern, turned to face the direction he'd been moving, and then pointed off toward the southeast. "It came from over there." He paused and considered the flare of light. "I think the flare of light came from the same direction."

"Light?" Jerrain asked.

"A flare of bright light."

"I was inside the caverns. Describe it to me."

As Hernande led them off the main path back to the village, heading to the hills to the southeast, Cory explained what he'd seen to Jerrain, answering the elder mentor's questions as precisely as he could. Hernande explained what he'd seen and felt from the village. Both he and Jerrain had experienced the same thing as Cory, but at what sounded like a more fundamental level; they'd known what it meant.

"I think it's similar to what the Wielders say is happening to the ley." Cory caught a significant look passing between Hernande and Jerrain. He'd seen looks like that from the mentors all through his tenure at the University as a student. "What? What am I missing?"

"The ley lines have been broken. What we're seeing now with the ley is a system that's seizing, trying to reassert itself. From what we've seen with the node in the caverns, I believe the theory that the quakes are related to the ley lines finding new pathways for themselves in the search for stability is correct. But what we just experienced with the Tapestry is fundamentally different."

"Why?"

"Because the Tapestry, as far as we know, isn't broken."

They'd reached the top of the ridge, the view still screened by trees. Cory thought about what Hernande had said as they began following the ridge toward where the trees dropped away and an outcropping of stone would give them a view of the southeast. Cory didn't see how the quakes and the ley were that much different from the contorted ripple he'd felt in the Tapestry—

Until he suddenly realized what Hernande meant.

"The Tapestry isn't broken . . . *yet*."

"What we felt could be the first sign that the Tapestry itself is suffering some kind of strain, that it may, like the ley system in Erenthrall, fail as well on some fundamental level."

"But we aren't abusing it, not like the Baron and the Prime Wielders were in Erenthrall."

"Weren't we? We were manipulating it just as they were manipulating the ley."

"But not to the same extent!"

Hernande held up a hand to forestall him. "I agree, in principle. And I don't think the shudder we felt has anything to do with our own manipulations of the Tapestry."

"But that doesn't mean that what happened to the ley lines isn't somehow affecting the Tapestry," Jerrain interjected.

"Recall what we were investigating with the sands. We were researching the connection between the Tapestry and the ley, and we used that connection to map the ley system. Mentors have known for decades that the two systems are intrinsically tied together, but we've never known exactly how, even though we used those connections in Erenthrall to help the Prime Wielders build the ley system. All of the ley lines—the conduits, the ley barge routes, the nodes—all of those are stabilized by manipulations of the Tapestry, so that the Wielders aren't needed to constantly supervise every junction and line. Even the creation of the towers in Grass came about through Primes and mentors from the University working together, the mentors warping the Tapestry into appropriate channels, the Primes directing the ley through those channels to sow the towers. Once you'd finished your studies at the graduate level, you'd have been taught how the Tapestry can be used to construct artifices and fields that would funnel the ley into whatever configurations the Primes needed. It only makes sense that if you damage one, you damage both."

"But the Tapestry didn't seem affected in Erenthrall after the Shattering."

"Not in any obvious way." The trees were beginning to thin. Ahead, Jerrain was pushing the lower limbs aside as they neared the edge of the forest and the outcropping. "But the Shattering was linked directly to the Nexus. Its destructive power was funneled through the ley line system. That's how it passed from city to city, until it covered the entire network across the continent, based on what we've seen of the cities within sight of the plains. I think it's safe to say that every city and town connected to the ley system was affected by the power surge to a great, most likely catastrophic, extent."

"But if the Shattering mostly affected the ley lines and not the Tapestry, why would it be reacting now?"

Hernande raised his hands to ward off the branches that were snapping back into his face as Jerrain let them go. The elder mentor could be heard muttering to himself and spluttering up ahead as he forced his way through the last of the trees. "Something must have happened that disturbed the Tapestry more directly. Something still connected to the ley, otherwise the Wielders wouldn't have had such an adverse reaction. Something—"

"Something like that."

Hernande shoved the last of the thick branches aside,

holding them so that Cory could pass. After the relative shadows beneath the trees, the direct sunlight blinded him, and Cory shielded his face, blinking into the distance.

When he finally realized he was seeing another distortion—one significantly more massive than the one in Erenthrall, although an orange-red-purple rather than the more familiar green and pink—his arm dropped to his side. "It's over Tumbor."

Hernande shifted a few steps ahead of him, toward the edge of the finger of stone that jutted out from the ridge at a slight upward angle.

"The sheer size of it . . ." Jerrain trailed off. "Think of the power necessary to generate such a structure. Where did it come from?"

"The distortion over Erenthrall was siphoning power from the remains of the Nexus and the lake of ley beneath the city. The singularity over Tumbor must have been doing the same for the past ten months." Hernande looked at Cory, as if for confirmation. "It's no surprise the result is so monstrous. There was no one there to halt or lessen its formation, like there was in Erenthrall."

Kara.

Cory's gaze shot toward Erenthrall. But the distortion there appeared unchanged.

"It's too bad we can't go study it." Jerrain was still eyeing the distortion over Tumbor. "Obviously its formation caused some kind of feedback or significant stress to the Tapestry. The formation of the one in Erenthrall must have done the same; we simply couldn't detect it. It must not have been as powerful."

"Or we were preoccupied with survival."

"Or that. I wonder if the damage to the Tapestry was more significant closer to Tumbor? Maybe what we felt was an echo. What would the manifestations of such damage be?"

Hernande began to stroke his beard in thought. "The distortion itself is damage enough. It's a fracturing of reality, isn't it? And isn't the Tapestry simply a more fundamental layer of reality, a layer beneath the surface that most people can't sense or manipulate? We probably should have studied the Tapestry and its connection to the ley more closely before using it."

"Human nature demands we use the tools we discover, even before we understand them."

Something flashed in the distance. Not from the direction of either Erenthrall or Tumbor. This was much closer, coming from beneath them, from the forest below.

Cory stepped up to the outcropping's edge and looked down. He scanned the nearest hills, but he saw nothing except treetops and patches of earth and stone through the foliage.

Another flash snapped his gaze to the left and a little farther distant, to where the trees were broken by a ravine. He couldn't see the stream that had cut its way through the stone, but he didn't need to. The raiders were at the top. Three of them. One of them was pointing in their direction with his sword, the sun glinting off its flat side.

A moment later, one of the others yanked a bow from off his back and began to string it.

Cory spun toward Hernande and Jerrain. "Raiders! Get back!" He lurched forward and shoved both of the startled mentors toward the forest, Jerrain staggering and falling to his side with a sharp cry of pain. Hernande stumbled but didn't hesitate, crashing through the nearest branches as Cory leaned down and hauled Jerrain to his feet, practically throwing the light-framed elder into the trees. Branches scratched across his face and leaves slapped his face, but the expected pain of an arrow embedding itself in his back never manifested.

"What in hells!" Jerrain cradled his arm against his side. "What's gotten into you? You nearly broke my elbow shoving me to the ground like that!"

"Raiders. They're on the lip of the ravine to the east. One of them was stringing a bow."

Hernande moved to peer through the trees. "Cory's right. How many did you see?"

"Three."

"There are more than three now. I see at least two dozen. And they're headed toward the Hollow."

# Eighteen

CORY CURSED AS A BRANCH slashed across his face.
By the tingling burn, he knew it had drawn blood, but
before he could reach to verify it, his foot skidded in
the damp, leafy slope and he fell, crying out.

Ahead of him, Hernande turned, then hurried back to
help him upright. They could hear Jerrain spitting and
thrashing his way down behind them, slowed by his age, the
trees, and the steepness of the hill.

"Are you all right?" Hernande pulled him up by one
arm.

Cory brushed dirt and leaves from the seat of his
breeches. "I'm fine. We don't have time—"

From the northwest, the Hollow's warning bell sounded.

"They're near the village!" Jerrain batted at the branches
surrounding him, then stumbled to a halt beside them, gasping. He sucked in a breath to continue speaking, but the
distant toll of the bell suddenly faltered with a harsh clang
and fell silent.

All three of them stilled.

"I think they're already at the village."

"We have to help them."

Hernande shifted his grip from Cory's elbow to his

shoulder. "You can move faster if you leave us behind, even with your bruised leg."

"Mentor—"

Hernande cut him off with a shake of his head. "There's no time to argue. We'll catch up. Go do whatever you can."

He emphasized the words with a shove. Cory stumbled, then straightened and ducked beneath the nearest set of branches. His pace was slow at first; he was still hesitant about leaving them alone and trying to be careful with his foot, but after their voices and the snap of branches as they followed faded, he gained speed. He plowed down the hill, dodged deadfalls and stumps, skidded in the earthy loam in soft patches and nearly tripped over hidden stones, but he stayed upright. His breath burned in his lungs, and within twenty minutes his side began to cramp. One hand raised to ward off branches, he dug a palm into the stitch and pressed onward. The landscape blurred into boles to be dodged, boulders to bypass, and exposed stone bluffs to circle. He headed toward the Hollow on instinct.

He splashed across a creek, feet and legs soaked to mid-calf, and then heard the first screams. He halted halfway up the far bank, one arm reaching for the root of a birch, and listened. Through the harsh sound of his panting, the clash of weapons sifted through the trees, so faint it could have been drowned out by the rustling of the leaves overhead if there'd been a breeze.

He snagged the root and pulled himself up the bank, then broke into a halting jog, moving more cautiously now, searching ahead for any sign of the raiders. The sounds of fighting increased, but it was the smell of smoke that brought him to another halt.

"No."

He darted forward and nearly missed the man standing guard at the edge of the path leading to the center of the Hollow. He was dressed in tattered black and gray, makeshift armor covering his shoulders and most of his chest and back. The man spun as Cory blundered forward, then grinned through his ragged beard, sword raised. His skin was pocked with red sores, and a single gold earring hung from his left ear.

"I knew someone would come running to me. It's why I didn't complain when they put me on sentry duty."

With a leer of anticipation, the man stepped forward.

Without thought, Cory reached out unnecessarily with one hand while simultaneously stretching out with his mind. He snagged the Tapestry with his thoughts, then abruptly twisted, his hand following suit.

The bandit gasped, free hand slamming into his substandard armor as he tried to clutch at his chest. He staggered forward, sword dipping down to the ground, then dropped to his knees. He caught Cory's gaze, eyes wide in shock, and emitted a horrible, gurgling croak, as if his lungs were filled with fluid.

Then he fell onto his side, twitched once—a spasm that ran through his entire body—and stilled.

Cory's arm dropped to his side.

He glanced around, the smell of smoke growing stronger, then lurched forward, falling to his knees beside the man. He grabbed the bandit's sword and shoved it away, out of reach, before rolling the body to the side. He pressed his fingers hard into the side of the man's neck, beneath the jaw, but he already knew he was dead. His skin was pale, growing grayer as Cory watched. A single bead of blood had blossomed in his black beard beneath one nostril, strangely dark and somehow more alive than the rest of him.

"It worked." Cory sat back onto his heels. A tremor coursed through him. He and the other University students had been practicing the knots for days, wreaking havoc on the slopes and forests around the caverns. But shattering rock and killing a man by opening up a knot in the center of his chest were utterly different experiences. He'd never felt numb when the stones splintered into fragments, never had this odd fluid sensation in his gut, as if his bowels were about to let go.

A scream pierced the numbness, jolting him. He jerked back from the body, tripped over the sword, then caught himself. Half-crouched, he ran his arm over his mouth, gaze darting through the forest around him and toward the thickening smoke. But the trees were eerily still, the pathway empty.

Standing, he scrubbed his hands on breeches and sucked in a steadying breath.

"It's what we practiced for." He flinched at the sound of his own voice.

He shuffled forward a few steps, then halted and returned for the sword. It felt familiar and awkward in his hands at the same time. He turned to the pathway and edged into the denser smoke.

Within twenty paces he was forced to hold his free arm over his mouth and nose or choke on the fumes. His eyes burned and watered as he coughed, but through the swirling tendrils he could hear moans and screams, the sounds of fighting oddly distorted.

Then he stumbled over a body, one of the villagers, a ragged wound in the side of his neck. He wore a surprised expression, as if he'd never seen the attack coming. Cory paused long enough to verify he was dead, then moved on, crouching down where the smoke wasn't as thick. Another body lay a few paces away, and he crawled toward it, but it was one of the bandits, his head stove in on one side, hair bloody and matted with brain matter and bone. Cory gagged and stumbled to the left—

And out of the smoke. He fell to one knee in surprise, coughing and blinking in the sunlight, vision blurred. Figures fought ahead, the clash of blade against armor and the grunts of effort shockingly clear and close. He recognized the shape of the village center, the communal oven and cottages to the left, the meeting hall burning to the right. At least two other buildings were on fire, but the bulk of the smoke came from the hall. He couldn't tell how many villagers and raiders were present, but it didn't appear to be many. Fewer than he'd expected.

Maybe the short warning signal they'd heard had been enough.

Then, eyes still watery, a shadow charged up from Cory's right, coming from the direction of the hall. Cory didn't have time to be surprised. He raised his sword to counter the half-glimpsed strike he knew was coming. A blade pounded down on his defense, numbing his arm, and he fell backward into a sprawl as he reached forward and twisted the Tapestry.

A squelchy crack—like a splintering tree branch, only wetter—sounded. The man bearing down on him howled in agony and dropped to the ground. Cory scrambled back farther as the man writhed. His vision finally cleared. Bryce,

Braddon, and a slew of the men and women recruited by the Dogs for training were hacking and slashing at the attackers as they slowly gave ground. The center of the village was littered with bodies, not all of them villagers. Those attackers not engaged with Bryce and the others were ransacking the cottages, heaving furniture and earthenware and anything else not of immediate use out into the square. They were being more careful at Logan's cottage, hauling out medical supplies and medicine and stacking it near a wagon. They were directed by a tall, thin man with a scruffy beard wearing a lord's jacket.

The man was watching him.

Cory swallowed, mouth dry, and his gaze fell to the man at his feet, whose howls had degenerated into low moans. He recoiled as he realized the man was clutching the lower half of his arm to his chest, the forearm hanging on by threads of skin near a wound at the elbow. Blood spurted from the ragged hole that had once been muscle and bone.

He'd missed the man's heart when he'd twisted the Tapestry and released the knot. It had exploded inside the man's arm, nearly ripped it from his body. He tasted bile at the back of his throat, but the leader of the raiders had caught the attention of three of the crew at Logan's cottage and motioned them toward Cory. The moans of the man were fading, his breath hitching now. Cory shot a glance toward Bryce and the others, but they'd retreated beyond the communal ovens, toward the barns and the fields beyond. Cory couldn't help them anyway, unless . . .

He fought back the bile and turned toward the leader. Reaching out with his free hand he grabbed the Tapestry and prepared to twist. But the man with the severed arm suddenly fell silent. No moans, no hitching breath.

No breath at all.

Cory sobbed and wrenched his hand back.

The three men had picked up weapons and were heading toward him. He lurched to his feet and back into the smoke pouring from the meeting hall, trailing along the length of the stone building's side. Sweat poured off of his face as he reached the far side of the smoke and the trees beyond. He leaned against the first trunk he came near, bent over, coughing harshly, lungs burning, but knew he couldn't linger. Shoving away, he stumbled deeper into the surrounding forest, his sight clearing slowly. He flinched when shouts erupted from behind him, ducking down behind a ragged stump. But the raiders hadn't seen him; they'd started a co-ordinated search, were spreading out, trying to track him. The smoke hindered their progress, driving them back as it shifted,

Gripping his sword tighter, his breathing more normal and his sight mostly returned, Cory waited until the smoke hid him from the others, then scrambled up and over the nearest ridge. He half ran, half limped away, heading deeper into the trees, and found himself following one of the many streams. He'd learned enough from Reiss and Quinn to know it was difficult to track someone through water, so he splashed through the center for a long distance, until his lower breeches were soaked up to the knee and his shoes squished, then climbed back out onto the bank. The chill water helped ease the dull ache in his foot. He hauled himself up the next ridge, aware that he'd started circling the village, heading for the caverns.

When the hand clamped onto his sword arm, he screamed. Another hand closed down over his mouth, cutting off the sound, and he heard Jerrain curse. "Keep him quiet! He'll bring them all down on us!"

"It's us." Cory could feel Hernande's breath on his neck. "Can I remove my hand from your mouth now?"

Cory nodded.

Hernande let go and Cory sucked in a ragged breath. He stepped back and spun to face the two mentors. They'd been hiding behind a hummock, an indentation where deer likely lay on the far side. He rubbed his arm where Hernande had initially caught hold of him, realizing the mentor had grabbed that arm so he could control Cory's sword.

"You're stronger than you look."

Hernande merely raised his eyebrows. "Did you make it to the village?"

Cory drew in a breath and regretted it immediately, as he coughed until his throat was raw. Wiping his mouth, he finally answered, "Yes. Bryce and some of his new Dogs were defending it, but they were in retreat. Headed toward the caverns I think."

"No, they aren't that stupid. They won't lead the attackers straight to our refuge." Jerrain began to pace. "Do you think Sovaan can hide the entrance? He's not as good at it as the rest of us."

"He'll do it. He always works better under pressure."

"Meaning he's fine if he's saving his own ass." Jerrain waved a hand in dismissal and turned on Cory. "How many of them are there? What did you see?"

"More than the last time. Over forty in the village, although I couldn't see everyone. They were inside the cottages, looting them. The town hall and a few of the other buildings were on fire."

"They won't find much of value in the village. At least, not what they're likely looking for."

"Agreed. Would you say they were rogues, or were they more organized than that?"

Cory thought about them carefully stacking the medical supplies next to the wagon. "Many of the men were scruffy and desperate, but they weren't exactly out of control. Their leader was calm. He sent men after me." He looked directly at Jerrain. "I used the knots. On people. You were right. It's horrific."

"I'm sorry you had to experience that."

"I'm certain it was necessary." Cory started to protest, but Hernande added, "You survived."

"So what do we do? If what Cory says is true, then their leader is going to figure out there are far too few people and supplies left in the village. Or in what's left of the refugee camp."

"Maybe they'll think that everyone left. Moved on."

"We aren't that lucky. Plus Bryce and the Dogs were still there. Whatever we do, we have to be careful we don't lead the attackers back to the caverns."

Hernande thought for a moment. "We need to find Bryce."

Aurek watched the Hollower dodge back into the concealing smoke, followed by his own men, then dropped his gaze back to the body lying on the ground. He eased forward while the rest continued to loot the cottages that lined this side of the village. A moment later, he stood over Billings' body. The man had been one of his guards before the Shattering. Mediocre but loyal, he got the job done when given a task, even if it wasn't always done quickly. He'd been found a few times blind drunk in the local taverns; something about drowning his grief over the deaths of his wife and two daughters after the fever swept through the northern plains five years ago.

Aurek knelt down next to the man, expecting to see his arm severed at the elbow. That's what it had looked like when the man had roared in agony and caught Aurek's attention. It had been a bellow of extreme pain, cutting through the more generic cries and shouts from the direction of the main fight. He'd turned to find Billings holding his arm to his chest, blood spouting from near his elbow, the Hollower sprawled on the ground. Then Billings had collapsed, writhing. The Hollower hadn't had his sword raised, but he'd had a sword. Aurek had assumed he'd caught Billings off guard.

"That's not a blade wound."

Aurek didn't flinch at Devin's words, even though he hadn't heard his second arrive. "No, it's not."

"Then what is it?"

"It looks as if Billings' arm exploded."

Devin hesitated, then knelt down beside him, looking at the wound more closely. "You're right. The bone is splintered."

"And the muscles and skin have been shredded, not cut." A dull throb began in the back of Aurek's head. He considered the tattered and mangled flesh of Billings' arm, the rounded knob of bone from his forearm visible through the congealing blood, then stood abruptly, turning toward where the few men and women they'd encountered had retreated.

"What could have done this?"

"I don't think it's a what. I think it's who."

Devin tore his gaze away from the wound to look up at him. "The White Cloaks."

"We know there are White Cloaks here. That scout, Joss, admitted as much."

"He only called them Wielders—"

"Wielders, White Cloaks, does it matter what he called them? They're here."

"They never did anything like this before the Shattering."

"They didn't have to. They had the Baron's Dogs to protect them. They were in a position of power. Not anymore. They're being forced to protect themselves. We need to find them and root them out, destroy them, before they learn to do something even worse."

He abruptly began moving toward the wagons where his men were stacking the supplies. Devin lingered a moment, then joined him.

"What do you want us to do?"

"Are these the only supplies we've found so far?" Aurek lifted the lid of one of the boxes, discovered stacks of torn linens, and shoved the box aside so he could root through the rest of the material.

"Yes, from the cottages and what we could drag from the town hall before it was engulfed."

Empty vials, blankets, mostly empty tins that smelled of dried herbs and spices, more linen and scraps of cloth, a few bottles of medicine so old their mouths were crusted with yellowed residue.

Aurek tossed a bottle to the ground in disgust. It shattered with a satisfying crack. "It's all old."

"What do you mean?"

"All of the medicine is old! Worthless! And the rest of these supplies are remnants, the last dregs of their lives, the things deemed not important enough to take with them." He spun toward Devin. "Call everyone back. Now. We need to regroup. The villagers aren't here. And set fire to the cottages. To everything. I don't want a single building in this village left standing!"

Devin stepped away, already shouting to the men to stop their looting and bring out the torches. Aurek stood beside the wagon and stared in the direction where the force they'd encountered when they arrived had retreated. They'd known they were coming. They'd been prepared.

But had they fled or were they holed up somewhere?

He glanced down at the now-scattered remnants of the supplies from the cottages, thought about the people they'd found here. The first few had been surprised, caught off guard, even though their group had been seen by at least a few of the villagers on their way here. Someone had managed to ring the damn bell, but the village had already been mostly empty. He hadn't seen anyone emerging from the town hall before they'd hit it. Or from the cottages. Those that had been defending the village had been clustered near the center—

"Near the wagons." He turned to Devin. "They're still close by."

"How do you know?"

"Because those we attacked were here with the wagons. They must have been loading up the last of what they intended to take with them. If we'd attacked another day or two from now, the village likely would have been empty."

"What if they were scavengers, like us?" one of the men standing nearby asked.

Aurek bristled. "We aren't scavengers. This village was housing White Cloaks. If you have any doubts, examine Billings' body over there. One of them killed him by using their power to tear his arm off."

Half a dozen of the men glanced toward the inferno that was the town hall, flames now shooting from the roof, and the body lying in the dust beneath it. Most of the men had gathered, only the scouts and those that had trailed after the defenders absent.

"Were they the ones that caused that flash of light?"

The men flinched, a few glancing toward the sky.

"Don't be stupid. That came from the south."

"From the south, yes. But we all know that's where the White Cloaks live, secure in their Needle."

"So what are we going to do?"

They turned to Aurek. He thought about the three people they'd seen on the outcropping not that far southeast of here. Could they be hiding that close? But no. His gut told him they would have run across signs of others if they were—trampled ground, signs of smoke from fires. And then there were the defenders here. The men they'd seen hadn't headed to the south. They'd fled west, the same direction their Dogs had retreated.

"They're hiding somewhere to the west." He faced that direction, noted the barns in the distance, the signs of fields beyond that. "Spread out, but not too far. We'll follow the valley. Keep an eye out for any signs of a fresh path worn into the ground—wagon tracks or fresh dung from their animals. They couldn't have gone too far, not with an entire village to transport."

"Who's there?"

Cory halted, searched the trees ahead where the voice had come from, but couldn't see anyone. Hernande and Jerrain came up behind him.

"It's Cory, with Hernande and Jerrain."

Quinn stepped from behind a thick bole, arrow nocked and readied, but not pointed directly at him. "How in hells did you three get out here?"

"It doesn't matter. The raiders are headed toward the pathway that leads to the caverns, and no one has had a chance to hide it as planned."

"What about Sovaan?"

"We never intended to have him hide the path. We aren't even certain he'll hide the cavern entrances. We always thought one of us would be there to take care of everything."

"But the Hollowers—"

"Take us to Bryce."

Quinn nodded at the command in Hernande's voice. Not the subtle demand Cory was used to as one of Hernande's students; this carried the steel of an alpha.

They wound down to the edge of a stream, where Bryce and the rest were gathered. Bryce and Braddon were deep in conversation with two others. All of the men turned at a shout from Quinn.

"You should be back at the caverns with the others," Bryce said.

"We'd gone to investigate what caused that flash of light from the south. We're here now, and the attackers are headed for the path leading to the caverns."

"They've already found it. Reiss just came back with the news. We were hoping we could lure them away, divert their attention, at least for a while, but it didn't work."

"Their leader appears far more intelligent than one would expect from a pack of bandits."

"He's dressed as a lord. Perhaps he was one before the Shattering."

"What do you suggest we do?"

"They've found the path, but they haven't started following it yet. They appear to be regrouping, now that they know where we've gone. There's still a chance to stop them before they discover the caverns. Braddon, send everyone to the eastern side of the path."

"The streambed?"

"That's our best option. The bank will provide some cover."

They ran, Bryce and the rest of the group outpacing Cory, Hernande, and Jerrain. The Dog's figure was a blur through the foliage, the rest of the men scattered farther forward and to either side. They followed the streambed, splashing across its length occasionally on stones submerged beneath a few inches of chill water. The stitch started in Cory's side again, but before it could grow into a seizing pain, Bryce slowed and signaled quiet.

They crept forward. Ahead, Bryce suddenly started giving orders with the Dog's silent hand gestures, men scattering, heading away from the stream toward the rutted pathway that had worn itself into the earth as they shifted supplies to the caverns. Within moments, the rest of their group had faded into the trees.

Hernande watched the tree line where the others had disappeared. "We need to get ahead of the attackers so we can hide the path."

"Both of you go. Bryce and the Dogs will slow the attackers down. You should have time."

"And what are you going to do?"

Cory brandished his sword. "Help them."

Hernande reached out to grip Cory's shoulder. "Good luck."

The two mentors moved off, keeping to the stream under the cover of the bank. Cory watched them until they rounded a bend up ahead, then he headed toward Bryce and the others. He moved as quietly as he could through the fallen leaves and branches, wincing at every crack of a twig. Within twenty steps, he picked out the backs and shoulders of some of Bryce's men, huddled behind boles or stumps or hummocks of earth. Bryce heard him approach, head spinning to look back like an owl's, but he didn't signal Cory back. He brought his hand to his mouth for silence and motioned Cory to the ground.

Cory crouched down low, heart thudding in his chest, as he caught the rustle of movement from the direction of the path. The earthy scent of loam tickled his nose, but he sank even lower, practically lying on the ground.

He stilled as figures appeared, moving along the path in a group, a few of them on the flanks winding through the trees. Their leader led them forward at a quiet, cautious pace.

Braddon signaled, but Bryce ordered him to wait.

The group of attackers edged past them, Bryce and the others shifting position so they remained out of sight. As soon as the last of the men had moved up the path, Bryce motioned everyone forward.

Cory exhaled with a gasp, tasted dead leaves and dirt as he inhaled and heaved himself back into a crouch, scrambling forward as the rest of Bryce's men broke cover and began sprinting toward the attackers from behind.

A moment before they struck, one of the attackers turned and saw them. He let out a shout, cut off in a gargle of blood by one of the trackers' arrows as it took him in the throat. But the short warning was enough.

The attackers spun as Bryce and the rest of the Dogs broke into roars and crashed into them. Swords clanged off of makeshift armor and men screamed as blood flew up in sprays. The sudden sound after the silence was deafening. Cory slowed. The section of forest ahead, cut by the ruts of the path, had fallen into complete chaos, men hacking and bellowing and surging back and forth like a tide. Bodies already littered the ground, blood pumping from chest wounds. Cory lowered his sword and reached forward, fingers ready to wrench the Tapestry, but the man's mangled arm flashed before his eyes. He gave a strangled cry.

He'd tried to train with the Dogs because he wanted to help defend the Hollow, but he could barely block with the blade, let alone kill with it. Killing the attacker on the ridge had been a fluke. Then he'd thought he could use the Tapestry in the Hollow's defense, but now he found he couldn't even do that. He was useless, worse than Sovaan, because he kept trying and could never follow through. At least Sovaan was up front with his pettiness and instinct for self-preservation.

Then he felt the Tapestry twist and heard an earsplitting crack. Cory staggered backward as earth and men erupted into the air like a geyser. Dirt and stone rained down as two more explosions tore through the attackers. Cory felt each knot form moments before it was released, their centers buried deep beneath the earth. They were tight, energy and tension compressed into a space the size of a fist, as they'd practiced since the last attack.

"Demons!" someone roared from within the attackers. "Mages! They're using the very earth against us! Fight them! Kill them before they destroy us all!"

Another explosion rocked the path, close enough that Cory raised his sword arm to protect his head from the dirt pattering down on him. Seizing the Tapestry, he reached out near the center of the melee before him, deep underground, and wrenched.

Earth erupted, flinging the bandits into the air and opening up a pocket of empty space in the fighting. The men he'd caught in the blast crashed down into their fellow attackers, knocking even more aside. Before they could recover, Cory reached left and then right, two new explosions breaking the attacker's loose formation, joined moments later by four more earsplitting cracks farther up the rutted road.

The attackers were screaming now, some in pain, others in panic.

"Stay close! Defend Baron Aurek! Stick with your units!"

But the unearthly attacks of the mentors and their students continued, some of the explosions stronger than others. Those engaged in fighting Bryce and the rest of his Dogs were the only ones not being targeted. Cory could see the sudden fear eating at the corners of their defense. Those farther up the path from Cory suddenly surged in retreat, piling into those fighting with the Dogs. When Bryce and the rest stood their ground, holding them back, a group of twenty broke toward the forest to Cory's right. Cory reached out, felt his fellow University students do the same, and earth and tree boles exploded. Three trees groaned, their trunks splintered by knots, and began to fall, the twenty men crying out and scattering to get out of the way, the earth continuing to geyser around them.

The raider's leaders roared orders, calling those who fled cowards and bastards, their comments broken by curses and grunts of effort as they continued to fight. Cory straightened, sword dangling, and noted that the main group of fighters had maintained position. Another group had broken for the trees and the stream to the left, most of them charging through the barrage of earth geysers and split trunks without pausing, oblivious to the snap and crack of branches as even more trees toppled. When a few of them made it through unscathed, more broke for the safety of the surrounding hills.

But not all of them. Those that stayed still outnumbered Bryce and his men, and were now fighting with fear-driven fervor and intensity. Cory unleashed another knot as he saw two of Bryce's Dogs cut down. Through the hole made as their bodies fell away, he caught sight of the leader, his lord's jacket splattered with blood. He fought with a calm focus and grim set to his jaw, eyes narrowed in anger and determination. He wasn't bellowing orders to regroup, or berating his men for fleeing. He simply fought.

Until he caught sight of Cory. Then he paused. He raised his sword and pointed it toward Cory.

Cory raised his free hand—he never even considered raising his sword—and reached for the earth beneath the lord's feet.

Before he could twist the Tapestry into a knot and release it, ley fountained up from the earth on all sides. It poured skyward in curling tendrils and sheeting curtains, hemming the attackers in on three sides, leaving them only one avenue of escape.

Those hardened enough to withstand the geysers of earth broke beneath the onslaught of ley, crying out in sudden horror. They surged forward against Bryce and his men, no longer trying to fight free, simply fleeing in terror. Those few who tried to hold ground, including the leader, were shoved aside. A few fell and were trampled as Bryce's defenders were overwhelmed. They charged down the path, directly toward Cory. He dodged to the side and into the trees, ready to unleash a knot if necessary, but none of them even glanced in his direction as they sped past.

"Cowards!" one of the remaining men shouted from his position near Aurek, the leader surrounded by a dozen stalwart men who'd remained behind. "Cowards! Come back and fight like the Dogs you pretend to be!"

Aurek raised a hand to silence him. "Let them go, Devin." He glanced around the rutted road, pocked with craters from the knots Cory and the others had thrown, littered with over twenty bodies. The wall of ley curved around his position, hemming him and his men in, although it hadn't moved. None of the Wielders had the skill to shift the ley into new pathways yet. They'd barely managed to control it without an established network like the one in Erenthrall during their practice sessions.

Aurek's gaze dropped from the ley to where Bryce, Braddon, and the others now stood, shoulders bristling, hands clenched tight to hilts. The Hollow's Dogs had regrouped after being thrust aside by Aurek's fleeing men. The two remaining groups were about evenly matched.

Aurek and Bryce locked gazes. Both groups tensed, men shifting positions subtly, Devin stepping slightly in front of Aurek.

"You're aiding Wielders." Aurek motioned to the gouts of ley behind him. "Hiding them. We've proof of it now."

"So what?"

"They nearly destroyed us all. They need to be eradicated, before they can finish the job. Give us the White Cloaks and these mages of yours and we'll leave you alone. We only want the Wielders and their compatriots."

"Like hells. You forget you were attacking our wagons before you even suspected we had Wielders. I don't believe for a second that you'll leave us alone once we've handed them over. And right now, I'd say they're our best protection against you lot."

"Why you little shit." Devin stepped forward, sword raised.

Aurek reached out and caught his fellow's arm, halting him. "You're making a mistake. I saw you fighting, Dog. We could use men like you in Haven."

"At the cost of those who saved me in Erenthrall and have protected me since."

"They'll turn on you, eventually, as they turned on us all."

"No one knows what happened in Erenthrall. Least of all you, Baron." Bryce twisted the title with contempt.

Devin's shoulders bunched again, and the tension ratcheted up another notch as everyone on both sides raised swords and settled their weights for another fight. But Aurek tugged Devin toward the path instead.

"We'll go. Quietly."

The two shared a look and Devin relented.

The attackers edged down the path, toward the remains of the Hollow, everyone moving cautiously, ready for any sudden moves from the other group. Braddon gestured to Bryce, asking to attack, but Bryce shook his head, his eyes never wavering from Aurek or Devin. When the attackers from Haven had shifted past them, the Dogs stepped out into the road, the ley a white fluid backdrop behind them, and watched as Aurek and his twenty guardsmen began trotting into the distance.

Cory stepped out from the trees. "Are you letting them go?"

"We don't have the men here to pursue them, unless you've suddenly become a master of the sword."

"Not recently."

"So what are we going to do?" Braddon asked. "They're running, but they aren't done with us yet."

"No, they aren't." Bryce raised his voice. "They're gone, for now. Who's out there?"

Behind, the spouting ley died down, sinking back into the ground without a trace, like water absorbed by the earth after a hard rain. Behind the curtain of ley, Cory was shocked to see Sovaan, flanked by Jasom, Raven, and Mareane. Mareane looked pale, obviously not fully recovered from her seizure earlier. As the ley died, she lowered her arms and sagged into Raven for support. Behind them, a group of two dozen Hollowers—led by Paul and brandishing pitchforks and knives—wiped the fear-sweat from their foreheads. Hernande and Jerrain appeared from the left.

"Where were you?" Sovaan huffed. "I had to cloak the cavern entrance myself!"

"We were investigating the disturbance in the Tapestry. Research. Perhaps you've practiced it a time or two."

"You cowardly little ... cloaking the caverns was your job!"

Hernande stepped between the two mentors. "I'm certain you handled it magnificently in our absence, Sovaan."

The pompous mentor settled down, rolling his shoulders back, chest pushed out. "Of course. It was nothing—"

Hernande didn't wait for the rest, shifting to Bryce's side. "What should we do? What do you need from us?"

"They're not going to retreat. My guess is they'll regroup back at the Hollow, then come after us again. We need to get everyone here that's been injured back to the caverns, then cloak the path and entrance as best we can."

"Paul, Sovaan, and the rest of you, see to the injured and get everyone back to the caverns. Jerrain, Cory, and I will handle hiding the path. Raven and Mareane, stay with us in case they return faster than we expect."

Paul motioned everyone forward, and they began checking all of the bodies, carting off anyone who was still alive. Raven made certain Mareane was recovered enough to stand on her own then began to help, doing triage on anyone with visible wounds. Mareane was still trembling, too weak to help, her pallor gray.

Bryce had turned to his men. "Quinn, you and Reiss follow Aurek." The two trackers took off, splitting up, each taking one side of the rutted path and vanishing into the woods. Bryce had already turned to Hernande. "We'll pull back to the caverns slowly. Are you certain you can hide the path?"

"We can."

Bryce glanced over the pitted ground with a frown. "Did you and your students do all of that?"

"We did."

"Well done. I doubt we would have driven them off without you."

"It was the ley that drove them off. We only scared them."

"True." Bryce switched to Mareane, since Raven was still dealing with the wounded. "I knew you Wielders would come in handy."

Mareane looked uncertain, as if she couldn't decide whether to be angry, affronted, or thankful.

"I thought you could use these knots of yours to kill, not simply move earth and fell a few trees."

"It's too risky. People move, the earth and trees do not. The knot you intended for their heart ends up in their arm or in empty air or in one of your own men instead."

Bryce considered for a long moment. "You'll have to work on that."

Paul approached. "We have everyone who's still alive, including two of this group's men."

"Good, we can question them about this 'Baron' Aurek and his Haven. Maybe we can find out where his main camp is located. In the meantime, how many dead?"

"Four of our own, ten of the attackers."

"Considering they outnumbered us at least three to one, I'll take it." The Dog surveyed the stretch of path between forest and hills. "We're done here. Let's get everyone back to the caverns."

As everyone began to pull back, returning to the caves, Mareane pointed to the sky behind them, in the direction of the Hollow. "Look."

Cory turned, along with many of the others. Above the trees, blotting out the blue of the sky and the front of thick clouds rushing toward them, a heavy column of black smoke rose.

"That's too close to be the buildings in the Hollow."

"It's the fields. They're burning the crops in the fields."

# Nineteen

A TREMOR SHUDDERED THROUGH the wagon, a counterpoint to the mind-numbing clatter of the wheels on the paved road, and brought Kara out of her light daze. As had happened during every earthquake since the quickening of the distortion over Tumbor three days before, shouts raced through the Kormanley group and the wagon ground to an abrupt halt. The enforcers closed in around it, while everyone else turned their attention to the gold-red-purple distortion that had grown on the horizon as they traveled.

"What's happening?" Adder reached to haul himself up from where he'd been sleeping into a seated position. He winced as he did so, his body still bruised from the fight. He raised a hand to the lump from the stone that had taken him down, still ugly, although the swelling had gone down appreciably.

Dylan handed over a flagon of water. "Another tremor. Not as bad as those first few after the distortion, but enough to be felt."

"Are the White Cloaks behaving the same way?"

"They've formed the circle, to the east this time." Kara waved toward where the enforcers were clustered protectively around Iscivius and the others, Marcus at the center. He'd driven a staff twice as tall as he was with a metal spike on the end into the ground as far as he could, then reached out to the others in the circle. Now he stood with head bowed down, eyes closed, as if he were praying.

"Any ideas at all about what they're doing?"

"I've been thinking about something Marcus said when they captured us, about the quakes redirecting the ley lines. I think they're checking to see if anything's changed since the last quake."

"So what's with the spiked staff then?"

"A divining rod of some sort, maybe." Both Kara and Adder turned to face Dylan. He shrugged. "We used to search for sources of water using a forked branch. Why not search for the ley the same way?"

"Like how Hernande and Cory use the sands. The rod helps them map the ley lines."

"It can't possibly be as precise, though. The staff probably helps them travel the lines farther than they could if they were doing it individually. I don't see how it could give them the entire picture."

"We could ask Carter."

Kara's gaze flicked from Marcus to Carter, who stood in the circle with the White Cloaks, Iscivius on one side, Irmona on the other. Both of them had kept a close eye on Carter since Marcus had declared him part of their group, but Carter had kept his distance from Kara and the rest of them, never coming within twenty feet of the wagon, and he'd kept a low profile amongst the enforcers and the White Cloaks. Even Riley had stopped watching him, leaving it up to Iscivius.

"I don't think Carter would tell us, even if he were still speaking to us."

Marcus suddenly shuddered and raised his head. His eyes locked with hers for a moment, before turning away to stare at the distortion. Then he broke his contact with the circle of Wielders and yanked the staff from the ground. He handed it off to Okata and began issuing orders.

"That was fast. They usually spend twice as long messing with that thing."

"Maybe there weren't that many changes. It was a small quake."

"Somehow, I'm not reassured."

The circle of White Cloaks scattered, Okata and Irmona heading back to the lead wagon and horses with Marcus, the rest ranging throughout the group. The enforcers raced to new positions as well.

Kara hesitated, then made for the back of the wagon.

"Where are you going?"

"I want to talk to Marcus."

But before she could climb down from the wagon, Riley grabbed her by the arm and thrust her back. Caught off guard—they'd been allowed out of the wagon to walk at various times over the past three days—she fell onto her ass, her elbow striking a crate with a painful jolt. Adder edged up to her side protectively.

"I need to speak to Marcus."

"Not now." Riley pointed at the wagon. "Stay here."

"Can we get out to walk?"

"No, stay in the wagon. We're almost to the Needle."

He stalked away, two other enforcers stepping up to take his place. They motioned them away from the edge of the wagon bed, and both Adder and Kara shifted backward.

As soon as they rejoined Dylan and Aaron at the back, Adder said, "Riley was afraid of something."

"So were the White Cloaks. They were moving with a little more urgency than usual."

"Riley said we were getting close to the Needle. Maybe that's it."

No one responded.

The wagon lurched into motion again, Aaron straightening enough that he could see ahead of them. "Look."

Kara, Adder, and Dylan shifted position so they could see over the driver's bench and around the driver and his enforcer guard. The guard glanced back at them, but said nothing.

Ahead of them, to the south, a thin spire rose out of the plains, black with a cold sheen to its sides, like obsidian. It cut into the horizon and blue sky like a blade, edged, and as the wagon rose over a small hillock in the plains they could see down into a wide, shallow depression at the spire's base. It rose from a massive, three-tiered temple that gleamed a dusky granite gray, stark against the yellow grasses and reddish soil of the land surrounding it. The temple exuded age, obviously built by masons, not Wielders, with stone quarried from a distance and carted here. The labor involved without the use of the ley to mold the stone must have been immense.

The temple and spire were surrounded by a ring of more mundane buildings built long afterward, with a city of tents around those. Spire, temple, buildings, and tents were enclosed by a circular stone wall. Blazing white banners flew from the walls and the temple, and they could clearly see guards, especially near the northern gates. More people were milling about inside the enclosure. Smoke rose from a few cook fires and chimneys, but Kara felt her skin prickling with the ley. She gasped as she recognized ley globes floating at various points around the ramparts, like those that had sat on the walls of the University in Erenthrall, although none of them were currently lit. They didn't need to be; it was midafternoon, the sun high. But based on the power she could already feel emanating from the enclosure, they'd be lit by dusk.

"That has to be the Needle."

"It's a damn fortress."

"No. It's a node. An active node." Kara tried to shift closer for a better view. "And based on what I can feel coming from it right now, it's the focus of all of the ley lines in the area."

"Like the Nexus?"

Kara grabbed the front of Dylan's shirt in one fist. "It's exactly like the Nexus. Remember all of the nodes and ley lines we found in and around Erenthrall?" Dylan nodded, one hand holding her wrist now, although he wasn't struggling. "They were channeling the ley in an odd direction. Not toward Erenthrall, but farther to the west." She released Dylan, who slumped back against the crates they'd been using as seats. She shifted to stare out the back of the wagon toward the northeast, toward where the distortion over Erenthrall squatted on the horizon, dwarfed by the much larger—and much closer—distortion over Tumbor. "They'd been altered."

"Because of the Shattering."

"No! They'd been disrupted by the Shattering, but since

then they'd shifted. We thought it was because the ley lines were trying to stabilize somehow, to return to some sort of natural order, and I think that's true. But they couldn't, because the distortion blocked the ancient nodes in Erenthrall, like the one in Halliel's Park."

"But that's not the case." She could tell Adder still hadn't made the connection to the Needle yet.

"The ley lines we found in Erenthrall haven't been rerouting themselves. They've been redirected on purpose. By the White Cloaks. They're creating their own Nexus here at the Needle, channeling all of the ley lines to this one point."

"And if they're right that the quakes are side effects of the ley lines reorienting—"

"Then the reason they check them after every quake is to make certain some of them haven't shifted their direction elsewhere."

They all considered this in stunned silence, the wagon bouncing as they crested the rise and began to descend toward the Needle. Ahead of them, a contingent of mounted enforcers raced ahead of the group, Kara assumed to announce their imminent arrival.

Another thought struck. "The quickening of the distortion over Tumbor must have wreaked havoc with the system. It must have cut off a significant number of ley lines connected to the Needle. The quakes must be those ley lines attempting to adjust, now that the nodes in Tumbor have been blocked."

"And if what happened after the distortion in Erenthrall is any indication, the quakes are going to continue, possibly become even more violent."

"That must be why the quakes around Erenthrall weakened in the last few months. The Kormanley stabilized the area by shunting the lines here."

"But that doesn't make any sense. The Kormanley were trying to destroy the Nexus. They wanted the ley returned to its natural order. Why would they be creating their own Nexus now?"

Kara drew breath to answer, but held it when she realized Adder was right. It didn't make sense. "I don't know. Maybe they realized that the ley wasn't stabilizing itself because the natural nodes were blocked, so they were trying to fix it themselves." But that didn't feel right either. She shook her head, more confused now than before. "Whatever it is they're trying to do, they need more Wielders. And now that Tumbor has quickened, they likely need them more than ever."

The wagon jolted and Kara grabbed the back of the driver's bench to steady herself. The enforcer there jerked. "Sit back down and stay there, unless you want to lose a hand." He shifted his own hand to the hilt of his sword for emphasis.

Kara pulled back, settling in next to Adder, Dylan and Aaron across from them. Both Dylan and Adder looked thoughtful, both churning over what they'd realized about the White Cloaks now that they'd seen the Needle and had some idea of what it was.

"What's going to happen to us once we reach the Needle?"

Kara didn't answer Aaron. Carter had probably already told Iscivius and Marcus that Aaron was just one of the Hollowers, there to help them with the horses and wagons. What did they do with those who couldn't control the ley?

Shouts rang out as they approached the gates, enforcers on the wall ordering those below to get out of the way. A bell clanged, atonal, as if it were cracked, announcing their arrival. Kara strained to see ahead of them, but the enforcer next to the driver ordered her back down again. She could still see out to the sides where a line of enforcers had formed, holding a group of men, women, and children back so that the wagons could pass through. The enforcers wore the same red shirts and black breeches as those that had captured them, although they were cleaner, but the people all wore clothing like what Kara had seen throughout the Eld and Stone Districts in Erenthrall before the Shattering. The cloth was faded and worn, but it had been cleaned recently. The people appeared healthy and well fed, and all of them were pointing excitedly toward the White Cloaks, Marcus in particular, their faces lit from within with a mixture of awe and hope, as if they were witnessing one of the lords or Barons walking amongst them. Most of them carried baskets or bundles of cloth or were loaded down with crates on their shoulders.

"They look prosperous."

"More so than even those of us from the Hollow."

Certainly more so than the groups Kara had seen scattered throughout Erenthrall.

"Maybe this Father they're all talking about isn't as bad as we think."

"Erenthrall was prosperous, too, but everyone was still beneath the Baron's heel."

As they passed into the shadow of the gate, Kara looked up. The stone archway was thick, at least ten feet wide, and riddled with small holes the size of her fist. The clop of the horses' hooves echoed oddly inside, deadened slightly by the heavy wooden doors banded with iron that had been swung open on either side. They passed beneath a slit with the sharpened points of an iron gate hidden in the shadows. She'd seen such things throughout Erenthrall—in the University gates in Confluence, as decorative spikes on top of the walls surrounding the manors of the lords, even as motifs in the mezzanines of the ley stations—but all of those instances had been decorative, or on gates rusted with age or disuse.

This gate had been cleaned, the spikes that drove into holes in the stone passing beneath them recently sharpened.

They passed into the Needle's courtyard.

The open area beyond the gates was crowded with tents, like a marketplace, but as they progressed toward the buildings surrounding the temple and spire Kara realized that it wasn't a market. The tents were homes, like what the refugees had used this past winter for shelter, except these tents appeared more permanent. Ley globes hovered inside the few that had open tent flaps, and she caught heating stones scattered both inside and out. They passed a ley-heated oven, shimmering with heat as a baker reached into the central chamber with a long wooden paddle and pulled out two fresh loaves. A shift in the breeze brought the heavy aroma of the bread, making Kara's stomach clench with a sharp pang of hunger as her mouth filled with saliva. Dylan craned his neck around to catch sight of the oven. More scents assaulted them as they pressed deeper into the tents—the spicy sizzle of roasting meat, both fowl and something juicier, like boar; the tang of lye and soap; the stench of butchering; and the reek of manure and livestock.

It was as if all of the districts of Erenthrall had been trapped behind the walls. A man herding five goats and a sheep fell in behind them for a time. Children raced around them, staying clear of Riley and the enforcers but otherwise running wild. A woman outside one tent stirred a deep pot of what smelled like beef stew, singing quietly to herself. A gaggle of two elderly women and a young girl were seated around pile of clothes, stitching. Two men were working on repairing a yoke and set of traces.

And scattered through them all, she caught sight of at least five other White Cloaks.

"It's unbelievable." Dylan couldn't mask the longing in his voice. "They all act as if nothing has happened, that nothing has changed."

"How did they get here? Where did they come from? This must have been a node before the Shattering. Or a junction, where the ley lines met before diverging toward Tumbor and the Demesnes to the west, possibly even the Horn to the south. It would have held maybe twenty Wielders for maintenance, their families, maybe enough others to call it a town if it was a waypost for the ley barges. Not this many people."

"They must have come here after the Shattering. Fled here, as we fled to the Hollow."

Kara sank back into the wagon. "This is exactly what I wanted for Erenthrall. I wanted to heal the distortion, stabilize the Nexus there, rebuild Grass and the central districts so that people could return." She gazed around the thriving tent city in shock. "The Kormanley did this?"

No one answered. Their cart trundled through the throng, everyone as stunned as Kara.

"Where are they getting all of their food?" They passed by a spit containing three succulent, charred hares. Dylan's gaze followed them with his eyes. "I didn't see any fields as we approached, or any barns with stock grazing the grassland."

"Because they don't have any."

Dylan and Aaron looked at her in confusion, but she could see Adder had already figured it out.

"They're getting it from the cities—Erenthrall and Tumbor. They must have been raiding both since the Shattering, but they had more people and were more organized. That must be why the resources in Erenthrall became so scarce so quickly. Remember the shards we found that had already been healed? They have Wielders. They must be raiding the shards for supplies, like us. And they were trading us for food. The Tunnelers wanted the supplies that were in these wagons." She patted the crates around them, most of which contained sacks of grain and nuts, linens and cloth, and glass jars of canned goods. Nothing perishable over the short term, or that would spoil because of heat. "Just like the Baron. The White Cloaks stole everything and are now using it to control everyone."

"Are they letting everyone come here?" Dylan asked, then answered his own question. "No, they can't be. The Hollow had already reached its capacity. They must have hit theirs here as well."

"That's why the Tunnelers were trading for food. Recall they didn't seem happy about it."

"They must not know where the White Cloaks are located, or where they're getting their food. And they're desperate enough to follow the White Cloaks' rules." Marcus' rules, Kara thought. Or at least those of this Father he spoke of.

She wondered how many of the factions who lived in Erenthrall were being forced to deal with the White Cloaks. She couldn't imagine the Rats trading for food or allowing anyone to control them in such a way. But the Temerites? What about the groups to the south and east of the distortion—the Gorrani and the others?

How many groups had there been in Tumbor before its distortion quickened?

Kara didn't notice they'd passed beyond the tents into the central part of the node until a shadow fell across her. She glanced up at the stone buildings to either side and the alleys and streets between them. She hadn't realized how noisy the outside square had been. There were still people in the streets, but the structures blocked most of the shouts and conversations. Windows were lit with ley globes and the warmer light of candles, reminiscent of Erenthrall before the Shattering. The buildings were only a few stories high, their architecture from decades earlier, before the Wielders had created the Nexus in Erenthrall and begun sowing their own towers and basing their construction on the ley. They reminded Kara of her flat in Eld, where she'd grown up, except these were even older, more like the dormitories at the University or the old Baron's manse at the University's heart.

Her gaze swept over the people on the street, to the shadowy figures seen through a few of the open windows, and then up toward the black spire that towered over them all. It reached into the sky, but not as high as the towers of Grass in Erenthrall. This was only a node, the spire marking the location of the junction of the ley in this area. It was only as high as the supporting towers of the Flyers' Tower had been. Still, its perfectly flat, glossy black surface sent a shudder through Kara's shoulders. It was narrow and thinned to a fine point, with no visible openings or balconies. It reminded her of the spikes on the gates, honed to an exquisite sharpness.

The wagon jerked to a halt, and Riley suddenly appeared at the back with six other enforcers.

"Out." He motioned with one hand, the other on his sword.

All four of them hesitated, but then Adder pushed Kara forward, hand on her shoulder. "Try not to get separated."

Kara slid to the end of the wagon's bed and off, Riley stepping back. Adder jumped down behind her. Dylan and Aaron followed, Dylan leaning heavily on Aaron's shoulder.

"Can't you get something he can use to help him walk?" Kara asked.

Riley flicked a dismissive look toward Dylan. "No."

He whistled and beat the back of the wagon with the palm of his hand. The driver pulled away, shouting to clear the way.

They were in a small square before a wide series of steps that led up to the temple that surrounded the Needle. This close, Kara could see that the temple itself was older than even the outer ring of buildings, the stone pocked. It dawned on her that it really was a temple, probably erected before the Barons came to power on the plains, certainly before Baron Arent seized control. Which meant this was one of the natural ley nodes, a source of power for the ley system before Prime Wielder Augustus created the Nexus in Erenthrall and subverted the ley for his own uses. The architecture was riddled with symbols and stone carvings, but before Kara could do more than take in that each tier's edge was lined with statues of birds and beasts, Riley shoved her forward, motioning toward where Marcus and the other White Cloaks clustered at the base of the stairs.

The square bustled with activity, mostly enforcers. A group trained off to one side, men and women working through parries, blocks, and stances without swords, focused on form. Another group sat cleaning, sharpening, and repairing weapons, armor, and tack. Based on the enforcers entering the building behind them, Kara thought it must have been a barracks, the men roughhousing and joking with each other, some already removing uniforms. A few paused outside near a barrel, using the water to scrub the grime off their faces. They'd obviously been outside the walls. Those at the barrel appeared shaken, unlike those that had already entered the building.

A breeze brought the scent of mutton and roasted vegetables from the opposite side of the square, where a cook stepped out of a doorway to toss a bucket of slop into another barrel. The sounds of a mess hall filtered out the door, along with the clatter of pans, dishes, and cutlery.

They reached Marcus and the others.

"—the distortion's edge about five days' hard ride to the southeast," an enforcer was saying as they halted a short distance away. His back was stiff, his tone formal, his face and uniform covered in dust and dirt. Kara could smell his sweat from where she stood a few paces behind Iscivius. Carter glanced toward her from his position between Irmona and Okata, but quickly dropped his gaze to the ground. "The distortion completely engulfed Tumbor and everyone inside it, along with a radius of nearly twenty miles on either side."

"Larger than we thought from our position to the north. What about our own men? How many did we lose?"

"There were three patrols and two excursion forces inside Tumbor at the time, taking tithes and gathering supplies. All of them are lost. Four more patrols were outside the city scouting or heading to or returning from their own rotations. Only one of them made it, although it was close. Once the distortion quickened, they ran for it and were only a hundred yards away from the distortion when it halted. We found them and brought them back with us."

"I'll inform Darius and Father. Go see to your men."

The man placed a fist to his heart and knelt before Marcus, head bowed. Marcus rested his hand lightly on the man's head, like a benediction, and when he removed it the enforcer stood and headed toward the barracks.

Marcus turned to Iscivius. "Father will want your report about what happened in Erenthrall. The rest of you head to the Needle. Help with the damage control caused by the quickening. I'll be down as soon as I can to see exactly how badly our network has been compromised and what we can do to repair it."

"What about them?" Irmona gestured toward Kara, Adder, Dylan, and Aaron.

"We're taking them to Father."

Irmona spun on her heel. Okata and the other White Cloaks trailed behind, leaving Marcus, Iscivius, Carter, Riley, and an escort of enforcers.

Marcus turned to Iscivius. "Father will likely be in the orrery." He began to ascend the steps of the temple, Iscivius a few paces behind him. The White Cloak glanced back at Kara a moment, then focused on Marcus' back.

Riley prodded Kara and Adder forward. They followed in Iscivius' wake, Dylan, Aaron, and Carter behind. At the top of the first tier, they cut left across a wide plaza. The stone statues of animals were separated by fat rounded urns that Kara had mistaken for crenellations from the plaza below. No plants grew in the urns, but they were filled with dirt. She could imagine what the temple had looked like with spiked grass or even small trees sprouting from them, the edges of each tier clearly defined. The use of animals for the statues also made more sense. As they moved toward a set of worn wooden doors with metal hinges to one side of the steps, she noted that the plaza itself wasn't a flat field of monotone stone. The flags were of varied browns and greens and yellows, all of different sizes, set in a pattern, like a mosaic. The result was a flowing river of color, oddly soothing, centered on a white stone circle. More urns lined the wall of the next tier between the windows and a few entrances, some with doors, some without, along with benches and scattered niches set into the walls. All of it was worn and faded with age and disuse.

Marcus shoved the door open, the hinges groaning, and they entered the ancient temple. The corridor beyond was lit with ley globes in niches to either side, revealing that the hallway wasn't rectangular. Instead, the walls angled slightly inward, the ceiling narrower than the floor. It was wide enough for two people side-by-side, but Kara still felt as if the hall was collapsing in on her as she and Adder followed Marcus and the other White Cloaks. The sounds of their footfalls and the rustle of cloth and scraping of armor from the enforcers filled the hall, Kara's skin prickling at the eerie echoes. They passed doorways and corridors, most shrouded in darkness, a few lit with more ley globes, but the sense of desertion lay heavy across her shoulders, even though the halls had obviously been cleaned. No one had lived here for decades, if not longer. She could smell the history on the air, dry and dusty and gritty, like stone.

They entered a huge room, twice as wide as it was deep, the far wall curved, the open windows looking out on bright sunlight and the shining black surface of the Needle. Without looking, Kara knew that the windows looked down on a hollow, likely filled with stellae, like the one she'd visited in Halliel's Park with Ischua. Except here, the Needle took up the center of the hollow, directly over the natural ley node. Before she could be drawn across the room to the node, like iron to a lodestone, she glanced upward, and her heart surged up into her throat, cutting off her breath.

In the hollow of the cavernous ceiling overhead, a large ley globe burned a brilliant red-gold, like magma, roiling and seething. Eight other ley globes surrounded it, circling in larger and larger orbits, each globe a different color—a swirling blue, a vibrant green, a dusky red, blue-green-brown covered in clouds, an orange striated with violet, a sickening yellow like pus, a cold white that burned, and a purple so dark it was almost black. They ranged in size from the purple, which was no larger than Kara's fist, to the orange-violet, which could encompass her entire body. The red and yellow orbs were encircled by rings. The largest four had smaller globes orbiting them, and between the orbits of the orange-violet globe and the blue-green-brown one, a blue-white light the size of the end of Kara's thumb pulsed, a tail of sparkling white light trailing behind it.

"What is it?" Adder asked, as Marcus and the White Cloaks headed off to one side, where a group of four men were seated at a large table. Riley started after them, but turned when he realized that all five of those from the Hollow had halted just inside the chamber. The rest of the enforcers paused around them, fidgeting.

"It's an orrery." Kara pointed. "That's our sun and the other eight are the planets. Those smaller orbs are the moons, and the one trailing light must be a comet. That one there, with the clouds, is Wrath Suvane. You can even see the continents through the cloud cover."

Kara's gaze dropped to Riley. "How did we not know this was here?"

"What do you mean?"

Kara gestured to the temple. "This temple doesn't feel as if it's been lived in or used for decades, and yet this orrery is by far the most beautiful I've ever seen depicting the heavens. The orbs are detailed in color. All of the moons are represented along with that comet. And without checking, I'd guess that the locations of the planets in their orbits, as well as the moons, are accurate. It's a stunning feat of ley manipulation. How is it that no one in Erenthrall ever mentioned it? The Wielders should have learned of it in our studies."

"Unless the Primes kept it secret," Dylan muttered behind her, too low for Riley to have heard.

Dylan was right. The Primes had kept many secrets. A hidden orrery at one of the old nodes would have been exactly the kind of thing they'd keep to themselves.

But Riley shrugged. "It wasn't active when we arrived here. No more gawping." He headed toward the table, heels clomping on the stone. The enforcers nudged them all from behind.

As they moved across the room, Kara noted that the walls weren't stone. They were paneled in wood and painted, the paint having flaked away in patches ages ago, littering the floor with dust. The wood appeared dry and cracked.

The end of the room where Marcus now stood with the others, speaking to those at the table, was lit with more of the mundane pale white ley globes.

They drew up to the table, the largest Kara had ever seen, with the capacity to seat at least twenty and, unlike the wood on the walls, oiled and polished to a high sheen. It was covered in miscellaneous objects—smooth stones, polished wood, small figurines. Platters containing pitchers of water or wine, glasses, fruits, and cheeses were arrayed at one end, a few plates and glasses sitting before or off to one side of those seated. The man Marcus spoke to had his back turned to Kara, so she could only see the back of his head, his hair black, streaked with gray. He wore a brown robe that reminded Kara of those worn by the Tenders like Ischua. The other three men were listening to Marcus as he described the end of their journey to the Needle. One of them was a White Cloak, but the other two wore enforcer uniforms, the cut and markings on shoulder and breast more formal looking than those worn by Riley and the others Kara had seen since Erenthrall. The eldest looked to be in his fifties, his face as scarred and pocked as the Dogs from the city, his eyes as brutal. Kara immediately thought of him as an alpha, the commander of the enforcers. His beta was at least ten years younger and wasn't as scarred. His hands were callused, as if he were used to heavy labor, and he didn't strike Kara as a fighter at all. The White Cloak had the thin face and build of a Temerite, with the trimmed beard common in the east.

"—when we met up with Iscivius and the others from Erenthrall. That's when the distortion over Tumbor quickened. We headed straight back to the Needle after that, checking the ley lines as we came."

"And what did you see?" The man—Kara assumed it was the one they all called Father—had a voice that cracked, as if his throat had been scarred. It was weaker than Kara had expected as well, solid but frayed around the edges.

"The lines are in chaos again. Everything we've managed to gain since the Shattering has been undone."

Father shifted in his seat, straightening. "Not everything. The lines coming from the north that were recently established using the old nodes are still active. Only the lines from Tumbor and Farrade have been severed. The others—Erenthrall and the nodes to the south and west—have been weakened and are erratic, but they are still holding. Our purpose has not changed. This is only a setback."

"It's still a setback."

"But it is one we will overcome."

"You aren't the one dealing with the nodes, attempting to rearrange the ley lines to suit our purposes."

"No, but I have faith that what has happened and what is happening now serves a single purpose—*our* purpose. I have known of you since before the Shattering, Marcus. I know you share that faith as well. Am I wrong?"

"Of course not."

"You were always impatient, if I recall. Don't let this setback throw you. I need you, as I needed you before."

Iscivius fidgeted one step to the side and behind Marcus. "Father, I have news from our excursion to Erenthrall—"

Father raised one hand.

"You say that the quickening occurred at the same time as you met up with the group from Erenthrall?" Father asked Marcus.

"Yes. Immediately after."

"I see."

No one spoke.

"I believe it is a sign." Father rose from his seat, the fingers of one hand steepled on the table. "I think it's time I met those you brought from Erenthrall, Iscivius."

He turned. Kara didn't know what she'd expected—a wizened old man? A hardened warrior to match the cracked voice?—but he was neither of those. She fought back a pang of disappointment. This Father everyone had been speaking so highly of since they'd been captured by the White Cloaks looked ordinary. She would have placed him in his forties except for the sense of age around his eyes. There, the wrinkles spoke of someone older, early fifties, perhaps. His skin was otherwise smooth, his hair pure gray around the ears, streaked with gray above. His face was round, his features plain. If his eyes hadn't been completely clouded over with white, he would have faded into any crowd in Erenthrall.

But those eyes. Even though the pupils were covered,

they cut into Kara when he looked at her. He should have been blind, with cataracts so advanced, but she knew he could see her. In fact, she sucked in a breath of shock as their gazes met.

She suddenly understood why they revered him. The intensity of his gaze, the fierceness and power behind it, instilled her with an uncertain awe.

He broke the look, glancing toward Adder, Dylan, Carter, and Aaron, before returning to her. He shifted closer to her, close enough she could smell his clothes. They reeked of some kind of pungent incense, over a layer of heavy smoke. His robe was clean, but there were small holes burned into it, especially near the cuffs of the sleeves.

Something familiar about the man's face niggled at the back of Kara's mind. "Who are you? Why have you abducted us?"

"I am the Father, the leader of the Kormanley. Or the White Cloaks, as we've begun to be called by outsiders. The real question is, who are you?"

Kara glanced toward Marcus. "He hasn't told you?"

Father shifted slightly, but did not look away from her. "No, he has not."

"Kara. Kara Tremain."

"Kara." It was said without inflection, but Father looked toward Marcus.

"It's her."

Father turned back to her. "A sign indeed. I think everything that we've fought for since the Shattering is about to come to fruition, as I foresaw."

Behind them both, Iscivius stirred. "She won't cooperate. She attempted to escape on our way here."

"And would you not have, Iscivius? I doubt that." Iscivius glared at the back of Father's head. Kara had the distinct impression Father knew. "I don't think it's necessary, at least in Kara's case, but Lecrucius, would you test them?"

The Temerite White Cloak stood and made his way around the table. He was slightly shorter than Kara, head tilted as he looked up into Kara's eyes. His expression was stern. "You may feel a tingling sensation." Then he reached out and rested a hand on Kara's head.

Kara tried not to flinch away, but her body tensed. A

moment later she realized what Lecrucius was doing. She'd seen the test performed on hundreds of students when she was attending school in Erenthrall, and had undergone the test herself after her parents' deaths at Seeley's Park. Lecrucius was a Prime. He was testing her to see if she had any talent for manipulating the ley.

She felt a prickling sensation course down through her body, but the prickling faded before she could draw another breath.

Lecrucius removed his hand. "She's strong. Stronger than everyone we've found so far. Definitely a Wielder. Most likely a Prime."

Adder gripped her arm.

"I'm all right," she said. "It wasn't like the first test. I only felt a faint tingling then, at the back of my neck. Like an itch. This was more intense."

"You've grown in strength since then." Lecrucius turned to Adder with a frown.

The Dog scanned the immediate area, as if preparing to run, but then his shoulders sagged. He bowed his head as Lecrucius reached forward, and Kara suddenly realized where the gesture of benediction she'd seen Marcus using out on the plains and inside the walls of the Needle came from.

After a breathless moment, Lecrucius removed his hand. "Nothing. He's simply a Dog."

Lecrucius moved on to Dylan, Carter, then Aaron.

"Both are Wielders," the Prime said, pointing to Dylan and Carter. "Not as strong as Kara, but stronger than most. The boy has a touch of power, but he's not strong enough to bother training. He'd never have been selected as a Wielder before the Shattering."

Aaron appeared startled by the announcement. Kara had to remind herself that he'd been born and raised in the Hollow. None of those like him in the Hollow would have been tested. Some of them could have the potential to be Wielders, and they'd never know unless their talent manifested like it had for Kara. But why would it? There was no ley node near the Hollow that would awaken the talent, like the one in Halliel's Park had for Kara. No one from the Hollow had been exposed to a significant amount of ley at all. They could live, grow old, and die without ever knowing they were a Wielder. The same would be true for any of the villages and towns significantly distant from the ley lines.

But for someone in the Hollow, whose residents shunned the ley, finding out they could manipulate the ley wouldn't be a welcome revelation.

"I could have told you that," Iscivius said. "We've been watching them since we took them in Erenthrall from the Underearthers."

"It's better to have it verified. Thank you, Lecrucius. We will discuss how best to use these new resources once Marcus has seen for himself the extent of the damage to the Needle."

Lecrucius returned to his seat but kept his gaze on Kara, his expression calculating.

Marcus cleared his throat. "Carter declared his intentions to become a White Cloak on the way here. I accepted, but told him you would have to pass the final judgment, Father."

"I see." He stepped toward Carter without pause. "You are Carter?"

The Wielder swallowed. "Yes."

Father's hand rose and gripped him beneath the chin, forced him to look into his white, filmy eyes. The man twisted Carter's head left and right, the young Wielder trembling, and then thrust him back.

"His intention is true—he does wish to join us—but his confidence in his abilities is flawed." Father turned his back on him. "Commander Ty."

The older man with the scars stood. "Yes, Father?"

"Take the two non-Wielders to a cell. We'll deal with them later. Marcus, escort our Wielders to their new rooms."

Ty began moving forward, Riley and the rest of the enforcers closing in from behind. When Riley grabbed her arm, she jerked away and shouted, "No! You can't separate us. I won't allow it."

Riley attempted to grab her again and she lashed out. Adder and the others began to struggle as well. Adder kicked out, foot slamming into an enforcer's chest, then punched another so hard Kara heard a crack and saw blood fly from the man's mouth. Another enforcer grabbed Aaron from behind, the Hollower yelling and beginning to squirm. Dylan tried to turn and fight, but with his injured knee, he could barely remain standing.

Kara kept her eye on Riley, dodging to the side when he reached out to grab her, batting his arm away. She didn't see Marcus until he'd reached around her from behind and pinned her arms to her sides. She spat a curse and began struggling, wrenching hard to the left, but Marcus tightened his hold and barked into her ear, "Enough! If you keep fighting, they'll both be killed."

Kara jerked one more time as the words sank in, then sagged in his grip. Aaron and Dylan had already been subdued. Only Adder remained free, facing off against Ty, the two Dogs glaring at each other, both ready for a fight.

"You'll regret this. I'll never help you, whatever it is you intend to do."

She'd intended the words for Marcus, but Father answered. "I think you will. I've foreseen it."

No one responded, the tension in the room shifting from Kara, Marcus, and Father to Ty and Adder.

"I was one of Daedallen's seconds. Do you want to test me, Dog?"

Adder's fists rose slightly, then lowered. "Not today."

Ty motioned the rest of his enforcers forward. They surrounded Aaron and Dylan, Riley seizing hold of Adder himself, and forced all three of them toward the door. Carter trailed after. Marcus didn't loosen his hold. His breath was hot against Kara's neck, his clasped hands tight under her breasts, his body pressed up hard against her back. She squirmed as the others disappeared through the door with Riley, Ty, and the enforcers.

"Let go of me."

"If you promise not to do anything stupid."

Kara nodded.

Marcus loosened his grip. As soon as his hands released, she shoved away, spinning to face him.

"Just like old times, huh, Kara?"

She flinched.

"Enough," Father interrupted. "Darius, accompany Marcus and our new Wielder to her rooms. I don't think she'll give us any more trouble. She knows her friends will pay the price."

The younger commander at the table rose and ushered her and Marcus into the outer corridor.

Marcus led her to the left, the side hallway curving almost imperceptibly ahead of them. Again they passed doorways and cross-corridors, only a quarter of the other halls lit with ley globes, most of the rooms to either side closed, those with open doors or without doors at all appearing empty or shrouded in darkness.

A short time later, they entered an area that was obviously in use, the corridors less dusty, the smell of ancient stone cut by incense, the savor of roasted meat and other cooking, and the sourness of sweat. Kara heard voices behind some of the doors, and a moment later they passed two White Cloaks. They nodded to Marcus, but kept their heads bowed as he passed and followed Kara afterward with their eyes. A room to the right held a woman sharpening knives on a whetstone, another held two children husking corn, unsupervised.

They passed a much wider corridor, continuing on its far side, the tenor of the hall changing. Here there were enforcers mingling in the halls or relaxing in their rooms, all with the air of rank. Kara assumed these were barracks for the commanders, more central than the barracks for the common soldiers she'd seen below. The men and women they passed eyed Kara critically, judging her potential as a threat, most dismissing her after a few seconds.

Then Marcus halted, shoving open a door to the left and motioning Kara inside.

When she hesitated, he said, "You don't have a choice."

The room was small, a cot against one wall, table with a pitcher and cup next to it, a chair tucked into one corner. A ley globe hovered overhead, but sunlight streamed in through the open window on the far wall. After pausing just inside the door, Kara headed to the window and looked down on a wide circular area at ground level, the black pearlescent stone of the Needle at the center, rising so far overhead Kara couldn't see its tip, even by craning her neck. The area around the Needle was paved in stone, the stellae she'd expected jutting up like fingers of rock. There was no obvious pattern to them, although she knew from her studies that the stellae at all of the ancient nodes had been placed with perfect alignment by their ancestors, their precision awe-inspiring.

Or they *had* been placed perfectly, before Prime Wielder Augustus had created the Nexus in Erenthrall. With that now destroyed, and at least two cities enclosed in distortions, who knew what the ley lines looked like.

Below, a group of three White Cloaks emerged from a door in the lowest tier of the temple, crossed the sand-colored area containing the stellae, and entered an opening in the side of the black Needle. Kara hadn't even realized the opening was there.

"I can't believe you're creating another Nexus, Marcus. After everything that the Kormanley did in Erenthrall to destroy the one there, after all of their preaching about returning the ley to its natural order, you stand here now and create another one all over again. Look at the damage you've done already!"

She turned when she heard a footfall behind her. Marcus had stepped into the room. Darius watched from outside. Marcus looked as though he wanted to approach her, put his hands on her shoulders as he'd once done in Erenthrall, before the Shattering, before the black-haired woman Dierdre had torn them apart, but he didn't, conscious of Darius in the doorway.

"You don't understand. It's not that simple."

"Then make me understand. What's not simple? It's seems fairly straightforward to me."

"You're right. We are creating another Nexus. Or we're trying to."

Behind, Darius stiffened. "Marcus."

"I know what I'm doing. She needs to know, especially if we're going to get her to help."

Marcus waited, but Darius remained silent.

"Yes, I was manipulating the ley in Erenthrall before the Shattering. There were others, but I was the one altering the Nexus that afternoon."

Kara's stomach dropped out from beneath her. Even though she had told everyone after the Shattering that

Marcus had been the one responsible, even though she'd seen the manipulation coming from Eld in the sands at the University, she'd harbored a small hope that somehow she'd misinterpreted events, that somehow Marcus hadn't been involved.

"You admit it. You admit to destroying the Nexus, to destroying Erenthrall and everything else the ley network was attached to."

"I admit to changing the Nexus, realigning it, before the Shattering. But I didn't destroy it. The surge of power didn't come from the node in Eld. The surge came from Tumbor."

Kara's mouth opened, but no words came out. She didn't know what to say, uncertain whether she believed him. He said it with confidence, but then he'd always been confident, even when he was wrong. She clutched tighter to herself, hollow inside, empty.

Marcus took a step forward, one hand outstretched, but she backed away, stumbled into the small table. The pitcher sloshed water; the cup rattled.

Marcus lowered his hand. "It was Baron Leethe. Dalton said he was the one who supported the Kormanley in their attacks on the city. He was the one who wanted Baron Arent's control of the Nexus broken."

"And you helped him." But then the full extent of his betrayal hit. "You helped the Kormanley, the group that killed my parents. You bastard!"

She'd shoved away from the table, knocking the pitcher to its side, and made it halfway across the room before Marcus shouted, "No!"

She halted. Not because of Marcus, but because Darius now stood in the room, sword drawn, point toward her.

She curled her fingers into fists and focused on Marcus. "You just admitted you worked for the Kormanley!"

"There were two sets of Kormanley in the city, Kara! One sect was the one who bombed Seeley's Park and killed your parents. They were violent. They were the ones bent on ending Baron Arent's stranglehold on Erenthrall by setting the city on fire. They set all of the bombs, including the one at the Amber Tower that set off the Purge. I wasn't part of that group. Neither was Ischua."

Kara recoiled. "Ischua?"

"Yes, Ischua. He was part of the Kormanley as well, the real Kormanley, the one led by Father Dalton."

"I don't believe you."

Marcus stepped forward, to within a pace of her. "Didn't you recognize him?"

"Who?"

"Dalton. Father. He's the man who ran into us at the market the day Ischua died. Dalton had been tracked down by the Hounds. He was attempting to escape them when he stumbled upon Ischua at that market. We were both there. He warned Ischua, told him to run, and fled. Then the Dogs showed up with the Hound and the entire market erupted into a massacre."

Images from that day flared across Kara's vision and she turned away. She barely noticed that Darius had lowered his sword. She heard the screams as the Dogs began slaughtering people indiscriminately. She saw Ischua standing up to them, saw the Hound sink his blade into her mentor's gut.

And she suddenly remember the man who'd started it all, the man who'd raced through the market, who'd plowed into Ischua and said . . .

*You have to run. The Dogs have found me. . . . If they found me, then they'll find the others. They'll find you. You have to warn them. Warn them all to get out of Erenthrall!*

"No." She reached out a hand to steady herself against the table, her palm landing in the water from the pitcher that had spilled across its surface and now dripped to the floor.

"The black-haired man was Dalton. He was talking about the Kormanley, Kara. He—and Ischua and Dierdre and then me—we were all trying to free the ley from the Baron's control. That's all."

As if he'd summoned her, Dierdre appeared in the doorway, clearing her throat to catch their attention. Kara stiffened, unable to suppress a surge of age-old hurt as she saw the woman. She'd aged since Kara had last seen her, before the Shattering—around the eyes and neck—but her hair was still long and a thick black.

"Father wants to know what's taking so long. He's waiting for you inside the Needle."

"He's been telling her about Father," Darius said. "And the Needle."

"Without Father's leave?"

Marcus spun toward her. "She'll only help us if she understands what we're trying to do here. I know her, Deirdre. Threatening her friends won't get her to cooperate. It will drive her further away."

"What have you said?"

"Nothing important."

"Only who Father really is. And Baron Leethe's part in the Kormanley. And what he did to the Nexus from Eld before the Shattering."

Dierdre considered Darius' words in silence. Then, to Marcus: "Nothing important?"

"We'll have to explain much more than that if we want her help. And we can't lie to her. I lied to her before, about you, about the Kormanley, and it only drove her away."

Kara switched her gaze from Dierdre to Marcus' back.

"Explain it to Father."

Marcus looked back at Kara over his shoulder, his expression troubled, then moved toward Deirdre. "We'd better not keep him waiting any longer then."

Dierdre took hold of him, wrapping her arm through his and twining fingers before they stepped from view down the corridor. Kara heard her say something, voice sharp, the words indistinguishable.

She turned her gaze on Darius. The enforcer sheathed his sword, then left, closing the door behind him. A lock bolt snicked into place.

# Twenty

"WAIT." The skin along Allan's forearms and across his shoulders prickled. He halted, the creek they'd been following toward the Hollow gurgling off to the right, their wagon creaking behind him. A breeze rustled through the leaves of the trees overhead, birds chirping the last of their early morning chorus, and Gaven and Glenn chatted excitedly with Artras at the wagon. They were close to the Hollow and everyone knew it.

But his arms still pricked with gooseflesh.

He hissed for quiet, one hand thrown back in warning. Artras broke off in midlaugh, startled, one hand going to her chest. The light in her eyes that had grown the closer they got to the Hollow suddenly dropped away like a stone. Glenn's transformation was even quicker, the Dog already sliding off the wagon's bench, a knife in one hand. Gaven jerked the horse to a halt, the animal snorting in protest. From the back of the wagon, Allan heard a low growl from the Wolf a moment before Cutter's head appeared, the tracker scanning the woods before slipping out of the back of the wagon. His arm was still bound to his chest, but he'd regained some strength. Not enough to draw a bow yet, but he'd been working it stubbornly since they'd left Erenthrall and entered the plains.

He and Glenn both moved to Allan's side.

"What is it?"

"We're close to the Hollow, close enough we should be hearing Bryce training the new Dogs, or the refugees working on the new cottages, if nothing else. I don't hear anything."

"They taught us to trust our instincts in the Dogs. What do you want to do?"

"I can scout out the village." Both turned to stare at Cutter's arm. "I can't draw a bow, but I can still sneak through the woods better than either of you."

"Don't go too far. I don't want to be sitting here in the open with the wagon for long."

Cutter took off, bounding over the creek and up the far slope, vanishing within five breaths Allan stood with Glenn, the Dog's gaze darting back and forth, searching.

"I don't like it either, now that you've drawn my attention to it." Glenn sniffed the air. "Is that smoke?"

"Yes, It is."

Both of them turned back to the wagon, toward Artras. She climbed down from the bench.

"I thought it was just a cook fire."

"Not a cook fire. It's stronger and darker. Older. I'm only getting it when the breeze gusts just right, but it's coming from the direction of the Hollow."

"What could have happened?"

"Anything. We've been gone almost three months."

The three of them fell silent, waiting.

All of them started when the Wolf grunted and climbed to his feet. He was tied to both sides of the wagon, tethered so that he couldn't reach Gaven at the front of the wagon, but with enough leeway that he could jump down from the back and walk behind if he wanted. They could cinch his lead from the front of the wagon without approaching him, force him back into the bed, but after a few days of failed attempts at escape with the new arrangement, he'd settled down in resignation. He let Artras approach him with food, but none of the others could get close without eliciting a low, deadly growl.

Gaven twisted to look at him, but the Wolf ignored him. Allan knew he'd reached the limit of his lead simply by standing.

The Wolf's nostrils flared, scenting the air. Then his lips drew back, the fur along his spine bristling. A low growl rumbled from his chest as he lowered his head.

"That doesn't sound good."

Glenn stepped to one side and drew his sword. Allan shifted in the opposite direction and drew his own. The minutes stretched out, the Wolf's growl never wavering. He'd shifted forward, his restraints taut, his ears forward. Gaven reached for the cudgel he now kept at his feet, letting it rest in his lap. The horse sidestepped, jangling its harness.

Then the Wolf's growl spiked. From the woods, a liquid gurgle sounded, followed by a rustling thump and the crackling sound of fallen leaves as something was dragged forward. The Wolf's growl ended in a huff, and he settled back down onto his stomach.

Cutter reappeared, dragging a body behind him. He brought it to the edge of the creek and dropped it before crossing over to their side. The man's throat had been cut, the wound gaping with the tilt of his head and the incline of the slope. He was in his thirties, with a thick, gnarled beard, eyes blackened by charcoal or ash. He wore makeshift boiled leather armor over chest and thighs, but nothing on his arms or lower legs. Allan didn't recognize him.

"Who's that?"

"The man on guard who'd seen us."

"He's not from the Hollow. Or at least, he wasn't part of the Hollow when we left."

"No, not from the Hollow. The Hollow's been destroyed. Burned to the ground. This man's with the group that did it. They've set up camp in the refugees' meadow. They aren't well equipped, but they're organized. Raiders, like those we ran into on the plains. It looks like they've been there for a few days at least, maybe a week. Some of the buildings in the village are still smoldering, although everything's been reduced to ash and stone. Most of the meeting hall is still standing, only one wall collapsed. The barns and cottages are nothing but charred supports. They even stove in the side of the communal oven."

Allan thought of his daughter, of Cory and Hernande, of all of those they'd left behind. Artras looked stricken.

"What about the villagers? Did you see Sophia or Paul? Hernande? Did you see any bodies?"

"There are some bodies in the village." He shot Allan a pained look. "I couldn't get close enough to identify them, but I don't think any of them were Morrell. There were maybe twenty in all, scattered, left where they'd fallen. I didn't see anyone from the Hollow in the attacker's camp. They either killed anyone they captured, or they didn't find anyone to take prisoner. I did a quick run around their camp and the village, but I didn't see anyone else except guards like this one, out on patrol or on watch. I don't think he'd warned the others we were here, unless he had a partner, but none of the others out on guard were in pairs."

Allan forced himself to think. "That doesn't make sense. Where'd everyone in the Hollow go?"

"Maybe they fled before the attackers arrived."

"Then why are there bodies in the village?"

"Because Paul and the other Hollowers wouldn't abandon their village that easily."

"Then maybe the villagers were caught by surprise. Most of them fled while some stayed behind to buy them time. That would explain the bodies. But why are the raiders still here? You said they've been camped here for days."

"Reveling in their victory?" Glenn offered.

Cutter considered. "I didn't see much revelry. In fact, I didn't see much of anything in the camp. No stacks of food or supplies. Not enough to account for what they'd have found in the village. And they have guardsmen everywhere, especially to the west. It's almost as if they're—"

"Searching," Allan broke in. "They're searching. Bryce wouldn't have sat idly by, not after we were attacked on the plains. He'd have had patrols. He was starting to organize them when we left. Which means the village would have had some warning. Maybe not much, but some. The Hollow isn't easy to defend—too open, too many directions from which to attack. He would have looked for some place to go to ground, to hide. The Hollowers must have fled to whatever he'd found as a retreat, and these raiders are now searching for them." He turned to Cutter and Gaven.

"Where would they have gone? Where could they have hidden themselves that's near the village?"

Gaven and Cutter eyed each other.

"It would be to the west. That's where the raiders are searching."

"There are caves to the west, not that far from the village. Children go there to play. Adults, too." Gaven cleared his throat self-consciously. "For, ah, a different kind of play."

"But the caves aren't that deep. I don't know if they would hold the entire village—"

"Is there anywhere else they could have gone?" When both Cutter and Gaven shook their heads, Allan said, "Then that's where they've gone, even if it's only temporary. Can we get there without running into the raiders?"

"I'll find a way." Cutter headed for the woods to the south and west.

"What about him?" Glenn pointed toward the dead raider. "They're going to notice he's missing eventually."

"We don't have time to bury him, but we can try to cover his body."

They had to backtrack. Cutter didn't want to risk running into the raiders out searching, and they'd widened their search area since his first scouting trip. Allan curbed his impatience—he wanted to see Morrell, wanted to know she was safe and unharmed—as they turned the wagon around and headed northward again. It was approaching evening by the time Allan called a halt.

"Are you certain we're close?"

"The caves should be on the other side of that ridge."

"Show me."

They left Glenn, Gaven, Artras, and the Wolf behind, circling to the north as they climbed the slope of the ridge. Cutter headed toward a fold in the land, the slope too steep. Shadows lengthened as they moved, Allan attempting to be as silent as Cutter, but the first scattered layer of autumn's leaves made it nearly impossible.

The darkness deepened as they slipped through the fold and passed into the lee of the ridge. An owl hooted as night sounds settled and nocturnal creatures began to stir. Cutter's form became ghostlike, seen only as he passed from tree to stone to tree.

Then he paused, Allan slowing until the tracker motioned him forward.

Without sound, Cutter gestured toward the stretch of clearing ahead, toward the ground.

Allan edged forward, confused, until the stench of death hit him.

It wasn't a clearing so much as a path. Ruts from wagon wheels had been worn into the undergrowth, except for a long stretch where the ruts had been broken. The earth looked churned and pitted, and trees had fallen across the road, their trunks splintered. Scattered among the debris were bodies, covered lightly with fallen leaves. The feathers of carrion crows glistened over a few, one of them letting out a harsh caw, while farther distant a wolf was dragging something deeper into the woods.

Allan lurched forward, but Cutter's hand clamped down on his shoulder, holding him back. He spun on the tracker, jerking out of his hold, but the tracker leaned in close to his ear. "They've been dead for days. And it's too exposed to check the bodies."

Allan was ready to check the bodies anyway—what if Morrell were out there?—but he knew Cutter was right. Even if no one was watching, they'd disturb the carrion eaters, and someone might hear their protests as they took flight.

They kept to the trees, slipping by the strangely churned earth and through a forest of splintered boles, as if the trees had exploded from within. They passed the last of the destruction, still following the ruts.

Within twenty paces of the last body, the road vanished. The ruts faded into the undergrowth, the ground undisturbed.

Allan shot a questioning look toward Cutter, but the tracker appeared as baffled as he was. They hesitated a long moment, then Cutter continued.

The slope grew steeper, Allan's breath coming in heavier and deeper huffs. The undergrowth vanished into rocks and pebbles and knobby tree roots. Allan hauled himself upward using overhanging branches or by grasping the trunks of the thinner trees. He slipped once, banging his knee into jagged granite.

Then it leveled out onto a rough landing, a stone wall obscured by dangling tree roots and vines to one side, before it grew steep again forty paces distant.

Allan bent to catch his breath as the tracker looked around in consternation. He edged toward the rock wall, searching, then turned to stare out into the trees and the surrounding hills, as if trying to get his bearings.

Allan straightened. "Where are they—?"

The point of a blade pressed itself into his back, cutting off his question. His hand twitched toward his own sword, but halted when more pressure was applied. Cutter spun, gaze flicking side to side. Judging by his look, there were at least three people behind Allan.

"We're right here, Allan." The familiar voice was close to his ear.

Then the sword dropped from his back, and Allan turned to see Bryce and three others grinning behind him. Two of them were obscured by the shadows and the trees, but the third was Claye.

The last time he'd seen the Dog, he'd been lying feverish on a cot in Logan's cottage. "Glad to see you made it. Glad to see any of you. Cutter saw what happened to the village. Where is everyone else? Where's my daughter?"

Bryce motioned toward the rock wall. "In the caves, which I assume you were looking for. The damn mages have covered up the entrances and any tracks leading up here with their illusions. We likely would have been found and rooted out days ago without them. But we shouldn't discuss this outside. None of the raiders are close at the moment, but I'm certain Paul and Sophia will want to speak to you."

"And I want to see Morrell."

"Is it just the two of you?"

"No. Artras, Gaven, and Glenn are waiting at the wagon. We also have a Wolf." Bryce's eyebrow rose. "Long story."

"Claye and Ritter, go with Cutter and retrieve the others. I'll take you inside, Allan. You can tell us all what happened."

"After I see Morrell."

Claye and Ritter stepped to Cutter's side, then all three

headed out into the darkness. Stars were pricking the sky overhead as the sun faded.

"This way." Bryce paused to give orders to Quinn—Allan recognized him as soon as he stepped from the shadows—and then he walked directly toward the rock wall. "It's a little disconcerting the first few times you pass through." He ducked and vanished. It appeared as if he'd slipped through the roots and vines, directly into the rock.

Allan hesitated a moment, then reached out, his hand passing through the stone as if it didn't exist, his skin tingling slightly. He stepped forward—

Into the entrance of a cave. Bryce waited for him on the far side. When he looked back, he could see out onto the flat area and into the trees beyond, as if the illusion of vines and stone weren't there.

"Do you want to see your daughter or not?"

The Dog led him down the tunnel, lit from deeper within by torchlight. They rounded a curve and the tunnel opened up into a large cavern stacked on either side with crates, trunks, barrels, and sacks. Four men stood guard as they passed through into another tunnel on the far side, this one descending deeper into the ridge. All four gave them cursory glances, until they recognized Allan. Shock brought two of them to their feet, but none of them said anything, although Allan could see the questions crowding their faces.

"This is the storage area. There's a second cavern and entrance where we're keeping the livestock. The raiders attacked us a few months after you left, but they weren't organized and we fought them off. I don't think it was their main force. We figured they'd return, so we started moving into these caves."

"Cutter said they wouldn't hold everyone, let alone all of these stores."

"The original caves wouldn't. But one of the walls collapsed, and we found more extensive caverns below, along with the ruins of some kind of ley node. The Wielders have been ecstatic. Once we knew we could harbor everyone here, we began moving in earnest. We didn't quite make it before they attacked again. We had enough warning to get nearly everyone in the village up here, along with most of the supplies, but we lost a few in the initial attack and the retreat. We would have lost many more if not for the University mages and the Wielders. They called up the damn earth and used the trees as weapons, while the Wielders used the ley like a shield. They're more dangerous than I thought."

They'd entered the far tunnel and were descending down a gentle incline. A second tunnel intersected theirs, the two merging. Ahead, a more intense light flickered against the wall from an opening to the right.

Bryce ducked into the opening. "Most of the villagers are living here or in the cavern farther down the tunnel. But Morrell is here because this is where the ley node is."

Allan stepped through onto the top of a rockfall, although someone had built steps leading down to the floor below. The room was filled with sheets and blankets rigged up like tents, riddled with walkways, cook fires, and staging areas for eating. Only the center of the room was open, where the stone fingers of stellae emerged from the relatively flat floor and white ley light fountained up inside their rough circle. The rest of the cavern was lit with torches, a few of them apparently created using the ley.

But Allan skimmed over everything, searching the faces of the crowded room below. Men, women, and children were hunched over fires cooking, mending clothes, scraping hides, conversing around buckets of wash. A few of them had paused to look up as Bryce began to descend the stairs. Some of those pointed, people Allan had lived with in the Hollow for years mingling with the refugees he'd brought from Erenthrall. They'd kept themselves segregated outside the caverns, but here they'd melded into one group. Conversations stalled as word spread, but still Allan didn't see Morrell. Or Cory or Hernande or any of the leaders of the Hollow.

Then someone screamed, "Da!" and suddenly Morrell was charging through the tents, Kara's yipping dog at her heels, people shifting out of her way as mothers brought trembling hands to their mouths and fathers clutched their own children closer.

Morrell pounded up the stairs, and a few short ragged breaths later she flung herself into his arms. Allan hugged her tight, down on one knee, his eyes burning as he stroked her hair and mumbled, "I'm back, poppet, I'm back." Max bounced and cavorted around them, front paws in the air, nose trying to pry in between them. Morrell sobbed into his chest, holding on so tight he could barely breathe, but he didn't care. For a tiny instant that felt like eternity, she was a child again, his child, his poppet. He drew in the honey scent of her hair, soothed her wracking body, smothered her fears with reassurance and murmured nonsense.

Her sobs quieted and she pulled back. She'd changed in the few months he'd been away. The lines of her face were harsher, more worn. She carried herself with more confidence and her eyes were harder, more serious. He could still see the child she'd been, but it was fading.

She was growing up, faster than he'd thought possible.

"Where's Kara?" She raised her hands to wipe away her tears. She didn't use the backs of her hands, like a child; she used her fingers, swiping from the corners of her eyes, down her nose, and across her cheekbones, the gesture decisive and dismissive and heartbreakingly adult. "Is she dead?"

The pang of realizing he was losing the daughter he knew cut across the sudden emptiness in his chest as he remembered what he'd come to the Hollow to do.

He reached down to calm Max's frantic excitement, then stood, "No, No, she's not dead. At least I don't think so." He glanced out over the room, where nearly everyone was watching them. His gaze picked out Cory immediately, Hernande, Paul, and Sophia standing behind him with Bryce. Janis waited patiently farther back.

His hands were on Morrell's shoulders and he turned back to look down into her eyes. She'd grown taller as well, he noted. "Don't worry. I'll explain everything."

Footsteps from behind announced the arrival of Artras, Glenn, Gaven, Claye, and Ritter.

"The Wolf?"

"We secured him with the supplies. We didn't dare move him to where they keep the livestock. The men there are watching him. They've also begun unloading what little we had with us from Erenthrall."

"Then we'd better go down and report what happened to the others."

They descended the stairs, people surrounding them as

they made their way toward the central ley node, where Allan had seen Cory and the others. Most welcomed them back and asked about the others, but Allan said nothing, intent on reaching Cory. He was aware that Artras stepped to one side with Jack's mother, a wail reaching him a short moment later, but he continued. Someone would have to find Kent's family as well, let them know he'd died protecting them in Erenthrall. He wondered if any of the members of their own families had died here, in the Hollow, when the raiders attacked. Had Gaven lost someone? Cutter? What would he say to Aaron's family?

What was he going to say to Cory?

And then the throng before him broke and there he stood, Hernande a step behind and to one side for support.

He halted, five steps away, and focused on Cory, met his gaze without flinching.

"She's alive, but she's been captured. And I intend to save her."

"I'm going with you," Cory said. It was clear that no one would be able to change his mind.

Allan had no intention of trying. He scanned the rest of those gathered around the fire. He, Artras, Cutter, and Glenn—Gaven had gone off to see his family—had spent the last few hours relating their trip to Erenthrall in between devouring whatever food and drink the others managed to provide for them. The roasted corn had tasted like ambrosia, and the fresh-baked bread with strawberry jam had elicited moans of pleasure from Glenn. They'd subsisted on roasted meat and whatever tubers and nuts they could find while returning. Green vegetables had been nonexistent. Allan couldn't get enough of them, even the cooked cabbage.

He caught Bryce's eye, Hernande's, then Paul's. "I'll take whoever I can get, but I don't think a few men and women are going to be enough. I'm going to need a pack, if not more. These White Cloaks had a guard, like the Dogs back in Erenthrall. It wasn't a ragged band of ruffians who could barely hold a sword, let alone use it."

"So you want to take all of the fighting men we have

with you? Who will protect the rest of us while you're gone? Have you forgotten about the raiders?"

Paul's voice had risen as he spoke, but Sophia quelled him by placing a hand on his leg. "Of course he hasn't forgotten about the raiders. Have you?"

"No, I haven't forgotten. And I don't know how to handle them either."

"We can't send anyone off to save some damned Wielder when we need everyone that can fight here to protect us!"

"She's not some damned Wielder. You didn't want any of us here in the first place." Cory turned to Hernande, then Allan. "We should just leave—all of the refugees. We should go find Kara and the others, let the Hollow fend for itself."

Hernande cleared his throat. "You don't mean that."

Cory's hardened expression fractured. "No. Not really. But it's Kara."

Hernande rested a hand on his shoulder. "We know. And we won't abandon her. I won't. And neither will Allan."

Paul rolled his eyes. "It's all well and good to declare your intentions, but you don't even know where she is."

"We know they were headed southward, along that road. I can certainly find that crossing again. We can follow the road."

"And how do you know they didn't leave the road an hour after you last saw them? They could be anywhere."

"The White Cloaks are Wielders, and they're actively using the ley. They'll have to be positioned somewhere near an active source, like the node here."

"So another node. That's a start. We can use the sands to figure out where they are."

"It won't be that easy. The 'south' is a large area, and the sands can only view a small portion of it at a time. It could take weeks to find a single node, and there would be no guarantee that it would be the node the White Cloaks are using."

"Not to mention that the nodes aren't particularly stable right now. The node you find might be dead by the time you get there, with the ley lines shifting around so much."

Artras gasped in realization and everyone turned to her. "That's just it. The White Cloaks wouldn't choose a node that isn't stable. They'd be actively working to stabilize it."

She turned to Allan. "Remember Erenthrall? We found signs that someone was manipulating the ley lines, redirecting them. We even saw signs of it before we reached the city, in that town where the old node had been activated. All of the lines were being directed to the southwest. I'd wager they're all focused on the same location, wherever the White Cloaks have chosen as their new home."

"Even this node here is directed southward," Raven added.

"The largest node southwest of Erenthrall is Tumbor."

Everyone fell silent for a moment.

"The White Cloaks aren't in Tumbor. The lines we saw in Erenthrall aren't flowing in that direction. They're angled farther west. They must be centered on another node, one of the junctions of the ley system from before the Shattering."

"So where are the junctions west of Erenthrall and Tumbor?"

Artras stared at him. "I don't know. None of us do. Only the Primes knew the ley system outside of Erenthrall. Most of us barely knew the ley outside of our own districts."

"Then we're back to not knowing where the White Cloaks are."

Hernande was chewing on the end of his beard, brow creased in thought. "Not necessarily." He reached into a pocket and withdrew a few pebbles. Allan had no idea where they came from, but they appeared to be simply river stones, picked up because of their color. Hernande placed two of the largest on the flat rock between himself and the fire, pointing to one, then the other. "Erenthrall. Tumbor." He then placed one farther west and slightly north of Erenthrall. "The Hollow." He handed one to Artras, who leaned forward and started placing the stone even before he said, "Place this one where you estimate the town with the active node is, the one you found before you reached Erenthrall."

"Here." She set the small white stone down northwest of the city-stone, not quite along a straight line between it and the Hollow.

"Good." Hernande grabbed three of the leftover skewers that had been used to roast some of their dinner over the fire, nothing more than sharpened sticks. He handed two to Artras and the third to Raven. "Place the skewers so they point in the direction of the ley lines from the Hollow, the town, and Erenthrall."

Raven frowned. "I don't know if I can do it exactly."

Hernande waved a hand. "It doesn't have to be precise."

Artras had already knelt and placed one of the skewers, starting at Erenthrall. Raven watched her as she placed the second, one end at the town. Then she sat back and Raven set the third down, fussing with it as it tried to roll to one side.

When she stood, everyone leaned forward.

The three skewers met in an area west of Erenthrall and slightly south, yet still north of Tumbor.

"The White Cloaks' node must be in that area. Cory and I will search the sands there and see what we can find."

Paul crossed his arms over his chest. "That still doesn't solve the problem of the raiders. They're waiting outside, searching for us. They aren't going to simply go away because you want to rescue this Wielder."

"Why are they still here? If you've been hiding out for days now, why haven't they moved on?"

"They want the Wielders. They want our 'White Cloaks' and those of us from the University. They want to kill us all for causing the Shattering."

"Who are they? Do you know?"

"Their leader is named Aurek. He calls himself a Baron, of a place called Haven."

Allan shared a glance with Cutter.

"The wagon train," the tracker said.

"What wagon train?"

"When we were on the plains, right after we'd left, we saw a fire in the distance. Kent, Adder, and I went to investigate. It was a wagon train, being attacked by raiders. We never heard the name of their leader, but after slaughtering everyone and burning the wagons to the ground, they said they were returning to Haven."

Artras looked horrified. "You told us it was nothing, a lone wagon, its driver dead, the bandits gone."

"Would you have felt better knowing the truth?"

"No. But I would have slept with my knife closer to my hand."

"So these are the same people that attacked us earlier then," Sophia said, "as we suspected."

"Yes. And based on what you've said, they aren't going to leave until they have what they want."

Allan stared into the fire, thinking. The others remained quiet, Artras poking a stick into the coals, Glenn chewing on a chicken wing, his beard already soaked in grease.

A long moment later, Allan looked up, met Hernande's gaze, then Bryce's. "I need to speak to this Baron Aurek."

All of them looked startled except for Bryce. Allan wondered if he'd already figured out what Allan had planned.

"Not right now. It's the middle of the night."

"No. Tomorrow. I need to get some rest. And I want to spend some time with Morrell." He turned to Hernande and Cory. "You two need to find that ley node." He started to rise.

Paul's face was twisted in confusion. "Speak to him? What are you going to do? What are you going to say?"

"I'm going to give him what he wants."

Allan emerged from the woods along the stream that ran close to the remains of the Hollow's village shortly after dawn. At a point where the water ran through the cracks in a lip of stone, he crossed and climbed the bank on the far side. The charred supports of one of the cottages stood off to his right, the garden that surrounded it blackened and trampled. He stepped through the barely discernible paths around it and out onto the main road through the village. He paused once, at what had been his own cottage, but it had been reduced to cinders and ash. He continued toward the center of the village, passed the rounded communal oven, one side crushed in like an egg, then Sophia's cottage, Logan's, others, and finally halted near one of the standing walls of the town hall. The small square of open space in the center of the village reeked of smoke and the dead. He counted seven bodies, the crows picking over two of them. He kept his eyes averted; he already knew who'd died here. Bryce had told him.

He picked a position out near the center of the square, shifting into the open, and then waited.

Twenty minutes later, the sun now angling down into the square on one side, two raiders appeared, both carrying buckets, chatting. One of them finished a joke and the other burst out laughing, and then they saw him.

Both froze, startled, then the one on the right swore, dropped his empty buckets, and drew his sword. The other did the same. They began to separate, circling him, so they could attack from two different directions.

Allan was forced to increase his assessment of their intelligence.

"I want to speak to Aurck."

The two raiders paused. "Who are you?"

"Allan Garrett, an ex-Dog and member of the Hollow. This hollow. I have a proposal for him."

Both of the men looked nervous when he mentioned being a Dog. Neither of them looked like they'd been trained extensively, dressed in rough clothes, with unkempt beards. He could smell their stench from here, even over the lingering smoke. But they *had* been trained, based on the way they'd reacted and currently held their swords.

They shared another look, a signal passing between them. Then the second lowered his sword and backed away, leaving the buckets where they'd been dropped. He vanished into the trees in the direction of the refugee camp.

Allan shifted his attention to the first, the one who'd spoken.

The man fidgeted. "He's going to inform Aurek."

Allan didn't answer, which only seemed to make the raider more nervous.

As they waited, something rustled in the trees to Allan's left. He knew Cutter, Bryce, and two others had followed him, but they would have been behind him, out of sight. He shifted his stance, trying to catch movement out of the corner of his eye. Another raider? Had they already circled around to his flank?

A shadow loped from behind a tree, through shade, to a section of concealing brush. Not human—too low to the ground, the motion too smooth. A wolf?

Or a Wolf?

He spun toward the left, hand falling to the hilt of his

sword. But the forest was silent. Nothing moved, even the leaves still.

"What is it? What did you see?"

Allan turned back. The raider had used the distraction to come closer. He stood only ten paces away now, his gaze flicking from Allan to the woods and back again in suspicion.

"Nothing." But Allan didn't drop his hand from the hilt.

Behind the raider, the man Allan had seen casually order the deaths of everyone in the wagon train—men, women, and children—emerged from the tree line surrounded by a dozen additional raiders. As he moved forward, his guard spread out. Half of them were archers, flights already drawn and trained on Allan. He assumed there were others now circling around him, unseen. He wondered if they'd find Bryce and the others. Or the Wolf.

As on the plains, Aurek was dressed in the rough finery of a lord, the fabric slightly worn, not quite as fine as what he'd seen while a Dog in Erenthrall. It was what the outlying lords might have brought with them to the city when invited by the true Baron to attend a party.

Aurek halted a step in front of the raider, who took a step back.

"Aurek."

"*Baron* Aurek."

"Lord of Haven, maybe, before the Shattering. No Baron."

"You said you had a proposal."

"You attacked us unprovoked. You've burned our buildings to the ground, looted what you could, killed whoever you could, yet you're still here. Obviously there's something else we have that you want."

"You are harboring White Cloaks. Hand them over to us and we'll leave."

"You're wrong. We don't have any White Cloaks here. We have only Wielders."

"Wielders are White Cloaks. They're the ones who brought the world down around us, with their Nexus and their ley. We want to make them pay for what they've done."

The men around him nodded in agreement. Allan scanned their faces. He could understand their hatred. They had probably been working in their town or village when the Nexus shattered, sending shockwaves through the ley network. They would have seen the flare of the explosion on the horizon, in the distance, would have wondered what had happened, what the Wielders and the Baron were up to now. But they would have gone back to their work, unaware that Erenthrall lay in ruins, or that the pulse from the Shattering was headed their way. If they'd lived near one of the smaller nodes, that pulse would have caused a surge, maybe even exploded as it had in Erenthrall. Their lives would have changed drastically, all because of the Wielders and the Baron.

And they had Aurek to keep that hatred fresh.

He returned his attention to the lord. "We'll need the Wielders if we're going to fix what's happened. They can heal the distortion over Erenthrall. They can stop the quakes, halt the auroras."

"Then why haven't they done that yet?"

"Because someone's killing them all off."

"You lie."

"The Shattering killed off all of the Primes. The Wielders who escaped aren't as powerful. They're regrouping, trying to figure out how to heal the distortion, how to stabilize the ley lines, which are what's causing the quakes. They need more time to—"

"Lies! Lies meant to protect themselves from justice. It's been months since the Shattering. They've done nothing in that time but sit back and watch the havoc and chaos the world's been thrown into. They don't deserve the chance to repair the damage they've done. The earth will heal itself in time." He spat on the ground at his feet. "You have nothing for me. Kill him. We'll find the Wielders without him."

Allan didn't flinch as bows creaked, the archers flexing muscles they'd allowed to relax during the conversation. "I know where the White Cloaks are hiding. The ones you're truly seeking."

Aurek's hand shot up, forestalling the archers and halting the few men who'd started forward with swords drawn and readied. He turned back slowly.

"You know where the Needle is?"

"Our Wielders can find it."

"The Wielders. Why would you tell me this? Why wouldn't you and your Wielders simply join the White Cloaks, then hunt us down?"

"Because they captured half of our party in Erenthrall. They killed at least one of us that wasn't a Wielder. I don't know what they've done with the others, but they were still alive the last time I saw them. Those of us that escaped followed them until they turned south, I'd guess returning to this Needle. We couldn't rescue them ourselves because of their guards—there were too many of them. We returned here to take back a larger force, but we found you here instead."

"So you have no love for the White Cloaks either. I don't think many do, especially those in Erenthrall. Like the Primes before, they use their power to control." He raised his chin. "You want to trade. The White Cloaks' location for your lives and those of your Wielders and mages."

"No, I want your men. I want to save my Wielders and the rest of my group from the White Cloaks. I need your men to do it. Our lives and those of my Wielders and mages come with it. I doubt you can get close enough to the White Cloaks and their Needle to do it without them. You've already seen what they can do."

Aurek's men fidgeted, a few glancing around sharply in fear, as if they expected the Wielders to appear out of thin air, ley boiling from their hands. But most turned to stare at Aurek, uncertain.

The lord of Haven had stilled. Allan could practically see his thoughts as he weighed the proposal. He didn't want to give up his position here—he knew he had the Hollowers trapped, that he could find their hiding place given time, that he could have their Wielders. But he didn't know how long they could hold out, or what the Wielders could do to defend themselves. He'd already lost men, and he didn't know how many more it would take to break the Hollowers. And for what, to kill a few Wielders? Perhaps lose the chance to find the White Cloaks?

All of that flashed through Aurek's eyes. Allan saw the moment Aurek decided to accept, his stance relaxing, weight shifting subtly.

And he saw the moment Aurek decided to betray them.

"We could simply attack you, capture you, force you to talk. Someone would break, eventually. Joss did."

"You won't risk it. Only a few of us know their location. If all of us are killed, you'll have nothing but a few Wielders and the White Cloaks will be lost."

"We'd find them eventually."

"Perhaps."

It was posturing, for his men, and both of them knew it.

"Very well. The location of the White Cloaks for your lives, and we'll let you tag along when we seize their Needle and cut their throats. Now, where are they?"

"You won't get it from us that easily. We'll meet here with all of our men and travel south together. You'll call off your search for the Hollowers. If we find your men anywhere west of the village, the deal's off."

"Agreed. But I'm not a patient man. We'll leave for the Needle within three days or I start searching for your villagers again."

"Three days then."

Allan turned his back on Aurek and his archers, his shoulders itching. He expected an arrow any moment, but nothing happened as he rounded the remaining walls of the meeting hall and passed from their line of sight. He increased his pace, passing a few more burned-out cottages before the trees closed in overhead, continuing northward longer than necessary to throw off anyone following. He heard nothing from behind, though, so after twenty minutes he cut west. At one point he heard the crackle of underbrush and halted, scanning for the raiders — and also for the Wolf — but saw nothing.

He'd made it halfway back to the caves when Bryce stepped out from behind a tree, Cutter appearing farther behind him.

"No one followed you. Aurek waited until you were gone, then ordered his men back to their camp. Cutter scouted around and he's called back his patrols as well."

"How many men does he have?"

"We've counted close to two hundred. But he sent a few east after settling in at the refugee camp. We think they were messengers, possibly calling for reinforcements."

"Or supplies. He may have decided to wait you out."

Bryce didn't argue the point. "You realize he's going to turn on us the moment he has what he wants. He won't give up our Wielders and mages, not after what they and Cory and the others did during their attack."

"I know. I never thought he'd keep the bargain. But he won't betray us until he knows where this Needle is. We'll have to be prepared."

"As long as you know." Bryce didn't seem bothered by the knowledge that Aurek would betray them as he fell in at Allan's side, but Allan reminded himself that Bryce was a Dog. Betrayal of others had been part of the job, when it aided the Baron or had been ordered by your alpha.

When Cutter joined them, Allan asked, "Did you see anything else out there?"

"What do you mean?"

"Anything besides Aurek's men."

Cutter looked at him oddly. "Nothing."

Maybe it *had* simply been a wolf.

"We have three days. Gather as many of the Hollowers and refugees as you think we can spare, but don't force anyone to come, let them volunteer. We need to leave enough Hollowers behind to defend themselves. Everyone else who can go and is willing needs to be with us."

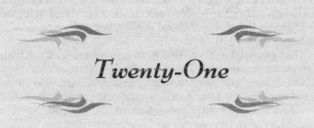

# Twenty-One

"I HATE TO SPARE THEM, but you're going to need a few wagons. Which means you're going to need all of our horses, except a few of the mares and the stud, of course."

"We can survive without them. There's no need—"

Paul cut him off. "You can't take forty or more people to battle without something to feed them."

Allan made to protest again, but caught himself. Paul was glaring out at the activity in the supply cavern, men and women and children picking through what they'd managed to put back, already loading up the backs of two wagons. Gaven appeared to be organizing them all, his orders curt, authoritative. Not the same meek and mild-mannered man who'd left with them months ago to find supplies in Erenthrall.

Paul had changed as well while they were gone. He was fidgety and short-tempered, as always, but based on the way he refused to meet Allan's gaze, it wasn't because he wanted to be confrontational. Three months ago, he would have gleefully kicked all of the refugees out of the Hollow without a second thought, glad to be rid of them, especially the Wielders. But not anymore. He wanted to help them, and he'd realized there was little he could do.

Nearly everyone who had been training under Bryce since the attack on the wagon that had killed Terrim had volunteered to join Allan to rescue Kara and the others. Bryce had been forced to single out a good portion of them to remain behind to defend the Hollowers. He'd selected Braddon as the alpha of those staying behind, since he was intent on coming himself.

That gave Allan forty-two men and women, along with Artras, Mareane, and Jude for the Wielders, Cory, Hernande, Jasom, and Jerrain from the University. Raven, as the eldest Wielder after Artras, would remain with the other Wielders for additional protection of the Hollow. Sovaan would stay with the remaining University students.

Fifty-one in their group. Two hundred in Aurek's. He hoped it was enough.

Allan realized he was still staring at Paul, the elder councilor twitching awkwardly where he stood. He reached out and clasped the man's forearm, shaking him lightly to force him to meet his gaze.

"You know you're needed here. You can do more good here than trying to fight on the plains."

"I wouldn't have believed it a year ago, but your Wielders and those people from the University saved our asses out there. And they wouldn't have had the chance without Bryce and his Dogs. None of us would be alive without them. Bryce practically forced us to move to the caves, and if we hadn't done that, we'd have all been slaughtered."

Allan let his arm drop, aware that the contact made Paul uncomfortable. "They might not have come if we weren't here."

"They'd have come eventually, if what you saw with that wagon train is true. They aren't hunting for Wielders alone. They're brigands, pure and simple, even if they have a leader they call a Baron and a cause to follow."

Allan didn't argue, because he believed it was true.

Paul turned to face him. "Go. Save Kara. And when you have her back—and all of the others the bastards took— come back here. The Hollow will always welcome you." His gaze flicked over Allan's shoulder, then returned. "Someone's here to see you."

Allan turned to find Janis standing behind him, waiting.

He went to thank Paul, but the elder had already moved away, wading into the activity surrounding the wagons, chiding a young boy who'd dropped one of the crates to slow down, it wasn't a race, before helping him lift it into the back of the nearest wagon and ruffling the boy's hair.

"He's mellowed some."

"Apparently." Allan motioned toward the tunnel leading down to the lower caverns. "I need to find Hernande and Cory, see if they've located the Needle yet. Did you need something?"

"Only a few minutes of your time."

"Of course. You took care of Morrell for most of her life, more a mother to her than anyone. What did you need?"

Janis didn't answer immediately, falling into step as they left the storage cavern behind, the walls of the tunnel closing in on either side. They'd almost reached the point where the tunnel merged with the one holding the livestock when she said, "It's about Morrell."

He stopped dead. "What about her? Did something happen while I was gone? She hasn't said anything."

"I didn't think she would. And no one else has probably thought to tell you. She healed people. First Claye, then Harper, and finally Cory."

"She's been working with Logan for a while. I'm certain she's helped heal many people."

"You don't understand. She didn't simply heal them, she *healed* them. She placed her hands on their wounds and within moments they were cured, or as close to cured that it still counts. Claye had an infection that Logan swore would kill him. Morrell touched him and the next day the infection was gone, washed clean out of him, and in another few days he was walking around. Unsteady and weak, but walking. Harper had a broken leg, the bone jutting out of the flesh. She touched him and within moments the bone was set. Cory's leg was trapped under a stone—one of those that fell from the cavern ceiling during the quake—but Morrell—"

"Healed him."

"Some of the Hollowers think she's a Healer, like from the stories. A true Healer. Others mutter about her under their breath, afraid of her. Superstitious heathens." Janis gripped Allan's shoulder. "But I'm most concerned about Morrell. She hears all of it, the good and bad. She doesn't know what to think. I spoke to her about it, but she's so hard to read sometimes. She keeps so much to herself."

Allan didn't know what to say, didn't know how he felt. Glad that it wasn't something bad, but also worried about what it would mean for Morrell. Aurek was here because of the Wielders and the University mentors, because of what they could do. What would he think if he knew Morrell could heal? Kara and Dylan were in danger because they were different, because the White Cloaks wanted Wielders. He could easily envision any one of the groups that they'd met in Erenthrall—the Rats, the Tunnelers, even the Temerites and Gorrani—seeking out a true Healer, simply to have her, to use her.

"I'll talk to her. Later." He began moving back down toward the ley node's chamber, where he knew he'd find Cory and Hernande.

Janis followed him.

They found them in the far corner of the node chamber, beyond the node itself, where the stone that had fallen in from the ceiling had been stacked. They'd used some of that stone to create a low rectangular wall about a foot high, sectioning off an area the size of a wagon bed that they'd filled with sand and pebbles from the scree and the pile of rock behind them. Both of them were standing over the sands, which were already in motion, shifting with a dry grinding sound.

"I'm not seeing anything of significance here."

"There's less activity to our west than I expected, although we haven't gone that far afield yet. There must be *something* remaining in the Demesnes."

"Someone will have survived there, yes, but who is to say how much of the ley system is still active? The Demesnes were never as densely populated as the Temerite lands to the east or even the Gorrani Flats and Archipelago to the south. Their ley system wasn't as extensive. It may simply have been cut off by the Shattering." Hernande glanced up as Allan and Janis stepped up to their sand pit.

"What have you found?" Allan asked.

"The sand we collected is coarser than what we used

back at the University—or even in the Hollow—so the maps we get aren't as refined, but I think we've found the Needle." He looked toward Hernande, who motioned for Cory to continue.

Cory knelt down to the sands, reaching forward and sweeping his hand over them. The tracks of shifting sand and pebbles that indicated the active flows of the ley ceased moving, but not for long. The sand began to move again, tentatively, as if feeling out their new paths. "It was more difficult to do that than it should have been."

"Do you use the ley to do it?"

"A small portion, to connect the Tapestry to the ley itself."

"Then it was probably my presence. I've been skirting the node as much as possible, so I don't interfere with anything."

"Interesting." Hernande considered him through narrowed eyes. "You affect the ley, but not the Tapestry. You didn't disrupt our illusions, for example. I wonder why."

Cory stood as the motion of the sands solidified. "We found this close to the area that Artras and Raven picked out on the makeshift map at the fire two nights ago." He pointed to where the sand swirled near the center of the pit, seven distinct lines of sand flowing toward the vortex. "We think that's the Needle. These two flows here are coming from Erenthrall, one from the north of the distortion, the other from the south. We think this thinner flow is coming from the old node Artras and Kara found in that town. And this one is from the node here. The others are coming from nodes to the west of the Needle."

Allan leaned forward, but didn't approach any closer. "What are these weaker lines here?"

Hernande answered. "Those are coming from Tumbor. Before the distortion quickened, they were likely much stronger, probably more so than the ones from Erenthrall, but they've been cut off. They're trying to reestablish themselves, but their anchoring nodes are now inside the distortion. The area around Tumbor is in utter chaos, worse than Erenthrall after the Shattering. There are likely massive quakes occurring there, along with eruptions of the ley like we saw in the city."

"Will you be able to find it once we've left the Hollow?"

"We can't take the sand pit with us, but Artras says that she can follow the ley line, now that we know it leads to the Needle."

"And you're certain this is where the White Cloaks have gone?"

"It's the strongest concentration of ley in the area."

Cory crouched down abruptly. "Look."

In the sands, one of the weak lines from Tumbor died out, a new, stronger line appearing slightly north of it, stretching from the Needle out toward—

"Farrade. Its anchor in Tumbor is gone, so it's shifted to Farrade."

"Or someone forced it to shift."

Cory and Hernande shared a look. "If we're right in our theory that the quakes are being caused by the shifting ley lines, then—"

Before he'd finished, the earth began to tremble. It started off light, then abruptly escalated. Allan crouched down, pulling Janis with him, shielding her with his body. People in the cavern cried out. The floor heaved once, twice. The ley at the node fountained higher, splashing the top of the cavern, but remained inside its circle of stellae. A scattering of fresh stone fell from the ceiling with a cascade of dirt, and a thin veil of dust filled the space, but the tremors stopped, the earth settling again.

Sobs echoed through the chamber, interrupted by harsh coughing. People began to move again, tentatively. Others began calling out to their families, verifying they were all right.

Allan stood, dust and light debris falling from his shoulders. He helped Janis upright, then turned to Hernande and Cory, both picking themselves up from the floor, Cory pale and shaken. "Everyone all right?"

"It wasn't that bad, because the ley lines being affected were so distant. The force created must be traveling through the ley network, affecting the areas along each line and node. And that force appears to be increasing with every change in the system. If this continues—"

"What?"

"The ley system may end up ripping the entire continent apart."

Allan stared at him, unable to comprehend what that meant. The ramifications were too immense, too incomprehensible.

So he turned away, headed toward the tented area where he now slept with Janis and Morrell. Janis followed.

"Where are you going?"

"To find my daughter!" Then, over his shoulder: "Make certain Artras can find the Needle."

He rounded the ley node, some of the Wielders clustered around it, including Raven. Allan assumed they were checking the ley after the quake. Raven opened her eyes long enough to nod in his direction, then resumed her work. When he reached the edge of the tents, he found people injured from some of the debris, along with a few of the tents collapsed. People were picking themselves up and dusting off, most shaken but unharmed.

He sped up as he neared his own tent, still standing, and ducked down into the opening. "Morrell?"

One look told him she wasn't there. He swore and backed out, glaring out over the cavern. "Morrell!"

A woman a few tents down from them looked up. "I haven't seen her since the quake, but she may have gone to find Logan and help with the wounded."

"Thanks."

"Logan's set up a makeshift infirmary in the other cavern," Janis said. "I'll show you."

They ascended the stairs built around the scree, still sturdy even after the quake, then headed deeper into the ridge, toward the second cavern. After a few turns and a sharp incline downward, the tunnel opened up into a chamber twice as large as the one containing the node. Lit by torches and cook fires, it housed the majority of the people from the Hollow, along with a sizable number of the refugees. Most of the smaller livestock—chickens, goats, sheep—were corralled off to the left, held in with hastily constructed rail fences. To the right, water gushed out of a crack in the wall, pooling below before running off through a crevice.

Logan had set up the infirmary near the water. At least a dozen people were waiting to be seen, one woman with blood dripping from her chin from a gash in her head, a man lying unconscious beside her. Another woman held a bawl-ing child, rocking the girl back and forth while hushing her and inspecting a bruise on her arm.

Logan was stitching up a man's sliced thigh. "Every time you move, it hurts worse." Logan saw Allan and Janis ap-proaching. "Where in hells is Morrell? I can use her help here."

"She's not here already?"

"No, I haven't seen her since this morning. She's proba-bly up staring at that Wolf again."

Allan stopped breathing. "What did you say?"

"That damned Wolf! She's been hovering around its pen ever since you brought it in here!"

But Allan wasn't listening any more. He was already halfway across the room. He knocked over a woman emerg-ing from her tent, shot back an apology at her outcry, but didn't slow.

From behind, Logan shouted, "Tell her to get her ass down here and help, if she wants to be a healer!"

Then Allan was in the tunnel, charging up toward the outer caves. He passed Paul on his way, the village elder startled.

Allan burst into the storage area, the men still working on loading the wagons. He sprinted toward the small enclo-sure where they'd placed the Wolf. Morrell stood at its en-trance, staring inside, her eyes intent, her mouth set in a stubborn expression that reminded him so much of her mother that it brought him up short.

Morrell turned to look at him. "I can heal him."

He was close enough to the enclosure now that he could see the Wolf inside, pacing back and forth at the end of his lead, as close to Morrell as it allowed. Its chest rumbled with a dangerous growl, its eyes feral, lips curled back. Patches of its fur were matted with dried blood from the meat it had been fed. None of the humanity Artras had forced him to see in it showed through now; it was only animal.

He reached for Morrell. "What do you mean?"

"There's a man caught inside the Wolf. I can see him. I can heal him."

She shifted toward the Wolf, but Allan jerked her back

as it lunged, choking as its lead snapped it back, ropes creaking with the strain. It huffed in exasperation and resumed its pacing.

"You can't, poppet. It's too dangerous."

"I'm not a poppet. And I'm not a child anymore."

Allan choked, as if he were on his own lead. He lowered his hands to his knees. "I know, Morrell. But—" He halted. He couldn't simply forbid it. She was too old for that. He needed to reason with her, like an adult.

"How do you know you can heal him? How do you know it will work?"

"I know I can. I healed Claye. And then Harper and Cory, and Cory's foot was crushed. I shouldn't have been able to fix that. But I did. And the Wolf—the man inside the Wolf—he hurts. I can help him."

Allan held her gaze for a long moment, thinking of Morrell's mother, Moria, of everything Artras had said as they argued over killing the Wolf, of the sparks of humanity he'd caught in the Wolf's eyes as they traveled here before the animal took over again.

Finally he lifted his eyes to the rock ceiling overhead. "Forgive me, Moria."

Then he grabbed Morrell's shoulder. "We'll let you try. But we'll have to secure him so that he can't hurt you."

It took the rest of the day and the cursing of three additional men to get the Wolf tied and muzzled in the enclosure. Allan stood two paces away, arms and back scratched, blood staining his shirt where it was torn, but the wounds weren't deep. He stank of sweat, his skin gritty and slick. He wiped his forehead with the back of his hand, redistributing the dirt, then turned from the panting Wolf to look behind.

A crowd had gathered, Morrell in the front, waiting patiently. She'd watched as they attempted to snag the Wolf to secure him, calling out orders not to hurt him, even after he'd latched onto one of the men's arms with his teeth before he could snatch it away. She'd healed that while the rest continued their work with the Wolf.

Behind Morrell, Paul, Sophia, Artras, Cory, Hernande, and what felt like half of the village watched, mostly in silence, only a few muttered conversations here and there. They sat or stood on the wagons. A few had climbed the stacks of crates and barrels against the far wall in order to see. All of them were watching Allan.

He eyed Morrell. "I'm still not comfortable with this, but if you want to try—"

"I do."

Allan stepped to one side to let her by, but didn't back off. He wanted to be ready to snatch her away if the Wolf so much as twitched. The Wolf began to growl as she approached, its eyes narrowed in hate. It struggled against the muzzle, teeth gnashing, lips curled back. Allan jerked forward when it tried to lash out with its claws. But the ropes held.

The growl deepened as Morrell knelt down at its side. It thrashed as much as it could. His daughter looked so fragile beside it, its strange size emphasized by her smaller frame. But then she reached forward with both hands and laid them gently against its heaving side and it yelped, the growl cut off, replaced by a heart-wrenching whine. Its thrashing ceased and it stilled, panting heavily.

Morrell glanced once toward Allan, as if seeking encouragement, then turned back to the Wolf and closed her eyes.

After a long moment of tense silence with nothing happening, Morrell's brow furrowed. Then it relaxed and she opened her eyes without removing her hands from the Wolf's fur. She looked over her shoulder. "Something's blocking me."

"It's the Wolf. Maybe he doesn't want to be healed. Maybe—"

"No, Da." Morrell met his gaze. "It's you."

Allan's mouth hung open in a moment of incomprehension, then snapped shut. Like the ley, he must somehow disrupt his own daughter's healing. That would explain why it hadn't manifested until now. He and Morrell had always been together, from the moment she'd been born. The only time they'd been apart for a significant amount of time had been during his runs into Erenthrall, both before and after the Shattering, and she'd only recently begun working with Logan. Had he held her back these last few years, simply by being with her?

The pang of guilt burrowed deep into his gut as he reluctantly backed off, those gathered parting to let him through, until he stood over thirty feet away. Bryce took his place without hesitation. Janis shifted back to stand by him, gripping his hand in hers without a word.

Morrell returned her attention to the Wolf. She closed her eyes again, tilted her head upward.

Everyone gasped when the auroral light began to flicker around her hands, purple-red, flecked with gold. The Wolf broke into another whine that increased in pitch until it became a low, mournful howl. The auroral light spread outward, followed by sickening pops and cracks, like bone snapping and splintering. The howl broke into snarls and the Wolf began to struggle again as the nauseating sounds continued. The people around Allan gagged, one or two shouting in horror. A woman screamed and fainted.

Then the snarls morphed from animalistic agony into human moans of pain. Beneath the aurora, the Wolf's fur shortened and receded, flesh appearing in patches. The forelegs shrank with a gruesome crunch and the paws elongated into fingers and hands. The chest cavity remained mostly the same, but the lower torso twisted and cracked, Allan thankful that Morrell's body and those standing between them blocked his sight of most of what happened there. The Wolf's muzzle shortened, along with the neck.

But before the transformation was complete, the auroral light began to dim, fading, as if it were seeping into the Wolf's body. Morrell's hands slipped from the man-beast's torso and she began to list.

Allan shoved through the crowd and caught her before she could fall, pulling her back as those behind broke into excited babble. Allan could barely speak as he twisted Morrell so he could see her. "Are you all right?"

"I'm fine, Da." He hugged her close until she began to struggle. "You're crushing me."

He kissed her on the forehead. "What happened? Couldn't you change him back completely?"

They both looked toward the Wolf. Except he wasn't a Wolf any longer. Most of him had been returned to its human form, but there were patches of fur here and there and his fingers still ended in pointed claws instead of fingernails.

His tail was gone. His face retained the most wolf-like features, with a stunted muzzle and pointed, furry ears, all but a patch on his throat still covered in black-brown fur.

But when he stirred and opened his eyes, they were human, no longer feral.

"I ran out of strength. I can finish it tomorrow, after I rest. Help me back to my pallet."

They turned, to find everyone watching them, most in awe, many with tears in their eyes. Morrell blushed and ducked her head as someone started to clap, joined by many others, and real conversations broke out.

Before it grew out of control, someone forced their way through the throng at the front, stepping between Cory and Sophia, and everyone quieted again. Paul reached out to stop Devitt as he moved forward, but Artras held the elder back.

Devitt approached Morrell slowly. He halted two paces away, then presented his deformed right arm. Allan remembered how Devitt's body had been twisted by the auroral lights in Erenthrall immediately after the Shattering. The clothes he wore now hid most of the damage, but not the odd turn of his arm.

"I didn't dare hope when I heard what you were going to attempt with the Wolf." He glanced toward the figure behind them, still tied up, then back. "Do you think you can fix this?"

Morrell stepped away from Allan and gripped Devitt's twisted forearm. "Not right now—I'm too tired—but I think I can."

Devitt broke into tears and his wife emerged from the crowd, running to his side. She nodded to Morrell and Allan in gratitude, then led Devitt away.

Paul came forward, trailed by a few of the others. Most of those behind began to disperse, returning to their work or to the caverns below.

"Damned fine work, young woman." Paul gestured toward the Wolf. "What do we do with him now?"

"Untie him. Bring him some clothes. See if he can talk, if he's hungry. I don't think he'll hurt anyone, although I'd be careful nonetheless. He still has some vicious-looking teeth."

"And those claws," Artras said. "I'll deal with him. He

knows me from the trip from Erenthrall." She called to two others and stepped past them, already talking to the Wolf.

Allan touched Morrell's shoulder. "I'm taking her back to our tent so she can rest."

"We still have a ton of work to get done before you can depart for the Needle."

"I know, but it can wait until tomorrow."

The following day, Allan never stopped moving. Cutter reported that Aurek and his men from Haven were staying east of the village, as promised, so Bryce took nearly all of those who intended to travel to the Needle outside to work on their fighting skills. Quinn worked with the archers, since Cutter still couldn't draw, Allan walked among the men and women—more women than he'd expected, certainly more than had been training when he'd left for Erenthrall—adjusting form or giving advice or encouragement where necessary, but then left the training up to Bryce, Claye, Braddon, and Glenn.

Inside the caverns, he checked in with Paul, who was overseeing the wagons. Two had been loaded and moved outside, two more were being stocked under Paul's careful watch. His helpers were mostly children and the elderly, with a scattering of others from the Hollow and a few refugees who'd elected to stay behind. Allan didn't begrudge those that wanted to remain behind; they couldn't strip the Hollow of all of its youngest and heartiest workers.

He caught movement coming from the Wolf's enclosure and headed over there, waving to Paul in acknowledgment. He didn't need to speak to him; the elder had everything well in hand.

At the enclosure, he found Morrell and Sophia kneeling before the Wolf. He lay curled up in a heavy blanket, shivering. The creature with claws and snout that had remained after his transformation yesterday was gone, replaced by a dark-haired young man, maybe thirty, with a sharp nose, narrow face, and green eyes. His ears were still slightly pointed, hinting of the Wolf he had been. His skin was pale and grayish looking, his eyes bruised, but aside from patches of hair on his arms and chest, the dark fur had faded.

The man started as Allan came up behind the two women, his nostrils flaring. Allan wondered if, like his ears, there were any other traits of the Wolf that still remained, like scent.

Morrell looked up at him. "His name is Drayden. Drayden Orilson. He's twenty-seven, and before the Shattering he lived in Erenthrall with his wife and two sons." Her tone turned somber. "They survived the Shattering, but he doesn't know where they are. He was caught in one of the auroral lights before they could escape the city."

Allan knelt down and met Drayden's gaze. "How are you feeling?"

"C-c-cold." A deep, throaty voice, with hints of the Wolf's growl in it.

"He's in shock," Sophia said, "and he's weak. The transformation is as rough on the patient as it is on the healer. It will take a few days for him to recover, maybe longer."

"I want to go—with you. To kill—the White Cloaks."

"We leave tomorrow. I don't think you'll have recovered yet."

He snarled, teeth bared, then broke into a fit of coughing.

Sophia reached for a cloth soaking in warm water and patted his forehead with it. "We'll feed him some good soup stock. That should help. But I don't think he'll have enough strength to travel by tomorrow."

Drayden bared his teeth again, but didn't argue.

"The Wolves. You have a pack in Erenthrall?"

"Yes."

"And who is your alpha?"

Drayden paused, wary. "Grant."

"He isn't entirely Wolf, is he? I saw him. He hunted me through the streets, but I escaped."

"Through the distortion. He hasn't stopped hunting you. He ordered us to find you, after you fled into the distortion. He sent us out searching for your scent. We knew when you returned, but he wouldn't let us attack you or those in your group." The words were twisted with disdain, but he caught himself, a look of shock crossing his face as he realized what he'd said and what it meant. The Wolf wasn't completely gone. "We followed you, staying hidden, watching."

"Why?"

"To see what you would do. You could enter the distortion. There are things in the distortion Grant wants. People."

"Like what? Who?"

Drayden fought off violent tremors. "He didn't tell the pack. Then he realized you had White Cloaks. They kill Wolves on sight, offer the other groups in Erenthrall food and supplies for our pelts, so they hunt us as well. And yet they weren't White Cloaks. They didn't smell right. So we waited, and followed, and then you were taken by the Rabbits and the Rats."

"Rabbits? You mean the Tunnelers. They took us to the White Cloaks, were trading us for supplies. Grant must have thought we were with the White Cloaks after all and had the Wolves attack us all at the trade-off. Or he wanted to make certain we didn't join with them."

"Yes."

"But we aren't with the White Cloaks. We never were. We were being traded like rice or fish."

"I know that now. I don't know about our alpha."

Allan thought of the Wolf he thought he'd seen in the woods two days before. "I think he does. I think he's been following us since Erenthrall. Would he do that?"

"Perhaps. For one of the pack."

Allan wondered what Grant would do once Allan left the Hollow with two hundred and fifty men, armed for a fight, headed toward the Needle.

Drayden's nostrils flared again and he half lifted his torso from the rough straw pallet he lay on. "She comes."

A moment later, Artras appeared, carrying a bowl of soup, its aroma filling the enclosure as she handed it over to Sophia and acknowledged Allan with a nod. "Straight from the pot."

Allan stood as she and Morrell helped Drayden into a seated position and began to feed him. He already appeared stronger, although he winced with nearly every movement.

In the two main caverns, families were preparing kits for those who intended to go. Bedrolls, clothes, a tin cup, a spare plate—anything that they thought their wife or husband or child would need or want. A few shed tears, quietly but grimly. Allan saw a few kissing wooden or clay figures of the gods before stuffing them into a satchel or backpack. Others had similar tokens of luck or protection—a lock of hair, a stone, a kerchief.

In the infirmary, Logan dealt with those more seriously wounded from the quake the day before while packing a similar kit full of medical supplies. He raised a hand in forewarning when he caught sight of Allan.

"Don't even try to argue with me. Paul has already had it out with me and Sophia has been glaring at me since this morning."

"What are you talking about?"

"I'm going with you. You'll need a healer."

"Who will take care of the Hollowers?"

"Morrell is quite capable, and I've been working with Sara since her husband was killed. Trust me, the Hollow will be fine. You'll need me more."

"I expect we will." He didn't want to argue. They likely would need a healer by the time they were done.

He checked on Bryce again, worked with the fighters for a couple of hours—he hadn't practiced much since they entered Erenthrall—then checked in again with Paul and Sophia. The wagons were ready. While he was sitting with Morrell and the Wolf—Drayden, he reminded himself—Cutter appeared with a report from the scouts. Another group of raiders had appeared, merging with those already camped out near the remains of the Hollow. That brought their number up to nearly three hundred.

"He must have had a secondary base camp somewhere east of here for the group to have arrived so quickly. Probably the camp they made when they were searching for the Hollow. He called in those reserves." Allan frowned down at the ground for a long moment, thinking, then looked back up at Cutter. "Warn Quinn. He should send someone out to make certain there aren't any others in the area. I don't want to leave here with Aurek only to have a secondary group of raiders from Haven attack once we're gone. I'll warn Paul and the others."

Cutter nodded and disappeared as everyone who'd been training outside flooded the cavern, sweaty and tired but in high spirits, joking with each other and clapping each other on the back as they filed down to the two rooms below. Glenn waved and Bryce nodded in acknowledgment as they passed.

When they'd cleared out, Allan turned to Morrell. "There will be a feast tonight, according to Sophia, since we're leaving tomorrow morning. Should we head down?"

She glanced toward Drayden, the man now clothed in donated garments, but with a blanket still clutched around his shoulders where he sat. He hadn't said much, listening to Allan and Morrell talk. Mostly Allan, recounting what had happened in Erenthrall again, since Morrell had fallen asleep the first time. She'd broken in with questions occasionally. At one point, she gave a halting account of the first attack by the raiders on the Hollow, waiting with the others, everyone huddled in their cottages, most of their guard up on the ridges in the rain. She'd been with Logan in his cottage, in case there were casualties.

Now, she asked Drayden, "Will you join us?"

The man pulled the blanket tighter about his shoulders. "I suppose I need to rejoin humanity at some point. It may as well be now."

But he halted at the entrance to the node's cave, nostrils flared. His lips peeled back from his teeth when Morrell returned and urged him over the threshold. "Too many people. Too many scents." But he let her hold his arm and accompany him down the rough-hewn stairs. Allan followed behind. People backed off to let them through, keeping an eye on Drayden.

As soon as they reached their tent, Janis trotted off to get them something to eat. She returned with Cory and Hernande, each of them bearing an extra plate of chunked and shredded venison that had been caught that morning and had been roasting all day. Bread sopped up the juices, and someone had baked potatoes and corn in the coals of the fire, their skins and husks charred. Janis produced a small crock of soured cream and another of butter.

Everyone dug in except Drayden, whose nose wrinkled at the potatoes and corn. He attacked the meat instead, but after the first bite he nearly spat it out, chewing slowly, swallowing with effort. "I'm not used to cooked meat."

They all shared a look, then Cory rooted through his portion, leaning over to shove part of it onto Drayden's plate. "It's the rawest meat I've got."

The rest of them followed suit, exchanging most of what Drayden had for their bloodiest pieces. He didn't thank them, but he did retreat to a corner of their fire and devoured what he could, body shielding his food, as if protecting it.

Morrell dove into her own food. She sat close to Allan, between him and Janis.

"How are the preparations going?" Hernande asked.

"Paul and Gaven report that everything is ready in terms of the wagons. I don't know what Aurek will be bringing, but keeping his own people fed is his problem. What about the Wielders and your own mages?"

"I hate that name, but it appears to have taken root. The Wielders and mages who are accompanying you are prepared. I'm reluctant to leave Sovaan behind as the head of the remaining students, but see no other choice. Jerrain insists on coming, although he'll likely have to ride in one of the wagons with its driver, and the others are too young to risk."

"Then I believe everyone is ready."

The group sat and listened to the raucous noise of the cavern, people laughing, at least two fiddles playing, a flute and drums twining through it all. The stomp of feet and whoops and hollers indicated someone was dancing. The energy was frenetic and tense, threaded through with worry and dread. Allan didn't doubt every nook and cranny where someone could meet in private within the cavern was being used at the moment. He recalled the tokens being packed earlier.

Morrell inched closer, leaning into him when he shifted and wrapped his arm around her shoulders. She grabbed onto his waist and nestled in tight.

A moment later, Hernande launched into a fable from the Demesnes, obviously attempting to lighten the suddenly somber mood. When he was done, Janis picked it up with a tale from her childhood. A line of dancers wove through their midst, led by one of the fiddlers. The flautist brought up the rear. She tried to get Cory to join them, but he simply shook his head.

Cory and Hernande excused themselves a few hours later, retreating to their own tent. Janis rose and busied herself inside theirs, after taking care of the cups and plates. Drayden had fallen asleep just outside their door, curled up like a dog.

Morrell started when Allan shifted, then drew back and wiped at her eyes. "Where did everyone go?"

"To bed. We have an early start tomorrow."

Morrell stood and ducked into the tent without a word.

They prepared for sleep in silence, Janis rolling over in her pallet to make certain neither one of them needed anything. Morrell threw herself onto her bed and turned her back to Allan. He and Janis shared a look. Allan fell onto his bedroll with a thump, exhaustion settling over his bones. He lay on his back, placed an arm over his eyes.

Morrell's blankets rustled. "I know you have to, for Kara's sake, but I don't want you to go. I want you here, with me."

"I know you do, poppet. But someone needs to help Kara, Dylan, and the others."

Morrell remained silent. Then: "I want you to help Kara, too. And don't call me poppet."

Allan tried to sleep, but the darkness would not take him. Hours later, after both Janis and Morrell's breathing had settled and the cavern's celebrations had fallen mostly silent, he rose and stepped out of the tent, back cracking as he stretched.

Drayden stirred and peered up at him with one eye over a crooked arm. "Don't worry, I will protect her while you're gone." Then his eye closed.

Allan was not entirely reassured.

An hour after dawn the next morning, Allan stood with Bryce, Gaven, Logan, Hernande, and Artras outside the cave entrance. Paul, Sophia, Raven, Sovaan, and Morrell faced them.

"Let Korma guide you." Paul shook hands with Allan. "Or whatever gods you pray to. Bring them back safe."

"As many as I can."

The elder stepped back. Gaven shouted to the wagon drivers, and all four of them hied their horses into motion.

The rest of the group fell into place around them as they headed toward the Hollow and their meet-up with Aurek.

Morrell suddenly dashed forward and hugged Allan tight. He crushed her to him, breathed in the fresh lavender scent of her hair, then released her.

"Bring her back, Da."

"I will." A motion near the caves caught his attention and he picked Drayden out of the shadows, the Wolf skulking near one entrance, watching.

He turned to Bryce. "Let's go meet Aurek."

When they pulled into the burned-out Hollow, it was empty, even the bodies that had littered the ground gone. They'd been hauled off and buried or burned. They gathered near the meeting hall, the wagons behind them. Cutter appeared briefly and waved the all clear; this wasn't an ambush. They waited, long enough for the fighters to start getting restless, before Aurek suddenly appeared.

He came out first, alone, striding forward confidently. His men emerged a breath later, filtering through the trees and the cottages behind him in a wide arc, twenty bodies across. Allan's own men shifted restlessly as Aurek's forces grew, first three deep, then five, finally dying out nine or ten deep. All of them were in ragged armor and carried weapons along with their own kits. Most of them looked hardened and grizzled, eyeing those from the Hollow with scowls of contempt. A few snickered or grinned.

Aurek stepped forward, one of his men a step behind him. Allan motioned to Bryce and the two moved to meet them halfway.

"Aurek."

"Allan. Allan Garrett, I believe. Formerly of the Dogs of Erenthrall."

Allan didn't remember informing Aurek of his full name. But then his gaze swept Aurek's men. He couldn't pick out anyone he recognized, not immediately, but it was possible some had known him from before, when he was a Dog.

He tried to relax. He didn't want Aurek to get beneath his skin, not this early. "I see you've brought more men."

"A few, from our original base camp. The others are tearing that camp down and will join us as soon as I tell them where we're going."

"South."

"That's not very specific."

"That's all you're going to get."

"Very well. South it is." He raised a hand and one of his men—leaner than the others, carrying a bow—took off into the trees, heading to the remains of their base camp, Allan presumed.

He focused on Aurek again. "It's probably best to keep our two groups separate. We wouldn't want any accidents or deaths brought on by misunderstandings."

"No. We wouldn't want that." Aurek looked their group over. Allan knew he was trying to pick out the Wielders and mages, but Allan had ordered them to blend in with the others. They were the Hollowers' only advantage, since Aurek's forces outnumbered them. Fear might keep his raiders in check; they'd already experienced what the Wielders and mages could do once before.

Aurek returned his attention to Allan. "Since you know where we're going, you can take the lead."

Bryce placed his fingers in his mouth and whistled, the sound sharp. Gaven shouted orders, and the wagons began to move, turning southward. Allan and Bryce melded into the group, walking alongside them, catching Cuttor's eye. The tracker nodded and broke away, vanishing into the woods. He'd keep an eye on Aurek and his men. Another scout was already checking the route ahead, searching for a potential ambush.

"He'll stab us all in the back the moment he sees it's to his advantage."

"I know. It's a long road ahead of us. But we have the Wielders and the mages. They'll be wary. And we know where they want to go."

"Knowing our destination is only an advantage for so long."

"By the time we near the Needle, I'm hoping Aurek's attention will have shifted from us to them."

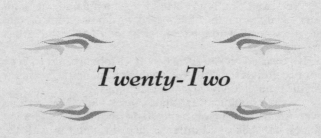

# Twenty-Two

THE QUAKE RUMBLED THROUGH THE NEEDLE, shaking the stone floor beneath Kara's feet. She caught herself against the wall, then snatched up the pitcher of water with a curse before it could fall to the floor and shatter. She'd seen the White Cloaks entering the black tower an hour earlier and had braced herself for the tremors that she'd realized would follow. This one wasn't as bad as that first one days before. That one had thrown her to the floor hard enough that her shoulder still ached, although the bruising had faded. There'd been a moment when she thought the entire temple was going to collapse around her. Based on the screams she'd heard from the corridor outside, some of the others had thought the same. She was fairly certain something had collapsed in the outer city; she'd seen the plume of dust from her window.

The tremors died and she pushed away from the wall, replacing the pitcher. Someone ran past her door and she crossed the room, pressing up against it to listen. An urgent conversation, then more running as orders were given. She couldn't identify the speakers, but the voices were hard, the tread of the feet heavy. Enforcers.

She stepped back, arms crossed over her chest.

She'd been kept in the room for four days. No one had visited except a middle-aged woman from the Demesnes who brought her food and refreshed her water. She never spoke, not in response to Kara's increasingly tense questions about Marcus or the White Cloaks, nor when she asked what had happened to Dylan, Adder, and Aaron. Expression stern, her darker-colored skin dotted with paint around her forehead and eyes, she merely deposited the trays of food and the new pitcher on the table, then turned and left, her multicolored wrapped dress swishing around her ankles, the enforcer stationed outside Kara's door stepping aside to let her pass.

Kara had considered the open window that looked down on the node, but it was too far to jump and she had nothing she could use to form a rope. The blankets covering her cot weren't enough.

Kara stalked to the window and looked down on the stellae of the node, watching the entrance to the black tower. A short time later, another quake rumbled through the temple, less intense, merely an aftershock.

"What are you doing down there?"

The knock at her door surprised her. The woman who brought the food never knocked.

"What do you want?"

"It's me. Marcus." The latch clicked and the door swung open. Marcus stood in the hall outside, an escort of at least three enforcers surrounding him. He carried a bundle of white cloth in his arms, the enforcers entering behind him, although only he crossed to Kara. "I brought you some clean clothes."

"I want to see Dylan, Adder, and Aaron."

Marcus set the clothes on Kara's cot. "They're fine."

"I want to see for myself."

"If I take you to see them, will you cooperate?"

Kara hesitated. But she needed to see the others, and the confines of the room were beginning to grate on her. Her shoulders itched, and she'd spent most of yesterday pacing relentlessly across the small chamber. "It depends on what you ask me to do."

"I don't intend for you to do anything, just look and listen." He motioned toward the clothes.

Kara moved and picked up the shirt, body going rigid. "These are White Cloak clothes. I won't wear them. I'm not a White Cloak."

"You'd rather keep your own shirt and breeches? They're beginning to stink."

"That's because I haven't been given the opportunity to wash them. Or myself."

"I'll have Marta take care of them. And bring you a wash basin with warm water."

Kara searched his face, but all she saw was edged impatience. "Stand outside."

He shook his head and motioned everyone out.

As soon as the door closed, Kara undressed, tossed her old clothes to one side, and threw on the shirt and breeches Marcus had provided. The fabric was surprisingly soft. The shirt was similar to what she'd seen Iscivius and the others wearing, but there was no cloak or Kormanley symbol, and the breeches were more like those worn by the enforcers. He'd even brought her new shoes. The freshness of the clothes made her skin feel rough and gritty. She definitely needed a bath.

Dressed again, she knocked on the door, which opened immediately.

Marcus looked her up and down in approval. "This way."

He must have arranged the detour to the rooms where they were keeping Dylan, Adder, and Aaron while she changed, for the guards at each of the two rooms were ready for them. Dylan was lying on his cot in a room similar to Kara's, but without a window; it was on the opposite side of the corridor. His knee had been splinted.

He caught her hand as she knelt by his side, his grip strong. "Thank Bastion you're all right. They haven't told me anything."

"Me either. This is the first I've been let out of my room." She looked him over, checking the splint. "How have they been treating you?"

"Well. They started working on the knee almost immediately. The healer comes twice a day. The food has been good." He tweaked the cuff of her shirt and raised an eyebrow in silent question.

"I had to agree to wear it in order to see you."

Marcus cleared his throat.

Kara gripped Dylan's hand again, held it tight, leaning in close. "I'll get us out of here."

Marcus stepped into the room. "You've seen him. Let's move."

Adder and Aarón were being kept in one room half the size of Kara's, containing only two cots and not kept as clean. It was in a section on the lowest tier of the temple, reached by a set of narrow stairs. A cracked pitcher of water rested on the floor and a dim ley globe flickered erratically in one corner.

Kara glared at Marcus as she reached up to steady the ley globe, strengthening it as well. Adder and Aaron shifted into seated positions on the edge of their cots. Adder sported a black eye and a fresh bruise along his jaw.

"What happened to you?"

Adder caught her arm before she could touch him. "A little roughing up by the enforcers. Are you one of them now?" His gaze flicked to her shirt.

"Of course not. He's forcing me to wear it. I don't know what they want from me. I've been kept in a room until today."

Adder released her. "What are they doing? Why are there so many quakes?"

"It has something to do with the node. Other than that, I don't know. Are they feeding you?"

Aaron answered. "Some. Mostly bread and cheese. Some meat."

"The only reason we're still alive is because of you. They don't trust us, but they need you enough that they can't risk killing us. You need to find out what they want. It's the only chance we've got."

Outside, a White Cloak appeared and muttered something to Marcus, whose mouth tightened into a thin line. "Enough. Time to go."

"Go where?" Adder asked her.

"I don't know."

"Be careful."

Kara retreated to the door, halting before Marcus while the enforcers closed and locked it. "Where to now, Marcus?"

"The node. I want you to see what we've been doing here."

He led her away, refusing to answer any of her questions. After a while, she fell silent, trying to take in as much of the temple as she could. But the strange corridors branched too often, and she hadn't paid enough attention when they'd descended to the lower level.

It was a shock when the lead enforcers opened up a set of double doors and brilliant sunlight spilled into the hallway. She raised one hand to shield her eyes, blinking back tears.

Then, following Marcus, she stepped out onto the stone of the node.

As soon as her feet hit the tan rock that formed the circular design centered on the black tower, power surged up through her feet. She gasped and recognized the temple for what it truly was—a pit, like the nodes in Erenthrall, but on a larger scale. The entire temple had been built to contain the node's power, the Needle itself a focal point. The ley coursed beneath the structure all around her and she reached for it without thinking, submerging herself in it as she'd done before in Erenthrall. But unlike the ley network in the city before the Shattering, this ley was chaotic—confined but wild. She allowed herself to flow through it, down its channels, noting the lines that stretched off toward the northeast, instinctively knowing that they connected with what remained of Erenthrall's ley structure. Another powerful line shot to the east, toward what she first assumed was Tumbor. But then she remembered that it couldn't be Tumbor, not with the recently quickened distortion; it was anchored too solidly. It must be reaching for Farrade. Another angled northward, which made no sense—there were no nodes in that direction, all of the cities in the Steppe were farther east—and two other weaker lines were directed to the west.

"I knew you'd connect to the ley as soon as we entered the node. You always understood it on a more instinctual level than anyone else."

His words were muted, as if coming from a distance, and Kara forced herself to focus, to draw herself up out of the feral ley trapped around her.

She centered herself and realized she hadn't moved from her first few steps onto the node. The enforcers had surrounded her, but they looked uncertain. Marcus stood a few paces away, watching her closely.

"What have you done?"

"As I told you before, we've tried to stabilize the network by building another Nexus. None of the strongest Primes survived the Shattering—at least, none that we've found—so we've done the best that we can with what we have."

He turned, heading toward the entrance to the Needle, crossing through the stellae that Kara could feel vibrating with the forces coursing through them. Kara hesitated, but even if she hadn't agreed to cooperate, she needed to see what Marcus and the rest of the Wielders here had done.

"After the Shattering—"

"How did you survive? I saw you change the Nexus from the node in Eld. You were there before the Nexus exploded."

"I was in the pit. If I'd been there when the pulse from the explosion spread throughout the network, I'd be dead, burned to nothing, like those closest to Grass when it happened. But when the pulse hit Eld, I'd climbed from the pit and slammed the doors behind me. The nodes in Erenthrall were built to withstand surges. That's why they have few, if any, windows, why the pits are protected by steel doors."

"So you had enough time to flee after you triggered the Shattering."

"It was Leethe!" They'd reached the entrance to the Needle and his voice echoed off of the surrounding walls of the tower. He spun toward her, grabbed her by the upper arms. He would have shaken her, but he controlled himself. "It was Baron Leethe. I told you before, the pulse that destroyed the Nexus in Erenthrall came from Tumbor. I felt it before it hit."

"But you were helping him, through the Kormanley. You were a part of it."

"I didn't know. I thought—"

But he didn't finish, releasing his grip and turning his back to her.

She massaged her bruised muscles. Her hatred of Marcus since the Shattering had become ingrained. Now, looking into his eyes, seeing the pain he harbored, she realized she believed him. He hadn't caused the Shattering, not intentionally. And he firmly believed that the pulse had come from Tumbor.

"So after the Shattering, after you survived, what did you do?"

Marcus didn't answer at first, simply stood, staring into the depths of the Needle. But then: "I fled the city, like many. I escaped before the quickening. I survived." He faced her. "Eventually I heard that the Kormanley had survived, that they had taken over the node here. Dalton was surprised to see me. He already had a few Wielders, mostly survivors from Tumbor. After a while, we realized that the ley wasn't correcting itself. It was trying to return to its natural order, but it couldn't, not with the nodes in Erenthrall blocked by the distortion. We needed to heal the distortion in Erenthrall. By then we'd found maybe twenty Wielders. We went to the city, but it wasn't enough. None of us were Primes, and the ley was too chaotic. And the city wasn't safe. Violent factions were forming—the Rats, the Gorrani to the south. We did what we could."

"The healed shards we found. That was you."

"We thought we could heal it a shard at a time. But the distortion is too large. It would take decades to accomplish, and we risked triggering the distortion's closure and losing everything inside."

"We came to the same conclusion."

"When we returned to the Needle, Dalton had found a Prime, Lecrucius. He suggested we create our own Nexus to try to stabilize the ley, here at the Needle. If we can't free up the nodes in Erenthrall, we need to bypass them. We've been working on that for the past three months, both here and in Erenthrall. We had a relatively stable system, until the distortion in Tumbor quickened. Now we need to bypass Tumbor, and I'm not certain we can do that. Not without more help."

Kara didn't want to trust him. But she'd seen what had been done in Erenthrall already—the healed shards, the shunted ley lines. All of it fit. And she was forced to admit that what he said made sense. He'd come to the same conclusions she had about repairing Erenthrall, only quicker, and had come up with an alternative.

But creating a new Nexus . . .

"The quakes—" she began.

"I know. Every time we shift a ley line, there's an aftershock. And they're growing worse. But the ley lines are shifting on their own, even without us tampering with them."

"There has to be another way. Even if we stabilize everything using the Needle as a new Nexus, what happens when the distortion over Farrade quickens? Or Ikanth? Each one will disrupt what you've done here. Each one will cause damage. One of them could set off another pulse, another Shattering."

"I know that! But what else are we supposed to do? Sit around and wait for the ley to destroy us on its own? I can't do that! I have to do something. But I can't do it alone. Even with Lecrucius and the Wielders we've gathered here, it isn't enough. We need help."

And Kara suddenly realized that beneath his anger and frustration lay guilt. For what he'd done in Frenthrall before the Shattering, for whatever part he'd played in the destruction of the Nexus. He wanted to atone for that mistake, had attempted to heal the distortion in Erenthrall shard by shard as penance, and now worked on the Needle for redemption.

She thought about all that Marcus had said, all that they'd seen in Erenthrall, all that had happened before.

Then, with resignation, she said, "Show me what you've done."

Marcus led her down into the Needle. The interior was as black as its exterior, but the walls were threaded with veins of ley light. No ley globes were necessary inside, all of the passages lit by the walls themselves. Kara ran her hands across the surface, fingers tingling with energy, but it was smooth as glass and cold to the touch.

The stairs spiraled down the outside of the tower, like at the node in Eld. As they descended, passing beneath the floor of the first level, it opened up into a large pit, the obsidian of the tower giving way to more ancient sandstone, what Kara assumed had been used when this node was nothing more than a sacred religious marker. The room was deeper than the nodes she'd worked in Erenthrall, lit from below by prisms of scintillant light and from above by the glow of the ley-veined ceiling of the black tower. Kara had never seen light like what lay in the pit below. She reached out toward it, sinking herself in the flows as they drew closer. Ley fountained up from below, and as she reached down with her senses she realized that, like the pit beneath the Nexus in Erenthrall, it descended far deeper than it appeared. Tunnels branched off of it in erratic directions—ley lines that had once connected to nodes in the major cities of the plains and those to the south and west. Some of those lines were still active, mostly to the south and west, toward the Gorrani Flats, the Demesnes, and the Archipelago. The largest of the tunnels were both dead. Kara felt their presence through the ley, since they were too deep to be seen. But new ley lines had been formed, the ley passing through the rock walls near where the old holes stood empty. Kara assumed they had held the original lines connecting to Erenthrall and Tumbor, and the new lines, slightly off-kilter, were those that Marcus and the White Cloaks had established to bypass the nodes in those cities. Prime Wielder Augustus must have carved out the tunnels when he built the augmented ley system around the Nexus, since even though ley could pass through stone, rock inhibited it. Augustus would have wanted the ley to be as strong as possible.

The stairs ended, leveling out on a wide ledge that circled the pit, the White Cloaks Kara had seen entering the black tower earlier that day scattered around its rim. Kara immediately moved up to the edge, kneeling and placing her hands on the lip so that she could lean out and stare down at the interplay of ley below. It took her a moment to realize panes of crystal hovered in the center of the pit, at least six of them, positioned precisely to capture and refract the ley. Their orientations augmented the power of the ley, while at the same time anchoring it more solidly here at the Needle. Most of the ley coursed through the node below the crystals, but from that pool, the ley arched up in thick tendrils, drawn up by the crystals.

"Is this what the Nexus looked like, before the Shattering?"

"No, the Nexus in Erenthrall was ten times this size. There were dozens of crystals, positioned to produce a hundred times this much power. And the building there had been built for that purpose. This node is ancient, altered by Prime Wielder Augustus to act as a junction, nothing more. Of the Wielders here, only Lecrucius had ever seen the crystals. And he and I were the only ones who'd ever worked with them. He and Iscivius figured out how to reproduce them. But because the ley isn't stable, we have to constantly align them ourselves."

Kara glanced up at the other White Cloaks, reaching out as she did so. She could feel them on the ley, watching, waiting, occasionally reaching out and adjusting one of the crystals into a slightly new position. "This is how you're creating the new ley lines."

"Adjusting the crystals strengthens certain lines while weakening others. It augments power in particular directions. Even with only six panes, it's immensely complicated. And we're learning this from scratch, with only what Lecrucius had learned as a Prime to guide us. The Nexus in Erenthrall was . . . I never saw it, only felt it through the ley, but it was beautiful. Almost alive. I don't know how Augustus and the other Primes managed to contain it, to control it."

"And yet you still meddled with it." The words were harsh, but she understood what Marcus was saying. Even here, with only six crystals, she was enthralled.

"Yes. Baron Arent needed to be stopped. He was a tyrant. What happened during the Purge proved that. To me at least."

Kara stood, dragging her gaze away from the mesmerizing ley below to face Marcus. "You seem to have done quite a bit here on your own. Why do you need me?"

Marcus didn't answer at first, shifting to stand beside her but staring down into the pit. "We weren't looking for you specifically. We were searching for more Wielders, to help control the ley lines. We've reached the extent of what we can do with those we have here already. We were hoping to find a few more Primes. But we found you instead." He turned toward her. "You were on the path to become a Prime. Everyone said so, even Ischua. In another few years, you would have been taken off the node work and trained to be a Master. And I wasn't lying earlier when I said that you have an affinity for the ley. You were the one that realized we could heal the distortions. No one before you had tried; no one had even considered it. The moment I saw you, I knew you'd been sent to help us. You can stabilize the Nexus here, and then the ley."

"I've never worked with these crystals."

"We'll teach you what we know. And I think your instincts will take over from there."

Kara couldn't argue about her instincts. Practically everything she'd done involving the ley had been instinct—healing that first distortion that had enclosed the seamstress' hand, raising the flying barge using the ley-saturated sails during the blackout, even attempting to heal the distortion over Erenthrall before it quickened.

Someone cleared their throat loudly from the direction of the stairs and they turned to find Dierdre waiting.

"Marcus, Dalton wants you. There's a situation."

Marcus motioned toward the enforcers. "Take her back to her room."

The enforcers closed in on her as he strode to the steps, then began to ascend with Dierdre at his side.

She cast one last glance back down into the pit, yearning to reach out and touch the crystals, to manipulate the ley. But she pulled the urge back under control. She wasn't certain she trusted Marcus yet, wasn't certain she believed his story.

She needed time to think.

"What's happened?" Marcus asked Dierdre as he reached the stairs. "Is it Iscivius? Lecrucius?"

"No, nothing to do with the White Cloaks."

"Then what? I was making headway with Kara. She was considering helping us, I could tell. Interrupting that right now might set us back by days, if not longer."

"She didn't help us before the Shattering. What makes you think she'll support us now?"

"Because circumstances have changed."

They'd reached the top of the steps, had emerged into the first floor of the obsidian tower. Dierdre halted, arms crossed protectively in front of her. "Do I need to be worried about you and *Kara*?"

"Of course not." He stepped close to her, placing his

hands on her shoulders. They were almost nose-to-nose, Dierdre's arms a barrier between them. "Kara and I ended our relationship years ago. You know that. You were there."

"She left you because of your association with me, with the Kormanley."

"Yes. And I could have abandoned the Kormanley for her. But I didn't. I chose you."

Dierdre wouldn't look at him, staring over his shoulder, but he could feel the rigidity in her shoulders loosening.

He leaned in to kiss her and she relaxed completely, her arms dropping and drawing him in closer.

He could hear the enforcers on the stairs with Kara. He broke off the kiss; he didn't want Kara to see them. With a faint nudge, he directed Dierdre toward the door out into the node's outer garden, the sunlight bright. "Now, what's the problem if it's not the other White Cloaks?"

Dierdre hesitated, as if realizing he was attempting to distract her. "It's the Gorrani who were camped out south of Tumbor."

"What about them?"

"Darius reports that they've broken camp and are on the move."

They were inside the temple now, climbing up to the second level, heading toward the orrery, Dalton's meeting room. "What does that have to do with us?"

Dierdre paused outside the door to the orrery and met his gaze. "Because they're coming here."

She yanked the door open and stepped inside. He followed her a moment later.

Inside, Father, Ty, Darius, Lecrucius, and Iscivius were already gathered, an escort of enforcers on guard a discreet distance from the large table. Ty and Darius were arguing, Lecrucius standing a pace away, attentive but not participating. Lecrucius had been worming his way closer and closer to Dalton. He'd been shocked to find him at the meeting when he'd returned with Kara and the others. Then to see him here now, already part of the council even before Marcus had arrived ...

*He* was the Son, the leader of the White Cloaks, not Lecrucius.

"—approaching from the southeast," Ty was saying to

Iscivius as they entered. "They're marching straight for the Needle. I don't think there's any doubt they intend to attack us."

"What brought this on?"

Ty didn't answer at first, eyes still roaming the makeshift map they'd created on the table. Large stones marked the major nodes in the immediate area—black for the Needle, near the center, sandstone for Tumbor, Erenthrall, and Farrade. Smaller chunks of quartz were used to approximate the nodes in the Demesnes and the Gorrani Flats that they knew of, while various pebbles indicated nodes that weren't associated to specific cities.

Mixed in with the stones were wooden blocks, representing different groups that had established themselves since the Shattering. Six blocks were scattered around Erenthrall, three to the north, two south, and one to the east. Farther north, another block marked Haven and the self-declared Baron who'd started his own Barony there, although they'd had little contact with his group, mostly violent encounters on the plains around Erenthrall.

There were more around Tumbor, the largest a grainy block to the southwest of the city that represented the Gorrani enclave that had established itself outside of the city's limits, between Tumbor and the southern land routes to the Gorrani Flats. But as Marcus and Dierdre approached the edge of the table, Marcus noted that the block had been moved.

"I'd say the distortion that's swallowed Tumbor forced them to move. They were looting the city for food and resources, like every other group that established itself in or around Tumbor. Many of those groups were caught in the distortion when it quickened, but the Gorrani enclave was much farther out, set up along the Ganges river. The distortion has cut the river off and it hasn't established a new bed yet. There's massive flooding all around Tumbor. Their water source may have dried up."

"Their food source definitely has."

"They were relying on Tumbor, shipping some of their food south to their homeland. They need a new supply."

"But why here? Why not raid the other groups that survived the quickening?"

"They already have. According to our patrols, they've

attacked most of the groups that were outside the distortion once it settled. Most of those groups were small and weak, the larger ones trapped inside. Only two were left alone, mostly because they're too well established in easily defensible areas. The Gorrani aren't going to bother if there isn't going to be a large payoff. They know we have plenty of food here. We looted Tumbor as much as they did. And they know we have Wielders. For all we know, they may think the quickening was done on purpose."

"So what do we do?"

Ty and Darius shared a glance. They may have been arguing when Marcus and Dierdre arrived, but they were in agreement as Ty said, "We prepare the Needle for an attack."

"Can our enforcers deal with them? How many of them are there?"

"We have approximately a thousand people within the walls of the Needle, three hundred of them enforcers. According to the reports, there are five thousand Gorrani marching toward us now."

No one spoke for a long moment, the shock settling like a grim mantle across Marcus' shoulders.

"We have the walls." Dierdre looked toward her brother for reassurance.

"Yes. And we have enough food within the walls to last us for months, if necessary. We can withstand a siege."

"But not forever."

"No, not forever."

Father suddenly stood and walked toward the far wall, staring out at the side of the Needle.

"I had a vision two nights ago. I said nothing about it, because I did not understand it. In this vision, a brown snake came out of the desert, slithering across the sands. Its tongue tasted the air as it moved. Occasionally, it would pause. It was marked with gold around its eyes, its throat yellow and white. It came upon a black stone buried in the sand, and upon seeing it, it curled around the stone, encircling it completely."

Father paused, those at the table exchanging a few glances. Dierdre and Darius were caught up in Father's vision. Lecrucius was openly skeptical. Iscivius took his lead from the Prime.

Dierdre stepped forward. "What happened?"

Father faced them. "The snake burst into flame. White flame. And the vision ended."

"White flame?"

"Yes. The vision is clear now. The snake is the Gorrani enclave, and it is the ley that will protect us."

Ty shoved back from the table. "The enforcers will protect us. We can hold them off for as long as necessary. We don't need the White Cloaks."

Darius also looked skeptical. "Can the ley even be used offensively?"

Everyone turned to Marcus. "It has never been used that way before."

Lecrucius stepped up to the table and rapped it with his knuckles to catch everyone's attention. "It can be used offensively, yes. It was something known only to the Primes, a guarded secret. It wasn't something we wanted common Wielders to be aware of."

"That was before the Shattering."

"Yes, it was."

"Why didn't you mention this earlier?" But Marcus already knew.

"It didn't cross my mind that no one else here knew. And the enforcers have been enough to keep us safe. But now that it's necessary, I suppose I can start training the White Cloaks in offensive and defensive techniques."

Marcus drew breath to protest, but Father had already straightened. "Do it."

Lecrucius nodded, then motioned to Iscivius, the two White Cloaks striding from the room, heads already bent in discussion. Marcus had known Iscivius favored Lecrucius—he'd latched onto the Prime as soon as he'd arrived at the Needle from Tumbor—but he hadn't realized how insidious Lecrucius' hold had become. How many other White Cloaks had already been drawn to the Prime's side? How many did he control outright?

"Marcus?"

Dierdre touched his arm and Marcus started. "What?"

Dierdre pointed toward Father, who had returned to the table and stood glaring at him.

"I said, you took that Wielder to the Needle today. Are you going to be able to force her to help us?"

Marcus steadied himself by gripping the back of one of the chairs. "I believe so. She isn't convinced yet—there's too much history between us—but I know her. She wants to stabilize the ley as much as we do."

"Then you may continue working with her. If she backs down and refuses to aid us, kill her." He turned to Ty. "Kill them all."

Ty straightened in acknowledgment. "What do you want us to do about the Gorrani?"

"Call all but our usual patrols. Bring in whatever resources we have from outside the walls. Then close the gates." He motioned Dierdre forward. "Prepare the plaza for a sermon. I'll need to prepare the people for the coming siege. Now that I understand the latest vision, I can assure them of our victory over the Gorrani snakes." He placed an arm around Dierdre's shoulder and steered her toward the outer door. "I'll want to do it toward evening, as the sun sets. And there should be drums."

Marcus hated the sermons—disliked all of the religious aspects of the Kormanley, though he'd found some of them useful, such as the blessings from the Son that everyone expected—but the gatherings in the plaza were grueling.

He tried not to attend them, but after what he'd seen from Lecrucius today, he'd have to be there, to make his presence felt, to remind the White Cloaks who the Father's Son truly was.

Ty and Darius were already bent over the table, moving blocks. One of the guards had been summoned forward and was sent with orders to the wall. Marcus watched impassively for a moment, then spun on his heel and left.

Two days later, Marcus stood at the edge of the roof of the first tier of the temple as the sun set bloody red on the horizon. A stiff breeze from the east snapped the pennants and sent the flames from the bonfires in the giant urns roaring, sparked embers gusting up into the sky. Marcus' white cloak tugged about his neck, choking him, but he stood silent as Father—standing at the end of a stone outcropping above the sea of avid faces below—bellowed about the white fire consuming the snake. "Korma will protect you! The White Cloaks will protect you!"

The crowd below chanted, "Fa-ther! Fa-ther! Fa-ther!" to the thud of a dozen drums. More bonfires blazed in the plaza below, closed in on either side by the buildings of the outer city. From what Marcus could see, nearly everyone who resided at the Needle was in attendance, except for the enforcers on the walls and at the gates. Father had made certain there were enforcers and White Cloaks mixed in with the people below as well; he could pick out their cloaks and uniforms easily.

Who had given that order?

"We certainly will protect them, won't we?"

Marcus tried not to flinch as Lecrucius stepped up on one side of him. Iscivius boxed him in on the other side. "Where have you been?"

"Organizing a little demonstration."

Marcus leaned forward, to better see the area Lecrucius and Iscivius were concentrating on. A section of the plaza had been cordoned off by the enforcers, a black stone spike jutting up out of the flagstone at its center. As he watched, Father's sermon coming to a close, three men raced out of a nearby temple door carrying a snake made of paper and wooden struts, almost like a kite. They made it slither toward the crowd, which backed away in horror before surging back as the men danced away. Then they circled the spike—obviously a representation of the Needle—and laid the snake down before vanishing back into the temple at a sprint.

A moment later, Marcus felt a surge on the ley from Lecrucius and, from the stone beneath the snake, white light bubbled upward. It fountained around the spike, completely obscuring the paper snake, and when it receded, the snake was gone, completely obliterated.

Those gathered went wild, the roar of approval bouncing off of the buildings. Father raised both arms to the heavens and the thunderous noise grew even louder.

Lecrucius stepped back from the edge of the roof. "Now all we need to do is make his prophecy come true."

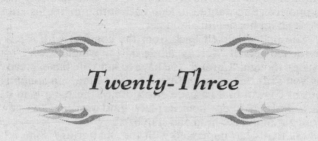

# Twenty-Three

"**N**OW HOLD THAT ONE STEADY and rotate the other crystal slightly to the left."

Kara barely heard Marcus' instruction, her eyes closed, her concentration on the panes of crystal floating in the depths of the Needle's pit below her. Sweat beaded her forehead with the effort. She could feel the flows of the ley around her, feel it surge and eddy. The pane she held steady vibrated slightly as she reached out to pull the edge of another pane closer to her. As it shifted, the currents in the ley reacted, new eddies forming. They struck the remaining four panes, tried to alter their orientations, but each one of them was being monitored by one of the White Cloaks that surrounded the pit near them. They held the panes in place while Kara worked. She could sense them on the ley, knew they were watching her more closely than even Marcus behind her, mostly with suspicion. All of them were ready to seize control of the crystals if Kara showed even the slightest hint that she intended to destroy them.

The situation was strangely and comfortably familiar: Marcus standing beside her, mentoring her as she learned something new about the ley, about her job as a Wielder. They had spent years like this, as partners, wearing the purple jackets in Erenthrall. That partnership had grown into something more, something deeper. Some of those old emotions rushed through her now, his presence soft and supportive. She wanted to lean back into him, let his arms close about her, let him hold her.

She pulled herself back from the comfort with a jerk, hardened herself. Marcus' subtle shift of weight wasn't lost on her, though. "Careful. You have to hold the panes steady as you shift one pane or they'll begin tilting and spinning out of control in a cascade effect. Once the pane is in its new position, keep them in place until you feel the new configuration take hold and stabilize."

"Is that what happened with the Shattering?" She felt the pane she was manipulating slip into place. But even as she held it, she felt a quiver of dissonance in the new setup. The alignment would hold once she let go of the panes, but it wasn't perfect.

She reached out, searching for what was wrong. It was like the stones Ischua had tested her with in Halliel's Park so many years before. She could feel what belonged, what didn't, and that the placement of the stones wasn't quite right, all through the energy seeping up from the ground through her feet.

"In a sense. From what we've been able to piece together here at the Needle, something catastrophic happened in Tumbor. It sent a surge through the system that hit the Nexus in Erenthrall hard enough that the delicate configuration of the crystals there was thrown off. I'm certain the Primes attempted to reestablish some kind of stability, but they were too slow. Or the surge was too powerful to overcome. The crystals shattered, and any chance that the concentrated power of the ley could be contained vanished."

Kara opened her eyes and faced him. "Boom."

"Boom."

She turned back to the crystals with a frown. "The new alignment isn't quite right."

"Show me."

His presence flooded the Nexus below them, flowing around her. She repressed a pleasant shudder. "There. The pane Irmona controls. Its bottom corner should be skewed a touch up and to the left."

"I don't sense anything wrong," Irmona said from her position twenty paces away.

"Can you correct it, without losing control of the Nexus?"

"Marcus! She's not one of us. She's not a White Cloak."

Marcus ignored the warning in Irmona's voice, kept his gaze steady on Kara. "Can you?"

She reached out toward Irmona's pane. Irmona resisted, refusing to release her hold on it, until Marcus said, "I am the Son."

She practically thrust the pane at Kara, retreating, but not far. Kara seized it before it could swing out of control, then steadied it back into position, but tilted the bottom just *so*.

The Nexus rippled with the new alignment, ley surging upward and curling around in thicker tendrils, the power increasing significantly. Everyone felt the backwash as it spread outward into the small city. High above, the veins of ley in the Needle pulsed brighter. No doubt all of the ley globes throughout the temple and streets below had done so as well.

In the pit, silence held, until: "There's a reason you weren't on track to become a Prime, Irmona."

She drew breath for some kind of scathing remark, but before she could voice it a rumble echoed through the chamber. Everyone tensed. "See! She's triggered another quake! On purpose!"

A wave of ley slammed into the Nexus from the direction of Erenthrall.

The entire pit heaved, tossing the White Cloaks and Kara to the stone. Okata cried out as his legs slipped over the edge. He clawed at the lip with both hands as ley fountained up from below. Kara scrambled to her knees. "It wasn't me! It came from Erenthrall!"

The building jolted again. Irmona crawled toward the stairs. The ley leaped higher, splashed across the ledge on the side opposite Kara, the White Cloak who'd been positioned there enveloped before he could raise his arms in protection. It burned him from existence.

Marcus snatched at Kara's arm and tugged her toward the steps, but she jerked away. "Okata!"

She stumbled to her feet, then staggered toward Okata. His torso had slipped down into the pit, so that he hung by his elbows, the edge tucked up under his armpits. His fingers dug into a crevice of the sandstone that made up the ledge, his knuckles white. Kara reached him as his right hand gave way. She snatched it and hauled backward. A moment later, Marcus appeared at her side, throwing himself flat on the stone and reaching out over the edge. He snagged a handful of Okata's white shirt. Together, they dragged him back onto the ledge.

All three scrambled toward the steps, where the rest of the White Cloaks were hunched over. No one had risked the stairs. Before they made it halfway, the earth heaved again. A raw, visceral crack resounded through the pit and debris rained down from above. Kara covered her head with her arms and flung herself to the stone floor as chunks of stone skittered around her. Dust filled the air, and she sucked in a lungful before covering her mouth with her shirt as she coughed.

But the quake was finished. The earth settled, the rumble dying out. Someone sobbed in the group of White Cloaks. Behind Kara, the geyser of ley began to subside.

"Irmona, Okata, Chekla, check the Nexus. Stabilize it if necessary. Everyone else, start checking the lines."

All of the Wielders broke from their huddle and made for the pit. Marcus turned to her. "Are you hurt?"

"Bruised, but not seriously."

"Can you help?"

"I don't know the layout of the ley lines you've established—"

"But you can follow them, see if they're stable or not."

He didn't wait for an answer, striding toward the pit. The others were already arranging themselves around the lip, even Okata. Kara could sense them reaching out and seizing the ley, reorienting the crystals, some of them stretching farther, traveling the ley lines out of the Needle toward their sources.

Kara climbed to her feet and brushed herself off, then paused. A huge crack ran up the stone wall of the pit, a gap maybe a hand wide, slicing through the stairs and jagging out onto the ledge they stood on, all the way to its lip. She couldn't see where it ended.

She turned her back on the fissure and headed toward the pit, her feet crunching in the grit that now coated the ledge.

Marcus gave her a sideways glance as she halted beside him but said nothing. She reached out, the ley in chaos, but Okata, Chekla, and Irmona appeared to have the crystals in hand. So she dove into the ley lines below, found the one leading toward Erenthrall, and followed it. As she traveled, she realized the line wasn't as strong as it had been before the quake.

Then she hit Erenthrall and she knew why.

"One of the lines in Erenthrall has been cut."

"How do you know?"

"I've been there recently. I know some of what you've altered there to set up the Nexus."

"It looks like the node in Dunlap has failed. It was feeding us a line from the northern Steppe—from Ikanth, Severen, and Dunmara."

"Was it cut on purpose?"

"I can't tell."

Kara followed him on the ley, stretching out from the network they'd set up around the distortion in Erenthrall to a node to the northwest. She realized with a wrench that the node he spoke of must be the one she and Artras had found in the small town just before they'd reached Erenthrall. There was a small line of ley leading toward it from the Needle, but then it dead-ended. No ley stretched off to the north.

Without a connection, they couldn't see what was happening to the north, whether natural or not.

Kara returned to the nodes around Erenthrall. The empty space of the distortion was like a gaping wound in her own body that she couldn't quite leave entirely alone. As she worked her way around the network, she kept probing it, unable to resist. She wanted to reach out and heal it, but it was too large. There hadn't been enough Wielders in the Hollow—

She halted, aware her body had stiffened back in the Needle.

"What is it?"

She swore silently. Marcus had noticed her sudden

tension. She shook it off, sought desperately for a diversion as Marcus' attention shifted toward her position.

"It's the network of nodes you have built up around Erenthrall." She cleared her throat, forced herself to talk slower. "It's not stable."

"None of the lines are stable anywhere."

"That's the problem. No matter what configuration you give the crystals in the Nexus, it won't be enough to hold the entire ley system in check. At some point, a line is going to shift, a node is going to give out. That's going to cause a ripple in the system, and that ripple is going to hit the Nexus here and throw those crystals out of alignment again."

"That's why we have White Cloaks here, constantly monitoring the system."

"How many White Cloaks do you have?"

"We had thirty-three. But we lost Sanderson today."

Thirty might be enough. Even if they weren't as strong as Marcus or even Dylan. And they had a Prime.

But could she trust Marcus? Or Lecrucius? They were Wielders. But was that enough?

There was too much history between her and Marcus, too much bad blood.

"Can you see a way to stabilize the nodes around Erenthrall?" Marcus asked.

"I don't know. It's too chaotic, the ley lines split. They're trying to compensate for the loss of the Nexus, but there aren't enough nodes." They needed the nodes locked inside the distortion. They needed to heal it so they could repair the damaged network. Or at least patch it. Erenthrall by itself wouldn't be enough anymore, not with Tumbor's distortion sealing away even more nodes, but it would be a start.

She pulled herself back toward the Needle, settling into her own body. "I'll have to study what you already have set up in Erenthrall to see what I can do to fix it, but we don't have much time. The quakes are getting stronger." She pointed to where the jagged crack ran up the side of the pit. "We need to find a solution before the Needle crumbles and falls down around us."

The first sign that something was wrong was when one of the horses in Aurek's group screamed and reared, legs kicking.

From his perch on the bench of the Hollowers' lead wagon with Artras, Allan glanced toward the Baron's group of men, keeping a discreet distance to the east after the first few days of travel near each other had erupted in three brawls and one near rape, broken up by Bryce and Aurek together. Allan and Aurek had agreed to keep the two forces separated by at least a hundred yards after that. Since then, the troubles had died down, although they still eyed each other warily across the distance.

Now, Allan stood, leg braced against the seat for balance, as the horse dropped down again to all fours, the shouts from the men nearby reaching them. "What's happening?" Artras asked.

Before Allan could answer, the wagon lurched. "What in hells?"

The horse pulling them began tossing its head and snorting. It jerked forward, as if trying to escape its harness, then halted abruptly, nearly tossing Allan over the front and onto its rump. Gaven cursed.

All four of their horses were acting odd, and more shouts came from Aurek's group. Far distant, a wolf began to howl, and on the plains ahead, a flock of at least forty geese took sudden flight, honking in anger. Three horses, saddled still, broke from Aurek's men, one of them with a man still caught in the stirrup. As they watched, the horse twisted and kicked him free. He lay where he'd fallen and didn't move.

At the front of their small caravan, Bryce suddenly spun and shouted, "Quake!"

A second later, Artras sucked in a sharp breath. "It's coming up the ley line."

Then it struck.

The earth heaved. The wagon Allan stood on bucked. The horse squealed, a hideous sound Allan had never thought to hear coming from any animal. If he hadn't been holding onto the front for support after the horse stopped so abruptly, he would have been thrown. Artras clung to the side, the entire contraption rattling in the tremors that followed. Men were bellowing, everyone crouched low to the ground. Aurek's men were doing the same.

After another, smaller heave, the trembling faded. Everyone began to pick themselves up, dusting each other off.

Artras righted herself. "That came from the Needle."

"Stronger than the few we've experienced in the past week."

"And the quakes are coming closer together."

Allan didn't know what to say. They were running out of time. "How far to the Needle?"

"Hard to say. At least three days at this pace, maybe more."

"Then we'd better start moving faster."

"Look!" Gaven pointed toward the west, where a plume of dust was rising from the land, blowing away from them. "What is it?"

"I don't know." Allan caught Bryce moving toward him, but motioned the Dog toward the west before stepping over Artras' legs and hopping down from the wagon. He turned back to the others. "Keep everyone here. Bryce and I will check it out."

"There's someone headed over from Aurek's group."

"Deal with them."

"Do you want to stop here for the day?"

"No! If Aurek's men are up to it, get everyone back in motion." He cut through the men clustered around the wagons, ignoring their questioning looks.

"Another quake," Bryce muttered as they intercepted each other, both trotting out toward the distant smear of dust. It was beginning to settle. "They're getting stronger."

"How did you know it was coming?"

"The animals back in the Hollow acted the same way before one of the stronger ones earlier."

They fell silent, moving swiftly. The dust settled completely. Allan's chest began to ache with effort, his muscles to protest—

Then Bryce's hand shot out and pulled him up short. "What—?"

But then he saw.

The earth had opened up before them, a fissure over ten feet wide, earth from the edge crumbling down into the depths. He heard stone hitting the sides as it fell, but he couldn't tell when it hit bottom.

Hernande's words echoed in his head: *The ley system may end up ripping the entire continent apart.*

"How long is it?"

Bryce took a step forward, then jumped back as a chunk of grassy earth fell away a few steps ahead of them. "Hard to tell. Long enough. It's not a sinkhole."

"No, it's not. Hernande warned us this might happen. I can't say I believed him, not truly. Until now."

They stared down into the fissure, neither one moving, until movement on the far side caught Allan's attention.

A Wolf loped into sight, appearing from behind a fold in the land. It trotted up to the edge of the fissure, its motions slightly unnatural, its tongue lolling out of its mouth. It halted and faced them, faced Allan.

"Tell me that you're seeing this."

"I am." Bryce didn't move. "There's a second one."

Allan didn't break the Wolf's steady gaze, but caught more movement to one side. The second Wolf was a dark brown-gray. The first one, larger, had black fur, frosted near the muzzle and ears. Its eyes were yellow.

Allan suddenly remembered the wolf's howl he'd heard before the earthquake. It hadn't come from this direction.

An indeterminate time later, the Wolf huffed and broke contact, jogging off to the right along the crevasse, the second one at its heels.

"Where there are two of them, there will be more."

"The entire pack is here. They're following us. But they haven't attacked." He recalled what Drayden had told him. The Wolves wanted the White Cloaks, just like Aurek.

"What's their game plan?"

"Hard to say. But if they intended us harm, they could have hit us at any point over the last week, assuming they've been here that long. And I think they have been. I thought I saw one of them back at the Hollow, before I spoke to Aurek that first time."

"No reason to show themselves now either. They want us to know they're there."

"He wants us to know."

"He, who?"

Allan turned away from his scrutiny of the western plains, giving up his search for more Wolves. The wagons had already begun to move. "Grant, their pack leader."

He broke into a light run to catch up.

Kara steadied herself against Dylan's cot as the floor shook with another quake. The tremor shivered through the stone before quieting. Dylan leaned forward from where he'd propped himself up against the wall.

"A small one." He shifted his legs over the side of the cot with a wince.

Outside in the hall, one of the enforcers on guard glanced inside at the movement, then turned away.

"But they're becoming more frequent. Something needs to be done soon."

Dylan massaged his knee then, with Kara's help, stood. They began to walk around the room, Dylan using Kara for support when necessary. "You said this Nexus they're creating won't work?"

"The Nexus is holding, but it's not going to repair the ley. I'd say that it stabilized it briefly. They built it slowly, about four months after the Shattering, when they realized that they didn't have enough Wielders to heal the distortion from the outside and that doing it one shard at a time was too dangerous and unrealistic."

"That's when we started to think the ley might heal itself. The quakes had lessened."

"The ley wasn't healing itself, it was this Nexus. But it's only a stopgap measure. It didn't fix anything, and now the ley is reacting, worse than before. Marcus knows it, but he doesn't know what else to do. Neither does that Prime, Lecrucius."

"But you have an idea?"

They'd circled the room twice, Dylan only faltering and grabbing onto her arm once. "Not a new idea. But they have enough Wielders here, with both of us, and a Prime, that I think we can heal the distortion exactly like we used to before the Shattering."

Dylan halted, one hand on her shoulder, skeptical. "It's huge, Kara. How many Wielders do they have?"

"Thirty-one, along with Prime Lecrucius. According to

Marcus, they're all of varying strengths, but mostly average or less. Some of them would never have been chosen for the college, but they're desperate. I've seen Lecrucius working with the ley and he's strong, and Marcus has grown since Erenthrall. With all of us—and with the Nexus that they've built—it might be enough."

"You mean, with you and the rest of us lending you our strength." Dylan sank back onto his cot and poured himself a cup of water. He drank, then leaned back against the wall again. "You haven't told Marcus yet. Why?"

"I don't trust him."

"Does that matter now?" Dylan waved a hand around vaguely. "This isn't about the White Cloaks or the Kormanley or what happened between you and Marcus before the Shattering. It isn't even about whether Marcus brought about the Shattering himself. If we don't do something about the ley now, it might destroy us. *All* of us."

"But—"

"Kara, is there a better option?"

"No."

"Then tell him."

Kara thought of the crack running up through the pit of the Needle. Not just a crack, a rent in the stone a handspan wide. And the quakes were intensifying. The next may be enough to bring the Needle down around the Nexus, destroy this node entirely, and then they'd have lost the best chance they'd had to repair the distortion over Erenthrall for over a year.

"It won't fix everything, even if we succeed. There's the distortion over Tumbor to deal with now."

"But it might buy us more time."

Kara wished she had Artras here to discuss this with. She hoped the elder Wielder had made it out of Erenthrall and back to the Hollow. Her and Allan and all of the others.

"Buy who more time?"

Kara recognized Marcus' voice. "Us. All of us."

Marcus glanced back and forth between the two. "What are you talking about?"

"Kara thinks that with the Nexus you've built, and the Wielders you have here, she can heal the distortion over Erenthrall."

"We'd still have to deal with the distortion over Tumbor, but we'd be able to stabilize the network using the nodes in Erenthrall, at least for a while. It will take everyone here working together, though. I don't see that we have any other option."

"How would you do it?"

Kara had thought he'd dismiss her idea out of hand. "I'd tap into the power stored in the Nexus, once we maximized the alignment. Then, with everyone—including you and Lecrucius—for support, I'd heal the distortion the same way we healed the distortions in Erenthrall before the Shattering. I'd envelop it and repair it from the outside in."

Marcus hesitated.

"You don't think I can handle it."

"No. I know you can handle it."

"Then what?"

"It's Lecrucius. He won't want to have you tap into that much power. He won't want you to lead the attempt."

"I've seen him working the ley. I'm stronger than he is."

"That doesn't matter. He wants control of the Needle, of the White Cloaks here. He's been undermining my status as the Father's Son, probably since he arrived here, biding his time. He has a good portion of the White Cloaks under his thumb, including Iscivius and Irmona. If he refuses to help, then so will the others."

"There won't be a Needle to control if something isn't done soon."

"I'm not certain he cares about that." He paused. "There's another problem."

Kara had learned to read Marcus decades ago. She stiffened at the look in his eyes. "What?"

"The Gorrani." At their looks of confusion, he added, "There's a force of about five thousand of them surrounding the Needle right now."

❦

"Where did they come from?"

Marcus had brought Kara to the Needle, but instead of descending down into the pit, he'd taken her up, to one of the highest windows looking southeast out over the plains. They stood at the edge of that window now, a cold wind whipping Kara's hair back from her shoulders in gusts. Below, the small city surrounding the Needle spread out in a circular pattern away from the temple and the node, a ring of stone buildings that merged into the tent city she'd seen from the wagon as they arrived. The tents brushed up against the outer wall, the gates sealed shut now, the top of the wall manned by the enforcers.

Beyond the wall, a massive group of men had gathered, keeping far enough distant to be out of archer range. They'd started to encircle the Needle, spreading out to either side of the main gates. Trailing out into the distance, in the direction of Tumbor, were rank upon rank of horses and Gorrani, marching toward them. A cloud of dust rose behind the column, the curtain blown toward the west and the setting sun. The fractured faces of the distortion around Tumbor gleamed with the orange light.

"They came from south of Tumbor. They'd established a community there along the river after the Shattering, so they could raid the ruins of the city and the groups struggling to survive there. They were far enough away to be outside of the distortion when it quickened."

"What do they want?"

"What we have."

Kara took a step closer to the window, squinting down as the Gorrani forces continued to grow. They had wagons, horses, and camels. Tents were already being erected. In snatches, the sound broken up by the wind, drums could be heard, and an occasional chanting roar. The setting sun glinted on armor and swords, and she recalled how nearly every Gorrani in Erenthrall had kept a distinctive curved blade in their household, even if they were forbidden to carry it on the streets. Every Gorrani youth was required to train with the scimitars, to be blooded with them, in order to be declared a man.

"Can they get in?"

"We've sealed the gates. According to Ty, we can hold them off, but not indefinitely. Father wants to use the ley against them. He wants to burn them from existence."

"We can't! That's not what the ley is for."

"But it was fine for Baron Arent and Prime Augustus to harness it and use it to control Erenthrall, to control all of the Baronies and wield power in the nations beyond the plains?"

"They weren't killing people with it!"

"His Dogs were. And his Hounds. They were crushing the people of Erenthrall beneath the Baron's heel. The Purge proved that. All for control of the ley. And you were willing to go along with it, to be a part of it, as a Wielder. You would have been a Prime, eventually. Then what? Would you have rebelled once you saw what they were doing, what they were keeping secret? Or would you have fallen into line and become one of Augustus' supporters?"

Marcus had a point. Except he didn't know about Hernande, Cory, and the sands. She hadn't run to the Primes with that knowledge. She'd kept it to herself. She'd like to think that such a small rebellion then meant she'd have fought back once she knew more. It had already begun, after all.

Maybe she wasn't as far from Marcus' ideals as she thought, although it galled her to admit it, even if only to herself.

"We'll never know, will we? But I won't use the ley to kill."

"We'll see." He motioned the enforcers that had accompanied them forward.

"Where are we going?"

Marcus turned away, speaking over his shoulder as he moved. "To the pit. Lecrucius is already there, preparing for tomorrow."

"Allan! Allan, look!"

Allan glanced back over his shoulder at Artras, then followed her finger. She'd stood up in the wagon and now pointed toward the south, the sun nearly sunk beneath the horizon to the west, the sky to the east already pricked with stars. The distortion over Tumbor hulked to the southeast, its purple-red and jagged lightning competing with the sunset, but directly south—

He squinted.

"Is that a spire?" Glenn asked.

"That's what it looks like to me."

To the east, a shout rang out in Aurek's group. A moment later, he saw Aurek and another rider take off toward the spire. The rest of his men ground to a halt.

"They've seen it, too. Bryce, stay here with the group. Set up camp. No fires." He hoped Aurek's men weren't stupid enough to light campfires either. "Glenn, you're with me."

They took off after Aurek and his man at a ground-eating trot, following the dust trail. The sun eased beyond sight, the last flares of day painting the clouds overhead before fading into dusk.

By the time they saw Aurek's two horses drawn to a halt on a ridge ahead, both he and Glenn were huffing. Sweat crawled down Allan's back and his face felt gritty with dust. He slowed as he picked out the others.

Aurek looked back as they approached, his face a pale blur in the deepening dark. "We've got trouble."

Allan and Glenn drew up beside the other two, gazed down into the flat below.

The entire area was lit with flames and ley light. An army encircled the walls of a small city, the black spire of what Allan guessed was the Needle rising out of its center. He'd seen similar spires in Erenthrall before the Shattering: the subtowers that the Primes had sown to support the Flyers' Tower. Ley globes lined the walls of the city and lit some of the buildings within. Fires also lined the walls, but the majority of the fire lay in a ring around those walls, highlighting where the army was encamped. A wide circle of darkness lay between the walls and the camp.

"Gods. There must be thousands of them. Who are they?"

"Gorrani." Aurek spat to one side. "I recognized their banners before the sun died."

"And their drums." Allan thought Aurek's second was named Devin; he hadn't dealt with him much since they'd left the Hollow.

Allan strained and caught snatches of a hollow drumbeat.

"How are we going to get through them and the wall?" Glenn asked.

"We have the Wielders and the mages." He emphasized the mages, watching Aurek. Now that the self-proclaimed

Baron knew where the White Cloaks were located, he needed another reason to keep Allan and the Hollowers around. The only advantage they had was the power of the Wielders and those from the University. "They'll be able to get us through the army and the walls. After that, it's up to us."

"Once we're inside the walls, you're on your own." Aurek jerked his horse around. "Stay out of our way. If you find your Wielders, get out. If we find them first—"

He didn't finish, kicking his horse into motion, back toward their camp. His second did the same.

The two watched them retreat in silence. "Can Hernande and the others get us in?"

"Doesn't matter. It's the only thing keeping Aurek and his men from attacking our group and killing us all right now." Allan turned to the Needle, frowned in thought, then headed back. "We need to talk to Hernande, Artras, and Bryce."

Halfway to their camp, the ground shuddered with another quake. He barely broke his stride.

# *Twenty-Four*

"THEY WILL ATTACK TODAY. They are readying their men to storm the walls as we speak. They spent the night constructing ladders."

"And driving us insane with their drums."

Commander Ty didn't acknowledge Lecrucius' comment.

Marcus shifted uncomfortably on their vantage at the highest tier of the temple, where he stood with Father, Ty, Darius, Lecrucius, and Dierdre. An escort of enforcers surrounded them. Father stood at the far edge, looking down over his city toward the walls and the army of Gorrani on the far side. They couldn't see them from here, the angle wasn't high enough, but they could hear them. They'd started chanting at dawn, the drums that had beat a steady rhythm all night long changing tenor and accelerating. The chant rose in waves, cresting, then starting over again. It came from all sides of the city.

The wind flapped in the sleeves of Marcus' white shirt and his cloak. The banners of the White Cloaks snapped behind them.

"Are the White Cloaks ready?" Father asked.

Marcus drew breath to answer, but Lecrucius beat him to it.

"We are, Father. We have been preparing all night. The white fires of your prophecy will burn the Gorrani from our walls at Commander Ty's signal."

A niggling pain crawled through Marcus' stomach. Ever since his confrontation with Kara the night before, he'd been uneasy. Five thousand Gorrani. Five thousand. Could he kill that many using the ley? He'd never killed anyone.

There was no other choice. If the Gorrani breached the walls, they'd kill everyone here.

Commander Ty glanced toward Marcus. "Until that happens, the enforcers are ready to defend the Needle and keep the Gorrani at bay."

Below, the Gorrani chant reached its latest peak and broke.

"Then get to the walls. Marcus, Lecrucius, to the Needle. Dierdre, what about the people inside?"

"Most have gathered in the plaza, Father. They're afraid."

"Then you and I will go down to the plaza and reassure them. By the end of the day, the Gorrani threat will have been eliminated and our cause proven righteous. The god Korma will prevail!"

Lecrucius, Darius, Dierdre, and most of the guards shouted out, "Korma!" but Marcus and Ty remained silent.

As they turned to disperse, a shudder ran through the temple, strong enough to knock a few of them to the ground, although Marcus remained upright. He caught Dierdre, keeping her steady, and she shot him a worried look.

"That's the fourth one since last night, and stronger than the last three."

"I know." As the rest of them regained their feet, he held her in reassurance. "Don't worry. Once the Gorrani are taken care of, we'll focus on the Nexus. I know we can stabilize it."

"Because of Kara? She doesn't have the strength."

"She's more powerful than Lecrucius, certainly more powerful than me."

"That's not what I meant." She grabbed him by the shoulders, looked him hard in the eyes. "You're stronger than her. Look at what happened in Erenthrall. She didn't have the courage to do anything about the Baron or Prime Augustus, but you did. Don't let her control you. Don't let Lecrucius control you either." She punctuated the last statement with a fierce kiss, then pushed him away. Father was already descending the stairs, Ty and Darius at either shoulder, a dozen enforcers surrounding them. She rushed to catch up.

Marcus watched their retreating figures, then turned to Lecrucius.

"Shall we, Son of the Father?"

"After you."

"Shit."

Allan couldn't have summarized the situation any better.

Behind the cover of the ridge they'd used the night before, he, Bryce, Hernande, and Glenn gazed down on the massive army of the Gorrani. They had completely surrounded the Needle—Cutter had taken scouts out to verify this overnight—although there were spots where they weren't as concentrated, mostly away from the three gates. Their chanting rose up from the flat below in waves, had been escalating since dawn had touched the east with a soft but striking orange. The rhythmic beats of the drums awoke something feral in Allan's gut, punctuated by the echo off the walls. From this distance, in the sunlight, he could see figures walking the escarpment, even a few on the rooftops of the temple and buildings within, but they were mere spots of color and movement, nothing more. He couldn't pick out faces; he could barely pick out individuals.

"Can the mentors get us in, Hernande?"

"We can break the walls, but I'm not certain how long it will take. Using the knots as we have in the Hollow isn't a precise science. It may take minutes. Or hours. It depends on the walls, what was used to construct them, how thick they are."

"But you can get us in."

"Yes."

Their safety from Aurek and his men depended on them delivering on their deal, even if Allan had no expectation that Aurek would follow through on his own end of the bargain. "So it's a matter of getting our mages to the walls and protecting them long enough to create a breach."

"I thought that's what Aurek's men were for."

Allan had thought to use the ley as a shield, as the Wielders had done in the Hollow, but Bryce's suggestion had merit. "It is now."

"Once we get inside the walls, what happens next?"

"We find Kara and the others, grab them, and get out."

"Easy. Where in hells are we going to look for them?"

Hernande shrugged. "The node. Kara will be close to the node, unless they're keeping her away from it purposefully."

"We'll start there. Work our way outward from there if necessary."

"It's unlikely Adder, Tim, or Aaron will be with the Wielders. If they're even still alive."

"But Kara or one of the others may know where they are. It's the best we can do."

As Allan finished, the ground shook, the tremor shuddering up from his knees into his chest. Everyone stilled, waiting to see if the quake would intensify, but it subsided.

No one said anything.

A patter of displaced rock came from behind them. Glenn looked back. "Aurek and Devin."

Allan crawled back to meet them, keeping himself below the edge of the ridge. No one on the flat below knew they were here; no use announcing their presence too early.

"What's the plan?" Aurek asked without preamble.

"The Gorrani have the Needle surrounded, but their force is weakest on the parts of the walls farthest from the gates. We'll wait for an opportunity when their force thins out after they've attacked and then hit the wall."

"How do we get past the wall?"

"Our mages will take care of it."

Aurek and Devin traded a look. "Are you certain they can get us in?"

"Yes. But they'll need time. Your men—and ours—will have to hold off the Gorrani while they work."

Devin looked doubtful. "The Gorrani are fierce. I've been to their lands in the south, seen them fight. They will not be easy to hold off."

Aurek was gazing toward the Needle, even though all but the black spire was hidden behind the ridge. "If they get us inside, it will be worth it."

Allan didn't understand Aurek's hatred of the Wielders,

but it surpassed a simple desire for justice after the Shattering. It went deeper, was more personal.

Before he could ask what drove him, though, the drumbeat from the Gorrani altered, speeding up, the chanting following along, catching up, rising to a higher pitch, echoing from the walls and bouncing back toward the ridge. Allan turned and scrambled up the low slope, heard Aurek and Devin on his heels. He threw himself flat to the ground and scanned the distance —

And the drums and chanting halted, sharply, as if cut off with a blade.

Everyone held their breath, the air still.

Then, with a roar that reverberated through the earth, the Gorrani charged the walls, defying the sudden flights of arrows that shot from the battlements, a slew of men among them carrying ladders. They converged on all sides at the same time, the tread of their feet thundering up and overwhelming their battle cry. Ladders began to rise, bases planted into the earth, men with ropes sprinting out ahead, lifting them up and over. Before they'd even struck the wall, Gorrani were scrambling up their lengths. From this distance, everything happened with excruciating slowness, all sounds subsumed by the general roar.

Beside him, Bryoo licked his lips and said again, "Shit."

Marcus and Lecrucius were in the outer stone garden of the node when the Gorrani chant escalated and broke off. Both of them halted, looking upward as they strained to hear what might come next.

The roar was deafening. Marcus winced, even though he knew it had been muted by the buildings and the distance between the node and the walls. The earth trembled, only this time it wasn't from a quake.

It was from the tread of five thousand Gorrani warriors.

"They're attacking the walls."

Lecrucius turned without a word and strode into the Needle ahead of him.

As soon as Marcus stepped through the doors, both of his arms were seized. He cried out in surprise, struggled briefly, but enforcers had hold of him, not White Cloaks.

"What is the meaning of this?"

"Isn't it obvious? I think it's time for a new Son to rise. A new dawn, so to speak." Lecrucius nodded to the guards. "Bring him. Place him with the rest."

"The rest?" Lecrucius didn't answer. He'd already turned and entered the stairwell leading down to the pit. Marcus struggled a moment more, until one of the guards twisted his arm, pain shooting up into his shoulder. He staggered forward, the guard only releasing the hold slightly when they hit the stairs.

The pit was active, ley spurting up in jets from the well below. White Cloaks ringed it on all sides, over two dozen of them. "Iscivius, is everything ready?"

"The Nexus has been aligned as you requested, Prime Lecrucius. And those you singled out have been secured."

Marcus' gaze shot toward a small group herded by a dozen enforcers against the pit's wall, near where the crack ran up from the ledge to the stairwell to the ley-veined obsidian ceiling. He picked out Kara instantly, along with Dylan and Carter, the younger Wielder from the Hollow sulking with arms crossed. Two others—Hartman and Jenner—were with them; not a surprise, since they were strong supporters of Marcus himself. But the sixth shocked Marcus to the bone: Okata.

They reached the bottom of the stairs, Lecrucius breaking away, heading toward Iscivius, the enforcers dragging Marcus toward the other group. They thrust him behind the enforcers already on guard, nearly slamming him into the wall. He steadied himself, nodded to the others, but kept his eyes locked on Okata.

"I thought you were one of Lecrucius' followers."

"He does not trust me because I am Gorrani."

"What's going on? We were in the middle of preparing for the attack on the Gorrani when suddenly the enforcers showed up and dragged Jenner, Okata, Carter, and I out of the group and stuck us with them." Hartman motioned to where Kara was partially supporting Dylan. "Iscivius said they didn't want us interfering."

Marcus leveled a glare at Lecrucius. "It seems our sole Prime has decided to take my place as the new Son, without Father's knowledge." Hartman gaped in astonishment, proving that Lecrucius had been right to single him out. Jenner pressed his lips together, although he didn't appear shocked.

"He could have trusted me."

Everyone ignored Carter.

"What about us?" Kara asked. "Why did he bring us down here?"

"He knows you won't help him against the Gorrani. He wouldn't trust you even if you agreed. But it would have been safer to leave you and Dylan both in your rooms."

Okata stilled. "Unless he intends to resolve all of his problems with some kind of accident."

Marcus recalled what had happened to Sanderson. He could see the same realization in Kara's eyes. "We can't let that happen."

"I can monitor them while they work—"

"You can't. Lecrucius will sense you. He's a Prime. He'll think you're attempting to interfere." Okata drew in a breath, his knotted Gorrani beard jutting up. "I'll watch for us. He may sense me on the ley, but as long as I remain far enough back he won't say anything."

"What about the rest of us? We just wait?"

The stone beneath their feet shivered.

Okata, eyes closed, had already sunk into the ley. "They're pulling in ley from the other cities. They've changed the configuration of the Nexus."

"How? What's the new alignment?"

"I can't tell, not without snagging Lecrucius' attention. But it's drawing the ley here."

Another rumble shook the chamber, and all of them turned to the pit as ley streamed upward, reaching for the ceiling. It rose in controlled spurts, unlike what had happened when Sanderson had been killed, but Marcus watched it with growing trepidation.

Kara sidled closer to him. "He's strengthening it using the Nexus, preparing to use it."

"The Gorrani have attacked the walls."

"So you still want to annihilate them with the ley?"

"We have no choice! We can't hold them off forever. They have to be stopped."

"You'll kill thousands!"

He was saved from answering by a jolt, the earth heaving. Some of the White Cloaks at the pit cried out, two of them falling to the stone floor near Lecrucius. "Hold on to the ley! Contain it until we hear the signal from Commander Ty! Iscivius, keep the crystals in alignment or we're all dead."

The quake continued, dust sifting down onto them from the cracked wall overhead.

"Their hold on the ley wavered during the initial jolt."

Kara snatched Marcus' arm at Okata's report, her fingers digging in as the rumble of the quake intensified. "He's drawing too much ley from the outer nodes. The system is trying to compensate, but it's already unstable. We have to stop him."

"You just want to stop him from using the ley on the Gorrani!"

"This isn't about the Gorrani! This is about the ley, about the nodes and the system. If he draws too much of the ley here, it will destabilize whatever fragile framework the ley has left!"

The chamber shuddered around them, more than just dust falling down from above now. Marcus knew she was right. He wanted to believe in Father and his vision, in Dierdre and the Kormanley, but using the ley against the Gorrani in such a way—

It was wrong.

He dropped his head in defeat, then raised it again with new purpose, catching Hartman's gaze, then Jenner's. "She's right. We have to stop him, before he brings the entire ley network crashing down around us."

But before anyone could do anything, the bellow of a massive horn cut through the low growl of the quake and Okata said grimly, "We're too late."

On the ridge overlooking the Needle, Allan hauled on the reins of the horse as the ground shuddered beneath them. The animal tossed its head, its eyes white in fear as it tried to dance away from him, but he held it in check.

"Keep him calm, Allan!" Glenn and the rest of the group from the Hollow were arrayed protectively around the wagon, Hernande on the seat beside Allan, Cory, Jason, and

Jerrain huddled in the back with Artras, Mareane, and Jude. Mareane and Jude were clutching each other as the wagon bed juddered, the rest gripping handholds on the sides. The supplies had been removed. Outside the circle of Hollowers, Aurek's men were standing with swords readied, everyone watching Bryce and Aurek at the front, both keeping an eye on the battle at the Needle's walls.

"What does he think I'm trying to do?"

Hernande, hands white-knuckled on the boards before them, didn't answer. Allan had originally planned on simply charging the walls once an opening appeared, but Artras had pointed out that neither she, nor Jerrain nor Hernande, would be able to keep up with the rest of the men in an all-out run. So they'd hastily flung the supplies from the wagon and brought it about. They'd move slower — would probably crack a wheel before they reached the walls — but it was the only feasible option.

They hadn't counted on the quake.

"It's not quieting," Hernande said.

"No. It's growing stronger."

And then Aurek raised his hand and shouted something Allan couldn't hear over the steady growl of the earth. It didn't matter. The shout from the raiders and their sudden surge forward told him everything he needed to know. With a snap of the reins and a "Heeyaw!" that he doubted the horse heard, he let the animal loose.

They leaped forward, the wagon clattering over the rough ground. Allan flew upward, his ass landing with a bone-jarring thud, and then he was hanging onto the bench with one hand, reins fisted in the other. Someone cried out from the wagon bed behind him, but he didn't dare look.

Ahead, the men who'd been in front of the wagon glanced over their shoulders, then cut away to either side to let them through. Allan yanked on the reins to slow the horse down, but it was no use. They were pulling out ahead of those on foot, only Aurek and the few men on horseback keeping ahead of them. The ragged battle cry from the raiders had died out as they ran for the nearest wall. Allan could see where Aurek was aiming, a section where the Gorrani had split to either side as the attack on the gate to one side intensified. To the other side, the southern warriors had managed to gain a slight foothold on the top of the walls with the ladders. A section of the wall was now clear.

"There! Are we close enough yet?"

"No!"

Allan wasn't surprised. The ridge they'd hidden behind to prepare was at least a mile distant. They hadn't even covered a quarter of that yet.

The wagon jumped—Allan couldn't tell if it was the quake or they'd hit a bump—but it landed hard, his teeth clacking together, nipping the side of his tongue. He tasted blood, swirled it around his mouth and spat to one side, while ahead the Gorrani had finally taken notice of them. A group of at least a hundred broke off from the back of those holding the ladders to the right, forming a line to meet them. They were close enough now to hear the battle even over the wagon, to make out individual faces. Their line was skewed, and Allan realized the Gorrani hadn't figured out they didn't intend to attack their flank.

He glanced back to see where the rest of their men were. Too far behind. The wagon and Aurek's horses would reach the Gorrani before anyone caught up to them.

He spun back around and hauled at the reins of their horse, no longer trying to slow him, simply trying to make him turn. A horn sounded from the walls far to the left, near the main gates. He bellowed "Aurek!" as loud as he could, saw the lord twitch, but he didn't slow. Allan heaved on the reins again and the horse began to angle left and slow. "Aurek!"

Someone's hand slapped onto the wagon bench beside him and he twisted, startled. Artras clung to the wooden headboard between the bed and the bench. "Stay back from the walls! Something's happening with the ley!"

Allan snapped around, the wagon now slowed enough he could stand. "Aurek! Fall back!"

The Baron twisted in the saddle, his expression dark with fury, but he pulled up short when he saw the wagon off course. Devin and the others with him all halted in confusion, horses milling about. Beyond them, the Gorrani looked bewildered.

And then white ley billowed up from the ground all around the walls like flames, starting at the base and rising higher and higher as it spread outward. As it grew in intensity, screams erupted from within and Allan flinched in horror. Aurek's horse reared up in terror, even though the flames were still distant, the Baron's face reflecting his own fear as he fought to keep his seat. The Gorrani who'd turned to face them glanced back over their shoulders, arms raised as if to shield themselves, and then they broke and ran. Those on the ladders to the right were smothered by the flames within a breath. Those on the ground below turned to flee, but only those farthest from the walls escaped the surging flames as they ran. Half of the men with Aurek kicked their mounts into motion, heading away from the walls, back toward Allan's wagon. A moment later, Aurek and the rest did the same.

Within the space of five heartbeats, the walls of the Needle in both directions were completely hidden by the eerily silent flames.

The sounds of battle almost completely died out.

The wagon drew to a halt, and Allan collapsed back onto the bench, his body numb as he stared at the sheets of ley. Even though they'd stopped, the wagon still shook from the quake. Those in the bed clambered forward to see.

"Gods," Artras muttered at his side.

Aurek reached them, cantering his horse in a sharp turn as Devin ordered the others who'd ridden beyond them back with harsh words and curses. The first of those on foot who'd been left behind formed up around the wagon, heaving and gasping.

"What is it?" Aurek asked.

"What do you think? It's a wall of ley."

"The damned White Cloaks."

The Gorrani beneath the wall who'd escaped the fire were no longer interested in their little group of three hundred men and a wagon. Those that were left were regrouping, well back from the still-burning white fire, maybe three or four hundred in all on this side of the Needle.

Aurek spun toward Artras. "Can you get us through it?"

"I doubt anything that was caught in the ley after the first few seconds still exists. The concentration of the ley is strong enough that anything organic that passes through it now will be destroyed. I could possibly shield some of us from the ley for a while, but I wouldn't bet my life on it, let alone others."

"What about the Gorrani who were caught in it?" Hernande's tone indicated he already knew the answer.

"Gone. Dead and gone. Not even Baron Arent thought to use the ley in such a manner. It's an abomination."

Aurek barked laughter. The lord turned to face them, his horse pawing the ground. "This is why we hunt the White Cloaks." He drew his sword, and suddenly the entire group tensed—Hollowers and raiders alike. They were all mixed in with each other, stragglers from the charge still filtering in, but as more and more blades were drawn, the Hollowers stepped toward the wagon protectively, Bryce taking up a position at the rear.

Allan didn't move, his eyes fixed on Aurek. "Not all of the Wielders are like the White Cloaks."

"So you've claimed before. I'd rather not risk it."

Artras climbed to her feet, using the wagon's headboard for support. The ground still trembled, although Allan didn't think anyone was paying any attention to that. "Don't you think if we were like the White Cloaks, with this much power, we'd have used it already? Why would we have let you raid the Hollow? Why wouldn't we have simply burned you out before you got there?"

"Because you *don't* have this much power!"

"Fool! It's because we choose not to use it!" She leaned forward over the headboard, her voice dropping. "We could have burned you at the Hollow. We could have destroyed you at any point on our travels here. And we could fry you where you stand right now if we wanted to."

More ley leaped from the ground, only this time it came up in front of Aurek's mount. Aurek shouted as his horse shied away from it, the rest of the raiders jumping back in fear. The Hollowers closed in tighter about the wagon, a few of them with looks as wild with terror as the raiders.

Aurek seized control of his horse again, but refused to back off. "You're bluffing."

The white tendril of ley rose higher, began to spread to either side. "Don't tempt me."

Allan glanced back and noticed Mareane and Jude both had their eyes closed, Cory supporting Mareane's limp body while Jasom held Jude.

Aurek's men fidgeted. Even Devin, his second, appeared

wary. He didn't lower his sword, but as the ley grew and flicked closer to his position, he stepped back.

Aurek held Artras' gaze, eyes narrowing as he weighed the truth of her words—

Then his lips curled into a smile. "You're lying. Kill them. Kill them all!"

Allan spat a curse, dropping the reins of the wagon as he stood and drew his sword.

At the same moment, a thunderous growl rolled out from the direction of the Needle and the earth lurched— once, twice—and then pitched upward with enough force that Allan was flung from the wagon. He slammed into the ground, one arm going numb, his sword slipping from his fingers. His vision swam and he groaned as he attempted to haul himself to his feet, but the earth rolled beneath him, no longer solid. Stone cracked and split, the sound shocking, felt as a thud in his chest that sucked the breath from him. A horse screamed. The air suddenly filled with dust. Choking, Allan crawled forward toward a body lying on the trampled grass—Hernande—and almost got caught beneath the wheels of the wagon as the horse panicked and bolted. Mareane rolled from the bed with a shriek, landing two steps distant, but he could see Cory, Artras, and a few others still huddled flat in the back as it passed.

"Mareane!" Allan snagged her attention as he continued toward Hernande. "Are you hurt?"

She answered by scrambling toward him, not trying to get to her feet. "It's not stopping."

Allan rolled Hernande over. Blood ran from a wound above his forehead, but the mentor stirred. "See if you can help him." He turned his attention toward the rest of the group.

The wall of white fire still burned in front of the stone walls of the Needle. Beneath it, the Gorrani were scrambling away from a massive crack in the earth, like the one he and Bryce had seen earlier. It radiated out from the wall into the plains, snaking farther out as he watched, widening as it grew. The raiders and Hollowers were all stumbling about, a couple bodies lying motionless, scattered. At least half of the raiders had bolted toward the north, away from the Needle, some of the Hollowers with them. In their panic, a few had run toward the crevice and were swallowed up before they could turn back. Among the men were three or four riderless horses. The wagon was a good distance away, headed northeast full tilt. Two figures clutched each other and flung themselves from the back, landing out of sight. A breath later, the wagon hit something hard, the bed leaping upward, splinters of wood flying. It landed, the rear wheels gone, dust billowing up as the horse dragged it another hundred feet before it fell completely apart, the animal tearing off into the distance with its traces and part of the wagon's support trailing behind it.

He didn't see Aurek or Devin, but Bryce staggered up to him, sword still out, his free hand clutching his shoulder. Glenn came up behind him.

"Glenn, go see who survived from the wagon. I saw them jump just before it broke up." Glenn nodded and trotted off toward the northeast, stumbling as the ground continued to shake. "Bryce, gather together as many of the remaining Hollowers as you can."

"What about the raiders?"

"Leave them, unless they attack you."

He turned back to Mareane and Hernande as he heard Bryce head off. Mareane had the mentor sitting up. He had one hand on his forehead, probing the wound, blood now trickling down between his eyes and along his nose, into his mustache and beard. He winced, brought his fingers away, and stared at the dark red coating his fingers. He didn't appear groggy at all.

"I must have landed on a stone when I fell from the wagon." He glanced up. His entire body stilled.

Allan felt the point of a sword dig lightly into his back.

"I should have killed you all back at your pathetic village," Aurek muttered.

Allan didn't answer. With each shudder of the earth, the point dug deeper, an inch from his spine, a hair beneath his shoulder blade. He could feel blood matting his shirt. If Aurek pressed hard enough, it would slide straight through him, most likely nicking his heart.

"Don't move."

Allan thought Hernande was talking to Aurek, then realized he was looking directly at him. "I don't intend to."

Hernande's attention shifted to Aurek. "Take your men and leave now, or I'll kill you."

"The White Cloaks are going to kill us all. But like that Wielder bitch earlier, I think you're bluffing."

Through the blade lightly embedded in Allan's back, he felt Aurek tense. He lurched forward and whirled, instinctively reaching for the blade he no longer had.

Aurek stood, face stricken, a rictus of pain, his free hand clutched to his chest, fingers a claw.

He gasped once, then collapsed to the side and lay still.

Allan propped himself up on one elbow. "What happened?"

"I burst his heart. I don't bluff." Hernande glanced around, taking in the walls, the white flame, the fissure opening up to their west. "But Aurek was right. The White Cloaks are going to kill us all."

"We have other problems," Bryce said, coming in from the side with a dozen men and women from the Hollow. He gestured behind them, toward the plains. "Devin is rounding up the raiders who haven't managed to escape." He glanced down at Aurek's body. "I assume he's going to be pissed you killed his Baron."

Kara felt Lecrucius release the ley. She was heartened to see Marcus looking aghast. Even Carter appeared troubled.

"What are we going to do?"

"We're going to have to wrest control of the Nexus away from him." The words held more conviction than Kara felt.

"How?" Marcus let his gaze slide toward the sixteen enforcers that surrounded them and the half dozen others scattered throughout the pit, his eyebrows raised in question. Most of them were focused on the fountain of ley and the White Cloaks that surrounded it, but two of them kept glancing back at the group of Wielders they guarded, eyeing them warily.

Isolated even from Kara and the rest, Carter had grown restless. Now he suddenly burst out, "I won't let you ruin this for me," and spun toward the pit. "Lecrucius! Lecrucius, they're planning to—"

Okata's fist connected with the younger Wielder's jaw and Carter's head snapped back. He collapsed to one side in a heap. The nearest guard turned, began to say, "Hey!" but Okata was already moving. He grabbed the enforcer by the throat, lifted him up as he snatched the man's sword from its sheath with a ringing hiss, then tossed him into the two nearest guards that were only now starting to react.

"Get behind me." Okata didn't wait to see if the other Wielders complied. With a single step, he stood over the three enforcers now on the ground, stabbing once, twice, a third time, one of the guards screaming.

Kara stood stock still, until Marcus grabbed her arm and shoved her and Dylan back toward where Carter lay on the stone, out cold. Hartman joined them, but as Okata stepped over to meet the remaining guards, half of whom had finally drawn weapons, Jenner grabbed one of the fallen guards' blades and moved in behind Okata.

The two of them stepped forward together, swords clashing and ringing, another guard falling by Okata's hand before Marcus suddenly stepped in front of Kara, cutting off her view. Her ex-lover's face was intent.

"He's a Gorrani." He gripped Kara by one shoulder, fingers digging in to focus her attention. "Let him handle the guards. You need to deal with Lecrucius."

Kara turned to Hartman. "Take Dylan. I may need you all as support."

Even before Dylan's weight had shifted from her, she dove into the ley, aiming straight for the Nexus.

But the White Cloaks were waiting. She sensed their presence a moment before one of them slammed into her, thrusting her to the side. They continued to buffet her, keeping her back from the crystals, from the pit where Lecrucius and the others were channeling the ley into the fiery wall she could feel surrounding the Needle. She circled the pit, probing, seeking a weak point. Behind her, Marcus, Dylan, and Hartman joined her on the ley, but they kept their distance and the White Cloaks left them alone. She heard the clang of swords where Okata and Jenner held the other guards off, but it was muted and distant.

She sank herself deeper into the ley, down toward where the lines connected with the pit, beneath the Nexus itself. The energy being drawn toward the Needle was immense, nearly knocking her away. She forged forward, noticed that the White Cloaks who had been hounding her couldn't follow, the current too strong for them to withstand. She followed the flow of the combined lines from Erenthrall, Farrade, and the nodes to the south, north, and west up from the pit toward the Nexus from beneath. No one tried to stop her; none of the White Cloaks could.

She braced herself to enter the Nexus—

And felt the surge coming from Erenthrall behind her.

She spun, managed to duck out of the Erenthrall line into the Farrade one for cover a heartbeat before it hit.

She didn't even have time to warn Marcus and the others.

The wave of ley hit the Nexus hard, the White Cloaks set to stabilize it screaming as they tried to contain the blast. At least three of them didn't survive, their presence on the ley snapping silent as they burned out. Up above, around the pit, Kara knew their bodies were hitting the floor as senseless as Carter's, except they'd never rise again. Their minds were wiped, if their hearts hadn't stopped.

But the rest retained control, Lecrucius' hold on the devastating white fire never wavering.

Then the quake hit.

It rolled up out of the earth with a growl, shuddering through the pit around Kara, its violence finding release above as the ground cracked and exploded, a fault line splitting the Needle's city in two. The White Cloaks who'd survived the surge were flung to the floor, Lecrucius' hold wavering. Two of them were jolted into the pit itself, screaming as they fell until the ley caught them. Kara shot out of the Farrade tunnel back toward the pit's edge, slamming back into her own body as the earth continued to shake.

She found Marcus, Dylan, and the others clinging to the floor, chunks of stone falling from the pit's wall overhead. Only Okata remained standing, feet spread wide, sword still ready in one hand. The enforcers that remained were crawling away from him, faces contorted in terror, as the quake continued to rip the city apart. The gap in the crack from the previous quake had widened by another two hands.

"Something's happened in Erenthrall!" Kara yelled over the grinding of stone. The quake had flung her body to the floor as well, but she grabbed Dylan and dragged him toward the pit's wall. Marcus and Hartman were already attempting to join them, Hartman snatching hold of Carter's body as he came. Jenner tapped Okata's leg from behind and motioned toward them, the two Wielders falling back from the retreating enforcers.

"We have to regain control of the Nexus. It's our only chance to stop this quake. Lecrucius has destabilized the entire network."

"I found a way in, but I'm going to need everyone's help."

"Do it! We'll support you."

Halfway around the pit, part of the ledge that they and the White Cloaks were huddled on suddenly split and fell away, dropping down into the well below, taking one of the White Cloaks with it. Kara dove back into the ley, the others following her one by one. She reached beneath the Nexus as she had before, but noticed that the line from Erenthrall now pulsed with a steady throb. It was feeding the quake, feeding the Nexus, the power escalating with each beat.

She had to break the cycle before it peaked.

Gathering the strength of the others around her, she aimed straight up through the torrent of ley energy and pierced the Nexus through the heart.

It was in chaos, the crystals barely held in place by Iscivius, Irmona, and the other White Cloaks. But she ignored them, focused on Lecrucius, the Prime still maintaining the wall of ley around the city.

"Help them stabilize the Nexus!" She wasn't certain the others could hear her, but she reached out through the ley and seized Lecrucius.

He roared in defiance, the sound muffled beneath the sounds of the quake but reverberating on the ley. The two locked hold of each other, grappling as the ley raged around them, Lecrucius managing to keep the protective wall raised. Every attempt Kara made to seize the lines supplying the wall was countered with a slap of force, knocking her aside. And now that he knew she'd slipped through his White Cloaks, he began constructing a shield around himself. She reached out desperately to block him.

But then Marcus was there. Distantly, where her body rested against the stone wall of the pit, she heard him say, "There's no time."

Marcus gathered up the excess ley spilling off of the

Nexus, concentrated it, and funneled it directly toward Lecrucius.

It hit him full force, shattered through the shield he hadn't yet completed and seared into his physical body on the platform. The scream he'd barely begun died out, only an echo of it rippling through the ley around them.

"Stop the wall of ley!" Marcus turned back to the Nexus, two of the crystals trembling, Iscivius and Irmona concentrating so hard they hadn't yet noticed that Lecrucius was dead.

Kara snatched at the lines holding the wall of ley around the Needle stable. With cold certainty, she snipped them off, channeling the ley back toward the Nexus.

It was too much. Irmona shrieked and crumbled to the stone as it overwhelmed her, the crystal she controlled released. Marcus leaped forward, seizing it before it could spin completely out of control. Kara rushed to help him, both of them straining to hold it. But they were fighting each other, Kara pushing while Marcus pulled. Both of them thought they knew how to align it correctly, at odds—

Until Marcus suddenly stepped back.

Kara leaped forward, struggling on her own now, wrestling the pane toward a new configuration. She could have done it alone, but when she felt Marcus behind her, ready to give her his strength, she accepted.

It was like working together as Wielders in Eld. They complemented each other, their power slipping together and melding smoothly. Kara gasped as they joined, but the pane held her entire attention. With their combined strength, the wildness of the pane's motion settled and stilled. It slid into position and immediately the chaos of the Nexus died out. The White Cloaks sagged in relief.

But the pulses coming from Erenthrall hadn't stopped.

Beside her on the shaking platform, Marcus said tightly, "I'll hold it. You go see what's happening in Erenthrall."

Kara didn't argue. Withdrawing from her connection to the Nexus—to Marcus—she paused to steady herself—

And then she dove into the ley line leading to Erenthrall.

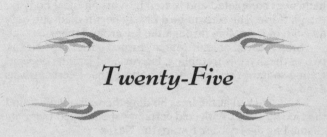

# Twenty-Five

"HOW MANY PEOPLE DO WE HAVE LEFT?" Allan could probably count them himself, those that remained grouped in a tight huddle behind him, Glenn at the back watching the Gorrani near the walls, he and Bryce at the front focused on Devin as he rallied the raiders.

"Thirty-four, including the Wielders and mages."

Allan's fist closed over the pommel of his reclaimed sword. He wondered who they'd lost and who'd simply panicked and run. "Devin has three times that."

"Aurek had six times our number before."

"But he had a reason to keep us alive. Devin doesn't."

"Maybe they'll simply leave."

Allan met his gaze with a raised eyebrow of incredulity, and Bryce grinned. The Dog was enjoying himself.

"We're too exposed here." Allan scanned the plains, seeing no reasonable place to make a stand, but then his gaze fell on the white wall of ley behind them, the Gorrani milling around to the east. "Let's shift everyone toward the walls. I want the ley to our backs, if possible, and the Gorrani to our flank."

Bryce let out a piercing whistle, catching everyone's attention. "Start shifting back toward the walls! Keep an eye on the Gorrani, Glenn. If they make any sudden feints in our direction, holler."

Devin noticed the moment they started moving, but he was still attempting to bring a semblance of order to his own group. Some of the men were arguing with him. Allan could hear him shouting back, berating them, threatening them as he rode his horse back and forth, sword raised. When two men broke ranks and tried to flee into the plains, he rode them down, slashing at one as the other fell beneath his horse's hooves. Neither one rose. No one else tried to run.

"He may be worse to deal with than Aurek."

Allan silently agreed.

They fell back toward the wall of ley, the ground still lurching at odd moments beneath their feet, the tremors a constant vibration in Allan's teeth. Halfway to the wall, Devin's group began trudging toward them. Then they came across Aurek's body, left in the grass where it had fallen, and any lingering doubts in the men Devin led vanished. He pointed down at Aurek with his sword, shouted something to the men, Allan only catching a few snatches of "honor" and "your Baron" on the wind—

Then the men bellowed in rage and began to run.

Bryce turned immediately. "To the ley walls!"

The Hollowers broke into a sprint, Allan at their backs now, charging after them. He caught sight of Cory guarding Hernande's side, Mareane and Jude with Artras. One of the others snatched Jerrain into his arms, the elder mentor cursing in protest. Jasom had drawn his sword and ran with the fighters in the outer edges, all of them urging the Wielders and mentors on.

The group halted when they came within thirty paces of the outer edge of the fiery wall. Allan glanced skyward, the flames reaching to the heavens, utterly silent. He wondered briefly if he could walk through the fire unscathed, as he'd walked through the distortions, but there was no time to experiment.

He turned and drew.

The raiders were almost upon them, Devin leading the charge. Aurek's second had aimed his horse toward Allan. He had a moment to register the sudden battle cry of the raiders, and then he was forced to throw himself out of the horse's path. Something tugged at his shoulder as he fell, followed instantly by a burning pain across his shoulder bone, but then he was rolling in the already trampled grass.

Before he could right himself, the rest of the raiders overran him.

Someone tripped over him, foot connecting solidly into his side. White-hot pain flared and he dropped his sword, reaching for his dagger as the screaming men surrounded him. He slashed to either side, struggling to pull himself into a crouch before some lucky kick connected with his head. His short blade scraped off armor and found flesh, men roaring in pain as blood pattered down on him. Fingers like claws, he snared one man by the breeches and hauled himself upright, jabbing his knife into the man's back before spinning him around and using him as a shield. Someone elbowed him in the kidney and he hissed the pain out through gritted teeth, orienting himself with one swift glance. He was trapped in the middle of the raiders, their focus on the huddle of Hollowers near the ley, Bryce and the rest defending the Wielders and mentors.

But the mentors weren't idle. Even as his gaze slid over him, Jerrain stabbed crooked fingers to Allan's right and the earth exploded upward, men flying with unearthly screams. Cory and Hernande stood protectively in front of the Wielders, doing the same. Devin's horse shrieked, the sound jarring, as the ground exploded beneath its feet and Devin was thrown from the saddle.

Someone realized he wasn't a raider. A gray-bearded man swung a wicked-looking knife, but Allan shifted the man he'd backstabbed. The graybeard howled as his knife sank into his fellow raider's chest. Before he could jerk it free, Allan shoved the dead man forward, unbalancing him. Both bodies fell beneath his feet, Allan already turning to sink his knife into another man's side. But it was a losing battle. He couldn't hold all of the raiders off, not when he was surrounded. Not even Bryce and his Dogs could hold off all of Devin's men.

Then the tenor of the screams around him changed. It took him a moment to realize it, another to realize the screams were punctuated by vicious snarls and growls.

The tide within the raiders shifted. Instead of everyone fighting toward where Bryce defended the Hollowers with his Dogs, the men around Allan now focused their attention backward, toward the plains, where the men that had been in the rear of Devin's group were attempting to flee as they were ripped limb from limb by Wolves.

Allan stood stunned for only a moment. Then he stabbed the man in front of him in the shoulder. Thirty paces away, a giant silver-gray Wolf slapped a raider flat against the ground with one huge paw and ripped the man's throat out with his teeth, blood splashing across all of those around them. Five more Wolves were wreaking havoc among the rearguard of the raiders to either side, while Grant, the leader of the pack, walked toward them with an escort of five more Wolves. With a gesture of his hand, three of those broke away and joined the melee, inciting fresh screams to the right. The silver-gray Wolf had lunged from his kill into the group on Allan's left, Arterial blood splashed in an arc, flecking Allan's cheek with warmth, but he didn't take his eyes off of the pack leader.

Until a gray-brown Wolf leaped toward him from the left, one claw slamming into his chest and pinning him to the ground. Claws dug five holes through his shirt and into his skin, but Allan's attention fixed on the animal's snout, inches from his face. Yellow, feral eyes glared down at him, and spittle dripped from black-red lips drawn back from yellowed, bloody teeth. Allan couldn't breathe, the pressure from the Wolf's weight on his chest too great. Tiny black dots began to dance before his eyes as the animal's hot, rancid breath exploded into his face. Its growl shivered into Allan's chest through the paw that held him immobile.

Then someone barked an order and the Wolf flinched. Its nostrils flared as it sucked in a breath, scenting him.

It drew back, head first, before lifting its weight free and withdrawing its front paw. But it didn't retreat. It stood over him, glaring to either side, its growl continuing.

Grant stepped into view, staring down at Allan from above. "Get up. The Gorrani are coming."

It took Allan a moment to figure out what he'd said, the words more growl than speech, but he couldn't move.

Grant reached down, lips curled in a half snarl, grabbed

him by his bloodied shirt, and hauled him upright, drawing him close to his malformed half snout. Allan's chest flared with pain where the other Wolf's claws had gouged into him. "The Gorrani." He pointed with his other hand.

To the east, the Gorrani who'd survived the wall of ley had finally formed up into a unit and were charging toward them.

Allan glanced back to where Bryce and the Hollowers had tightened up on the Wielders and mentors, looking on in confusion as the Wolves ripped the raiders apart, leaving them alone. The fiery ley still rose up behind them.

Allan turned back to Grant. "There's nowhere to run."

Grant's fist tightened in his shirt, the pack leader's eyes flashing a lambent yellow—

But then the wall of ley that surrounded the Needle suddenly collapsed downward into the ground, leaving the stone walls bare and the ground beneath littered with hundreds of weapons, buckles, earrings, nose-rings, and other assorted metals. Even the ladders were gone.

Everyone spun, the fight pausing for a few heartbeats.

Then Allan yelled, "Jerrain! Hernande! The wall!"

The mages spun—Jerrain, Hernande, Cory, and Jasom—and a breath later the stone wall surrounding the Needle exploded outward with a single splintering thunderclap. The sound rolled across the plain into the distance, but Bryce was already shouting for the Hollowers to withdraw into the breach, massive chunks of stone still crumbling down to the metal-littered mud where the majority of the Gorrani army had died. The Hollower fighters herded the Wielders and the mentors toward the hole punched through the wall, climbing over the heap of stone toward the opening they'd created, like the scree in the caverns near their village.

Grant grunted and set Allan down with a jarring thud, but didn't let go. He snarled and barked out orders, the Wolves breaking away from their kills and retreating with the Hollowers, harassing any of the raiders who attempted to follow them. Bodies littered the ground, nothing more than torn and shredded meat, the sight turning Allan's stomach, but he forced himself to look.

He didn't see Devin anywhere.

Then Grant shoved him toward the crack in the stone wall. "Move."

Allan ran, Grant loping along beside him. He scrambled up the rockfall, swearing when it shifted beneath him because of his weight or the still shuddering earth. Bryce pushed the last of the Hollowers through the opening, then ducked inside. The Wolves clawed their way up the rocks and through as well. Behind, Allan heard the Gorrani approaching at a run, their battle cry growing louder.

When he reached the opening, he turned. Grant paused a step below him. The remains of the raiders were scattering toward the plains, but they wouldn't make it. The Gorrani — over a thousand now — were closing in, cutting off their escape. On the field before the rockfall, two Wolves were still worrying at their kills.

Grant whistled sharply. One of the Wolves' ears pricked and he looked up, muzzle stained black with blood. He glanced toward the approaching Gorrani, then streaked toward them, leaping up the stone fall.

The other ignored them.

Grant turned and shoved Allan through the narrow opening. Allan clambered through the rough breach, fine dust and small rocks cascading down from above as he picked his way over the thick, broken wall. He sucked in a lungful of air and emerged coughing hoarsely on the far side.

"Get down!" Bryce urged him down with a frantic wave from halfway down the slope of the much smaller rockfall on this side. Allan stumbled toward him, still coughing, and Bryce hauled him off the rock as soon as he was within reach. Grant and the last Wolf from the other side leaped clear. "Seal it up now!"

Allan ducked as another splintering thunderclap rolled across the wide courtyard, stone pattering down, a boulder the size of his chest slamming into the flagstone beside him, cracking in two. Arm raised protectively over his head, he twisted and saw the rock wall above the gap the mentors had just made collapsing downward. Men on top of the wall staggered back from the collapse, many of them pointing down toward them with fingers or swords.

"Allan!"

Allan turned to see Bryce gesturing him toward the sea of tents that filled the courtyard beyond the wall. "Keep moving. The White Cloak enforcers are headed this way."

Allan sprinted from the wall to the tents, following Bryce and the others as they wove through the makeshift city, the haphazard housing scattered with cook firepits, laundry drying on lines, and the scattered detritus of humble lives, reminding Allan forcibly of the Hollowers huddled in the caverns near the village. But he had no time for memories, even those of Morrell. He ran, lungs burning, keeping Bryce in sight. Out of the corner of his eye, he caught flickers of Grant and a few of the Wolves, heard yelps of shock as they ran into some of the people who lived here. But the tent city was surprisingly empty. He only startled three people, a woman emerging from her tent with a cast iron pan in one hand, a basket of eggs in the other—who screamed and ducked back inside as Bryce flew by—and two men seated around a butter churn, trading off the handle, even though the city was under attack and the ground was still shaking. Both paused and frowned at them as they ran by.

Ahead, what sounded like the shouts of a thousand voices rose in a wave, then descended. Allan nearly stumbled as the tents abruptly ended, opening up into a plaza, more than half empty. Members of their group were standing at this end or emerging from the tents to either side, gasping and holding their chests or sides. Grant stepped onto the plaza twenty paces away, the Wolves padding out softly behind him, all of them still streaked with gore. He took in the scene, then faced Allan, but he didn't approach. At the far end of the open area, stone buildings to either side, the people Allan had expected to run into in the tent city were gathered, most on their knees, hands raised toward a figure standing at the edge of the first tier of what looked like a temple. The man held his hands to the sky, his white robes flapping around him as he shouted down into the crowd.

Glenn trotted up to Bryce and Allan, his expression disturbed. "It's some kind of religious gathering. It sounds damn similar to what the Kormanley were preaching before the Shattering, along with something to do with snakes and fire and retribution."

"Any sign of Kara or the others?"

"None. Aside from the priest up there, I don't see any of the White Cloaks, unless they're in commoner clothing and mixed in with the crowd." Glenn staggered as the earth lurched, a sharp wail of fear rising up from the crowd ahead. The priest raised his voice, as if volume would stop the quakes. "I only see a few of the White Cloak guards here, mostly up on the tier with the priest. The rest must be at the walls."

"Kara will be at the node." Cory pointed to the obsidian spire rising behind the priest. "She'll be at the center of it all, at the Needle."

"Are you certain? She wasn't cooperating with the White Cloaks the last time we saw them."

"She'll be there."

Bryce, Glenn, and Allan shared a look.

"It's as good a place to start looking as any."

"Right." Allan glanced over their group. Only twenty-four left. Then there were the Wolves. He counted an even dozen of them, not including their pack leader. "Let's see if we can find a way into the tower."

Kara fought her way through the pulses coming from Erenthrall, each one threatening to shove her back down the ley line to the Needle. The farther she stretched from the Needle, the more she pulled at the combined strength of the other Wielders there and the energy generated by the Nexus.

But when she finally reached Erenthrall, she gasped. "Gods."

"What is it?"

Even though she was hundreds of miles distant, Marcus' voice cut through her shock. She shook herself, began assessing the damage. "Erenthrall is in chaos. It's suffering massive quakes, worse than those we're feeling here. The ley system you and the other White Cloaks set up is gone." She wished it were an understatement, but the nodes Marcus and the others had established had been ripped apart. Active nodes had gone dead, and inactive ones were now connected to ley lines that hadn't existed even a few days before. She scrambled from one node to the next, attempting to get an overall impression of what had happened, but it didn't make any sense.

"There's too much ley." She passed through junction after junction. Some of the lines slammed up against the distortion, ley spilling up and out into the city. Others hit nodes and branched, surging around the distortion or arrowing off toward more distant locations like the Needle. All of them were suffused with ley, as if the system had somehow tapped into a huge reservoir—

Kara thought suddenly of the lake of ley resting far beneath the city. The Nexus Prime Augustus had created had siphoned off ley from that lake, and when the distortion had first formed as a piercing white ball of radiance over Erenthrall after the Shattering, it had fed from it. Kara had used it in her attempt to heal the distortion before it quickened.

But the distortion had cut off the lake from the remaining ley system. The main conduit to the lake lay near the center of the distortion, in the center of Erenthrall, in Grass.

Not anymore. Even as she dove down beneath the city, beneath the distortion, deep underground, following the ley lines there—those natural and those created by the Primes—she knew what she would find.

Near the bottom of the distortion, where the original conduit was blocked by the distortion, a secondary pool of ley had formed in a massive underground cavern. It was being fed by the lake deep below, had probably started filling up as soon as the distortion had blocked its original path. But the new reservoir had reached full capacity and had spilled over, searching for a new outlet.

It had found it in the shambles of the ley network the Primes had built around Erenthrall. Like water, it had sought the easiest pathways after it filled the reservoir to its brim, and the destroyed network was there, waiting. Now it was flooding the system.

Kara's body sagged in defeat. Rough stone pressed through her clothing, scraped at her cheek. "It's going to destroy us all."

"Kara!" Marcus' voice was distant, which was odd, since her body felt so close. Her pulse thudded through her arms, her throat, hot and heavy. It roared in her ears. Her breath rasped from her lungs, choked with fine grit thrown up by the quake. Yet the screams and moans of the other Wielders and White Cloaks were muffled.

Then someone grabbed her jaw with one hand, fingers digging in, pain stabbing through the numbness. "Kara! Do something! The Nexus here will not hold much longer!"

"I don't . . ." She'd intended to say she didn't know what to do. The problem was too immense, like the quickening of the distortion after the Shattering. But she'd managed to do something then, even though it had only been her and four other Wielders.

Mentally, she picked herself up. Deep beneath Erenthrall, she stepped back from the wall of the ley line she'd clung to since discovering the secondary pool of ley and centered herself, forced herself to think. Not like a Wielder, but like a Prime.

There was too much ley. The system couldn't handle it, because the only parts of the system left in Erenthrall were the secondary lines outside the center of the city. These were the nodes that had powered the outer districts, the barges, the heat, the ley globes that lined the streets and lit the interiors of the buildings of those that could afford to pay for it. All of the major junctions and the Nexus itself were sealed up inside the distortion.

"There's nothing left that's strong enough for this much ley to anchor itself to." She was aware that Marcus was still shouting at her, that the pit at the Needle was heaving under another quake, that part of the pit's wall had collapsed. "Everything that we could use to control the ley is locked inside the distortion."

She turned from the awe-inspiring view of the secondary reservoir overflowing its boundaries toward the distortion overhead.

"It all comes back to the distortion. We have to heal the distortion."

She still wasn't certain there was enough power in the Nexus and strength in the White Cloaks and Wielders remaining to do it, even with the reservoir so close, but they had to try. Erenthrall was being torn apart.

Far distant, in the pit at the Needle, she grabbed Marcus' arm. "I'm going to try to heal the distortion over Erenthrall.

It's the only way to stop the surges coming from the city. We need the nodes locked inside. I need you to channel as much of the energy from the Nexus as you and the White Cloaks can handle to me." She tightened her grip. "Send it even if it might burn me out."

He tensed, ready to argue with her, the emotions felt more through her fingers than seen. Her concentration was on the distortion in Erenthrall, on its edges, on not allowing it to daunt her. Then Marcus breathed out, the air a gust in her face.

"All right." His voice was laced with an old pain. "Give us a moment."

He leaned in and kissed her, a light touch on her lips, and then he pulled out of her grasp. She focused on the distortion. She stretched herself outward, as she'd done as a Wielder before the Shattering, extending herself so that she could feel the edges of the fractured reality, the planes and facets, the jagged arcs of lightning and the brilliant-colored arms. As she sank herself into its surface, noting the fractures that were smaller and should be healed first, the intricacies of the shards and how one would collapse upon the other if healed too quickly, images of this distortion forming played across her mind. She'd been lying on the stone steps outside the Nexus, the Wolves led by Hagger closing in, all of her strength gone. Artras had stood over her protectively, dagger glinting in the distortion's pure white light above. Then that light had flickered. Its penetrating whine had cut off and it had collapsed down to a pinprick, then nothing.

And exploded outward, the thick arms swirling overhead, reaching greedily toward the city, reality breaking in an elegant, beautiful whirl of energy that had consumed all of them there on the steps—Allan, Artras, Dylan, Hagger, the Wolves, and Kara.

Then it had slowed and set, reality halting in their shard, time stopped. Only Allan had been unaffected. Without Allan, they would have all been lost.

How many others were trapped in the shards even now? It wasn't the same distortion as before. There were ragged holes in the edges now, from where Kara and the White Cloaks had healed individual shards before realizing how useless a solution that had been. But they'd seen what had happened in a few of those shards—like the group that had hoarded their food supplies but ultimately killed themselves when they realized no one was coming to free them. Yet there were thousands of shards, must be thousands of people still trapped, still alive in shards where time had slowed or been halted.

Her goal since surviving the quickening had always been to free them, however possible. That drive had been forgotten as she fought to survive and the realities of the new world after the Shattering had taken over. Now she *had* to heal the distortion. Not simply to save those caught inside, but to save everyone else on the plains as well, before the fractured ley system tore the land apart.

She settled herself around the spherical distortion, drawing herself up around the edge where she knew she and the White Cloaks had healed shards. Those points would be the weakest, the most likely to destabilize the distortion and cause a catastrophic collapse as she worked.

"We're ready."

She drew in a few deep breaths to steady herself. The ground heaved at the Needle again, but she ignored it. Through the ley, she could feel the earth around Erenthrall shifting as well, felt buildings collapse as fissures opened up through the streets. Strangely, the areas closest to the distortion were the most stable.

The distortion itself wasn't being affected.

"I'm ready."

Far distant, Marcus said, "Now."

Kara felt the wave of ley roaring toward her, channeled up from the Needle's junction, funneled through the Nexus, guided by the White Cloaks and Wielders down the ley line that connected the node to Erenthrall. She braced herself for its impact—

And still it nearly carried her away when it struck. She screamed. She knew she'd screamed, but the whitewash noise of the ley pummeling her drowned it out. With monumental effort, she seized hold of the power thrust upon her and focused it on the distortion. Her reach doubled, then tripled, expanding around the distortion until she completely enclosed it. But unlike her attempt to heal it before it had quickened, this time she had no immediate support.

There were no Wielders here to lend her strength or guide her. They were all intent on maintaining the new Nexus. So she drew upon all of her training as a Wielder, all of the intricacies of the clocks her father had allowed her to help repair before his death, and she began to work.

The rough edges where shards had already been healed came first. She held the rest of the distortion together as she began smoothing the edges down. Carefully, first one shard, then the next came free. The arms that were the backbone of the distortion trembled as each shard released, and she paused until she was certain she hadn't started a collapse. Then she continued, the energy from the Nexus still roaring through her. She handled it by dispersing it around the distortion, letting it flow out, around, and back toward her again until she could use it.

She'd already smoothed out three areas that the White Cloaks must have dealt with when she turned her attention to a new area. A small shard had been isolated from the rest of the distortion, and she realized it was the piece that contained the wagon and family being attacked by Wolves. They hadn't been able to figure out how to repair the distortion without also freeing the Wolves, and there would have been little chance they could stop the Wolves before they tore the family apart. So they'd left the shard alone, and then been caught up in the war between the Rats and the Tunnelers.

She hesitated over the isolated shard, afraid to heal it, since it would mean the family's almost certain death, then set it aside and returned to the distortion. She could return to it later.

She attacked the distortion again, running the ley energy over the fractures, the cracks slowly sealing, melding the shards back to reality as the fissures withdrew. Her confidence grew and she began to work faster, the ley pulsing around her. Without thought, she reached for more, drew ley from the reservoir that had overflowed and started the current crisis, integrating the two flows from beneath the distortion and the ley line from the Needle. She began sweeping over the distortion in waves, as if she were polishing it, the fractures thinning and retreating as she worked, but it was so large.

And the one engulfing Tumbor was even larger.

She refused to let the thought rattle her.

Everything was healing smoothly until another violent heave in the pit at the Needle threw her body to the floor. Staggering pain sizzled through her shoulder and something cracked in her chest, a bolt of white-hot agony ripping through her lungs. She jerked back from the distortion involuntarily, her concentration broken. The disruption rippled through the ley—

And the distortion quivered.

"No."

She was already reaching forward to seize control again. But it was too late.

The quiver intensified, and then the entire distortion began to collapse.

"No, no, no!" Those at the Needle were screaming as more of the pit fell apart around them, but back in Erenthrall, the distortion began chewing up the streets and buildings caught in the shards that were suddenly snapping closed around them. Images of the seamstress' hand being torn to shreds in front of her, blood splattering her cheek— and the distortion that had killed her dog Max's original owner—jolted through her. Except those had been minor distortions compared to this one.

This distortion would reduce the center of Erenthrall— Grass, Stone, Confluence, and her home in the Eld District—to rubble.

And the collapse was accelerating.

She wasted precious moments stretching out with the power of the ley in the hopes of surrounding the distortion and stabilizing it that way. But that had never worked before. The collapse was drawing inward, toward the center. She was on the outside. There was no place to grip the distortion, to counteract the inertia pulling it into itself. All of her efforts only aided the collapse.

Frantic, she raced around the distortion once, twice, seeking a crack, a fissure, anything that she could pry open to get at the inside, as the distortion continued to shrink. But there was nothing.

"No!" White-hot agony seared through her chest again.

Everything in Erenthrall inside the distortion was going

to be destroyed. Everything she had feared from the moment she'd escaped its clutches was playing out before her eyes.

She couldn't let it happen. She needed to halt the destruction. She needed to get *inside*, needed to heal it from inside out, not the outside in.

Steeling herself, she gathered up as much of the ley as she could, focused it into a single blade. No. A needle, narrow and thin. A path. She needed a path of least resistance. A conduit.

The well of the original Nexus.

Diving deep beneath the distortion, down to the reservoir of ley, she seized the needle of power she'd created—

And then she drove it up through the ley line that connected the original Nexus to the lake of ley far below. The wall of the collapsing distortion fractured as she pierced it, the shards shattering as she shoved the needle deeper and deeper, until it exploded into the heart of the distortion, into the shards surrounding the cracked crystal dome of the building that had contained the Nexus. She hovered over the jagged openness of that dome, the sheared-off towers of Grass—including the Amber Tower—like spikes beneath her. If she'd looked, she would have seen the bodies of Hagger and the Wolves below on the steps, but she didn't take the time. With the ley funneling through her, she sent it out into the distortion in an explosion of power. Here at the heart, she had access to all of the structural arms, the jagged edges, the facets and faces. Everything connected to this one place, and so she sent the ley through those arms, sent it screaming out toward the destruction drawing steadily toward her from all directions.

The entire distortion lit from within with a fiery incandescence, like a white sun. It sizzled through her mind, scorched through her body, and seared into her bones.

And then everything went black.

In Erenthrall, the distortion trembled, a motion barely discernible from the heaving of the earth that surrounded it. Then it shuddered and began to shrink, slowly drawing in upon itself, leaving churned up buildings, bridges, streets, and parks in its wake. The implosion accelerated, the swirling arms that had swallowed the center of Erenthrall whirling back in upon themselves. The splintering of stone overwhelmed even the tortured grinding of the quakes around it.

Then a white-hot fire bloomed in its center. The light expanded outward in a sudden flash, flaring brighter than the sun. It swallowed the distortion whole and blazed beyond, visible across the plains, from the small town in Haven to the Hollow to the scattered groups huddled around the new distortion in Tumbor. Commander Ty and his enforcers on the walls at the Needle looked up from their battle with the Gorrani below, then shaded their eyes before being forced to turn away, the light too bright. Caravans of Temerite refugees to the far east cowered beside their wagons at the second sun on the western horizon. To the north, beneath the blazing white eyes of the Three Sisters, the light seared through the gray-black clouds and sheets of auroral lights that drifted through the mountains and gave the tortured souls there a fleeting burst of hope. And in the west, the people of the Demesnes paused in their prayers at the basilicas or halted their marching armies as the eastern clouds burned in a stunning wash of white that hurt the eyes.

In Erenthrall, those that had survived the quakes quailed and fell to their knees, or screamed at the heavens, or bowed their heads and wept, all of them—Rats, Tunnelers, Temerites, Gorrani—convinced it was a second Shattering.

But the intense light merely blazed over them. Those that stared at it were blinded, some for a few days, others weeks, some permanently.

Then it died, imploding down to a pinprick, a scintillant star.

And then it winked out.

In its wake, the ground continued to shudder, but the distortion had vanished. The center of the city—surrounded by a ring of chewed earth—remained intact, the buildings that had survived the Shattering freed from the distortion. The quakes began to subside.

The uneasy silence held for nearly an hour before a hideous rumbling crack rocked the entire city, the shockwave of sound heard hundreds of miles away. With a slow, shuddering grind, the entire city of Erenthrall sank over a thousand feet down into the plains, the grassland around it fracturing, riddled with hundreds of fissures. Buildings and towers that had withstood the Shattering, the quakes, and the distortion fell inward, columns of dust rising in plumes. Fires broke out. Geysers of ley shot upward.

But the earth settled and the quakes stopped.

And after a day of quiet—no tremors, no aftershocks—the survivors began to stir.

# Twenty-Six

"**T**HIS TEMPLE IS A GODS-DAMNED MAZE!"

Bryce's voice echoed in the odd corridor far ahead of Cory. The entire building shook with the quakes that were now one continuous roar of grinding stone and teeth-rattling tremors. He staggered against the side wall, reaching forward unconsciously to steady Hernande as they followed Allan, Bryce, the Wolf leader and two of his pack, and a half dozen of Bryce's Dogs deeper into the building. They hadn't had any problems finding a door—most of the guardsmen appeared to be at the walls, defending against what remained of the Gorrani, or stationed near the plaza where most of the citizens of the Needle were gathered.

Another lurch of the ground beneath them caused someone behind to shriek, but Cory didn't pause to find out who. They were spread out along the corridor, Cory with Hernande and Jerrain, a few more Hollowers immediately behind them, then the Wielders and the rest of the Hollowers, the Wolves interspersed here and there. Whenever they reached a corridor or side room, the Wolves would scent the air, one of them occasionally breaking away to lope into the flickering ley-lit halls to investigate before returning. The main group didn't pause as they made their way straight toward the center and the black tower, passing darkened rooms with barely a glance. Dust drifted down from the ceiling as the ground shook, and once or twice a pebble struck Cory's head or shoulder.

He barely noticed, his focus ahead on the black tower, on Kara. He needed to find her, needed to see her, hold her, smell her. He needed to know she was alive. It pushed him forward even when some of the others quailed. It had driven him since they'd left the charred remains of the Hollow behind, since Allan had appeared at the top of the stairs in the caverns with Artras, Cutter, Gaven, and Glenn, since he'd told them all of their capture by the Tunnelers and the betrayal of Kara and the rest to the White Cloaks.

Those ahead suddenly stopped, Jerrain and Hernande crowding up behind them.

"What is it? Why have you stopped?"

"The Wolves may have something. A scent."

"Yes." The pack leader's voice was the low rumble of a wolf's growl. "Your Wielder has passed through this cross-corridor before. I can smell her."

"How long ago?"

"A day at most."

Weakness buckled Cory's knees and he caught himself against the angled wall, Hernande now reaching back to steady him. "She's still alive."

"I can't tell which direction will lead us toward her, though. We'll have to split the group."

Allan cleared his throat. "Bryce, take Grant and four others and follow the left corridor. The rest of us will take the right."

They split without words, Bryce angling down a corridor to the left that looked identical to the one leading to the right. Cory could see farther ahead of them now, with half of the men up front gone. Allan was trotting, a Wolf at his side, two Hollowers behind, then Jerrain, Hernande, and Cory. Doorways and halls intersected the new corridor, like the one they'd just left, but this corridor curved subtly.

And these rooms were in use.

Allan noted the sudden appearance of cots and chairs and habitation an instant before Cory did, slowing, but not quickly enough to avoid plowing into a woman emerging from one of the rooms with a handful of wadded laundry.

She screamed as they both fell to the ground, clothes flying, the Wolf erupting into a low, menacing growl Cory could hear over the constant thunder of the quaking. The woman continued shrieking as she and Allan thrashed about, the two Hollowers standing over them, swords readied, but then the woman's cry cut off.

Allan had a hand clamped over her mouth, his other arm around her waist, but her frightened eyes were glued to the two swords leveled inches from her face. They flicked toward the Wolf and widened even further. She struggled again for a moment, then subsided, her chest heaving. Cory noted her darker Demesne skin and nudged Hernande.

"The Wolf won't hurt you," Allan said. "None of us will hurt you. We're here for our Wielders and those who were with them. Where are they?"

Allan removed his hand from her mouth. "I'll tell you nothing."

Hernande stepped forward, crouching down in front of her. He pulled back the sleeve of his left arm, revealing a scattered array of tattoos across his bicep that looked like a constellation of small stars. Cory had never seen them before; they'd always been concealed by Hernande's clothes.

The woman's eyes flared with fear. "Oransai! But Prince Valladolid slaughtered all of the oransai and their families at Barakaldo."

"Not all. A few escaped."

The floor heaved, a curtain of dust cascading down on them all as they staggered. Cory glanced up, noted a crack running down the length of the ceiling, then resolutely dropped his gaze back to Hernande.

"Tell us where the Wielders are."

The woman stiffened, defiant, but then her eyes dropped to the tattoo. "My parents always said Valladolid was wrong in what he did, that the oransai deserved better." She met Hernande's eyes. "The Wielders are at the node. Prime Lecrucius had them taken there."

"Prime?" Artras had come up behind Cory, the other Wielders behind her.

The Demesnes woman sniffed. "Yes. Prime."

"Where is the node? How do we get there?"

"I'll take you."

Allan released her and they followed her through the corridors, Cory slowly realizing that these were the servants' quarters. They passed a kitchen, men and women bustling over steaming cauldrons and roasting pits, no one noticing as they ran past. A few ducked out of their way, startled, the Demesnes woman shouting something at them, and then they reached a much wider cross-corridor that led to a door, which the woman flung open.

The sunlight was shocking, everyone drawn up short as they raised a hand to shade their eyes. Cory stepped forward, wiping away tears, as the woman pointed toward the base of the black tower across a field of stone and stellae. "There!"

As soon as Cory saw the opening in the tower, he charged forward.

Behind him, Hernande and Allan both shouted, "Wait!"

He ignored them, rushing through the entrance, pausing in the darkness beyond, eyes adjusting yet again to the pulsing ley light that ran through the walls of the tower. He spun around in desperation, caught sight of the stairs to the left, and bolted for them. He heard the skittering of claws on slick stone and knew the Wolf was right behind him, then the sound of cursing and the tread of boots.

He emerged into the pit's massive chamber as the earth heaved violently. Below, white-cloaked figures were arrayed around the fountaining ley in the center of the pit. They screamed, half of them thrown to the ground, a few of them no longer moving. Another group cowered on the floor near the pit's wall. Cory's gaze latched onto Kara, leaning crookedly against the wall, Dylan half holding her upright, another figure crouched before her, back to him, others scattered around them.

"Kara!" He clutched at the stairs as the ground heaved again—

And then the wall next to Kara and the others cracked and exploded outward. Chunks of stone spilled down to the ledge of the pit, some the size of a man's torso, dropping into a section that had already crumbled away. Kara was tossed to the floor, her body strangely limp. She struck the stone floor hard with her shoulder, rolled onto her back, and then cascading stone buried her, a sheet of dust blocking her from view.

"Kara!" Cory scrambled down the stairs, leaping a gap without thought, nearly tripping over the side.

He sprinted across the ledge, shoved someone out of his way as he fell to his knees, and began scrabbling at the stone that had buried most of Kara's body. Only her head, shoulder, and part of an arm and leg were visible. He tossed rocks aside, digging through the loose rubble beneath, aware that others were helping him, that some were digging nearby for more buried in the debris.

Then Kara coughed, a horrible wet choking sound. Cory paused, a stone half lifted from her still mostly buried body.

Kara drew in a ragged breath, then exhaled slowly, her head sagging.

Cory threw the stone aside, then leaned over Kara's head and shoulders. Tears fell onto her face, dark splotches in the dust that had settled there. His hands hovered over her cheeks, trembling. He was afraid to touch her, afraid he'd break her, even though she was already broken. He couldn't even tell if she was breathing anymore.

"Cory!" Someone shook his arm. People were still digging around him. "Cory, she's still alive."

His head shot up, but everything was blurry. He wiped at his face with his arms, focused—

"Marcus?" He couldn't think. It didn't make sense. Marcus was dead. He'd died in Erenthrall, after disturbing the Nexus and bringing about the Shattering.

"Marcus." He vaulted to his feet. His arm snapped out, fingers like claws as he formed a knot in the center of Marcus' chest. The Wielder—no, the White Cloak—gasped, hand leaping to his heart as he staggered back—

But then another hand latched on to Cory's arm, grip tight, commanding. Hernande stood calmly beside him.

"Let it go."

Cory released the knot, his hand cramping as it relaxed. Marcus sagged. He shot Cory a look of pure hatred.

But then, between them, kneeling at Kara's side, Artras said, "Her arm's dislocated, and I think she bruised the hell out of her ribs, but she'll live."

Cory fell back to his knees. "I thought she was dead."

"Unconscious."

Marcus stayed a few paces away. He still clutched his chest, but his breathing had settled and his natural color was returning. "She healed the distortion over Erenthrall." His voice cracked and he cleared his throat. "She nearly burned herself out, but she did it."

Only then did Cory realize that the earthquakes had stopped.

Kara moaned, and Cory reached out and touched her forehead, pushing a lock of stray hair out of the way. She rocked her head side to side, then opened her eyes. "C-Cory? What are you doing here?"

"We came to save you, of course."

Kara tried to sit up, but sucked in a sharp breath and lay back down, sweat sheening her skin. "My shoulder hurts."

"It's dislocated," Artras said. "We'll need to take care of that as soon as possible. It's going to hurt, especially with the bruising you got from the falling rock, but it needs to be done."

"Then do it."

"Hold her."

Kara screamed, but she cut it off by biting her lip as they settled her back to the ground.

"You'll have to stay immobile for a few days, in case it isn't just bruising and you do have a fractured rib."

"No one's going anywhere at the moment," Allan said.

Cory started. He hadn't been paying attention to anything other than Kara and the immediate area. But as he looked up at Allan, standing at the top of the stairs, he realized that the White Cloaks were clustered to one side. Marcus stood back, eyeing Allan, while a few of the White Cloaks hovered over another who'd also been dug out from the rubble, a Gorrani man. Dylan sat propped up against some of the rock nearby, massaging his knee.

Aside from Hernande and two other Hollowers, none of the rest of the group who'd come with them were in the pit.

"Where are the others?"

"Bryce found Adder and Aaron. They're all at the entrance to the black tower, holding it. The commander of the

Needle's guardsmen wants to speak to either Lecrucius or Marcus."

Allan escorted Marcus out of the pit, the ley that lit the corridor dying out within twenty feet to both the front and back of Allan as they moved. He'd made certain he didn't actually enter the pit below, not knowing how he'd affect the node itself. He kept his hand on one of Marcus' shoulders as they pushed through the Hollowers crowded around the Needle's entrance, Adder and Aaron both hanging back. Grant stood in the corridor leading off from the entrance to the center, nostrils flared, a few of his Wolves beside and behind him. None of the men were close enough to the entrance they could be picked off through the doorway by archers, but all of them had their swords drawn. He didn't see Cutter among them and wondered briefly where the tracker had gone off to, but shifted his attention to Bryce, the Dog waiting where he'd left him.

He tugged Marcus to a halt. "Any change?"

"He's waiting about halfway between the doors to the temple and the tower. There are a couple of stellae to either side. It's difficult to tell if he has any archers in the windows above, but he has men ready at the door. Cutter's taken a few of our own archers up into the higher levels of the tower to see if they can gain an advantage there. We haven't found any other entrances to the tower besides this one."

"There aren't any," Marcus said. "This is the only way in or out, except for the tunnels currently filled with ley. However, there are three other entrances into the stone garden, one each at the four compass points. He could be sneaking in soldiers through those doors, although if he were doing that, I assume you'd have heard about it by now from this Cutter."

Bryce glanced toward Allan. "Do we trust him?"

"For now."

Bryce ordered someone to check out the other doors and see what Cutter had found. Men shifted to fill in the gap. Allan released Marcus and stepped to the side of the entrance, tipping his head out for a quick look around.

The commander stood where Bryce had said, a plinth of stone three paces behind him and to the right that was tall enough to provide cover for a single man. The nearest stone on the left was five paces to the side, shorter, but wide enough that someone could be crouched down behind it. He counted seven men in the shadow of the opposite door in the temple, with a minimum of three windows above that could conceal archers.

He took another look, this time focusing on the man, not his surroundings, then turned to Marcus. "What's the commander's name?"

"Ty."

"He was a Dog."

"Dalton ran into him after the Shattering," Marcus said. "He recruited him and the others for protection. It's the only reason he survived the first few months, before he found this place."

It sounded like what had happened to the refugees before they'd made it to the Hollow. Allan doubted that those who'd fled the University would have made it far without Bryce and the other Dogs watching their backs.

Their courier returned. "Cutter placed the archers in windows a few levels up. They have a sightline on the commander and the door here. The other three doors are closed. He reports no other activity in any of the windows of the temple—no archers, no watchers, nothing."

Allan and Bryce exchanged a troubled look. "He should have at least put watchers up there."

"I would have already had men filing into the stone garden, archers in all of the windows." Allan turned back to the entrance, watching the harsh sunlight and the sharp shadows it cast as it edged toward sunset. "What's his strategy? We're trapped here, with no way out. He knows that."

Marcus cleared his throat. "Commander Ty is a reasonable man. And like me, I don't think he's bought into Father and his visions. Unlike his second, Darius."

"Who's this Father?"

"Dalton. He's the man who established the Needle. He pulled all of these people together, brought them here, all based on visions he claimed to have. He convinced them he saw the ending of the Nexus and the Shattering. He told them he could save them all, that he could heal what had been destroyed, that we could begin again on the correct path." Marcus' eyes flicked toward Bryce and the others. "Before the Shattering, he was the head of the Kormanley."

The Dogs in the group spat curses and shuffled around, the tension in the small entrance room doubling.

Allan kept his focus on Marcus. "But Commander Ty isn't a believer."

"No, he's not."

"That could mean anything."

Allan considered. "Let's find out."

He motioned Marcus toward the door, then fell into step behind him, but off to one side. He didn't place his hand on Marcus' shoulder as he'd done before; Marcus had earned at least that much.

As soon as Marcus stepped into view, Allan called out, "I've brought Marcus. We're coming out."

Marcus paused a step beyond the door, letting his eyes adjust, Allan guessed, then walked toward Commander Ty. Allan had to blink away the harshness of the sun, but he never took his eyes off of Ty. The man was older by ten years, face scarred and pitted like anyone who'd spent time as a Dog. His stance was solid, shoulders wide, back stiff. A sword sat sheathed at his hip, but his arms were crossed over his chest as he watched them cross the short distance to his position. His light hair, thin and wispy, glowed in the sunlight, his body framed behind by the shadow cast by the stone plinth on the left.

Marcus halted three paces from him without any direction from Allan. A quick glance revealed that no one was hidden behind either of the nearest stellae.

Ty caught the look. "No one is lying in wait. And no one is preparing to flank you through the other entrances to the stone garden." He didn't wait for a response, shifting his attention to Marcus. "What's happened here?"

"What happened to the Gorrani?"

"They have been routed. The fires that Father Dalton foresaw—that I assume your White Cloaks provided— destroyed nearly all of them. Those that remained regrouped after a disruption at the walls"—he stared at Allan for a moment—"but we held the minor breach. Once they realized they couldn't take the walls—not with only a thousand men—they retreated. Returning to the southern flats, I presume. We have scouts trailing them.

"Now, what's happened here?"

Marcus had paled at the mention that only a thousand Gorrani remained. "Lecrucius and the other White Cloaks used the Nexus to bring you the ley fire, but it destabilized the network we'd established. That's what caused the extended earthquake. We nearly lost the Nexus completely. It would have caused another Shattering. Not as destructive, but devastating nonetheless."

Ty's only reaction was a slight tensing of his shoulders.

"With the help of Kara—the Wielder Iscivius captured in Erenthrall—we managed to bring the Nexus back under control. But the damage had already been done. The network around Erenthrall had collapsed. Kara attempted to repair it, but it triggered the distortion. As it imploded, she managed to heal it. The distortion over Erenthrall is gone. The ley lines to the nodes in the city have reinitiated and stabilized the ley. That's why the quakes have stopped, at least for the moment."

Ty's eyebrows rose. "She healed the distortion in Erenthrall? By herself?"

Marcus waved a hand. "She had the support of the White Cloaks here, and the Nexus to draw power from, but essentially, yes."

"And what did Lecrucius have to say about this?"

"He didn't survive the near collapse of the Nexus."

Ty nodded, as if he'd expected that answer. Oddly, the tension in his shoulders eased.

He turned toward Allan. "Which brings us to you and your men. You breached our walls, and then sealed them back up. Not without damage, of course. The height of the wall in that area has dropped by nearly thirty feet. That's a weak point that we'll have to watch and repair sometime in the near future. How did you do it? We saw you approach with that other group. You had no siege weapons, no ladders. No one on the walls saw you set any black powder."

"It doesn't matter." Allan had no intention of giving up such an obvious advantage. "We came for our people, those that this Iscivius captured in Erenthrall. Return them to us and we'll leave."

Ty's gaze shifted toward the burn scar Allan had received when the Kormanley priest had set himself on fire at the sowing of the Flyers' Tower.

"Allan," he said, as if testing the name out. Then his arms dropped, hand falling to the hilt of his sword. "Allan Garrett. You were a Dog. You ran, abandoned your brothers. Commander Daedallen had the entire pack searching for you, until we were distracted by the Purge. He even sent a Hound after you."

"No one leaves the Dogs."

"No one dared. Yet you did. And you survived. How did you escape the Hound?"

"I didn't. He found me at the edge of the city. He could have killed me easily, but he let me go."

"Strange bastards, those Hounds. I could never stand being near them." He paused in thought, staring first at Allan, then up at the black tower behind them, then back down at Marcus.

"I have a problem. I don't much like Father Dalton. I don't trust him, or his visions."

"His most recent vision appears to have come true."

"Did it? He predicted that a fire would destroy the Gorrani snakes, but only after Lecrucius revealed he could use the ley as a weapon. Did he have a vision, or did he make that up after he found out the Gorrani were coming and that Lecrucius could destroy them with the ley?"

"What would your second, Darius, say about that theory?"

"Darius is overseeing the main gates. What would your lover, Dierdre, think?"

"She'd flay me for doubting Father."

"And yet you don't believe him either."

Marcus hesitated. "Not his visions, no. But I do believe in some of what he preaches, in his hatred of how the ley was being abused before the Shattering, and his conviction that it needs to be returned to its natural state."

"And yet you've created a new Nexus."

"Nothing like what Prime Augustus constructed. And we're using this Nexus to repair the ley system. Once that's finished, we intend to destroy it."

"I don't think that was Lecrucius' intention," Ty said.

"Lecrucius is dead."

"Convenient."

Allan cleared his throat, both Ty and Marcus looking toward him. "What are you suggesting, commander?"

"A truce. I control the enforcers. I could kill Father Dalton and seize control, except he has a strong hold over the people. I'm not certain, even with the enforcers, that I'd survive long after Dalton's death. And I have no desire to rule. I'm content as commander of the guard. It's a higher position than I had before, as a Dog in Erenthrall, and it doesn't have half the responsibilities of a Baron. Even with the people on my side, as unlikely as that would be, I'd still have to contend with the White Cloaks. Based on what I saw today, none of us could survive if they took exception to us. The White Cloaks need to be controlled. I feared what would happen if Lecrucius seized power, and yet I saw no way of stopping it. I'm glad he's dead."

"A truce. Between you, Marcus, and Dalton?"

"Yes. I control the enforcers. Marcus, you control the White Cloaks. And both of us control Dalton. Let him continue with his preaching and his visions. Let him assuage the people's fears. But don't let him rule. He's gained too much power since we found the Needle. He needs to be curtailed."

"And what of my men and those we came to get back?"

"Take them. Go back to where you came from. We won't follow you, or seek you out." An edge came into his voice. "And you agree not to come back with whatever—or whoever—you have that can break our walls so easily."

Allan suspected Ty already knew how they'd managed to crack the walls. "Agreed. We have no reason to return here."

But Marcus shook his head. "It won't work."

"Why not?"

"Because the White Cloaks will never accept me as their leader, declared Son of the Father or not. I lost that role to Lecrucius before the Gorrani laid siege to the Needle. They won't take me back now." He faced Allan. "But I know who could take control."

Allan stared at him for a long moment. "Kara."

"She proved herself to them today. None of them could

have held the Nexus together and then healed Erenthrall. None of them could have controlled that much ley. I doubt even Lecrucius could have done that."

"Not all of the White Cloaks will back her."

"Iscivius and Irmona are likely already plotting how they'll seize control themselves. But I can guarantee that nearly every other White Cloak will rally behind her. Definitely Okata, myself, Hartman, and Jenner. Others based on what happened today."

"I came here to rescue her, to take her back to the Hollow."

"We need her here."

Commander Ty shifted, breaking the argument before it could heat up. "Perhaps you should ask this Kara what she would like to do." He turned his back on them both, heading toward the open double doors of the temple.

"Where are you going?"

He paused, looked back over his shoulder. "I'm going to protect our good Father Dalton with a proper escort and see him safely back to his rooms after he's finished appeasing the fears of the populace." He started walking again. "You can find me in the orrery afterward."

"Orrery?" Allan had no idea what an orrery was.

"You'll see."

They watched as Commander Ty stalked past the enforcers on guard at the door, his men pulling back.

"Even if we can get Kara to agree to stay, it won't be as easy as Ty makes it sound. He'll have to contend with Darius, his second. And I'll have to deal with Dierdre." Allan didn't understand why Marcus grimaced, but the White Cloak shrugged whatever the issue was aside and faced Allan. "We should return Kara to her rooms, make certain a healer sees her, and let her know about Ty's proposal."

"I'll want my own men guarding her door." Allan intended to do that himself. "And the rest of the Hollowers in the rooms around her."

"Of course." He glanced back toward the node. "Your men should also stay here at the node and hold the tower. Not necessarily to keep the enforcers out, but to keep the White Cloaks in. Until this is settled, I think we should all stay here, at the Nexus. It's the base of our power."

"I'll leave Bryce here. We'll take care of Kara and anyone else who was wounded, and then we'll see what she has to say."

~~~

"I have to stay."

Everyone in the room stilled—Artras, Hernande, Cory, Allan, Grant, and Marcus. They'd explained to her what Commander Ty proposed. She'd listened in silence, and when they were finished and that silence had stretched, they'd begun quietly arguing with each other about what should be done—all except Grant. The pack leader stood in one corner and watched them, muscles in his face occasionally twitching, nostrils flaring as he scented the air. Cory wanted to pack up all of the Hollowers and head back to the Hollow immediately. Now that he knew Kara was safe, he was concerned about how the quakes might have affected the caverns where the Hollowers had taken refuge. They could travel slowly. The Needle could provide them with wagons, supplies—they owed them that much. Or at least owed Kara. Artras agreed. Marcus, of course, argued that Kara should stay. If she didn't, if they didn't put a stop to Dalton now, his power and influence would continue to grow. He'd become more erratic, his search for surviving Wielders more desperate. Who knows what he'd do, what threat he'd pose the Hollow in the future, especially knowing there were powerful Wielders hiding there. Allan watched her as they argued, but she could tell that he agreed with Marcus. This Dalton—this Father—was a threat, and would remain a threat, no matter whether Ty thought he could control him. It would be better to have a presence here.

Hernande argued both sides, chewing on his beard the entire time.

But now they'd stilled, focused their attention on her. She didn't look toward them but stared up at the ceiling over her cot, her torso wrapped in an ice pack. Her entire body felt bruised. Her shoulder and arm throbbed where it had been dislocated, and if she breathed in too deep, a sharp pain cut into her chest. The healer had said one of her ribs was cracked and had given her some horribly bitter medicine to help deal with the pain, but it hadn't taken effect yet. She could still taste it on her tongue and in the back of her throat, even though she'd drunk at least three glasses of water to wash it away.

"I have to stay. The quakes may have stopped, but the ley system is far from stable. The damage in Erenthrall is extensive. Nodes will have to be repaired, and the reservoir of ley that overflowed and caused the most recent quakes will need to be dealt with. Then there's the distortion engulfing Tumbor. It will need to be healed. Along with the ones we can see hanging over all of the other major cities that haven't quickened yet. The only way to do any of that is to work with the Nexus Marcus and Lecrucius built here."

She rolled her head so that she could see their reactions. Cory looked angry, Marcus satisfied. Allan had bowed his head, and Hernande nodded in agreement. Artias' lips were pursed.

"Besides, didn't you say the Hollow had been burned to the ground?"

"Yes. Yes, it was."

"We were worried about feeding everyone for another winter even before that. Can everyone survive there now without shelter? Food? They must have lost most of the crops."

"They have the caves for protection. That is, if the quakes didn't collapse them." Cory caught Kara's gaze. "We can survive the winter there."

"And the food?" Kara shifted on her cot, wincing at the pain. "We went to Erenthrall looking for supplies because we were already short. We brought back nothing, Cory. With the raid on the Hollow, I'm certain Sophia and Paul and the others have even less than they anticipated."

"We have plenty here at the Needle," Marcus threw in. "Enough to feed everyone at the Hollow. Bring them all here."

"They wouldn't come. Sophia and Paul and the rest of the true Hollowers—not the refugees that they took in, but those that have lived there their entire lives—they won't abandon it. Not even when all that remains now are the charred husks of buildings. They've probably already started rebuilding."

"We can't abandon the node there now anyway. It's too important. All of the nodes are important, old and new.

We'll have to have Wielders there to watch over it, and others to protect them." Kara reached for Cory, and when he stepped forward hesitantly, she took his hand. He knelt down beside her cot so she wouldn't have to stretch. "It wasn't working in the Hollow. The refugees and the Hollowers—we didn't mix. Those from Erenthrall were restless. They never fit in, and while the Hollowers wanted to help us, they're too used to being isolated. We barely tolerated each other. But here . . . this is what I wanted for Erenthrall, what I hoped to build after healing the distortion. A place of safety people could flock to, one that could be protected, one that we could use as a base to repair the ley. We have all of that here."

He took her hand in both of his, twined their fingers together. "The Hollow changed after you left, after the first attack by the raiders. It's different now. You're right, though. We wouldn't all survive the winter." He raised his head, squeezed her hand. "We'll stay here."

"Then it's settled." Marcus turned to Allan. "I'll inform Commander Ty and the White Cloaks that Kara will stay, that he has his alliance." At Allan's uncertain nod, he left.

Artras stepped forward. "I think we should let everyone from the Hollow decide on their own what they'd like to do, but I intend to stay here with you."

"Those of us from the University will stay as well. I can't see Sovaan remaining in the Hollow, and Jerrain would be better off here. The students will come with us, of course." Hernande drew in a breath. "We've realized that the ley and the Tapestry may be more connected than we first thought. Recall that in Erenthrall, the Primes and mentors worked together to build their towers and junctions, to keep the ley system working properly. I think, if you want to stabilize the ley, that you'll need us. Besides, you may need our protection while you're here. This will not be an easy alliance."

Kara shifted herself into a seated position, setting the soggy towel wrapped around the remaining ice to one side. It didn't hurt as much as she expected—the pain medicine must have been kicking in—but she still thought she could hear bone grating against bone as she moved. "Will you stay here, Allan?"

He glanced toward the door, the floor, then back to her.

"It will depend on Morrell. She's only known the Hollow. She may not want to leave."

Kara had grown used to having Allan around since the Shattering. If he stayed in the Hollow—

She shook herself mentally. Allan had to do what was best for himself and his daughter.

"So you're staying?" Nearly everyone started at Grant's voice; they'd forgotten he was there.

"Yes. Yes, I'm staying."

Grant stepped forward, the motion somehow menacing. Kara drew back slightly, her hand clenching tightly onto Cory's.

"We came to slaughter the White Cloaks, for hunting us down in Erenthrall, for ordering our deaths, even though *they* caused the Shattering, *they* brought forth the auroras that changed us into Wolves. When we attacked your people in Erenthrall, we thought you were with them, or that you would soon join them. Now we know otherwise." He lifted his head slightly, shoulder tensing. "What do you intend to do to us now?"

"If you can control your pack, then nothing. The hunting will stop. I'll make certain Commander Ty—and Marcus—understand that."

He snorted, lip curling, body bristling, but then he backed down. "We will stay. To protect you, and to watch you. But there are brethren in Erenthrall, trapped in the distortion. And others."

"If they survived the partial collapse, then they're free now."

"But they do not know of this agreement. They are feral. I would like to find them, bring them here, if they are willing to be part of my pack. And I would like to search for my wife."

"Of course."

Artras cleared her throat, then frowned at Allan. "Tell him. He deserves to know."

"Tell me what?"

Allan glared at Artras before shifting his attention to Grant. "Is one of your pack named Drayden?"

"Drayden attacked you in Erenthrall and was wounded. We followed his blood scent to your Hollow, to your caves. Does he live?"

Allan crossed his arms over his chest. "He survived, thanks to Artras." Grant shot a look at the elderly Wielder. "But he's no longer a Wolf."

Grant stilled. "What do you mean?"

"My daughter healed him. She transformed him back into a man." His brow creased. "Mostly."

Grant uttered a few short muffled snorts and snarls of disbelief. "You lie." The words rumbled with a dangerous undertone.

"You can return to the Hollow with me and see for yourself. Perhaps she can return you and the rest of your pack back into human form."

Grant huffed a few times, uncertain, but then said carefully, "I would like that. But some of my pack may be too far gone. There is little human left in them."

Kara sagged to one side, unable to hold herself up any longer. Cory caught her and gently lowered her back to the cot. A fog was settling over her, brought on by the medicine. She had barely followed Grant and Allan's conversation, especially at the end. But still she protested. "I'm fine, Cory. Sit me back up."

"No, you're not. You're hurt and still recovering. Lie back down and get some sleep."

"But there's so much to do."

"Let us deal with it."

She fought to sit back up again, heard the others talking behind Cory as he leaned over and adjusted the pillow, pulling a blanket up over her. But her strength was gone. She merely fumbled with the blanket, and as soon as her head settled back—a twinge coming from her cracked rib—her eyes closed and she found herself drifting.

"Cory." The name slurred. She reached out again, her arm waving, feeling oddly detached from her body, but she felt him take hold of it, felt his mouth press to the back of it in a kiss.

"What, Kara?"

"Stay with me. Stay . . . here."

He leaned over and kissed her forehead. "Of course."

Dalton sat in a chair before the massive table in the outer room of the suite he'd taken for himself in the third tier of the tower. A tray of fruit and bread sat before him, along with a decanter of wine, a glass already poured but untouched. He'd poured it after being escorted by Commander Ty from his sermon. He'd stayed even after the quakes had ceased, expounding about the White Cloaks, how they'd saved everyone from the backlash caused by the misuse of the ley by Baron Arent and Prime Augustus, how activating the old nodes had succeeded, how this was proof that returning to the natural ley system would heal the world. He hadn't known then that the distortion over Eren thrall had vanished. He could have used that.

When he'd finally brought the meeting to an end and sent the people of the Needle back to their tents, Commander Ty had been waiting.

He resisted the urge to lash out with a hand and fling the wine across the room. Ty hadn't forced the issue, but it was clear that he and the six other enforcers—none of them true believers, he'd noticed—intended him to accompany them. There hadn't been anything he could do. So he'd straightened his shoulders and allowed them to escort him to his own rooms.

Then they'd left. But before the door had closed behind them, Dalton had seen the guards settling into place to either side of the door.

He'd stood in the center of the outer room for at least ten minutes, before walking stiffly to the table and pouring the wine.

Then he sat down. To wait. To think. To plan.

And as expected, voices rose outside the door. Someone shouted—a command—and then the door flung open, Darius striding into the room.

"How could he?" He crossed the room, not even looking at Dalton. "I'll slit his throat for this. The temerity! Restricting you to your rooms! Placing guards on the door! You're the Father! Without you, we never would have survived the aftermath of the Shattering. We never would have fled Erenthrall before the distortion quickened. We'd all be dead!"

Dalton reached for the wine. "You exaggerate." He took a sip. All of the anger he'd been stewing in since arriving at his rooms under guard had died, as if vented through Darius' ranting. He contemplated the wine.

Darius came to an abrupt halt before him. "You're taking this rather well."

Dalton looked up, took in Darius' disheveled appearance, his wildly mussed hair, the sweat and grime that coated his face and armor. And soot. He could smell fire, and realized that Darius had come straight from the wall. Someone must have informed him of what Ty had done.

Which meant not all of the enforcers would side with Ty in the end. If it came to such an end.

"No." He set his wine aside. "No, I'm not taking this well. But there's nothing that can be done at the moment. We must bide our time. There will be a reckoning for Commander Ty. And for Marcus."

"Marcus. Dierdre will take care of Marcus."

"I'm certain she will. But for now, we wait."

"Wait!" Darius began pacing, hands clenching and unclenching. "I want to strangle Ty now."

"We wait. We wait and watch and see what visions may come. We will be given a path to follow. Look at what happened with the Gorrani. Did I not foresee their destruction?"

Darius shot him a look, then halted and visibly calmed himself. "Fine, Father. We'll wait. For now."

Dalton stood, placed a hand on Darius' shoulder in reassurance. "We will prevail. We are ordained to prevail. Now go find Dierdre. Convince her not to do anything rash regarding Marcus. Convince her to keep her rage in check. She may be able to use him to keep abreast of whatever he and Ty are planning."

Darius nodded, then bowed his head before departing. He gave the guards outside a scathing look before closing the door behind him.

Dalton took another sip of the wine, but it tasted bitter to him. He drifted into the bedchamber, prepared himself for bed. He stared out of the high window at the black tower of the Needle and the sunset beyond, darkness descending in a flare of vibrant colors.

Then he turned and lay down on his back, eyes toward the heavens, arms at his sides.

Hours later, he drifted into sleep.

He dreamed of snakes and snarling dogs, and three piercing white stars exploding against a darkened sky.

Deep inside Erenthrall, at the center of the city, beneath the remains of the towers of Grass, the dust cloud that had risen and obscured the city after the massive quake had sunk it below the level plains had settled. Nothing stirred beneath the shattered dome of the Nexus. Bodies littered the cracked steps—one with a sword thrust through his chest, a few Wolves, the rest human. But the Wolves that had been frozen within the distortion for the past year had long ago shaken themselves off and run after being freed. They'd paused only to sniff the bodies and howl in grief and anger.

Nothing had moved since. Not here.

Until—deep in the shadow of the Amber Tower's main entrance—a man emerged. He stepped out onto the wide steps that led up to the tower, feet kicking up plumes of the thick dust that had collected there. They swirled in the gusting breeze. He surveyed the destruction of the center of the city, his expression impassive.

Behind him, three more figures emerged. They moved with a strange smooth grace that exuded danger and death, like a blade drawn lightly down skin, drawing blood along with silvery pain.

They hesitated on the edge of the steps, then descended, passing out into the newly released city streets.

The Hounds of Erenthrall had been unleashed.

Didn't get enough?
Want more?

Read a deleted chapter from
***THREADING THE NEEDLE,***
"Inside Erenthrall"
now at Joshua Palmatier's website!

Visit www.joshuapalmatier.com
and click on "Extras."

Then check out all of the other
interesting links and projects
from Joshua Palmatier, including:

• The "Throne of Amenkor" series
• The "Well of Sorrows" series
• Zombies Need Brains

and more!